FRANKLIN HORTON

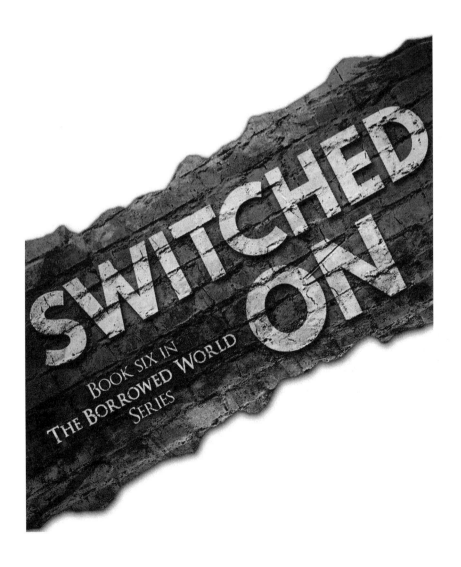

SWITCHED ON

BOOK SIX IN
THE BORROWED WORLD
SERIES

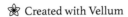 Created with Vellum

PROLOGUE

For Jim Powell, the collapse began on a routine business trip. Jim's job at a local government agency required frequent travel from his home in southwestern Virginia to the state capital in Richmond, a distance of several hundred miles. He'd made this trip twice a month for over a decade without a hitch. Then the country was hit with a devastating coordinated terror attack.

Terrorists hit infrastructure targets around the country causing disruption and chaos. Most of the attacks were not mass casualty events but they ended life as Americans were accustomed to living it. Within hours the grid collapsed, followed eventually by cellular connectivity. Like Americans saw in natural disasters, such as hurricanes Katrina and Sandy, looting began immediately.

Jim and his group of coworkers were not friends. Some were not even on friendly terms, so there was some disagreement on how to proceed. Jim made it clear that he was heading for home immediately, with or without them. There was a vote and the group decided to leave, though there was still tension.

On the trip home they encountered lawlessness, struggling drug addicts, and a government response fully unprepared for the scale of the events unfolding. As millions of travelers were stranded on the highways FEMA established emergency camps, but were ultimately unable to support them in the long term. Eventually, people who went there seeking shelter realized there was no plan for getting them home. Many struck out on their own but had lost critical days thinking the government was going to fix this for them.

Jim Powell had no such delusion. Although he was what some people referred to as a prepper, Jim didn't see himself that way. He was from the Appalachian, or hillbilly, part of the state. He came from a line of people who had weathered economic hardship and deprivation. They believed in taking care of themselves and their families with little regard for the way outsiders and the government conducted their business. It was the way he had been raised.

Jim had long suspected there would be a collapse of some type and had prepared his family. They knew how to run the home in his absence. He left them well-equipped with guns, ammunition, and a long-term supply of food and water. While they did not live a fully sustainable lifestyle, raising all of their own food, they did live in the country with access to clean water and property for growing food.

Jim's trek home was not an easy one. They lost a member of their group in the chaos that soon ensued. Eventually, the group split in half over a disagreement on the best way to get home. Jim, his friend Gary, and his coworker Randi set out on their own. Alice and Rebecca chose the FEMA route, trusting that the government would house them in a camp, then bus them home. It did not work out as promised. Alice would eventually make it home but Rebecca did not, dying at the hands of a mentally-ill traveler named Boyd.

After a brutal struggle to get home, Jim found his family engaged in a conflict with desperate neighbors who saw no problem with stealing from those who had resources they did not. While Jim had to kill on his journey, so did his wife at home. Even his young son was not spared from pulling the trigger on a neighbor.

He had no time to appreciate being home, finding himself immediately embroiled in the chaos of having to rescue his mother and son from neighbors who had taken them. When he resolved that, again having to kill, he hoped the worst was over. He was home now.

He and his family were together. They could hunker down, bury their heads, and weather the hard times.

If only it were so easy.

No one in Jim's original group found their return home to be as idyllic as expected. While Jim tried to get settled back into life in his valley, his friend and traveling companion Gary was dealing with his own issues in the town where he lived. Gary was also prepared for hard times, though the location where his family built their home was not defensible. Living on the edge of a densely-populated town, they were vulnerable to attack.

When Gary communicated with Jim and found that there were empty homes in the secluded valley where Jim lived, Gary made the tough call to pack up his family and leave their home. He was not able to do so before he lost a son-in-law in a violent episode that left Gary's daughter depressed and catatonic. In their rattled state, they made the journey and moved into an empty house not far from Jim's.

Randi lived with her two daughters and her grandchildren miles from any town. They lived near her father's farm, a thirty minute drive from Jim's house. Randi's family could have survived indefinitely on the resources of their farm and the knowledge in the heads of her parents. Instead, they fell victim to a long-standing feud that boiled over with a neighboring family. One bad decision by Randi's brother led to a vicious outpouring of violence that resulted in Randi's parents being murdered and her family home burned to the ground. Despite her earlier assurance to Jim that she would be fine, she ultimately took Jim up on his offer to join him in the valley where he lived.

Inevitably, those things that made Jim's valley attractive to him also made it attractive to outsiders looking for a place to weather the storm. Several times Jim, his neighbors, and his friends found themselves fighting off outsiders intent on stealing their homes and their resources. With each encounter Jim was finding diplomacy had little place in this new world. Discussion only seemed to buy you time until the guns came out.

He struggled to keep his family and friends safe, but he also struggled with an underlying guilt because there had been times when he'd wished for this—that the world would reset, that the government would collapse and reveal itself for the fraud he knew it was.

The thing he had not bargained for, the thing he had not anticipated, was how much violence, heartache, and hardship would come with the collapse. He was tired of killing and tired of seeing people he knew die.

Most recently, his coworker Alice, with whom he had a difficult relationship during their working career, had decided to come join them in the valley. She'd lost her husband and her mother. She saw the valley as a way to provide her son with greater protection.

She did not even have the opportunity to settle in before she got herself killed helping save Jim's life. For Jim, that was just new guilt on top of the old.

Jim didn't know what he was going to do. He did not want to be in charge but found himself as the de facto leader of this group more often than not. He just wanted to be left alone, but it had been easier to hide in the world before the collapse. Now, those that hid would find all that they worked to preserve stolen from under their noses.

Could Jim continue to shun responsibility or was it time to step forward? Was it time to own the blood he'd spilled?

1

Three Months Earlier

THE COAL-FIRED POWER plant at Carbo, Virginia, had never looked so desolate in its seventy year history. Until the world stumbled, the power plant was constantly busy. There were coal cars delivering fuel, operators monitoring gauges and switchgear, and heavy equipment zipping around. Sitting idle now for months, the facility was covered with a fine layer of gritty fly ash, oily coal dust, and soot. Perhaps that patina would never go away.

Cecil Hughes had worked at the plant for nearly forty years, the last thirty of those years in the machine shop. The machine shop was a medium-sized steel building, roughly the size of a fast food restaurant. Its outer skin was pea green metal of the type often found on industrial buildings in coal country. The inside of the steel structure had thick insulation that was covered in seventy years of dust and grime.

The building had that particular character that only old shops have. The floor was oil-stained and worn smooth by many decades of boots. The walls were lined with vintage lathes, milling machines, drill presses, and racks of metal stock. The smell of cutting oil still hung in the air despite the fact that no machining operations had taken place in months. This was Cecil's domain. He was the shop foreman and most of his waking hours for the last thirty years had been spent in this windowless, poorly-lit building.

Cecil worked at the plant up until the day they sent him home. The plant was still able to produce power but it was no longer able to get that power where it was needed. After the grid was damaged in the initial attacks, no one followed the urgent plea to throttle back their power usage. Washington, D.C. and Northern Virginia wanted more power, and plants tried to make that happen. The cost was that components were fried trying to meet demand. With the roads blocked by disabled vehicles and fuel becoming difficult to obtain, the power companies couldn't dispatch workers to replace the substation and power transmission components. So the operators at the Carbo plant did something they rarely did; they let all the fires in the boilers burn out. Coal suppliers had already warned them they were experiencing difficulty getting fuel, so the shutdown was inevitable.

Cecil lived in a nearby hollow. A lot of his family lived close by on his property. Both his son and his daughter had mobile homes in the same hollow and Cecil enjoyed that. It kept his grandchildren close by so that he could be a part of their daily lives. Cecil's mother was still living and she lived in the family's old home place at the mouth of the hollow. Cecil had grown up poor, so he was not as concerned as some might have been when the power went out. He knew how to get by with very little but his children and grandchildren did not.

When the weather got cold, they had trouble heating their homes because they had not followed Cecil's advice to install a woodstove in their homes for backup heat. They didn't want the mess, didn't want to cut firewood. They all ended up at Cecil's home, where he had a woodstove, but it was less than ideal. His mobile home was over-crowded to the point of misery.

Desperate for options, Cecil decided to move them all to the machine shop. It was basically his second home anyway. He had keys to get through the gates and into the shop. The machine shop also had an enormous coal stove and while there was not enough coal stockpiled to keep the power plant itself going indefinitely, there was more than enough coal lying around to keep that coal stove going for several winters. Over the course of several days, Cecil's wife, mother, kids, and their families moved into the shop, taking beds, cots, sleeping bags, and everything else that mattered to them.

When the weather permitted, they fished the river for largemouth and smallmouth bass, catfish, pike, muskie, and even alligator gar. They trapped turtles and beavers, and hunted the slopes around the plant for deer, possum, rabbits, coons, and black bear. Cecil's wife always grew a big garden and she brought her canning and cellar vegetables with her. While the family wasn't thriving, they weren't starving either. They were already planning on a much bigger garden the following summer and had been stockpiling seeds.

It was not quite winter yet but fall was on the way out. The nights and mornings were getting colder. Soon winter would be fully upon them. There was a lot of variation in how severe central Appalachian winters could be. Some were mild but others were utterly arctic in nature. Cecil wondered what this winter would bring. He hoped he was ready.

On one particular morning, he was the first to wake. He lit a Coleman lantern and shook the ash and clinkers from the stove grate, then added more coal. The shop would be warm for his family when they woke up. He never slept well anymore. He worried too much. His bladder was also determined to wake him up early each day.

From within the windowless shop, Cecil and his family had no way to know that an eight-man team was converging on their location. The team of top tier operators were led by a civilian known simply as Boss. Despite his lack of rank, he was as armed and lethal as any of his team members. Perhaps he was even more lethal since he lacked the discipline and structure a military background might have instilled in him. Yet his team had all seen him in action and had forged a bond of trust despite the difference in their backgrounds. They all trusted him.

Boss also had a special position of trust with the group currently running the government. Although he was separated from their most powerful placeholders by several layers of insulation, *everyone* knew his name and they knew his work. A certain level of government official knew there were jobs only Boss was perfectly suited for, and this particular assignment was one of them. He had been hand-selected. He had been briefed by someone near the top and had anything he required at his disposal. In this period of deprivation and scarcity, he had choppers, fuel, rations, ammunition, and anything he asked for.

Boss's team wore mil-spec uniforms in a Realtree camo pattern that blended perfectly with the Appalachian terrain. Except for a designated marksman, all of the men carried suppressed bullpup rifles and .45 caliber Sig 227 pistols. There were no rules of engagement for this operation. Whatever Boss asked, they had clearance to do. If they left a wide trail of bodies and debris, no one cared.

As long as they succeeded.

The team watched the machine shop for an hour. Their intel, derived from the most powerful satellite images available, told them there was a small force residing here. Perhaps a dozen folks. Those satellite images placed most of them in the machine shop, but Boss took nothing for granted. After watching the facility, after seeing that smoke only rose from the chimney at the machine shop, he was more comfortable in accepting that this entire facility was abandoned except for those folks living in the shop. That made now as good a time as any to make their move.

"I want Group Two on overwatch. Group One will breach," Boss said. The team wore wireless throat mikes and earpieces. It was state of the art, with encryption that left him with no concerns anyone would overhear their conversations.

The two group leaders confirmed their instructions and Boss raised his binoculars to watch what unfolded. He was pretty certain he knew how this would turn out, but you never knew how crazy hillbillies would act. He'd worked with a few over the years and they could be full of bluster or they could cut you. You never knew which one you were getting.

The breaching team approached the machine shop, taking advantage of the clutter around the property to conceal themselves. They flattened out against other structures, against rusting front-end loaders, and run-down forklifts. The lead man carried a battering ram.

They were perhaps ten seconds from piling into the structure when Boss's urgent warning came across their earpieces. "Group One! Take cover! Take cover!"

Each man in the entry team took cover where he could find it, hoping his camo did its job. The entry door to the machine shop had just opened and a man emerged in partially-laced boots with his hair sticking out in all directions. He'd obviously just woken up and he did not appear to have a weapon.

"Hold steady. See what he's up to," Boss instructed.

Everyone on the team remained in their cover, not moving a muscle, even their respiration slowing to the bare minimum. The man who'd come from the shop staggered over to a pickup truck and yanked down his zipper. He threw back his head and peed on the tire like a dog who'd been stuck in the car for a long road trip.

"Have I got someone near this guy? Give me some clicks."

There were two distinct clicks, their signal for an affirmative response.

"Okay. Whoever responded, take the whizzer out. Use a blade," Boss instructed.

There was no hesitation. Immediately, a figure rose from near invisibility at the front of a forklift. In a fluid movement, he was on the peeing man, clamping his gloved left hand over his mouth and drawing his head back to expose the neck. With his right, he unsheathed a custom Bowie from its holster behind his Sig. It was a single, flawless movement that came faster than the blink of an eye—covering the mouth, jacking the head back, and slicing completely through the subclavian artery as easily as if he were gutting a fish.

Cutting the throat was never as efficient as they made it in the movies. It was not an instant death. The first reaction was a wet, drowning cough as blood ran down the exposed windpipe of the still living body. That provoked a cough reaction, which sprayed the blood from the wound. From there it was a race as to what was going to kill you faster, the blood loss or the blood filling the lungs, drowning you.

Boss witnessed the whole thing, pleased with the cool efficiency of the kill. "Good job, T.J. Group One move forward. Prepare to breach. And check that damn door. No sense using a battering ram if you don't need to."

T.J. moved to the door and twisted the handle. It was indeed unlocked. He raised a high thumbs up, hoping everyone on the team caught the gesture.

"You're clear to breach," Boss announced.

The team stacked up, their weapons held ready and selectors set to burst fire. When everyone nodded that they were ready, T.J. triggered his light and slipped inside.

Unlike the drug raids seen on TV, where officers ran in announcing themselves, this raid was executed in near silence. That was, until the gunfire started. Boss was pleased to hear that all of the gunfire was suppressed weapons. No shotguns, no deer rifles. He took that to mean there was no return fire. This was his men cleaning house.

Boss said nothing. He did not want to distract his men even though he was curious how it was going. When they were done, they would let him know.

"We're clear," came T.J.'s announcement. It was less than a minute later but seemed much longer.

"Roger that," Boss said. "Any injuries?"

"That's a negative."

"Group One, clear the buildings. Group Two, secure the perimeter."

When the groups acknowledged their orders, Boss went to see the scene in the workshop for himself.

"It looks like some kind of family group," T.J. said. "They didn't put up a fight."

Boss nodded. "After we've cleared the facility, toss the bodies in the river. The snapping turtles will clean up the mess."

2

Present Day: Winter

THE SCENE in Jim Powell's living room made it almost seem like a typical winter power outage. It could have been the aftermath of an ice storm or a heavy snow, but it wasn't. The United States had been shaken to its core and his family, like many others, was struggling to keep their heads above water. Jim, his wife, his two kids, and his parents were sitting around the room trying to stay occupied. Jim's mom had taken to crocheting, something she hadn't done in nearly twenty years. Pops was reading a nine year old issue of *Outdoor Life*, learning how to snag springtime lunkers. The rest were playing a game of *Sorry*.

Except for Jim. He was pacing the house restlessly, feeling like a caged animal. He was not an *inside* person.

The impression that the lack of power could be attributed to a winter storm was compounded by the fact there actually was deep snow outside the French doors. It was nearly two feet deep in the drifts. It was the type of storm this region usually only got once every ten years or so. That it came in a winter already brimming with hardship was par for the course. Nothing had been easy for them, a trend that apparently would continue.

Were this a typical winter storm, the kids would be rejoicing in the school closures. They would be outside riding sleds and snowboards, enjoying the novelty of feeling like they were camping in their own home. But now, after seven months with no power, the novelty was long gone. Everyone was tired of camping in the house. Everyone was tired of the struggle. They all wanted life to go back to the way it was a year ago.

Everyone, even Jim, dreamed of power being restored. As a lifelong survivalist, Jim had to admit that there were moments over the years where he wished the country would collapse just to wake people up. He imagined a good dose of hardship might bring some reality into the lives of people that seemed totally oblivious. He felt like people had gotten too dependent on the government and too used to lives of relative ease. They'd forgotten the lessons of previous generations. They'd forgotten that no one would ever care about the safety of your family as much as you would. They'd forgotten that, ultimately, your fate and your survival was in your own hands.

Though everyone in Jim's family was still alive they'd all been touched by hardship. There was chaos and violence everywhere, even in small town America. They'd all had to make hard decisions. Some had been forced to kill another human and none had been spared the anguish of having to bury people they knew and cared about. With survival came suffering, but it was the only option. This was not a family that gave up. This was not a family of sheep that would lay down for slaughter.

Jim knew his family was faring better than many around him. They had resources accumulated from Jim's years of obsessive preparations. On this cold winter day they had warmth from the fireplace, light when they needed it, spring-fed running water, and they would eat a hot dinner. Though Jim carefully rationed food, they had not known deprivation or starvation. He would do his best to make sure that remained the case.

Despite their comfort, Jim was starting to experience cabin fever. He was used to being active during the day. He'd already done a lot of shoveling and there were paths to nearly everywhere on his farm that he might need to go. He and his son were also taking turns maintaining watch at the various observation posts around the valley. He just didn't like being inside so much. He went to the group of tall windows that looked out over the yard. The view hadn't changed since he looked out this same window just a few minutes ago. It was a beautiful view despite the circumstances, with billowing clumps of snow clinging to cedars and a pristine overlay of white that almost made one forget what a dirty, gritty, and violent place the world had become.

"This reminds me of the big snows we had when I was a kid," Jim said.

"Were they really bigger or are just we getting older?" Ellen asked.

"They were bigger," Nana said. "It seems like every winter we had at least one really bad one. Now you may go an entire winter with just a dusting of snow that melts right off."

"What was it, '77 or '78, that we had that really big one and missed two months of school?" Jim asked.

"I think it was 1978," Nana said. "The snow just kept coming. Every time it melted down a little, more came."

"I was four. I don't remember it," Ellen said. There was about eight years difference between her and Jim.

"The sledding was great," Jim said. "We didn't have any close neighbors really but I met up with other kids that lived on the same road. We would find a good spot and sled there all day. We'd find a cedar tree and build a fire under it. They had dense foliage that the snow couldn't get through. You could strip the bark off for getting the fire going."

It was yet one more of those things that kids these days probably wouldn't have the opportunity to experience. Parents couldn't let their kids be gone like that all day. Things could happen. Freaks could steal them. Social Services would come investigate that they were unsupervised.

"You remember that day you went sledding with Mr. Fairlane?" Nana asked. "It was during that same storm."

Jim smiled. "I'd forgotten about that. He was a nice man."

Nana smiled. "A wonderful man."

"Who was Mr. Fairlane?" Ellen asked.

"He was a retired teacher that was one of our closest neighbors," Jim replied. "I guess he was going stir-crazy too. We heard a knock at the door and were kind of surprised because our road was impassable. We went to the door and there was old Mr. Fairlane in a snowsuit."

"It was funny," Nana said. "He was like a kid asking if Jim could come out and play."

"We went sledding there by the house," Jim said. "Rode for hours and then he went back home."

"That's cool," Ellen said.

"It was," Jim agreed. "I hadn't thought about him in years. What happened to him?"

"He died when you were away at college," Nana said. "His wife stayed on in the house by herself. They had two kids but the daughter died when she was a teenager. The son moved to California and rarely came back."

"What happened to Mrs. Fairlane?" Jim asked.

"She's still alive as far as I know," Nana said. "I saw her out in town sometimes. She had friends from church who came by and took her out shopping."

"Wouldn't she be over a hundred years old by now? They were old when I was a kid."

"Kids aren't good judges of age," Nana said. "But anyway, she was twenty years younger than him. She was fresh out of the state teacher's college when he scooped her up. Age differences meant less then. People weren't as concerned with marrying a peer."

Jim thought about it. Even with the age difference, that would put Rosa Fairlane in her mid-eighties. He couldn't imagine that she'd survived to this point. The elderly were the hardest hit. They weren't able to get medications. Their pantries didn't have the padding that working families might have due to limited income or outliving their savings.

He walked over to the bookcase and picked up a pointed rock from a shelf. It was a Native American relic, a digging tool of some sort. Mr. Fairlane had given it to him when he was a kid. The man had started collecting relics in the 1930s, long before most people had any interest in them. He had an extensive collection and had given Jim many small items over the years.

The man had been something of a relic himself, of a time when men, when people in general, were different. He'd been born around 1910 best as Jim remembered and had come up poor. He'd worked and saved, putting himself through Virginia Tech at a time when they were only handing out a couple of dozen degrees each year. He was genteel and intelligent while remaining as homespun and country as anyone around him. It was the kind of thing that educated people from the area tried to erase within themselves anymore. They wanted the *country* gone. The wanted the *hillbilly* gone.

Jim put the relic back on the shelf. "I'm going to do some work in the shop." The place was well-insulated and had a woodstove. It wouldn't take long to get it warmed up. There were always things in there that needed tinkering with, experiments and things he never got around to finishing.

As he dressed, Jim thought of the impish Mr. Fairlane with his thick white hair and bushy white eyebrows. He could almost remember his voice, although he found it strange that it was the most difficult detail to recall. His face, his clothes, and his gait were not difficult but Jim struggled with the voice.

When he got his coat and boots on, he grabbed a handgun and a rifle from hooks by the door then stepped out into the cold. Perhaps that served to focus things for him. Then it came to him. He heard the laugh, then the voice came with it. When it came to him, he heard it clear as the crisp day that lay before him.

"Would you mind to check on Rosa for me?"

There's no way she's still alive, Jim thought. She seemed in frail health thirty years ago, at least to his child's mind. But he would check out of respect for someone who helped make him who he was. He would check in honor of a world that he missed.

The door opened behind Jim.

"Dad?" It was Pete. "You forgot your radio."

Jim checked his empty radio pouch. "I didn't notice."

"I wouldn't have noticed either, but Hugh was calling you on it," Pete said.

"Thanks," Jim said, patting his son on the shoulder. He raised the radio to his mouth. "Hugh, you still there?"

"*Yes sir,*" Hugh replied.

Hugh was an old friend. They had worked together at Jim's first job. They hadn't crossed paths for years but made contact again when Jim found out Hugh was working as a radio operator for a group of rogue cops who had taken over the local superstore. When those folks took Jim prisoner, Hugh played a role in his escape, and ended up moving into the valley with Jim's group. He was an amateur radio operator and spent the cold months of winter getting his radio equipment operational. He was now scouring the airwaves for any information about the state of the world. He radioed Jim with an update every day.

"How are things up on the mountain?"

"*Any better and I wouldn't be able to stand it,*" Hugh replied.

"So what's going on?"

"*I've been logging contacts ever since I got this equipment up. There's been chatter all winter about helicopters, trains carrying troops, occupying foreign armies—all the usual conspiracy-type bullshit. It's all so fragmented that none of it makes any sense. But the feds started blasting a message everywhere last night.*"

"What do you mean by *blasting*?"

"*They've got a loop repeating on all kinds of frequencies—ham frequencies, commercial VHF, AM, FM, weather—all over the damn place.*"

"Saying what?"

"*Saying power restoration will begin next week.*"

Jim was so shocked he had to sit down on the steps. "Next week?"

"That's what they said. No details but to continue listening for updates next week."

"Jesus," Jim mumbled, uncertain if he'd even keyed the mike or not.

"This explains all those flickers of power over the winter," Hugh went on. *"They were working on shit, testing. Maybe we're at the end of this."*

Other families in the valley who were monitoring the same frequency began bombarding Hugh with questions. He did his best to answer them with what little information he had. As word spread over the next couple of days, each person would struggle to make sense of this crazy chapter of their lives. They would hope that, as Hugh said, they were at the end of it.

What would be ending would not be what any of them expected.

Jim shoved his radio in the pouch on his vest. He went back in the house and stood on the rug by the door allowing his eyes to adjust to the light.

"Back so soon?" Nana asked.

Jim didn't immediately answer, still processing Hugh's information.

"You okay?" Ellen asked.

"Did you guys hear Hugh on the radio?" Jim asked.

Ellen looked around. "I think I left my radio in the bedroom." It was something Jim fussed at her about. The radio did no good in an emergency if you couldn't hear it. She prepared herself for a lecture but it didn't come.

"Hugh says there's been an official transmission about the power," Jim said. "Restoration is supposed to begin next week."

All eyes turned to him, questioning. When they saw he wasn't joking, Ariel jumped to her feet and began cheering. Everyone else soon joined her. They were lost in their reverie and didn't notice Jim slip back out the door.

~

JIM STOOD on the porch and surveyed his kingdom, shading his eyes against the reflected sunlight with a raised arm. The sun may be bright but it was still too cold for any significant melting to take place. In other projects accomplished out of boredom, wide paths were shoveled to the woodshed, the barn, and the shop building. When Jim got tired of sitting in the house, carrying firewood was usually the remedy, but the wood rack on the front porch was already stacked full. Even in these cold temperatures, there was probably enough for a week or longer.

The information Hugh had delivered was stunning. Admittedly, there were no details, but the pieces made sense. There was a power plant within twenty miles of the valley. Surely if it was restored, they would have access to power soon. Jim tried to stay in the present and not let his mind run away with him. Even on that little piece of information, it was racing. He even found a part of himself already doing an after-action report on this entire SHTF period of his life. What preparations had worked and what hadn't? What would he do differently next time?

Next time?

He definitely hoped there was never a next time.

His churning thoughts were interrupted by a shout. Times being what they were, the shout provoked him to step back toward his house and move the M4 to a low ready position until he'd assessed the situation. The sun reflecting off the snow made it hard to get a good look in all directions but he soon noticed a bundled figure making its way across the field toward him, coming from the direction of Randi's house.

"That you, Randi?"

He couldn't tell through the layers. Between the scarf, sunglasses, jacket, and gloves, there was no flesh exposed. Although he could usually tell folks by their gait, in this case it was little more than an overstuffed waddle that told him nothing.

"Yeah, it's me. I had to get out of the house. My family, God bless 'em, is driving me bat shit."

Jim laughed. "I feel your pain. I'm starting to pace the house like a lion at the zoo."

He went down the steps and waited while she staggered closer, letting herself through the wide cattle gate that separated the pasture from the yard.

"I needed to get out for a while," she said. "I told them I needed to check the horses and make sure their blankets were still tight or some shit like that. It was just an excuse to get out. The kids and grandkids have watched *Finding Nemo* on a tablet four times today already. I can't take it anymore."

"Well, I was going to build a fire in the shop and tinker with a few projects. You're welcome to come hang out in there."

Randi shrugged beneath the layers, at least that was what it looked like. "Is there a chair? I ain't sitting on any uncomfortable stool. I'm old and cranky and a stool won't help that."

"Even better. There's a comfortable couch. I've slept on it before when one of the kids was having a rowdy sleepover with their friends. I'm pretty sure there's even a few bottles of liquor stashed out there somewhere if that's what you need."

Randi shook her head. "Despite Lloyd's best efforts, I'm not quite as fond of day drinking as he is, but don't take that as a hard no. That is subject to change."

They headed in the direction of the shop, Randi following Jim down the shoveled path. The snow crunched and squeaked beneath their boots.

"I'm thinking about making a run into town tomorrow," Jim said. "Think we could take your horses?"

"Only if you take me with you."

"Of course you can go. Seems like you need out as bad as I do."

"What's the mission?"

"Mission?" Jim asked.

"Yeah, there has to be a mission. There's *always* a mission. Why are we going to town?"

Jim stopped and turned around to face Randi. "It's kind of a long story, but there was this old neighbor man who was really nice to me when I was kid. He was like a grandfather you weren't related to. He's probably been dead for twenty-five or thirty years, but my mom mentioned this morning that his wife was still alive when this whole mess started. I had no idea. I hadn't thought of her in years. I know this sounds crazy, but when I was inside a few minutes ago I could feel this guy asking me to go check on his wife."

"You could *feel* it?"

Jim took a deep breath. "I told you it sounded crazy. This guy was asking me to go check on his wife Rosa. It wasn't in my ears. It was in my head."

"With all the shit we've been through in the past six or seven months, you're going to tell me you think that sounds crazy? If you told me a year ago that the country was going to get knocked on its ass, I would have told you that was crazy. If you told me a year ago that we'd be living without power now, I would have told you that was crazy. If you told me a year ago I would walk all the freaking way home from Richmond, I would have damn sure told you that you were crazy. Everything that's happening around us is crazy. So when you tell me that you feel like a dead friend wants you to check on his wife, that just doesn't even meet the standard of crazy anymore. In fact, it's probably the most reasonable thing I've heard in a while."

"You have a point," Jim said. "Either way, I can't imagine she's survived. She's old and in poor health."

"Well that's a positive fucking attitude," Randi quipped.

"Just being realistic."

Randi shook her head. "You know, Jim, your people skills are sorely lacking. You need a lot of work in that department. A little positivity, a little sensitivity, would go a long way."

"Now you're starting to sound like my family."

"Maybe they have a point. If you can listen to a dead guy, maybe you should think about listening to the live folks around you."

Randi was wearing her lecturing face. Jim could imagine it was the one she used when delivering tough love to her kids. She'd even used it on him a few times.

Jim turned around and kept walking toward his shop. "Everybody has some opinion on something I need to improve," Jim growled over his shoulder. "I'm about to the point of not giving a shit anymore."

"Oh, quit pouting."

"I'm not pouting. I'm just embracing my inner curmudgeon. I'm owning it."

"There's better things to own."

"There's better things to talk about too. Like the power coming back on," Jim said.

Randi stopped in her tracks. "Excuse me?"

Jim stopped and faced Randi again. "Did you not catch Hugh on the radio? The way he got bombarded, I assumed everyone must have heard it."

"The power is coming back on? When?" She was practically salivating.

"We don't know exactly. Hugh says the government is playing some kind of recorded message on a lot of different channels saying that power restoration begins next week."

"Next week?" Randi's eyes were wide and she seemed on the verge of breaking into dance.

"*Begins* next week," Jim repeated. "That doesn't mean that we will have power here in this valley next week. In fact, I don't know exactly what it does mean but it sounds like they'll start powering things back up next week. That's why we saw those lights flickering this winter. It had to be them testing the lines."

Randi took a deep breath. "That's a lot to think about. What will that be like? What about all the dead people? What about having a job again? What about insurance? Are they going to be fixing peoples' houses?"

Jim shook his head. "One thing at a time. How about we walk up to Buddy's house and see if he wants to go with us tomorrow? I'm tired of your lectures about what I need to be working on to make myself a better person. I'm sure you're missing Lloyd, anyway."

"Whatever, asshole. You need all the constructive criticism you can get. You should take it and run with it."

"I need to grab my pack if we're going up the road," Jim said. "Feel free to keep talking while I'm gone. It will have the same effect."

Randi scowled and started to give Jim the finger but she was afraid Ariel might be watching out the window. Ariel would tell on her for sure. She was at that age where she loved to rat out the adults.

Jim trotted toward the house, climbed the steps, and stomped the snow off his boots. He went through the front door, careful to stay on the rug so he wouldn't track snow any further into the house. He grabbed his go bag from a hook by the door.

"Going somewhere?" Ariel said. Jim smiled at his daughter. "Randi showed up to check on her horses. We're walking up to Buddy's house. I'm going to see if Buddy wants to go into town with me tomorrow. I should be back before too long."

"Don't drink any of Lloyd's liquid jelly," Ariel said with the smugness and sarcasm that only a pre-teen girl possesses.

"Liquid jelly?" Ellen asked, frowning at her daughter.

Ariel nodded. "That's what Lloyd told me he keeps in those jars. They're different flavored jellies. They're just *liquidy* because they're not in the refrigerator. He said because of that you have to drink them instead of putting them on biscuits."

"Don't be listening to anything that Lloyd says about that," Ellen said. "He's full of liquid jelly, especially between his ears."

Ariel laughed.

Jim tossed a hand up. "I'll see you later. Don't let the fire burn out."

"I'm on it," Pops said.

Jim slipped out the door with his armload of gear and headed back across the yard. He found Randi sitting in the barn ruminating on something. Jim didn't ask her what it was. Everyone had a lot of dark thoughts to process these days and needed time to do so. It didn't necessarily mean you wanted to talk about them. He knew that if she reached that point, she'd come out with it.

"Ready to go?" he asked.

She rose stiffly from the chair, finding that the layers she was wrapped in didn't provide a lot of flexibility.

"You need help, Grandma?"

"Bite my ass," she growled. "I'm fine."

"And you said *I* didn't have people skills."

UNFORTUNATELY THERE WAS no shoveled path from Jim's house to Buddy's. Jim and Randi traipsed down his driveway and went through a red tube gate to access the paved road that ran the length of the valley. There they found some tracks—horse, man, dog, and deer.

There were no vehicle tracks. Usable gasoline was almost entirely gone from the valley now. There may still have been caches out there remaining in undiscovered outbuildings, vehicle tanks, and lawn-mowers, but they weren't turning up often. Without the addition of fuel stabilizer, most of what remained was turning to a useless shellac. While Jim and his group still had a little diesel and home heating oil, they were trying to be extremely conservative. They had no means to replace what they used and there were no signs fuel would be in production again anytime soon.

"This snow reminds me of being a kid," Jim said. "They didn't plow the roads until the snow stopped falling. Four-wheel-drive was less common then and families didn't have six vehicles like they do now. On a snowy night there wouldn't be anyone out. People stayed home because they had better sense."

"I'm about your age," Randi said. "I remember. Different high school but the same county."

"I remember this one time when I was a teenager," Jim continued. "I was staying with a friend in town. There was a deep snow like this and we went out walking around. There was nobody anywhere. We sat in the snow underneath the red light in the middle of town and just shot the shit. We must have sat there for an hour and we never saw a car. Those were the good old days."

"So this walk ain't recapturing the magic of your golden years?" Randi asked.

Jim shook his head. "Not quite."

"Maybe those were the good old days because you knew you still had power at your house," Randi suggested. "That's where the freedom to do things like sitting in the snow in the middle of town

came from. You do something like that now you would need someone
with a gun watching your back. You might get shot in the head for
your warm clothes. And these days you wouldn't be going back to a
house for a cup of hot chocolate or a bag of barbecue corn chips."

"Shit!" Jim groaned. "I wish you hadn't mentioned those. I haven't
thought about those things in forever but God I loved them. I would
probably shoot someone right now for a bag of them."

"You probably would, being the cold-hearted bastard you are, but
let's not get started on the things we miss. If we do, shit is going to get
real sad real fast."

In the deep snow each step was a post hole. They had to raise
their legs high, moving slowly and burning lots of energy. Conversation died off, the focus moving to just making progress. What was
normally a ten minute walk took about thirty, but eventually they
were tromping up the steps to Buddy's porch. The gray painted
planks were clear of snow. Jim went over by the front door and leaned
against the wall, unlacing his boots.

"You think Lloyd cleared this porch?" he asked.

Randi laughed. Clearly she had her doubts.

There was no need to knock. As the pair took off their shoes they
could already hear someone walking toward the door. Buddy opened
the door, a lever-action hunting rifle in his hands. Through the open
door, Jim could hear strains of banjo music.

"Aren't you tired of that racket yet?" Jim asked.

Buddy shrugged. "Beats listening to my old joints creak."

Jim shook his head in disagreement. "If you say so."

Buddy held open the door while Jim and Randi slipped inside.
Buddy kept the house superheated, like a lot of older people. The
living room was probably close to 80°. Jim started to shed layers soon
as he was in the house.

Lloyd stopped playing and looked at his oldest friend.

"You know how you can tell if the stage is level at a bluegrass
show?" Jim asked.

"No," Lloyd replied cautiously.

"The banjo player drools out both sides of his mouth."

Lloyd slapped his knee and snorted with fake laughter.

"I thought I'd get the important things out of the way first. Insulting the banjo player," Jim said. "So what's this you told Ariel about drinking liquid jelly?"

Lloyd look sheepish. "She heard me say something about drinking blackberries from a jar. It was all I could think of on short notice."

"And with limited sobriety," Randi added.

"And then there's that," Lloyd agreed.

"So what brings you all out in this weather?" Buddy asked. "Everything okay?"

"Things are fine enough," Jim said. "But I was thinking about going into town tomorrow to check on the wife of a friend. Wondered if you might be interested in going."

Buddy nodded seriously. "I would. Appreciate the offer. What brought this on?"

"Just a feeling," Jim said, not ready to get into the story again.

"Well, count me out," Lloyd grumbled. "I'm tending the fire."

"Nobody ever counted you in," Jim said.

"We walking?" Buddy asked.

"Horses," Jim said. "I've still got a little fuel in my truck but I'm not sure I could cross the river in this mess and get up that bank on the other side, even with chains."

"Horses?" Lloyd snorted. "I definitely ain't going."

"I already told you that you weren't invited," Jim pointed out.

"Just us?" Buddy asked.

"I thought about asking the sheriff," Jim said. "Didn't know if he might need a break or if he might want to see what was going on in town."

Buddy twisted his mouth and shrugged. "I talked to him yesterday. Saw him outside carrying wood and went over there. I think they're on a death vigil for his mother. She's not eating or drinking. Her kidneys aren't working and she hasn't woke up in days. They're pretty sure this is the end but she just won't give in to it."

Jim nodded. "I'll leave them alone then. I may ask Deputy Ford instead." He took a seat on the couch.

Randi spotted a jar of moonshine on the mantle and opened it. She took a deep whiff from the open lid. "Hmmmm...blackberry jelly."

"Smartass," Lloyd said.

Randi took a sip and offered it to Jim. Jim had one also.

"Just help yourself, why don't you," Lloyd said with mock offense.

"Planned on it," Jim said.

"Guess I'll have one," Lloyd said. "I hate to see a man drink alone."

"Randi is drinking too," Jim said.

"I hate to see two people drinking alone," Lloyd corrected.

"What you mean is you hate to see people drinking booze without you," Jim said.

"Same thing," Lloyd said. "Manners are manners."

"So did you hear Hugh's transmission on the radio?" Jim asked, looking from Lloyd to Buddy.

"I caught some of it," Buddy said. "There was a lot of chattering and I couldn't make it all out. Sounded like there was news about the power?"

Jim repeated everything he'd heard from Hugh. Buddy and Lloyd nodded, taking it in but not displaying the same excitement that Randi or Jim's family had demonstrated.

Randi leaned over and punched Lloyd on the arm. "Didn't you hear what he said? The power will be back on soon? That's good news."

Lloyd regarded her, cradling his banjo. "I heard him but I don't share the opinion that it's good news. I prefer the world a little more natural. A little darker."

"Well you can sit in the damn dark then," Randi said. "I, for one, am ecstatic. What about you, Buddy?"

The old man shrugged noncommittally from his seat at the kitchen table. "Things won't go back to the same. They can't. Too much has happened. I don't know how they'll fix it."

Everyone understood that Buddy was right to some extent. They talked about it until the sun dropped to the shoulder of the distant mountains. Jim and Randi rose to pull their layers back on and return to their crowded houses.

They planned a departure time of 8 AM the next morning. Buddy said he would trek up to the deputy's trailer before it got fully dark and see if Ford was interested in going with them. To no one's surprise, Lloyd reaffirmed that he would make certain the fire did not go out while they were gone to town.

3

Rosa Fairlane awoke to a completely silent house. Quiet was not unusual or off-putting to her. For the twenty-five or so years since her husband died, the house always seemed quiet. Despite the passage of time, he was still what she listened for each morning. Him in the kitchen fixing a cup of coffee, building a fire, puttering around his office, or his footsteps just moving through the big house.

She did not even notice the absence of modern sounds like cars, television, and the hum of appliances. She had been born into a world without those things and it seemed fitting to her that here toward what was most certainly the end of her life she should find herself again in a world without those things. It was almost as if the electronic age had merely been a noisy blip in the middle of her life.

She threw back the covers and managed to swing her stiff legs from the tall bed. Out of habit and ritual her feet automatically found the fuzzy house slippers she always wore. Oddly enough, in this time of deprivation and want, those were one thing that she had no concern about running out of. When you reached her age no one knew what to give you as a gift so all you ever got were nightgowns, robes, and slippers.

She and her husband always lived on one level of the house. There were two bedrooms and a bathroom upstairs but she hadn't been up there in years. One of the bedrooms had belonged to her son. He lived in California now and she didn't think she'd ever see him again. He had not come back home to visit often but she understood. He was busy and his personality was such that he had found it easy to cut himself free of the mooring of family.

The other bedroom was perpetually that of a teenager of the 1960s. There was a white portable record player on a table with a 45 rpm record on the turntable. It was the Guess Who. There was a poster of The Doors and one of Jim Morrison solo. Another poster featured signs of the zodiac. There were beaded curtains at the window and a flowered bedspread that her daughter had picked out from the Sears catalog. A blue hairbrush on a mirrored tray held strands of hair that Rosa had stroked hundreds if not thousands of times, her eyes closed, her memory placing the warmth of a child's head beneath those strands.

Rosa knew the room by memory but could not even recall the last time she went in there. Ten years? Twenty years? It belonged to her daughter Pat. Her daughter had been seventeen when she drowned on a canoe trip on the Clinch River.

It was a hot summer day and there were several canoes full of teenagers, all part of the church youth group. Capsizing a canoe on the slow moving river would not have been a big deal had Pat's legs not become entangled in a submerged tree. The powerful river had folded her over at the waist, submerging her head. She could not disentangle herself nor could she straighten out to get her head back above water.

It was several minutes before enough people got to her that they could free her legs. They were also fighting the current and the underwater entanglements. When her limp body was finally freed, her spirit was no longer in there. She was gone.

It was 1969. There were no cell phones and no med flights. At that time, in that place, the drowned were dead forever. There was no resuscitation and lingering hope. Part of Rosa died that day too, but

Charles would not let her go fully with her daughter. He tethered her to this word and made her continue living.

Charles had already owned this house when she married him. He was a resourceful school teacher and bought a hulking brick Victorian on the edge of town that was falling into disrepair, making it his own over the years. He always had his eye out for interesting architectural features or found materials that were available for free or cheap. Their entry foyer was made of the dark walnut paneling from an old attorney's office. The living room had the hand-planed wainscoting of a church that was being torn down. The mantles came from a colonial-era mansion that was repurposed as a hay barn.

When a modest pioneer home was being torn down to make way for a grocery store, it bothered Charles deeply. The home was one of the oldest on Main Street. He got permission from the property-owner to salvage what he could but he was only given a weekend over which to do so. Charles hired several strong-backed farm boys for a day and they helped him remove several trailer loads of hand-hewn logs and beams. He was always hiring students and former students to help him with jobs. He found he much preferred to work with younger folks. Over time, Charles found a way to integrate those logs into the boring Victorian kitchen, giving it a totally unique pioneer charm.

That was the way of Charles Fairlane. He had a respect for the past and was always trying to find ways to integrate it into the present. Being married to him had been an adventure. Rosa was a teacher also, and they both had summers off. In the early years of their marriage and when the children were small, they took long road trips across the country, visiting national parks. They camped on floorless tents or sometimes just on blankets beneath wide-open sky. It was something that Rosa had never imagined herself doing during her sheltered upbringing.

Charles had been a brave man in his way. He had not been afraid to venture forth into the world and to be who he wanted to be. Over the years since he died, she often found herself drawing on the strength that had come from him. While that strength was present in her memories of him, it was also present in everything around her. It was present in all his projects and his collections. It was present in the remodeling projects that made their home so enthralling to guests. She drew on all that strength now, keeping herself alive in the months since the world had regressed.

When she and Charles had been married their home was on the fringes of town. They often saw deer, bear, and coyotes. Foxes and rabbits were plentiful. The town eventually made its way out to them, swallowing their little enclave of privacy. There were modern homes built and mobile homes parked, making their street noisy, requiring streetlights that erased the stars from the night sky. Unlike the neighborhoods of her childhood, neighbors here no longer had any relationship with the people around them. In fact, she had barely seen anyone since the world fell apart, except for those unpleasant visitors she preferred not to think about. She was certain her father would not have approved of the way that turned out.

She didn't even know if the homes around her were occupied any longer but certainly no one had come to see her. She didn't even know the current state of the world. All she knew were the bits and pieces she picked up on the radio before everything went dark and quiet. It was enough to tell her the story.

The ladies from her church who usually helped her with her shopping and her regular doctor appointments had not been by either. She had lost track of time but the arrival of winter told her it had been several months since she'd run out of medications. She could feel the effects on her health. There were moments of weakness and dizziness. She tried to take it easy and to treat herself with home remedies to relieve what symptoms she could. She couldn't remain idle. There was way too much to do. As in the pioneer days, even as in her childhood, staying alive required work. Lots of it.

Long before the use of the term *permaculture*, Charles had planted the grounds of their country home with fruit and nut trees. He didn't do this imagining the need for these things as part of a long-term survival scenario but because it was the way people he knew had always done things. It was only common sense that your property should feed you year round.

He always encouraged her to can and preserve their harvests during his lifetime and she continued to do so in his memory. She preserved walnuts, hickory nuts, and chestnuts in their earthen basement. She preserved apples, grapes, and blackberries. Each summer she planted as much of a garden as she could manage, and usually a little more. She was on a cane or walker most days and working in the garden was the extent of the physical exercise she was able to get. Her husband had often used one of the kid's little red wagons to assist in his garden chores and she continued doing so, though the wagon was now as old and rusty as she herself felt.

Her husband had harvested seeds of his favorite varieties, not because he was a homesteader by name but because that was how he'd been raised. He knew plant varieties not by their scientific or commercial names but by association with the people from whom his seed stock originated. There were Aunt Theodosia's cucumbers for pickling, Uncle June's striped tomatoes, and old Miss Wells' crook-neck squash growing by Cousin Albert's sweet bell peppers.

Some of his special names she remembered and some she sadly did not. Those names had faded from her memory like the embossed Mrs. and Mrs. Charles Fairlane had faded from the yellowed envelopes she used for storing seeds. In the absence of knowing her husband's original names, she wrote the only name she could assign them. There was Charlie's zucchini, Charlie's tommy-toe tomatoes, Charlie's corn, and so on. She kept the seeds in an old cookie tin in the basement so they would remain rodent proof.

For the past several months, since the time no more visitors came and the phone quit ringing, she lived from her pantry and from her canning. It concerned her that she could see an end to this, a point where all of the shelves in the pantry would be bare, where the buckets and bushel baskets in the basement would be empty. It was already hard enough to even get down there now and retrieve anything.

If her health stayed decent and she could make it a few more months, she could plant a garden again. There would be a lot of hoeing required since she assumed she could no longer hire anyone to till the soil for her. Lettuce and peas would come up quickly even in cooler weather. She was not scared to die but she would prefer not to starve to death, but anytime she thought about dying she knew whatever fate she met could not be as bad as that of her daughter. While she did not want to imagine her daughter trapped under the cold water, struggling for breath, she could not stop herself from going there.

"However I go, you knew worse," she said to her empty house.

LIKE MOST MORNINGS, Rosa went to build a fire first thing. In its better days, the home was heated with a coal furnace. She had it checked out each year at the beginning of heating season and it was becoming harder and harder to find anyone who knew how to work on those old behemoths with their peeling asbestos and grimy auger-fed stokers. It had become equally hard to find folks who would deliver coal to her home and shovel it into the coal bin in the basement. Everyone told her that she needed to modernize and get a heat pump, to quit fooling with that dirty and labor-intensive heating system. She didn't want to spend the money, nor did she want to change the house in that way. She wanted it to stay the same until she died, then replacing the heating system would be the problem of the new owners.

The old kitchen with its log beams had a Majestic wood-fired cook stove. It was original to the house. Even as he added electric appliances over the years, Charlie insisted on keeping the with cook stove as a throwback to his childhood.

"There ain't no biscuits like woodstove biscuits. It's the only way to cook a breakfast. Fried potatoes, eggs, gravy, fried ham. None of it tastes the same on an electric range."

That woodstove was what had allowed her to survive this winter. On the really cold nights she'd slept in the kitchen. She didn't have the strength to move her bed down there, which would have been her preference. Instead, she set up a folding cot in the kitchen and slept on it. She always awoke stiff and aching the next morning so she preferred her own bed when she could tolerate the cold nights.

Charlie had died with a full shed of firewood. During the last years of his life it wasn't often that they had a fire, but every time somebody he knew lost a tree, Charlie insisted on cutting it up and storing some of it. It was just the way he thought about life. You didn't let those opportunities to put away a resource pass you by. Some of it he used for woodworking projects in his little workshop. Some of it they occasionally burned in the backyard, having campfires long before backyard fire pits were in vogue.

It was difficult for Rosa to carry firewood and she again utilized the little red wagon. With Charlie dead around thirty years, she assumed some of the wood had to be over fifty years old. In fact, some of it had completely rotted to dust. She found mouse nests and delicate old snake skins but none of those worried her. The dry wood burned quickly. She supplemented it with scraps from Charlie's workshop. There were shelves full of odd little bits of wood that he had saved for this project or that. She filled buckets with them and fed them into the stove piece by piece.

Some she recognized as having been part of a particular project, and those flooded her with memories. There were fragments of handmade patio chairs, bookcases, and children's beds. There was cedar Charlie had cut and planed himself for cedar-lined closets and hope chests. There was painted pine from a toy box, stained oak from a coat rack, and cracked blue-painted poplar from a pie safe. More than once she found herself in tears as she fed the fire.

When the scraps were dwindling, it was with great remorse that she began to break apart projects from the workshop. There were incomplete tables and bookcases, unassembled oak chairs. Some of those projects could have started fifty years ago. She couldn't remember. She always looked at them with a sort a reverence, as if Charlie lived on in them. Part of her hoped he might come back sometime and complete them. She knew that would never happen but it had kept her from discarding them.

Now she understood that there was no hope their children would complete them either. These incomplete projects would never be meaningful to anyone but her. She knew if Charlie could speak to her, he would tell her to break them apart, to take what she could from them. In that manner, he could continue to provide for her as he had when he was alive. They had built a life together, and now she was erasing it one piece at a time, starting at the farthest periphery. Were the winter to go on long enough, she would eventually burn the furniture in the house. She would tear his precious paneling and wainscoting from the walls and burn it too if she had to. She would burn the salvaged doors, the wormy chestnut bed, and each and every baluster from the stairs.

Rosa had continued using the toilet. She'd grown up without indoor plumbing and was no stranger to the use of a slop jar. Their house had rain barrels below the downspouts because Charlie insisted that his vegetables preferred the natural rainwater to public water. Rosa used that water for drinking and flushing toilets. Lately she'd been melting snow so the rain barrels could fill back up. Her kitchen was filled with containers of melted water. There were jars, thermoses, old Tupperware pitchers, and whatever she could find. If all other sources of water eluded her, there was a trickle of a brook at the corner of the yard, though she knew she would have trouble carrying much more than a half-gallon at a time across the yard.

She filled a kettle with water she'd melted yesterday and set it on the cook stove while she built her fire. The tinder she placed in the wood stove that morning was pages torn from a Compton's 1964 encyclopedia of the *Year in Review*. There was nothing in that book that anyone cared about anymore. The kindling she put on top of those crumpled pages was split from wide, rough-sawn cedar boards that Charlie had used to apply board-and-batten siding to the back patio during a 1960s update. He'd saved all the scraps and had built many bird houses with them over the years. Some of those houses still sat on fence posts or hung from trees in the backyard. Others fell apart as the thin nails rusted to nothing.

Rosa was long out of coffee, but as she had inventoried her pantry early on she found no shortage of Jell-O. She attended a lot of church functions and Jell-O was always an ingredient in some dessert. A couple of spoons of the powder mixed with hot water made for an acceptable morning beverage. It was not Maxwell House but it would have to do. She had some homemade teas but she preferred those for an evening beverage.

With her mug in one hand, she took her cane and walked to the window overlooking her backyard. There were three deer back there nudging around beneath a barren apple tree, hoping to find something under the snow. Rosa thought of shooting one of the deer. If she was certain she could get it to the back porch, she would do so in a heartbeat. The problem was that she didn't have a way to hang it. Even as a proper young lady, she'd seen her father butcher animals. She knew what to do, but knew she'd have to hang it to properly preserve the meat and keep it from predators.

It still might come to that. She eyed the shotgun sitting on the kitchen table. An open box of buckshot sat beside it. After the last time she'd been forced to use it, she thought it wise to keep the weapon close at hand. There were ways she was willing to die. There were also ways she was not.

4

A somber party of four rode out of the valley on horseback the next morning. Jim rode lead because he wasn't feeling too talkative. Buddy, Randi, and Deputy Ford followed. While the clear sky and strong morning light held promise of a warmer day with hopefully some melting, they weren't there yet. A strong, cold breeze blew steadily from the southwest, keeping morning wind chills in the upper teens. The riders huddled over their saddles, trying their best to ward off the cold and keep their flesh covered. The one thing they could not deflect was the nagging reluctance to head into the unknown of town. Those trips rarely ended well. That awareness clawed at each of them.

Jim didn't look down on the townspeople so much as he just couldn't figure them out. He didn't understand how a man could think with so many other people crowded into his psychic space. If your home was the place you went to relax and unwind at the end of the day, how could you do so when you couldn't even go outside without being scrutinized by your neighbors? When Jim went outside, he didn't want to see people. If he was enjoying the scenery, the mere appearance of people pissed him off. Except for his family and a few friends, he found people and mosquitoes to be very similar

—a buzzing, hovering nuisance that only reappeared after being swatted away.

The path to town was unbroken trail. No one had been out that way since the snow fell. Despite being an uncomfortable and untrained horseman, Jim knew the trail best. Most of it was familiar farm road and of little concern until they got to the creek crossing. It was large creek, what some areas of the country might consider a small river. At these temperatures, its edge would have turned to an icy encrustation where saturated snow froze into a sharp rind.

When they reached it, Jim waded in carefully, encouraging his horse to tromp down the icy edge and clear a path. With that knocked out of the way, he tried to follow the same path he'd taken his truck through. That track was relatively smooth, the larger rocks having been chucked out of the way a century ago when this river crossing was the primary route into the valley, before bridges were added.

Past the river they immediately rode into their first bad memory. Despite the beautiful snow covering, this had been the scene of a battle. A wrecked car marked the spot where another deputy, Ford's friend, had been killed by some rogue cops. Though no words were exchanged, Jim knew everyone was in a dark place.

Beyond this scene was the cornfield behind the shopping center, the place where Alice had been killed after she'd rescued Jim. He felt the hammering of complex emotions, guilt at what happened to Alice and sadness for her son Charlie. They made a wide circle around the superstore that had been a base of operations for the rogue cops, where so much had taken place. Jim had been held prisoner and many men had died. It was where they found Jim's old friend Hugh, who now lived high in their valley and had spent the winter putting together a battery of radios that should improve their access to information.

The group followed the road at the edge of the parking lot, keeping a wary eye toward the boarded façade of the superstore. A thin tendril of smoke rose from a hastily erected stovepipe punched through a skylight on the roof. Somebody was still there. Someone that had nowhere else to go. Jim just hoped it was not someone intent on avenging a death he may have played a part in.

Past the shopping center, Jim paused at an intersection, turning his horse. Buddy rode up alongside him, though it was hard to tell who was beneath the insulated face mask, the hooded Carhartt jacket, and the Carhartt coveralls. He peeled the mask up, revealing an ashen face. There was no trace of the resilient man whose eyes often glinted with amusement at his new friend Lloyd. The hard man was back. The man forged from loss, killing, and inconceivable pain.

"Reckon this is where I get off," Buddy said. "Where we going to meet back up?"

"You going to be a while?" Jim asked.

"I ain't talked to my baby in a while. I've got a lot to tell her."

Jim nodded somberly. He couldn't imagine having to do what Buddy was on his way to do right now. To visit his daughter and speak to her through the layers of frozen ground.

"Then how about Plan A is we all come meet up with you at the cemetery when we finish our business. Plan B is that we meet right here on this spot. If for some reason you decide to leave the cemetery or some shit happens, this is where we meet up. Sound good?"

Buddy nodded.

"Everybody get that?" Jim confirmed with the others.

More nods.

"Keep that rifle handy," Jim warned, eyeing Buddy's lever-action deer rifle. "Keep it strapped to you and not the horse in case you have to get away on foot."

"I was carrying a rifle when you were still shitting green, but your concern is noted." Buddy also been in a war where getting too comfortable with your surroundings got you killed. He knew about situational awareness. He gave the group a nod and a two fingered wave before heading off.

"I worry about him going off by himself," Randi said. "Town could be different since we were here last. People here probably have cabin fever just like we do. They're scared, cold, and hungry. That's just for starters."

Deputy Ford shrugged. "Yeah, well, if that's all, what could possibly go wrong?"

Randi frowned. "You guys suck."

"He's more than capable of taking care of himself," Jim said. "I worry more about the poor souls who mess with him."

Buddy was a hard man from a line of hard men, yet still he walked the Earth with a relatively dependable moral compass. He could be gentle with his friends but was not afraid to kill those who needed killing. He understood there were those for whom death was the only medicine.

The deputy looked curiously at Jim, not knowing all that Jim knew about Buddy's past. He didn't know about Buddy's daughter overdosing and the piece-of-shit boyfriend that Buddy had burned alive. He didn't know about Buddy helping Randi seek revenge on the people who had killed her parents. Ford was still a relative stranger to the valley and he didn't know the secrets yet. He didn't know where the bodies were, quite literally, buried.

The remaining three rode together for another two miles, with both the emergency operations center and the Fairlanes' home being in the same general direction. The miles reminded Jim of pictures he'd seen of war-torn Bosnia and Czechoslovakia. Clean, modern buildings reduced to shambles, people living in preindustrial squalor among wrecked and useless technology. It further brought home Buddy's comments of the previous night, about how restoring order and normality would not be so simple as turning the lights back on.

Evidence of scavenging was everywhere. Stores had been looted, vacant homes ransacked. People were desperate for anything that might give their family a better chance. Perhaps the biggest change since his last trip through town was the change in weather, which forced people to turn their scavenging efforts toward things that could be burned in their fireplaces or woodstoves. The town pre-dated the nation and even the sacred Colonial era buildings in town had been stripped of trim and clapboards. Doors had been carted off to be split for kindling. Oak mantles and hand-planed maple stairs had been pried loose of the square nails that had so securely retained them for centuries. Even decorative trees growing along Main Street and on the school campuses had been sawn down and hauled off.

Such desperation would only lead to more death as people attempted to burn fires in unsafe fireplaces that hadn't been used in decades. When those heating systems fell into disuse, the chimneys were often blocked by birds or squirrel nests. Many residents may not even think to go outside and confirm their chimney was still there. Sometimes when homes were reroofed people knocked the chimneys down to below roof level and roofed over them to save the expense of repairing them.

People were moving around here in town, whether for social purposes or to scavenge. There were tracks and compressed sled trails. They came to another intersection where a powerless traffic light hung uselessly over an intersection.

"Where we meeting back up again?" Deputy Ford asked.

"Let's just stick to what we told Buddy," Jim said. "The cemetery is the primary. If that goes south, the intersection near the superstore is the backup."

"All right. You folks be careful." The deputy peeled his horse away from the group, plodding on into the deep snow.

"You be careful out there too," Jim called after him.

"He doesn't seem like the careful type," Randi remarked.

"Nope," Jim agreed. "He doesn't."

THE FAIRLANE HOUSE sat on what used to be a main road leading out of town. When the town grew up, it grew in other directions and that part of town didn't grow with it. A four-lane highway carried traffic in the opposite direction and the old neighborhood became much quieter, retired like the Fairlanes themselves. Their Victorian was of brick construction, the walls three locally-made bricks thick. The interior walls, joists, and rafters were framed from rough-cut sawmill oak that was now so hard with age a nail could not be driven into it.

The steep roof was covered in embossed Victorian steel shingles discolored by rust at their edges.

The yard was vast and rolling, the house guarded by ancient maples so large that three men could not encircle them with their arms. The trees dropped red and yellow leaves in the fall. Mr. Fairlane had estimated those to be nearly three hundred years old. When Jim was a kid, Mr. Fairlane pointed out all of the history that the trees had been witness to.

"Daniel Boone could have taken a nap right there," Charlie had said, pointing toward the base of one of the broad trees. "An Indian brave could have stopped there to eat jerky or have a smoke."

Jim studied those trees again, recalling those old days, the way Mr. Fairlane had made history so much more interesting than his teachers at school. He and Randi stopped their horses at the entrance to the property, taking in the scene. There were swinging wrought-iron gates hinged to tall posts of recycled bricks. They were not original to the property but a feature that Charles Fairlane constructed himself in the 1960s. A man in town wanted to get rid of a brick root cellar and offered Charles all of the bricks if he would tear it down. Having more strength and enthusiasm than money, he'd jumped on the project and those bricks now greeted visitors to his home.

There seemed not to have been any visitors in a long time. Jim studied the immaculate snow between the road and the house. "Looks like no one's been up there."

"Nope," Randi agreed.

"I can smell smoke."

"I don't see anything coming out of the chimneys," Randi said. "Could be a neighbor."

"That doesn't mean a lot. If she's burning old wood, like furniture and building materials, there might not be any smoke."

Jim made no effort to venture onto the property, still lost in his reverie of the old home, his memory of the old man.

"We going to go up there and look or you just going to do this whole thing by ESP? 'Cause if that's what you're going to do, I could have stayed in bed."

Jim cut Randi a dirty look. "Lot of memories here and I just ain't anxious to see the old lady dead. Let's get it over with." Jim clucked his mouth and nudged his horse forward.

"There you go with the negativity again," Randi said. "Think positive."

Jim steered his horse to the unbroken snow of the Fairlanes' gravel drive, trying to remember what lay beneath this snow. Halfway up his horse stumbled. It recovered but Jim, not a confident horseman, was a little shaken. "What the fuck? That a fallen branch?"

"That ain't a tree branch," Randi said, pointing.

Jim spun his horse back in that direction and looked at the ground. A waxen face with an ice-encrusted beard stared at him from the snow. His horse had stumbled over a body. "Jesus!"

"I think there's more," Randi said, pointing at another distant mound partially exposed by the windblown snow.

Jim hadn't noticed the bodies. The yard was rippled and banked with windblown snow. He noticed a third body then and had a thought that the Fairlanes' yard looked like the corpse-strewn slopes of Mount Everest where bodies laid permanently frozen, even being used as navigational markers. "I'm not sure if this is a good sign or not."

"Maybe it's a sign you best be calling out from that saddle before you get shot out of it," Randi said. "If Mrs. Fairlane is in there, she doesn't look like much of a negotiator."

With that comment, it dawned on Jim that if these men had been shot from the house, he and Randi were now within range. He turned his horse back toward the house and waved an arm over his head. "Mrs. Fairlane! Mrs. Fairlane! Are you home? It's Jim Powell. Don't shoot!"

Jim turned back to Randi. "Maybe that'll stop her from mowing us down like these poor bastards."

Randi looked uncertain. "I guess it depends on how long ago you turned into an asshole. If she remembers you as an asshole kid from thirty years ago she might just go ahead and shoot you anyway."

"My asshole attitude was a more recent development."

"That's hard to imagine," Randi said. "You've taken so naturally to it."

Jim was preparing his retort when the sound of a heavy door bolt carried across the front yard from the house. The door swung open and the twin black orbs of a double barrel shotgun emerged from the gap. In the shadows behind it, Jim thought he saw a pale face hovering over the stock.

Jim held both hands up and waved toward the house. "My name is Jim Powell! Is that you, Mrs. Fairlane? I'm a friend."

There was a reply from the house. It was so faint Jim couldn't understand it, but Rosa Fairlane was always a soft-spoken lady. When he didn't respond to her words, a wispy hand extended through the crack of the door and beckoned them forward.

"I don't know about this," Randi said. "It could be a trap."

"It *could* be her," Jim said uncertainly. "I just can't tell from here. I'll have to get closer. You hang back."

Randi swung an arm wide in a gesture that said *be my guest*. Jim nudged his horse forward, turning off the driveway, which continued to the back of the house, and steering his horse directly toward the front door.

When he got within earshot, he said, "Is that you, Mrs. Fairlane? My name is Jim Powell and I used to know you and your husband when I was a child. I visited you many times when I was a kid. I was just coming by to check on you."

The gun leveled at his head made him uncomfortable. He could clearly see the pale face of an elderly woman through the crack in the door, a cloud of frizzy, unkempt hair surrounding it. He couldn't see her eyes but there must have been recognition because the gun lowered. The door swung fully open and a lady wearing a fuzzy blue bathrobe used a walker to shuffle onto the porch. She looked frail as a bird but it was Mrs. Fairlane all right.

She regarded him, her eyes narrowed, looking down her nose. "I used to know a Jim Powell but I haven't seen him in decades. Figured he must be dead since he didn't come visit. Why, out of the blue, would you get the idea that you needed to come check on me? That doesn't make a bit of sense."

Jim smiled at the elderly lady. She had to be in her mid-eighties but she was obviously still sharp. "I'm not sure you'd believe me if I told you."

She huffed at him. "Well, you all come in then. We're letting the heat out and my feet are getting wet." With that, Mrs. Fairlane turned her walker and shuffled back into the house, closing the door behind her.

As she went, Jim noticed that she was wearing fuzzy blue house slippers that matched the robe. Jim cracked a grin, then waved Randi forward.

They tied their reins off to the substantial wrought iron porch rail then clambered up the steps in their heavy snow boots. The porch had not been shoveled but a generous porch roof kept most of the drifting snow a few feet from the door. When they reached that circle of bare porch they stomped off their boots.

The door in front of them was heavy oak with many layers of crackled white paint. The peeling door had been pushed to but not shut. Jim pushed on the door, the hinges groaning. Just inside the large entry foyer dark stairs climbed to the left. To the right was a hallway that led to French doors, then to a formal parlor. On the floor was a colorful Moroccan rug that was likely a prized possession when it was purchased new. Patches were worn threadbare by a life of foot traffic.

Jim stopped on the rug and began unlacing his boots.

"You're really taking your shoes off?" Randi asked.

Jim nodded.

"What if we need to bolt out of here in a hurry? You prepared to run for it in your socks?"

"This is the *Fairlane* house. You don't enter this house without taking your shoes off."

Randi rolled her eyes. "Jesus Christ, Jim, when have you ever been sensitive to decorum?"

Jim looked around, considering. "Probably only here."

Randi groaned then began unlacing her own boots. "If I have to take off running without my shoes, you're carrying me. I do *not* like this."

Jim ignored the comment. "Mrs. Fairlane is a lady, so be on your best behavior."

Randi wrinkled her brow and pursed her mouth. "I'm offended by that on so many levels. First off, I'm a lady too, and I don't see anybody being on their best behavior for me. Second, there's the implication that I don't know how to act among civilized folks."

Jim shrugged and headed down the hall, pushing through the French doors. Warmth and the smell of wood smoke greeted him. The heat was welcome after the cold ride into town. It wasn't uncomfortably hot, like his own house became sometimes, but probably upper sixties. The parlor was empty and Jim moved on through toward the kitchen. This was the source of the heat. He found Rosa Fairlane at an antique wood burning cook stove. She was pouring water from a copper kettle into a teacup. The rich smell of mint hit Jim's nose.

"I caught a chill out there in that hallway," Rosa said. "Do either of you care for some mint tea? The water is already hot and I have plenty. It grows along the creek in the backyard, even in winter."

Jim remembered that creek and the spot where the mint grew. He remembered Mr. Fairlane showing him the dark green leaf, crushing it between his fingers and holding it beneath Jim's nose. He was the first person to ever tell Jim about the variety of useful plants that grew wild in their mountains.

"I think I will have some," Jim said. "Randi?"

Randi had finally gotten her boots unlaced and was just now entering the room. She smiled at Mrs. Fairlane and extended a hand. "I'm Randi. Nice to meet you."

The frail lady slowly took the proffered hand, not so much shaking as clasping it for a moment. "I'm Rosa Fairlane. I used to know this young man when he was much younger and had better manners."

Jim immediately understood what she was referring to. When he graduated high school and left the area, he never again stopped back in. He never came to express his condolences to Mrs. Fairlane after her husband Charles passed away. He been by this house hundreds of times while visiting his own parents yet he had never thought to stop. The more time passed, the more awkward it seemed. He was just your average impolite, self-centered young guy. In those days, life was about him.

"I apologize, Mrs. Fairlane. Honestly, I always thought a lot of your husband but I never knew you as well. I guess I didn't realize my visit would've meant anything to you."

Rosa shuffled to an ornate china cabinet and removed two fine porcelain cups with saucers. She placed them on the counter and dropped a pinch of mint leaves in each, then poured hot water over top of them. She turned to Jim, her heavily lidded eyes sagging. "You'll have to carry your own cup and join me at the table. I'm too shaky these days to carry much."

Before Jim could offer to take hers, Rosa made her way to the table, her teacup in one hand, the other resting on the counter for support. Already chastised, Jim rushed to the table to help Mrs. Fairlane with her seat. When she sat down, he helped her scoot up to the table, then he returned for his own cup.

"As I said, I didn't realize my visit would've meant that much to you. I am truly sorry if I offended you. Your husband was one of my favorite people during my childhood."

Rosa Fairlane gave a barely perceptible shrug. She spoke slowly, like someone who might have had a stroke at some point in the past. If that were the case, it would explain the difficulty she had with walking. "It's not entirely your fault. Matters of decorum are certainly different these days and I don't suppose we'll ever return to the polite society we once had. Why, when Charles and I began courting, he had to come to my parents' house and ask permission to even speak to me. I remember it like it was yesterday. He showed up on horseback in fancy riding breeches with shiny brown boots. He sat in the parlor and had coffee with my parents. I wasn't even allowed to come into the room that first time. It was just them getting to know him before they would even grant permission for matters to go to the next step. I think that went on for a year before I was ever alone with him for even for a moment."

"Where did you meet your husband?" Randi asked.

Mrs. Fairlane turned stiffly to Randi. "Why, in church."

She said it as if it was the only place that anyone ever met, as if it was the most obvious thing in the world.

Jim cleared his throat. "Well, again, I apologize if I did anything to offend you or hurt your feelings. That was certainly not intentional."

Rosa dismissed it with a wave of her hand. "It's not you. It's the world. And if you're going to start apologizing for the world, where does it end?"

The conversation fell silent when Jim had no answer for that, no response for the sincere question in Rosa's clear brown eyes. Looking out the wide kitchen windows at the snow-covered yard, Jim recalled the bodies.

"There were dead men in the driveway. Do you know anything about that?"

"I didn't know for certain they were dead but I'm glad to hear it since I went to all the trouble of shooting them. They tried to break into my house. It was dark and I wasn't certain I hit them."

"Oh, you hit them all right," Randi said. "They're dead as fish sticks."

Rosa gave a little nod and smiled, pleased with herself. Perhaps she was relieved to know she'd resolved the situation and those men would not be coming back.

"How are you getting by?" Jim asked.

Rosa took a delicate sip of her tea and replaced the cup on its saucer. "I think not too bad considering the condition of things. This is much more like the world I was born into. This old house of ours is perhaps better outfitted than most to live without the modern conveniences."

"It's quite warm," Randi said. "It feels nice. Are you getting enough to eat?"

"At my age, eating is not the treat it once was. Feeding my family was a treat. I always enjoyed that. Feeding myself is just a chore, but it's one that thus far I've been able to accomplish. I raise as big a garden as I can manage each year. I have a lot of canning put back. I've also been drinking quite a bit of Jell-O."

"Jell-O?" Jim asked.

Rosa nodded, her chin trembling slightly as she waited for her eyes to focus on him. "Served as a hot beverage, it seems to have some nutritional value."

"And that's all you've had?" Randi asked.

Mrs. Fairlane glowered at Randi disapprovingly. "Is that all? I think I've done quite nicely for myself, young lady. I'm eighty-four years old. I think I've done better than most people. I've been able to eat every time I've been hungry and I'm not certain every family out there could say that."

"You have a point. I'm sorry if I offended you," Randi said. "I was just concerned."

"Look, I know it probably seems strange us just showing up out of the blue," Jim said. "The truth is I've been so absorbed in this disaster that I haven't really thought about anything or anybody outside of my own immediate family. I know that sounds selfish but that's just the way it is. But this morning I was examining an Indian relic that your husband gave to me. Crazy or not, I felt him asking me to come check on you and that's why I'm here. Is there anything we can do for you?"

"I'm sure we could find somebody to take you in if you feel like you need to get out of this house," Randi said.

Though Randi's intention was sincere, this was exactly the wrong thing to say. The normally dignified woman slapped the palm of her hand flat on the dining table, the noise thunderous in the still house. The cups rattled on their saucers, startling both Jim and Randi.

Rosa Fairlane set her jaw and spoke to them in a low, angry voice. "I've been doing just fine, thank you very much. Just because I crossed your mind suddenly after thirty years doesn't mean you're obliged to take care of me. I am not interested in your charity or your welfare."

"Geez, I'm sorry. We're not here to piss you off," Randi muttered.

"That crass expression does not fully capture the magnitude of my irritation," Mrs. Fairlane said. "This town is probably full of elderly folks just like myself who are getting by. We're of tougher stock than you produce these days. While I'm sure many of them could use a hand, I feel certain that most still retain enough dignity they're not interested in being anyone's burden."

Jim stood and put a hand on Mrs. Fairlane's shoulder. "I appreciate that and I'm sorry if we upset you. We'll be going. I just wanted to see if there was anything we could do to help."

Rosa turned shakily toward him and raised her fiery eyes to meet his. "I neither want nor need your help, young man."

"Then we'll be leaving. By the way, there's a message being broadcast on the radio that they're going to start restoring power next week. We haven't heard any details yet but that's what we know. Maybe if they at least get some of it on we can find a more comfortable location for you. Maybe they'll operate shelters or something."

Rosa Fairlane gestured around her at the large empty house. Her fingers were gray and spotted, the palms pink and worn smooth. "This house means nothing to me anymore. It's the empty husk of a family that lived here and died. I'm like a little hermit crab that needs to crawl out and leave it behind. If there's a better opportunity, I will consider it."

"Then give us a few days to see what the government has planned then I'll be back to check on you."

"Well, just be aware that if it takes thirty more years for you to get back to me you'll probably find nothing but dust and gnawed bones," Mrs. Fairlane said.

"Thanks for clarifying that," Jim said, his mouth spreading into the fakest smile he could manage. "I'll see if I can be more expeditious."

5

Deputy Ford reigned in his horse near the emergency operations center and sat watching the dark building. A year ago, the place was a hive of activity. People were in and out twenty-four hours a day. County, state, and town law enforcement stored vehicles there. Drug raids were launched from there, dispatchers worked from there, and confiscated vehicles were stored there. Now, from all appearances, it was as dead as the rest of the town.

It had been a couple of months since he'd been here and he assumed he'd find the place looted, but it didn't appear to be any different from when he was here last. The building had plate glass windows on the front and although Ford expected to find them shattered, they appeared intact. They didn't house inmates here since it was only a dispatch center, and the building had none of the hardened surfaces a jail or temporary detention center might have. It looked more like an office building, which in fact was what it had been before the county purchased it.

By nature, he was the cautious type, and Ford decided to ride the perimeter of the facility before he went any closer. The front of the building only gave him a little of the picture. The entrance was on the north side and everything there looked exactly as it had been when he last saw it. He rode to the right. The west had no entrances but was lined with narrow, recessed windows that looked into offices and conference rooms.

The back side of the building looked undisturbed as well. It was a solid block wall with three heavy steel exterior doors and no windows. He steered his horse closer to those doors and saw no signs of tampering or prying. This surprised him, but then again, the emergency operations center was hidden in an industrial park on the fringes of town. Aside from Jim's parents, who lived within sight of the building, there weren't many folks living out in that area.

The deputy circled around the last side of the building, where a large parking lot provided parking for employees and emergency vehicles. There was a surplus MRAP, a HUMVEE, and a boat used for water rescues. There was a discreet black van for surveillance operations and drug raids. Several retired police cruisers were clustered together, some sitting on flats. There was a pickup that trustees used for trash collection on the highway medians.

This side of the building was lined with more of the recessed windows but did have a single staff entrance at the end of a narrow sidewalk. The windows all had the same low-E reflective coating that appeared bronze in the strong sunlight. As Ford rode along, he looked at each window to make sure it had not been busted open. Each gave off the same identical reflection.

Except for one.

The deputy paused, studying the window. The windows were fixed panes of glass, which were non-operative. They didn't open. There was really no reason that one window in a line of identical windows should be giving off a different reflection unless it had been tampered with. The deputy looked around and saw no footprints coming or going from the building. There was nothing but undisturbed snow. Still, something seemed wrong about it.

He dismounted his horse and tied it off to a light pole. He unslung his department-issued AR and held it at a low ready position. He moved close enough to the building that he had eyes on both the questionable window and the one next to it at the same time. Comparing the two windows side-by-side he could see that the decorative aluminum cladding on the frame of one window was missing. He didn't see those trim pieces anywhere but it was possible they were beneath the snow. Because the exposed gasket around the window was black it did not look altogether different from the dark bronze trim of the undisturbed window next to it.

It was curious that someone would go to this extent to conceal their attempt to enter the building. Most people these days threw rocks through windows with complete abandon and didn't give a shit who knew it. Why would someone go to such lengths to make the building appear undisturbed? Maybe they were taking shelter there and didn't want anyone else to know? Could that be it?

The reflective coating on the windows made it difficult to see inside the building. With the bright sunlight shining against them the only way to really see inside was to get right up against the window and cup your hands around your eyes to keep the ambient light out. The move made the deputy a little apprehensive but he had come too far to turn around because of a suspicious window.

The deputy crept closer to the building, set the butt of his rifle in the snow, and leaned it against the building. He pressed his nose to the glass, cupping his hands around his eyes to cut out any stray light. He looked into the dim interior of an empty conference room, and right into the face of a young girl. By the time he figured out what he was looking at in the dim light, she erupted into a terrified scream.

Ford raised his hands to assure her that he meant no harm but she bolted across the room toward an interior doorway.

"It's okay! I'm not going to hurt you!" he called, trying to follow her with his eyes.

He caught a glimpse of movement. He squinted, trying to make out what he was looking at. It was the barrel of a gun.

"No!" the deputy screamed, dropping to the ground.

There was a deafening boom and glass rained down on him. The deputy kicked his feet out, shoving himself back as close to the wall as he could get.

Boom.

Another shot rang out and the remaining glass was blasted from the frame. Ford frantically tried to come up with a plan. There was no cover for at least fifty or sixty yards. He would have to get to one of the abandoned vehicles in the parking lot and hope he didn't catch lead in the backside while he was doing it. Whoever it was inside had already shown a willingness to shoot and he couldn't imagine he could get that far without them taking another shot. He had no choice but to try to buy himself some time, hoping that he might be able to bargain for his life.

"I'm a deputy! I don't mean you any harm. I was just seeing if the building had been broken into. I was going to grab some supplies."

There was no response but he was certain whoever had shot at him was still there. He could feel it. They were probably just waiting for him to pop up and reveal himself. Then he would die.

"Honest! I'm a deputy. I don't mean you any harm." There was desperation in his voice and it was real. He didn't want to die.

"Then you better be raising a badge," came a terrified voice. "If I don't see a badge you're a fucking dead man."

It was a woman. A woman who sounded just as scared as he was. When he processed her words, he experienced another moment of panic. He wasn't certain he had his badge. He hadn't been wearing it because he didn't want to distinguish himself as a law enforcement officer and draw fire from someone with hostile feelings toward the police.

He prayed he had shoved it in a pocket somewhere. He patted his chest and his sides. He patted his front pockets. Nothing.

"I'm waiting!" the woman called, her fear increasing his own level of fear. Scared people made bad decisions, such as pulling the trigger on a cop.

"I'm looking! Hold on!" He checked his back pockets, furiously shoving a hand into the damp material. There it was. He found it.

"I've got it!" he called.

"Raise it up slowly to where I can see it. If it's not a badge, you're going to draw back a nub."

He hurriedly extracted the badge and raised it cautiously to the blasted out window, expecting that at any moment his hand was going to disappear into a spray of blood. "Can you see it?"

"I see something but I can't tell anything about it. You just sit still while I get a little closer. If you move, I'll shove this barrel through the window and drop buckshot right into the top of your head. You got it?"

"I got it. Just settle down. I'm legit." He continued holding the badge up. His ears were ringing from the gun blast and he couldn't hear any indication of anyone moving around inside. He was terrified, wondering if at any moment she was going to shoot him in the top of the head. His scalp tingled at the thought, at the knowledge that he probably wouldn't even hear the shot before he was already dead.

"Okay, so it's a damn badge. How does that prove you ain't here to try to hurt us?"

"I'm a cop, lady. I don't go around hurting women and kids."

"You *used* to be a cop. A lot of people used to be a lot of different things. Now they're all something else, just like you might be something else. A badge don't mean shit."

"You're right. I reckon it doesn't. If I was in your shoes I'm not sure if I would believe me either. You just have to take my word for that part. I swear to you that I'm not here to hurt anyone."

"I ain't big on people's word. Matter fact, I ain't big on people," she grumbled.

Ford almost smiled. "Sounds like we would get along fine then."

"I ain't looking for anyone to get along with!"

"Easy there, I didn't mean anything by it. I just meant that I'm not big on people either."

She didn't miss a beat, not disarmed at all by his casual conversational tone. "So why were you out there scaring my little girl?"

"This building was the emergency operations center. This is where I worked from. I've been staying out of town, but I came into town this morning and I thought I'd make another run through to see if there were any supplies I missed."

"Well, my daughter and I have been staying here. We've found a little bit of food but not enough to share. Reckon you're just going to have to get out of here."

"I don't mind to move on as long as you won't kill me when I stand up."

"Don't do anything that deserves killing and I won't."

She had a point there. "How did you get in there anyway?"

"I worked in construction before. I know how these windows go in. If you know that, it doesn't take much to get one back out again."

"I barely noticed anything."

"That was the plan," she said.

"There may be more supplies in there you can use. That's what I came to look for."

"You going to tell me where to find them?"

"I don't know where they are but I might be able to help you find them. There's several places they could be and I have the keys to get into those places."

"How do I know I can trust you?"

"I reckon you don't. All I can give you is my word."

She mulled that over but hunger and concern for her daughter beat out caution. "I'll let you in but you have to leave your guns outside. I'm not letting you around my daughter carrying your guns. I don't trust you."

"Fair enough," Ford said. "But if someone steals my shit I'm going to be pretty damn mad."

"Not my problem," the woman replied.

"Well, I'm standing up. My hands will be empty. Don't shoot me." Ford pushed himself to a squatting position then thrust his hands over his head.

The woman gripped the gun tighter and stared as Ford's hands appeared in front of the blasted out window opening. They were empty, as promised. He eased up, not liking the feeling of the gun pointed at his back.

"I'm turning around now."

"Slowly," she said.

He turned until they were face-to-face. "Can I lower my hands now?"

She nodded. "You can come on in but keep your distance. This gun is staying on you. Don't make me nervous or something ugly might happen."

Ford didn't like the sound of that, knowing that the ugliness that might happen would involve him bleeding out in a gory mess. He used a gloved hand to rake the small chunks of tempered glass free of the opening, the delicately climbed in. In his thick layers, he was not very graceful and ended up falling to the floor.

"Don't shoot," he said, afraid that she might mistake his clumsiness as aggression.

"I'm not shooting you for being an oaf."

"Thanks," he mumbled, embarrassed. "I guess."

"Now find those supplies you were talking about," she said.

"What's your name?" Ford asked.

"None of your damn business."

Ford frowned. "What does it hurt to tell me your name?"

"Was this just a trick to get inside? Do I need to kill you and roll you back out the window?"

Ford sighed and got to his feet. "If you I help you find supplies will that convince you I mean you no harm?"

"If you help us find supplies then get on out of here and leave us alone I will be convinced."

Ford started toward the hallway. The woman backed away nervously, training the shotgun on him again. "You go easy. Don't make any sudden moves."

"Where's your daughter?"

"That ain't none of your business either."

"I was just asking to make sure she was okay."

"She's fine. She's hiding. I know where she's at."

"Got it," Ford said. "Let's start in the locker room."

He made his way down the hall and pushed through a door on the right with a sign that said *Private*. There were no windows and no light entered the room. Ford pulled a flashlight from his pocket and shone it around the room. Inside were six-foot tall lockers, a tile floor, and showers. It looked like any high school locker room.

"The lockers are all locked," the woman said. "The cops must not trust the other cops." She smiled at that comment.

"Locks just help keep people honest," Ford said. "Besides, I know where the master key is." He went to a locker with no padlock on it, opened the latch, and removed a set of bolt cutters.

"That's the master key?"

"Even cops forget their keys sometimes," Ford said, starting down the row and snipping off padlocks with surprising ease.

The woman rushed to one and started pulling the broken padlock from the locker.

"Easy now," Ford said. "Some of these lockers have personal belongings in them. I'd rather you let me go through them. I'm just going to check for any food or snacks the guys may have left behind. I don't want you going through their personal shit. I figure if they haven't come back for the food by now they're not coming."

The woman hesitantly conceded and backed away, taking a seat on a bench while Ford finished moving through the padlocks. When he was done, he slipped the cut lock out and opened the door.

"So how did you guys end up here?" he asked, trying again for conversation.

The woman looked at him, a snide comment on the tip of her tongue, but she held it back. She sighed, rubbed her head in what seemed like frustration or exhaustion, and looked away from him.

Ford found an unopened box of ten protein bars and pulled them out. "Here we go. All yours." He tossed her the box.

She reflexively laid the shotgun across her lap to catch the box, then panicked when she realized what she'd done, yanking the gun back up. Ford hadn't moved. Hadn't made any effort to go for her.

"I'm not going to hurt you," he said. "I'm serious. This is why I came here. To look for leftover supplies."

"Then why should you share them? How do I know you're not going to hurt me and my little girl and just take all of it?"

"Because that's not who I am. That's all I can tell you." He looked long and honest at her, trying to convince her, but uncertain if he was getting through whatever damage had been done to her.

In the next locker he found a few of unopened bags of beef jerky. He tossed her two of them and kept one for himself.

"Why is this food here?" she asked.

"Long hours," he said. "We don't always know when we're getting home or where the next meal is coming from. It's good to be prepared for those times we can't just run to a fast food place."

Ford moved on to the next locker and found a plastic grocery bag beneath a change of clothes and some toiletries. There were some candy bars and a couple of cans of tuna. He took one of each and gave the rest to the woman.

"My name is Nicole," she said as Ford moved on to the next locker. "My daughter is Paige."

Ford regarded her for a moment and nodded. "Good to meet you, Nicole. You can call me Ford."

She was looking away and did not acknowledge his comment. "There were men came to our house looking for food. My husband went outside to tell them to go away and they killed him. When I saw that, I grabbed Paige and we ran out the back door. We hid in the woods until they were gone, then I grabbed what I could from the house and we took off. I couldn't stay there knowing they could come back anytime."

"Where did you stay?"

"We slept in somebody's old shed for a couple of nights but when it got really cold I knew I had to find something better. We were walking through here, taking a shortcut to town, when I noticed there were several buildings out here that looked empty."

"Most people wouldn't stay out here in the winter because there's no way to heat them," Ford said. "How have you been doing it?"

Nicole shook her head. "I haven't. We stay in sleeping bags most of the time. We read and color and do stuff like that. Things you can do from a sleeping bag."

"What have you been eating?"

"We had a little food that the men missed when they broke into the house. I've even been back there a time or two to get more stuff. I made Paige hide here while I went. It takes about an hour to walk there and a little longer to get back if I'm carrying a lot of stuff. We also found a few cans of food in the lunch room here and I broke the front out of the vending machine."

"That's a crime," Ford said.

Nicole looked at him with a look of incredulity but found that he was smiling at her. "Oh, a joke."

"Not much of one," he acknowledged.

"I'm going to get my daughter out here and give her something to eat," Nicole said. "She's not had anything today. You promise you're not going to try some shit?"

"If that was my plan, I would have done it already," Ford assured her. "I told you exactly why I was here. You've got the proof in your hands."

"There aren't many lockers left. Was this the only place you knew to look?"

Ford shook his head. "I've got a few tricks left up my sleeve."

Nicole yelled for her daughter, not quite ready to leave Ford alone in the building. After several attempts, the little girl skulked into the room, her head lowered while she glared at Ford.

"I'm sorry I scared you," he said, assuming that was the reason for her expression. "You scared me just as bad as I scared you."

That admission put a brief smile on her face. Nicole handed her daughter a bag of jerky. Ford expected another smile at that or some expression of joy but what he saw instead was a ravenous, desperate look overtake her. Her hands shook as she tore into the bag and shoved a large piece into her mouth, chewing the tough jerky as hard as she could.

"Easy there," Ford said. "You're going to get choked if you don't slow down."

"He's right," Nicole said. "Go slower. Stop to take a drink." She handed her daughter a well-used water bottle.

"Where are you getting the water?" Ford asked.

"From the gutter downspouts," Nicole said. "It looks clean but it's got a little bit of an odd taste to it."

"I've got a couple of more places to check," Ford said. "You coming with me or do you trust me enough to let me go by myself?"

Nicole studied him and seemed to concede from weariness rather than any quality she saw in him. "I'll let you go. I'm going to have a bite to eat with Paige. If you find more food, will you bring us some?"

Ford nodded. "It's a promise."

Nicole set the shotgun to the side. "Then go on."

"I'll leave you this light. I think there's another in the room I'm going to."

Ford left the locker room, returning to the conference room where he'd entered the building. He left the food he collected on the table and headed down the hall to the locked room where they kept the load out assault gear. The room was locked but he had a key. The lock to the unmarked door was undamaged so he assumed no one had been in there. It was not lost on him that many of the men who might have been tempted to break into this room were dead already, many of them killed at the superstore after they sided with Barnes.

The room had no windows and he propped the door open with a fire extinguisher so some ambient light from the hallway would reach the room. The first thing he looked for was a flashlight to replace the one he'd left with Nicole and Paige. There was a shelf with several heavy D-cell Mag-lites on it and he tried one. It worked.

This was the room where they kept the specialized gear that they might use on a drug raid or in the extremely infrequent hostage situation that might pop up. There were department-issue tactical vests, body armor, bump helmets, and belts with every kind of holster and pouch. There was also a wall with a dozen Go Bags. Ford knew that each Go Bag had a hydration bladder as well as a couple of bottles of water. There would be several MREs, a trauma kit to enhance the individual first aid kits that each man already carried, and a few other items.

There were some large black duffel bags stacked on a shelf. They kept those in case someone had to grab gear from this room and haul it to the location of an unfolding emergency. Ford decided it would be easiest to sort what he found if he started one bag for him and another for Nicole. He shoved two full Go Bags into each of the cavernous duffels and then split the contents of the remaining Go Bags. He grabbed a tactical vest for himself and shoved it in the bag he was keeping.

He placed a couple of flashlights and some batteries in the bag for Nicole and her daughter, then added the remainder to his bag, along with several headlamps and tactical lights. Finding a weapons-mounted light reminded him of the small armory in the building. It was not as large as the armory at the sheriff's department but he assumed this one had been looted based on what the sheriff said. Still, he couldn't leave without checking. Just the presence of the woman now living here told him that the building might be fully ransacked the next time he came back. And who knew how long that might be.

Ford strapped on a headlamp to free up his hands. He dragged the two heavy duffels down the hall to another unmarked door. He fished out his keys and found the one that opened the door. The only thing in the room was a gray cabinet that dominated the wall across from the door. It was eight feet wide and seven feet tall, made of heavy steel mesh that allowed air to flow freely. A padlock secured the cabinet and a flat steel shield prevented anyone from reaching the lock with bolt cutters.

The deputies were not allowed to have individual keys to the padlock but there was a key box on the wall, openable with their door key and containing the padlock key. Ford opened the key box and was pleased to find the locker inside. He approached the cabinet and pressed his head against the steel mesh, shining his light into the interior. He couldn't hold back a smile when he found the locker was still full of weapons.

He opened the locker and stood admiring the contents. Since this was only a secondary armory, it just held a few weapons, but they were good stuff. There were several pump-action Mossberg shotguns. There were three Colt Law Enforcement Only M4s that looked similar to what Ford was carrying now but with one significant difference. They had a selector switch instead of a safety, allowing the weapon to be in Fire, Safe, or three-shot burst modes. One had a 40mm grenade launcher for tear gas.

There was a suppressed H&K MP5 that ran full-auto as well as two FN SCAR Subcompacts that were select fire. Additionally, ammo cans stacked in the bottom of the cage held thousands of rounds for each weapon. Ford knew there was no way he could leave any of it. He would set Nicole up with more rounds for the shotgun but he was taking the rest of this if he had to strap it on his horse and walk alongside it.

"Poor fucking horse," Ford mumbled. "If you knew what was coming, you'd be heading for the hills."

6

Randi and Jim were mounting their horses outside of Mrs. Fairlane's house when they heard distant gunshots. They looked at each other nervously.

"You think that's Ford?" Randi asked.

"Sounded like a shotgun," Jim said. "Ford was carrying a rifle."

Randi nodded, understanding they were both probably thinking the same thing about now, that Ford may have been on the receiving end of the gunfire rather than the giving end. "Should we check on him?"

"I want to go by my parents' house and check on things anyway. The emergency operations center is right there close by. We could swing over and check on him."

"If you want to check on him, I'm going to go check on Buddy," Randi said.

Jim frowned at Randi. "Buddy said he wanted to go alone."

After some effort Randi finally managed to climb on her own horse and settle in the saddle, struggling in the bulky layers of winter clothing. "What people want and what people need aren't always the same thing."

"Buddy is pretty plainspoken. If he tells me he wants to go it alone, I take him at his word."

Randi frowned. "Well, you're pretty plainspoken too. In fact, you're about the grumpiest damn person I've ever met and if it was you up there, I'd still go."

Jim realized that an argument with Randi was time wasted. She was clearly his equal in terms of hard-headedness. He'd have about as much luck telling the snow to melt as telling Randi not to go. He sighed and gave up. "You be careful."

"I always am."

"Make sure you have a round chambered," Jim said. "And keep those guns handy."

But Randi was already gone, her horse trotting down the driveway and steering clear of the dead bodies frozen to the ground.

"Yeah, I'll be careful too," Jim said to the empty yard. "Thanks for the concern."

Jim nudged his horse onward, down the drive, and through the gate to the road. Instead of retracing his steps to where he and Ford had parted ways, Jim went in the other direction. As a child, he'd walked to Mr. Fairlane's house on an old road that had since been abandoned. He thought it might still be passable if he took a shortcut through a nearby neighborhood. At the end of that neighborhood was an area that had once been the town dump, all traces of it now long buried. There were a few places where he might have to cut through a gate but he had bolt cutters with him for that purpose.

He plodded on for around a quarter mile before emerging onto the dead end street. There probably weren't a half-dozen houses on the street, most dating from the 1950s and 1960s. The neighborhood had never been desirable because no one wanted to live on the road to the town dump, overrun as it was with rats, cats, and stray dogs.

At the end of the street, Jim reached the artificial contours of the reclaimed dump with its perfectly angled hills and flat planes. It had been forty years since they closed it. Weeds, brush, and trees were making some progress and probably did a decent job of hiding the unnatural landscape when they were fully leafed-out, but the unnatural shapes were obvious now.

Jim played there as a kid, after the dump was closed but before the reclamation. He remembered it as a good spot to find cool old bottles and other odd bits of junk. There were even a few old vehicles scattered on the fringes of the property that had managed to avoid the crusher. He'd sat in those as a kid and imagined being able to drive them from where the trees formed cages around them.

At the end of the dump he cut the padlock on a gate the county put in. After taking his horse through, he returned the chain and padlock to where they appeared undisturbed and continued on his way. Ahead was a ridge lined with dark green cedar trees. His parents' house lay on the other side of that.

He followed an overgrown farm road that had fallen into disuse. The cedars that lined both sides of the road were heavy with snow, the lower limbs so burdened they sagged to the ground. There were no tracks on the ground other than birds and squirrels, though Jim had taken to keeping an eye on those things. After the Great Depression, the deer were nearly depleted in this area and the population needed almost forty years to recover.

He approached the emergency operations center from the back side. Had he been using the roads, he'd have come to his parents' house first, but this route saved him nearly three miles. He spotted Ford's horse where he'd left it tied to a light pole. Jim approached the horse and saw the tracks leading to the building, not to a door but toward a bank of windows. Then he noticed Ford's rifle leaned against the wall and the blown out glass peppering the snow.

The hair on Jim's neck stood up and sirens went off in his head. All those windows and all that glass. Him sitting there in the open. He dropped off his horse, placing it between him and the windows, and walked it to a nearby truck. He tied the horse off to the bumper and crouched down while he studied the building. The reflective windows made it difficult to tell what was happening in there.

Jim was familiar with this building, and knew there was no approach that offered decent concealment. He assumed Ford had to be in there and he couldn't imagine him leaving his rifle outside by choice. Something had happened and Jim had to know what it was.

Using the parked cars for cover he slogged his way toward the front corner of the building. It was far from safe but it was the least visible approach to the building. When he reached the last car in the parking lot, he slung his rifle to his back and un-holstered his pistol. He crawled toward the corner of the building, a distance of no more than thirty feet, but thirty *open* feet. The feeling of being exposed made him wish he'd fashioned a poncho out of an old white sheet to offer him some sort of camouflage against the snow. He expected a shot to come at any moment and he prayed their aim would be poor.

Within eight feet of the building, he rose to his hands and knees and scurried the remaining distance, flattening himself out against the base of the wall. He listened for a moment and heard nothing. The windows were about three feet up from ground level and Jim crawled along toward the shot out window, hoping he was close enough to the wall that a shot would be difficult. It was awkward going, his M4 jostling around and banging against the wall at times, nearly choking him at others.

When he finally reached the window he stood upright, flattening himself against the wall between the windows. He took a double-handed grip on his pistol and spun toward the open window, weapon raised. At that moment, a black duffel bag nearly the same size as the opening came sailing out. The sudden emergence of the black bag startled Jim and he backpedaled. In the deep snow, he lost his balance and fell backward.

With his finger planted on the trigger, Jim nearly sent a round flying through the open window. He hesitated, wanting to lay eyes on his target. What he found was Ford staring at him curiously through the opening.

"Fuck!" Jim said. "I almost shot you."

"What are you doing out there?"

Jim holstered his pistol, rolled to his side, and clumsily got to his feet. "I was going to check on my parents' house. When I heard gunfire, I thought I should probably come down this way and make sure everything was okay."

"I almost got scalped with buckshot earlier but it's cool now."

"Who are you talking to?" came a panicked voice from inside.

"A friend," Ford called back. "He heard the shots and came to check on me."

"Who are you talking to?" Jim asked.

"It's not important," Ford whispered. "I'll explain later." He came out the window, carefully avoiding any remaining shards of glass. He picked up his weapons from where he'd left them in the snow, holstered his pistol, and slung the rifle over his shoulder. He reached back through the opening and grabbed several smaller backpacks, dragging them back out through the open window.

"Those look heavy," Jim commented.

Ford smiled. "You got no fucking idea, man. This is good shit."

"I'm intrigued."

"Help me with this."

Jim grabbed one of the two backpacks and found it shockingly heavy. "What's in this? Rocks?"

"Ammo," Ford said.

Jim shared that same devilish grin now. Even though they were not in short supply, more ammo was always a good thing. They decided the best plan was to hang both packs on the rear of Jim's horse, fastening the packs together like saddlebags. When they returned to the window, Jim had to help Ford with the duffel bag, each of them grabbing a strap and hauling it between them.

"More ammo?" Jim asked.

Ford shook his head. "I thought the gun locker had been hit but it hadn't. There was a small armory in the building. Several Class 3 items."

"Select fire?"

Ford nodded. "Oh yeah."

"Did you get all of it?"

"I left a riot gun with the people inside but got all the other stuff."

"Good man," Jim said.

"You're assuming I'm sharing anything," Ford said.

7
***

B uddy rode to the cemetery with a focused reverie. From the very moment he was en route to visit his daughter his mindset changed. He became increasingly somber and his heart began to pull his mind to places beyond his control. The sights before his eyes—the snow-covered road, the darkened houses, the looted and vacant businesses—faded to the background, overshadowed by a grainy montage that played before his eyes like a home movie.

He saw a scene from dating his wife that blurred into moments from her pregnancy with his daughter Rachel. There was a vivid flash of her birth, of waiting at the hospital with his wife's family while his daughter came into the world. There was a vignette of taking Rachel to school on the first day and how he'd laughed at his wife for becoming emotional over that milestone, and then he was overtaken by tears after walking her to class. He saw a picture she had drawn when she was only four years old. It still hung on his refrigerator. He watched her sitting at the kitchen table with a glass of milk, eating Oreos, and drawing that picture. He remembered taking her fishing for bluegills at a local lake and their mutual surprise when she reeled in a long, toothy Northern Pike.

Buddy's chest constricted and he forced himself to suck in a deep breath, then slowly let it out. It felt like more escaped him than his exhalation, like a piece of his spirit left to join Rachel, unable to wait on him to die. Every time he visited her it affected him differently. After she died last summer, he hadn't really cared if he lived or died. Then the world went to shit. He hadn't really expected to make it this long but he had. In some ways that disappointed him. He did not relish the fact that he was here alive, alone, and still feeling this pain of her loss like it was yesterday.

His horse stopped and Buddy looked at it curiously, then looked up to notice he was at the cemetery gate already. His horse was waiting as if confirming this was indeed their destination. Buddy was not certain how long he'd been standing before those gates or even how long it had taken to get there. He could not recall the trip, only the somber streaming recollections of his old life.

He knew it was unsafe to travel in such an inattentive state but it was too late to do anything about it now that they were there at the iron gates. Had Buddy been more vigilant he might have seen that his ride into town had not gone unnoticed. In riding past the short block of identical rental houses he'd drawn the attention of a young man sitting on a front porch mulling over his frustrations. They were a multitude and of much greater consequence than the decisions he'd previously faced in his life. He was concerned about where his next meal was coming from. He was concerned how he was going to keep his grandmother alive.

The kid was seventeen years old and had been raised by his grandmother ever since the courts took him from his mother. He'd never met his dad and could never really get a straight answer on who or where he was. He'd stayed with his grandmother for periods throughout his childhood, but the last time his mother overdosed, she ended up in jail. The courts decided enough was enough and they gave his grandmother permanent custody. She'd done her best to raise him but making her single fixed income cover two people was a struggle.

With the snow muffling sound and the lack of vehicle traffic, the town was silent on this day. The boy hadn't even heard the rider, just noticed him as a movement in the periphery of his vision, a flicker of movement like a squirrel jumping in the shadows. The boy's eyes locked onto Buddy and he intently watched him ride by. He didn't move and was fairly certain the rider had not seen him.

When the man paused at the cemetery gate, the boy rose and quietly entered the house. His grandmother had pulled their electric stove into the living room with the boy's help. Using an axe they chopped a hole in the back of the stove of adequate size to receive a section of stovepipe. The old rental house had a chimney that had not been used in decades but the grandmother, who'd grown up with wood heat, had checked the chimney out. She determined it was sound and functional.

They used pieces of aluminum foil to close the gaps between the back of the stove and the stovepipe, shoving them in like chinking between logs in a cabin. The grandmother removed the wire baking racks from the oven and replaced them with an old car wheel set on the bottom element. She used this as a base for her fires. The stove was smoky and far from ideal but it kept them alive. They burned everything they could find.

While they had heat, food was getting scarce. They were never able to get ahead, so the pantry was always sparse. Over the winter, the other inhabitants of the town determined which houses were vacant and those had already been looted of any remaining food. Grocery stores and the convenience stores had been cleaned out. Finding food was purely a matter of resourcefulness and determination at this point. Searching cars for any leftover snacks, looking under the shelves in ransacked grocery stores, and looking in desk drawers in empty offices. Even those resources were producing less and less bounty. In the last week the only thing they managed to eat were a few squirrels that they'd caught on glue traps designed for rats.

Inside the house, the boy found his grandmother feeding the fire, shoving in a chunk from a rickety picnic table they'd busted up. The boy looked at the woodpile and saw it was getting slim. He'd found a stash of old pallets behind the tractor shed at the cemetery and figured he was going to have to drag a couple home. They were hard to bust up but they burned really well.

"I just saw a man on a horse," he said. He guessed it was a man, though it was hard to tell through the layers.

"A horse?" She let the stove door bang shut and watched the fire for a moment through the soot-covered glass.

"He stopped down at the cemetery. Looked like he was going up that way."

"Into the cemetery?" She fixed her ice blue eyes on him. They seemed young and vibrant despite being inset in a face crackled like old pottery. "Bad day for paying your respects."

"I wish we had a horse," he said. "We could search a lot more places for food. It would be easier to bring home wood. Or we could just decide to get out of this place and go somewhere else."

"Where could we go?"

"We could find a cabin somewhere in the woods. A place we could fish, hunt, and raise a garden."

"I growed up that way, boy. Ain't an easy life."

"This ain't easy either," the boy replied, gesturing around them.

The grandmother had been overweight most of her adult life and now was just fleshy, like an air mattress with a slow leak. Loose folds of wrinkled skin hung from her face and arms. She was missing all her teeth and no longer cared to wear her dentures. She looked away and thought, then back at the boy shortly, her eyes cutting. "There's a lot of meat on a horse."

"Meat?" the boy asked. "On a horse?"

His granny nodded. "Horse eats the same things a cow eats. I haven't ate one but it can't be a whole lot different. Right now I'd probably eat one even if it tasted like the south end of a northbound mule."

The boy looked concerned. Though he'd wanted the horse too, admittedly for a different reason, he hadn't thought through actually taking the horse. Having grown up poor, his grandmother was more resourceful than him.

"How would we get that horse, Granny? We ain't got anything to trade and I'm sure he ain't going to give it up without a fight."

His granny pointed a withered, sun-damaged finger at a gun rack on the living room wall. "Yonder deer rifle should do it."

The rifle was a thirty ought six that belonged to his grandfather. The boy didn't know much about it. In fact, he didn't know much about his grandfather either, since he'd been a baby when he passed. All he knew was that his grandfather had killed many deer with it over the course of his life.

"I never shot that gun," the boy said.

"You've got a .22 just like it. Bolt-action, scope, and safety works the same, just kicks harder."

The boy looked at the rifle, mulling over the process, thinking out each step in his head. He examined the possibilities. "What if he shoots back?"

His grandmother dismissed the idea with a wave of her hand. "Aw, he ain't going to fight back. You shoot that horse and he'll think he's next. He'll run like his ass is on fire."

"I don't know if I could kill a man if it came to that."

His grandmother gave him a weary frown. "You don't take that horse, you might be killing the two of us. How much longer you think we can live off squirrels, candy bars, and the odd can of vegetables?"

The boy understood she was right but also that this was a pivotal moment in his life. No matter what happened down the road—the power coming back on, him going back to school, him getting married and having children—he'd always have to live with the fact he'd killed a man to take his horse...for food.

The boy went to the gun rack and removed the rifle he'd been forbidden to touch up until this moment. It was heavy and solid. He drew the bolt back. The mechanism operated with a solid precision that his .22 rifle lacked. He opened one of the sliding doors on the bottom of the gun rack and removed a worn box of shells. The flaps were worn smooth, as if they had been carried into the woods many times without wasting any rounds.

The rifle's box magazine loaded differently than anything the boy had ever used before and his grandmother helped him load it. He thumbed several rounds down through the open chamber, hoping he didn't have to fire any of them at the man, hoping that he indeed fled as his grandmother assured him he would.

"Let me get my coat," his grandmother said. She disappeared into an adjoining room and returned in a few minutes in an old purple coat. The excess room inside it after she buttoned it up was indicative of just how they were wasting away. She had a large butcher knife in her hand.

When the boy's eyes landed on the knife, they went wide. "You going to stab that man?"

His grandmother looked at him like it was the dumbest question she'd heard all day. "That horse ain't going to cut itself up. We have to butcher it and haul the pieces home."

The boy nodded but still looked at the knife uncertainly. He'd never butchered game before the world fell apart. In fact, had only seen meat for most of his life shrink-wrapped in foam trays at the store. Since last summer he'd learned to butcher squirrels, chipmunks, possums, raccoons, and even cats, but he'd never done anything as large as a horse. He couldn't imagine it.

"You know how to do that?" he asked.

She nodded. "I've done cows, hogs, and deer. Ain't much difference betwixt them."

The grandmother, understanding her grandson was a little apprehensive about the situation, did not want to give him too much time to think about it. With her eyes, it was unlikely she could hit the horse with the scoped weapon. With her lungs, damaged from sixty years of cigarette smoking, it would take her too long to get down there. The rider may be gone by the time she made it. If he could get down there and fell the animal, she would come along in time to process it.

They exited the front door, and from the yard could see the rider was no longer at the cemetery gates. The cemetery had seen little traffic since the snow fell and there was no broken trail to the interior roads.

The grandmother shaded her eyes with her gnarled and wrinkled hand. "Whereabouts do you think he is? Can you spy him?"

The boy had already caught sight of Buddy. He pointed. "He's about halfway between the gate and the mausoleum. Straight up the hill."

The grandmother squinted, but with distance and the glare off the snow she couldn't make out anything. "That's why I need you, boy. I can't see nothing anymore. Just an old broken down woman."

They plodded through the snow, high-stepping it to Main Street where a beaten trail awaited them. When the boy slowed to wait on her, the old lady urged him forward.

"You ain't gonna get anywhere waiting on me. You keep going. I'll get there when I get there."

The boy nodded somberly, understanding the weight of this lay on his shoulders now. Their fate, their future, their survival—all of it was on him and his actions. He couldn't separate this decision from what his grandmother had done for him when he was a child. She couldn't afford him. She didn't have the means to provide for him, and didn't know how she was going to be able to do it. But she had. Now a decision of the same gravity lay before him.

When the boy got nearer to the cemetery, he came to a group of tall pines that shielded the cemetery from the road. He lost sight of the distant rider. He angled off the road and cut up a steep bank. In the wet snow, he ended up having to crawl, pushing the rifle ahead of him. He wished he'd thought to make a sling for it like his .22 rifle had.

He stopped at the top of the bank and looked back for his grand-mother. She was still chugging along, puffing hard, and trying to catch her breath. Even following in his footsteps, it was hard going for her. When she looked ahead and caught him waiting, she gestured for him to keep moving. He conceded and disappeared through the wall of pines.

This cemetery didn't use raised markers. Everything was flat to the ground, offering no cover whatsoever. There were a few trees and he decided that keeping a tree between him and the rider at all times might make him less noticeable.

Buddy reached Rachel's grave and slid off his horse, dropping the reins. The horse pawed at the ground, tried to nudge snow away with its nose, and found nothing of interest. It snorted loudly, exhaling clouds of mist. Buddy didn't notice the horse's effort. He was lost in reverie. In his mind, he saw his daughter. Her old bed was set up here in the snow and she lay on it beneath a thick layer of blankets. Her eyes were closed and she looked like she had when he last saw her. It was to this girl that he spoke, not the girl beneath the ground, not the child in his memory. He saw and felt her. In his head, he was kneeling at her bedside, speaking to her sleeping form.

"I'm sorry it's been so long since I came to visit you," he said. "Times have been hard."

He waited for a reaction on the face he saw but there was none.

"I've struggled, sweetie, but there have been good people around me. There's a man named Lloyd living at the house with me and he's a crackerjack. You would think he's hilarious." Buddy sighed heavily and imagined his daughter living back at the house, interacting with Lloyd.

"I've tried to help people. I've tried to be a good man, but I've lost too much. I'm frozen to the core with pain and grief. I understand now it will never thaw. There's nothing in this world, nor will there ever be again, that will produce enough warmth to reach the core of me." Buddy reached out and stroked her head, feeling the cool skin, the cool hair.

The boy was within seventy yards now. He watched with confusion as the kneeling man reached before him and moved his hand in the air. Although he couldn't see anything, it appeared as if the man did. Was he seeing a ghost? Perhaps he'd gone mad, driven insane by the random cruelty and endless suffering.

The boy noticed the horse sniffing the air and was concerned about being detected. He was here now and had to follow this through. There was no way to back out without having to face another night of hunger. He could not disappoint his grandmother.

He could not be the cause of her suffering. He dropped to his knee and put the crosshairs of the scope on the horse. He didn't understand the anatomy enough to know exactly where the heart was but he assumed it had to be somewhere in the region of where the shoulder joined the body. That was where he aimed, trying to calm his surging heart and wavering barrel.

He flipped the safety off, put a finger on the trigger. He tried not to think about the crazy man touching things that couldn't be seen. The horse filled his scope as it filled his mind. He pulled the trigger.

The rifle boomed and the recoil startled him. He nearly fell over, having failed to brace himself against it. In his gyrations, he lost sight of the horse in the scope and lowered the rifle. In the distance he saw the horse stagger and drop. He looked for the old man and found him raising a rifle to his shoulder. It was aimed directly at him. The boy screamed and lunged forward, dropping himself flat on his belly in the snow.

The old man's rifle boomed and the boy yelled out again, hearing a round whizz by him. He heard a different voice screaming, not his own this time, and looked down the hill. His grandmother was cursing at the man and trying to run toward them. The old man turned toward her now, raising his rifle.

The boy panicked. Was the old man really going to shoot her? He couldn't let that happen. He worked the bolt and chambered another of the long rounds. He dropped an eye to the scope and fought to get the crosshairs on the old man. He jerked the trigger, more interested in scaring him than in getting a perfect hit. He didn't care if he hit the old man or not, he just wanted to distract him from firing at his grandmother

But the round found its target.

Buddy spun as if hit by a sledgehammer. The round caught him high on the shoulder and blood sprayed onto his face. He dropped into the snow.

The boy got to his feet and looked toward his grandmother. She'd fallen onto all fours but was looking in his direction, uncertain if that first round had hit him. The boy was concerned and started downhill toward his grandmother.

"No!" she bellowed. "Check him!" The cry took all the wind she had and she sagged back down. She coughed, trying to catch her breath.

The boy had forgotten about the old man. He jacked another round into the rifle and staggered toward where the old man fell. He found the man face down on the ground, blood pouring from a vast open wound on what used to be a shoulder. The man's left arm hung crooked and useless, barely attached. It was a gory sight and the boy fought the urge to throw up. It wasn't just the nature of the wounds but the fact that he was responsible for them. He had done this.

He couldn't tell if the old man was breathing through his thick layers. The boy approached him and kicked Buddy in the leg. In a flash, Buddy rolled over and raised his .45 Colt automatic. The boy was staring straight down the barrel. The gun was less than four feet from his face. Buddy knew he was going to die and he planned on taking on his attackers with him. He didn't pull the trigger though.

"Just a boy," he gasped.

That hesitation, that merciful instinct to spare a child's life, cost him his own. It gave the boy just enough time to level his own rifle at the hip and pull the trigger. The round caught Buddy just below the sternum. He arched and sucked in air, dropping his Colt. Buddy kicked once and tried to crawl away, his bloodied arms creating a crimson snow angel, a bloody angel of death.

The boy staggered backward in horror. He ran into his grand-mother. She was gasping too hard to speak but took the boy's arm and pulled him away from the dying man, wishing to spare him the sight, to spare him from bearing witness to the fruit of his harvest. She led him to the horse, breathing hard and shuddering on its side. The old woman took one look at the boy, into his eyes, and relieved him of his rifle. She chambered a round, shouldered it, and put one in the horse's head, ending its suffering.

The boy stared at his grandmother, tears in his eyes. "Was this worth it? Was all this worth it?"

His grandmother had no means with which to answer that question. It was done now and they would have to see it through to the end. She pulled the butcher knife from an inner pocket of her coat. "We got work to do. Get back to the house and bring me your sled. I'm going to roll out its innards and quarter it."

8

R andi hadn't grown up in this town but she was familiar enough to get around. In better times, it was where she came to renew her driver's license, pay her property taxes, and buy groceries. She plodded in an easterly direction, following their earlier trail until she hit the defunct red light. She got on Main Street there and headed into the central part of town. She passed an old garage that had been in business for more than fifty years. The parking lot was full of cars for which the repairs would likely never be completed.

Strangely, she noticed the plate glass windows on this particular business had not been broken out. Perhaps it was a small gesture of respect. The owner had helped many people over the years, fixing vehicles they needed for getting to work even when he did not have any assurance they could pay for the repairs. He gave payment plans to people who had no credit. Over the decades, hundreds of young men got their first job pumping gas from his tanks.

She passed the town hall and a bank, both showing signs of break-ins and vandalism. This main street looked identical to that of hundreds of thousands of small towns across the country. It was a hodgepodge of old houses and old businesses. There were several churches, a grocery store turned into a pharmacy, an elementary school, and a middle school. There were indications of foot traffic around the old school buildings, as if they were used as shelters and may still be housing some displaced folks.

She passed through the center of town, by the snow-covered Confederate statue and the town's original red light. This was the oldest part of town, built in the 1800s. Some of the buildings were stone, hewn by Greek and Italian stonemasons. She passed several closed restaurants, a defunct coal company headquarters, and in that whole time did not pass a soul stirring on the streets. There were plenty of signs of people collecting firewood or trying to find empty homes where they might scavenge a bite of food.

The sun was higher in the sky and along Main Street, sheltered by the row of businesses, the breeze dissipated to the point it almost felt warm. The sound of the snow under the horse's hooves changed, indicating there may even have been a little melting going on. That would be welcome. The snow made everything in their lives even more exhausting than normal.

Randi squinted into the distance and could now see the gated entrance to the cemetery. She was glad she'd brought her sunglasses. The sun bounced off every snow-covered surface and without them she knew she'd be suffering from a headache. When she turned through the iron gates she automatically looked to the distance where she knew Buddy's daughter's grave was located.

Had the weather been warm, she would expect to see him sitting or kneeling beside the unmarked grave, just as he had through all of their other visits. He would be speaking softly to his daughter as if she were right there with him. With the snow on the ground, she expected to see him standing beside the grave or sitting on his horse but she couldn't find him. The hair on the back of her neck stood up and her heart began to beat a little faster.

She dismounted and tied her horse to the gate hoping that no one would come along and steal it. She scanned the area behind her and saw nobody, but that didn't mean anything. There was a neighborhood back there. There were houses visible and she would be just as visible to them if they were looking out. They could be watching her right at that moment.

She looked back toward the cemetery thinking perhaps she was disoriented by the snow cover and looking in the wrong direction. She shaded her eyes and expanded her search area, scanning the entire swath of ground where she thought the grave to be. Her breath froze. She spotted two figures on the ground, hunched over a shape. She never could see well, even with glasses, and couldn't decipher what lay before her.

Was one of them Buddy?

She couldn't tell what was going on but she slipped into her dark place. Something felt wrong. She confirmed there was a shell in the chamber of the shotgun she was carrying and hurried toward the scene ahead of her. In the deep snow, she could not make good time and it was further than she could have run on the best of days. Admittedly, she was in better condition than she had been at any time in the past twenty years because of how physically taxing life was now. Still, she was not at peak cardio fitness. Her adrenaline pushed her forward, sweeping her up the hill. It took perhaps five minutes to get closer to the scene but it felt like an hour. With each step she feared the people would turn and see her. She prayed one of them was Buddy but she still couldn't tell.

She wished that this was a cemetery with monuments she could hide behind. The flat markers made for a barren landscape that offered no protection, no concealment. When she was perhaps thirty feet away she could clearly see that neither of the two were Buddy. It was two strangers and they were butchering her horse, elbow deep in gore. Her stomach lurched at the sight of the blood, of the pieces of meat.

That had been one of her father's horses. He was dead now, along with her mother. Nearly everything she owned had burned with the family's home. It seemed as if the world was intent on taking everything that meant something to her. It was tearing her to shreds one little nibble at a time. She leveled the shotgun at the figures.

"What the fuck are you doing?"

She could hear fear and uncertainty in her voice, but there was rage there as well. It was not fear of these people but fear she wouldn't be able to stop herself from doing to them what they were doing to her horse. She hoped they heard it too. She hoped it made her sound unbalanced and half-crazy because that was *exactly* what she was at the moment.

The figures froze. One was mid-slice, intently removing a chunk of warm meat from the body. The other was stacking the slippery chunks on a bed sheet. She couldn't imagine Buddy allowing this to happen while he still had breath in him. She risked a sideways glance but couldn't see him anywhere. She returned her attention to the people in front of her.

"I asked you a question. What the fuck are you doing to my horse?"

An elderly woman, big, and perhaps around sixty years old, started to turn around.

"Don't you move! Don't turn around!"

"This is our meat," the old woman hissed. "We killed it fair and square. You best go on your way and leave us alone."

Randi wanted to kill the woman right then for her admission. "Where is the man that was on that horse? What did you do to him?"

When the figure next to the old woman spoke, it was clear from his voice that he was a boy, probably fourteen or fifteen years old. "All he had to do was give up the horse. He didn't have to fight." It was not defiance in his voice but remorse.

"Did you hurt him? Did you kill him for this horse?" Randi asked, her jaw clenched.

The boy started to speak again but the old woman elbowed him. "You don't have to tell her a damn thing. You just keep your mouth shut."

Randi's heart pounded. Keeping her gun on the pair, she took in a wider scan of her surroundings and froze when she found a disturbance in the snow she'd missed before. It was a bloodied tangle of limbs. Randi returned her glance to the people in front of her just in time to catch the old woman easing a pistol out of her jacket pocket.

Randi fired with no warning. At close distance, the 12 gauge round wrought instant death. The old woman pitched forward across the horse, her neck ending in a venous, shredded rag of meat. What had been her head was now a spray of pink texture that settled onto the snow. Her blood spilled silently onto the cooling meat.

The boy jerked sideways and fell away from the body. He skittered away, pushing with his feet. "Granny! Granny!" he bellowed in horror and revulsion.

"You stop right there!" Randi screamed. "You have any weapons on you?"

He pointed at the other side of the body, where the deer rifle lay on a tarp.

"I killed a boy your age once before," Randi said. "It didn't sit right with me. I still have nightmares about it. But I had to do it and I'm willing to do it again. You've got *one* chance. You get off your ass and you run as fast as you can down this hill. If you stop running, I might change my mind about letting you live. If you come back, or if you bring other people back, you're doing to die. They'll all die. You got it?"

"Can I have my granny?"

"Fuck no. Leave her for the coyotes and the buzzards."

The boy looked at Randi, trying to comprehend what he saw as incomprehensible cruelty. She looked him in the eye, clearly seeing that he didn't understand the parallels between what he had done and what she had done. It was the selfishness of youth. He was the center of the universe. All he understood was that she'd killed his grandmother, he couldn't see his own role in it. Couldn't see that the two of them, he and his granny, had started this ball rolling.

When the boy didn't move, Randi shouldered the shotgun again and put the bead on the boy. "Time's up. Run or die."

He struggled to his feet and scrambled through the snow, falling several times. Randi fired, churning the snow several feet behind him, wanting him to know that she was serious. Wanting him to know that she could live with the guilt and bad dreams if she had to.

When he was halfway down the hill, she turned to where Buddy lay in the distance.

The adrenaline ebbed from her body and a great sadness overwhelmed her. "Oh, Buddy. I said I was done crying over this world. Please don't make me break that promise."

She staggered toward him, each step revealing more of the carnage, each step hurting more. He was lying across the wooden marker that she and Ariel had made for his daughter's grave. His blood ran across the carved sign, filling the letters and numbers in. Randi dropped to her knees. Her nurse's instinct was to check for a pulse but there was too much trauma. Even if he'd still been alive, they could not have saved him. That these wounds were fatal was merciful.

Randi peeled off his knit facemask. While the mask had been blood-spattered, the face beneath it was clean, though pale and flaccid in death. She touched his face; his cheek was cool.

"You were important to us, Buddy Baisden," she whispered. "We all looked up to you. You kept us headed in the right direction."

She stroked his hair, remembering how he'd helped her set things right for her parents' deaths, remembering what he'd done to the people who allowed his daughter to die. "I hope you're with your family now. I hope everything is right with them and that you're happy again."

A single tear pushed its way free and rolled down her cheek. She had promised herself she could not cry anymore. There was too much loss, too much suffering, to let it all inside. She removed her hand from Buddy's face and put it in her lap. She dug her thumbnail into the back of her other hand until the urge to cry was replaced with a dull pain. By the time she quit, her own blood was rolling down her fingers.

9

Charlie Watkins was the son of Alice, one of the original group stuck in Richmond with Jim. Alice's journey home had been quite different. She parted ways with Jim, Gary, and Randi early on. She had a much rougher go of it due to an early insistence that FEMA's rescue efforts would get her home before Jim's reckless fantasy of a cross-country hike. When FEMA failed to live up to its end of the bargain, Alice and Rebecca, another coworker, made the decision to try to do the same thing that Jim and his party had done. By choosing this option so late, they lost the option of traveling with a group they could trust even if they didn't always get along.

Alice's journey was ill-fated from the beginning. They joined forces with another traveler who ended up murdering Rebecca. Alice thought she was safe but crossed paths with him again later and ended up imprisoned in his basement. By her own tenacity, she escaped and got herself home. The experience hardened her but it did not change her luck.

She lost her mother and husband soon after she made it home to her family. At that point, she decided she and her son Charlie should accept Jim's invitation to join them in the valley where he lived. Her acceptance wasn't an admission she needed help. Instead, she was becoming increasingly aware she was going through some emotional trauma from experiences on the road and she wasn't able to give Charlie what he needed. She wasn't really able to be a mother to him anymore. She needed to get him around people who could help him. He needed to be among people who could still experience empathy and compassion.

Just as they were reaching the valley, Alice and Charlie saw Jim abducted by a group of former law enforcement officers who were holed up at the local superstore. Despite having butted heads with Jim often in their professional lives, Alice developed a begrudging respect for Jim when his predictions of social collapse materialized just as he'd said they would. She made the decision to send her son Charlie on to the valley, to warn Jim's family of his abduction, while she followed along. She was successful in helping Jim escape but it cost her her life. During the extraction, she took a round to the back of her head and died in a muddy cornfield before ever reaching the valley.

Despite having children and grandchildren of her own to take care of, Randi took Charlie in. She and Alice were never close. In fact, they butted heads on numerous occasions, but she did it because she was one mother trying to help another. She hoped if the situation were reversed Alice might have done the same for her children. In the few months Charlie lived with Randi, he had become close friends with Jim's son Pete.

They'd gone to school in different parts of the county and never met but they were similar in that they both rose to the occasion during this period of societal collapse. Both had easily fallen into the routine of providing food and security for the people they loved. Neither seemed to be experiencing any depression or feeling of loss over what the world had been. Everyone else seemed to be going through it but the two boys showed astounding adaptability. They'd easily taken to carrying guns and living in survival mode twenty-four hours a day. No one in the valley knew where the world was going, but wherever that was, young men like Pete and Charlie were ready for it. They would be the leaders of their community. They would be the future of their tribe.

There were not a lot of places the two boys could go but they been granted an increasing level of freedom within certain parameters that Jim set for them. As long as they were careful, Jim allowed them to fish in the nearby stream. They were instructed not to confront anyone they saw and, should they encounter anyone, they were to retreat quietly and come back home. They were also allowed to hunt and established a trap line that was providing a variety of fresh meat to supplement their dehydrated meals and survival rations.

Wild game was not the only meat available. Some farmers in the valley were culling their cattle herds, since they were having difficulty feeding them through the winter. Some hay had been stored before the collapse and before the food ran out, but managing the large bales without machinery was a struggle.

Being that the valley was farm country and there were dozens of barns where feed had traditionally been stored, rats used to be a problem for farmers. Their numbers were dropping as people ran out of cat food and cats were forced to work for their supper. There was still a good supply of rat traps to be found in barns throughout the valley. The boys scoured those barns and found dozens of wooden rat traps with wire bales. Most of the people they spoke with didn't need them anymore and were glad to let the boys have them.

Rather than sitting in the woods all day with a rifle, Charlie was putting traps to work for him. Using a trick he'd learned from an old man, he made squirrel poles and leaned them against tress where he saw indications of squirrels. The poles were about eight feet long and intersected the trees at about chest level. After being in place for a few days, squirrels took to using the poles as shortcuts to the ground. Charlie allowed them to get used to the pole before placing a trap on it.

When a few days had passed and the squirrels had become accustomed to using the squirrel poles, he mixed up a little dehydrated peanut butter and baited his rat traps, which were nailed to the squirrel poles. Each day now Charlie and Pete walked a path in the woods and checked their rat traps. Nearly every day they found a squirrel in one.

They also used electric fence wire, which they found in abundance, to build snares in which they caught rabbits, groundhogs, raccoons, and even deer. When so much work needed done around the various farms, it made a lot of sense to let snares do the hunting for them. They just had to check them each day, rather than exerting time and energy hunting the woods for an animal they may never encounter. Such trapping methods may not have been legal or ethical in better times, but rules and laws were mostly out the window at this point. People had taken on a pioneer mentality, doing what they had to do to survive

Sometimes, while checking their trap lines, the young men would go visit Hugh, the radio operator who'd recently joined them in the valley. Hugh was a longtime friend of Jim's whom he had not seen in many years. They hadn't gone to school together but Jim had worked with Hugh at his afterschool job.

The boys enjoyed visiting Hugh because he was full of stories. The man had an interesting career trajectory that gave him a vast knowledge of survival, weapons, and tactical operations. Hugh was vague about his background and not forthcoming about how he'd built his knowledge base. Jim suspected that Hugh worked around the world as a civilian contractor in the security field. Hugh would neither confirm nor deny, though sometimes if the homemade liquor was flowing, his tongue would loosen and he would tell a new story, redacting and sanitizing it of time, location, and detail.

At some point in his career Hugh realized that he possessed the computational and electronic skills for being a radio operator. Whatever line of work he may have been involved in, he made an effort to grow and improve those skills. By the time Hugh returned home to Virginia he was quite knowledgeable in the various radio bands and an antenna theory.

There were several abandoned homes in the valley Jim had been able to offer to Hugh with the approval of the neighbors. It was no surprise to Jim that Hugh picked the most remote home, a trailer located high on the slope of the mountain range bordering the southeast side of the valley. It was an older mobile home that had been dragged into position with a bulldozer and placed on a shelf cut into the side of the mountain. The location required a four-wheel-drive vehicle to access it in the best of times but here, in the worst of times, it was foot-access only, which was fine with Hugh.

A wood stove took care of heating and cooking. At the border of the property was a mountain stream that ran year-round and allowed Hugh to have a gravity-fed water system in his home. Besides being attracted to the remoteness of the location, Hugh was happy that the elevation of the site gave him excellent options for placing radio antennas.

When Hugh decided to join them in the valley, Jim made sure Hugh had plenty of muscle for transporting his radio equipment from the superstore. The activity required armed guards since there was still concern of retaliation. Some of the residents of the superstore had been killed by folks from the valley. Some families of the dead were still living in the superstore and the resentment threatened to boil over at any moment.

Jim had months to ponder that the lack of long-distance radio equipment was a major failure in his preparations. Gary had some equipment but he was a novice and had unrealistic expectations of what he would be able to do with the equipment he purchased. He found it wasn't nearly as capable as he'd been led to believe.

When Hugh joined them, it took very little convincing to get Jim on board with putting together a serious ham setup. Soon after his arrival, the folks from the valley conducted a massive push to gather all the equipment Hugh might need. The biggest deficiency was in the area of antennas.

Besides the radio equipment he brought from the superstore, Hugh also had knowledge of various pockets of radio equipment situated around the county. On scavenging missions they found wire, antenna components, and other electronic components that Jim had no understanding of. Hugh knew of two radio operators who had passed away in the last year and whose widows had been unable to part with their equipment.

He intended to pay visits to both of those widows and see if he could barter for the equipment, but neither was to be found. Hugh loaded up the equipment, knowing that the original operator would understand. To keep a clear conscience, Hugh left a note in each location vaguely explaining who he was and why he had taken the equipment. He did not leave an address where he could be found, but he did write down a frequency where he could be reached if the equipment needed to be returned or the widows wanted to take him up on the offer of barter.

ON THE MORNING JIM, Buddy, Randi, and Deputy Ford went into town on horseback, it wasn't long before Charlie showed up at Jim's house looking for his sidekick. He asked Pete if he wanted to check traps and maybe do a short hunt for some bigger game. Even in the cold and snow, checking the traps was preferable to sitting at the house and doing chores. Pete asked his mother and she was agreeable, pleased that Pete had found a role for himself in their new reality. While he didn't have enough experience that he could do all of the things the men did, he was able to help fill in the gaps by providing security and food. While Jim's family was doing better than many of the others due to an extensive pantry, there were plenty of people in the valley pleased to find a gutted squirrel hanging on their doorknob.

"Take a radio, and I want you to check in every thirty minutes," Ellen said. Pete didn't object. It was a small price to pay if it got him out of the house.

It took Pete a few minutes to pull on his outdoor clothing and grab a rifle. The whole time he was getting dressed he had to endure a lecture on being safe from his mother, Nana, and Pops. He did a lot of nodding and agreeing but was for the most part ignoring the lecture that he'd already heard dozens of times over.

The boys soon found checking the trap line in the deep snow was no picnic. They complained to each other but at the same time they saw it as an adventure that beat the hell out of sitting around the fire. They checked over a dozen trees where they utilized their squirrel poles, finding three squirrels and two chipmunks. Even the chipmunks would not go to waste. They could feed them to the cats or boil them outside over a fire for dogs to eat. At such times even the domesticated animals became less picky.

After they slid their last frozen critter into a sack, Pete radioed his mother.

"This is Wombat calling with required check-in. We're going to go check on Hugh and see if he spotted any large game high on the ridge."

"Acknowledged, Wombat. Be careful."

Pete rolled his eyes, but was pleased his mother followed proper radio protocol.

No one had seen or heard from Hugh in two weeks. While that was not atypical, the boys wanted something to do and visiting Hugh was always entertaining.

It took them nearly an hour to get from their last trap to Hugh's mobile home. High-stepping in the deep snow was exhausting. They were forced to stop every ten minutes to cool off and rest their muscles. When they reached Hugh's home he was standing on the porch, already waiting on them. He had a cup of coffee in his hand and a grin on his bearded face.

"You think you boys can make any more noise? There won't be a possum left in this county after all the noise you made."

Pete and Charlie looked at each other suspiciously, fairly certain they'd made very little noise at all. Pete took the bait.

"Noise?" he asked. "We didn't make any noise."

"Then how did I know you were coming?"

The boys shrugged. They didn't have a clue. Hugh clambered down the trailer steps, wearing jeans, tall snow boots, and a T-shirt. The steaming coffee mug in his hand read: May Contain Whiskey. "Let's retrace your steps and you can tell me where you screwed up."

"It took us an hour to walk up here and now you're wanting us to walk back?" Charlie whined.

Hugh regarded the boy with hard blue eyes. "Do you want to learn something that might save your life one day?" He didn't wait for an answer.

How did one answer a question like that? Of course. If someone had information to offer that might save your life one day, you certainly wanted access to that information. The boys reluctantly fell into step behind Hugh and retraced their path for a good hundred yards back downhill.

When he reached a particular spot, Hugh paused in the set of tracks they left earlier and gestured around him. "This is where I first became aware of your presence. I would tell you to look for the alarm but you wouldn't find it if I gave you until summer."

"What was it?" Pete asked. He was ready to get inside and warm up for a few minutes. If Hugh said he wasn't going to find it, then Pete wasn't going to take him up on the challenge and spend more time outside than he had to.

"Basic tripwire. Two pound test fishing line. It breaks when you hit it. You'll never even know you walked through it most days. It was buried under snow so you probably charged right through it and never felt a thing."

Hugh crouched and fished around in the snow, snagging the broken fishing line where it passed through an eye hook at the base of a tree. "Knocked down a whole stack of cans on the back porch. That was the alarm."

Satisfied that the boys understood what had happened here, Hugh started back up toward the mobile home. Along the way he pointed out two different sets of electronic security that also alerted him to the boys' arrival. One method used a transmitter and reflector. When the boys interrupted the light beam, a wireless transmitter triggered an alarm in the mobile home. The final alarm used thermal sensors. All of these devices were simple battery-operated devices that come from home improvement stores.

"If you're just one man by yourself you need devices that are going to be working for you while you're sleeping or doing other things. It's like trapping. The trap is working to gather food while you're doing other things. Even with the state of the world being what it is, you need to automate as much as you can. You need systems that are gathering water while you're doing other things, and systems that are providing security while you're doing other things. You need as much in the way of simple, unsophisticated, and inexpensive automation as you can afford."

"We've been using the squirrel poles and rat traps just like you showed us. We got three squirrels today," Charlie said.

Hugh nodded. "That's good. I've got several squirrel poles set out myself, as well as a few deer snares."

"How's the radio business?" Pete asked. "Heard anything else about the power coming back on?"

Hugh scratched his head and looked off in the distance as he was prone to when collecting his thoughts. It was almost like his own head became an antenna, gathering the information he was preparing to relate. "Just a lot of chatter about what this official transmission really means."

"I thought it meant that the power was coming back on," Charlie said.

"Power restoration could take a long time. It can take months to get one city back online after an ice storm. Multiply that by what we have here. They have to assess each area before they restore power and make sure the infrastructure wasn't damaged due to overload when the grid was collapsing."

The boys looked dejected.

"I was looking forward to playing video games online again," Pete said.

Charlie nodded. "Me too."

"Maybe at some point," Hugh said. "I think you had better take it one day at a time. Don't be getting your hopes up for things that might not happen and most certainly might not happen anytime soon."

PETE AND CHARLIE spent a few minutes warming up by Hugh's fire, swapping stories and updating Hugh on the little that had transpired in the rest of the valley since the snow came. When they left, they promised Hugh they would update Jim on the things he had mentioned. They departed after Pete radioed in again to his mother to let her know they were at Hugh's. He told her they were leaving for a short hunt before descending back into the valley then signed off.

Hugh asked, "Where do you intend to hunt?"

"I thought we'd follow some of these old logging roads," Charlie said. "Work our way up higher on the slope."

"I've been doing some recon of my own. I think it would be worth setting up a little blind where that power line crosses the top of the ridge. With the power company maintaining a cleared right of way, you should have sight lines down both slopes. One of you could look down the east side, the other could look down the west side, and you could cover a good bit of ground without walking around."

"It's a good idea," Charlie said, and Pete nodded.

"There's some bear moving around too," Hugh cautioned.

"Shouldn't they be hibernating?" Pete asked warily.

"They don't always go into deep hibernation around here anymore," Hugh said. "The winters don't stay cold long enough so the bears take little naps and then get up and move around. They're moving around in this snow because I've seen the tracks."

"You need a dog," Pete said. "You'll be overrun with bears in the summer."

"That's high on my list for spring," Hugh said. "Tripwires and electronic measures are nothing compared to a good dog."

They boys departed with a wave and the promise they would return in a week or so.

"Let Jim know if I hear anything of interest," Hugh told them, "I'll venture down into the valley to pass on the information."

The flat ledge of earth Hugh's mobile home sat on had been carved out by a dozer during a logging operation. It was part of the landing and staging area where knuckle-boom loaders stacked logs on trucks. Because of the logging operation, there was a network of trails and skidder roads starting immediately behind Hugh's home leading deep into the hills. The Clinch Mountain range had steep shoulders at this level, becoming even steeper as you crested the summit. The logging roads were the best way to get around whether you were on foot, four wheeler, or horseback. The boys headed for a logging road cutting away from Hugh's backyard, trudging into deep snow.

Slogging through the snow, their muscles already sore, the boys began to question the wisdom of their hunting trip, of climbing the steep ridge in the deep snow. Turning around was not an option. Had they been older they may have turned around and gone home, but these were young men on a young men's adventure. Retreat was not an option.

The logging roads allowed them to reach the top of the mountain much sooner than if they had been following a game trail or bushwhacking. Still, it took them an hour and a half to reach the crest of the ridge. They were tired and sweaty, despite opening zippers and shedding layers to keep from soaking their clothes. Although it was already late afternoon and the days were short, they were not concerned because they knew that going downhill, with gravity assisting, they could descend in half the time.

The ridge top was not a jagged peak, but a broad, rounded, densely-wooded plane strewn with boulders the size of shipping containers. There were magnificent views of the snow-covered valley below them and they stared, taking it in through the clouds of their puffing breath. When his breathing slowed, Pete radioed his mother again to let her know that they had reached the spot they were going to hunt. Pete could almost see the house and hoped he could reach her.

He keyed his microphone. "Wallaby, this is Wombat, come back?" Pete was always coming up with new call signs. He and his sister Ariel thought it was hilarious but no one else found it as entertaining as they did.

He repeated his message twice before his mother responded. *"This is Wallaby,"* she replied dryly.

Pete cracked up hearing her say it. Even Charlie thought it was funny.

"We're on top of the ridge, right where the high tension line clearing is. You can probably see it from the front porch because I can nearly see the house."

"Roger that. I'm standing on the front porch right now and I can see exactly where you're talking about. Don't stay long because you need to allow yourself time to get home."

"We have lights if we need them but I expect we'll only hunt for about an hour or two. It's really cold and windy up here."

"That's fine. Check-in before you start down."

"Got it. Wombat out."

While Pete was on the radio, Charlie was wandering around examining vantage points and scouting the area. He pointed at something on the ground.

"What is it?" Pete asked.

"Hugh was right. Bear track."

"No kidding?" Pete got up from the rock he was sitting on and went to examine the track. He had seen a few bear tracks over the years and this was indeed a bear track. "Can you tell anything about the size?"

"Looks like a yearling. Not massive, but if he's wandered around in this mess he's probably hungry. Keep your eyes open. You might not hear him coming."

Pete looked at Charlie with a frown. "That's comforting."

Charlie shrugged. "It is what it is."

"So how you want to do this?"

Charlie pointed at the massive high tension tower approximately fifty yards from their position. "Let's go to the clearing. You can watch one side and I'll take the other."

"Fine with me."

"If you spot something, give me a heads up before you shoot. That way I know I won't think I have to rush over and stop a bear from gnawing on you."

For nearly two hours they maintained vigilance, each watching the cleared right-of-way beneath the dead power lines. Pete realized that if something drastic didn't happen, if the country didn't recover and get the power back on, these clearings would grow back quickly. It didn't take long for trees to overtake an area that wasn't taken care of. Pete fished a cut of jerky out of a crumpled plastic bag and shoved it in his mouth. Before they split up, he and Charlie split some food Pete brought. There was jerky, old Halloween candy, and a couple of biscuits with homemade blackberry jelly.

Neither saw any deer or other game moving around. Perhaps the deer were smart enough to know it wasn't a good day to be out wandering around in deep snow. They were probably bedded down somewhere waiting this mess out. Perhaps Pete and Charlie should have been doing the same thing, but it was still better than a day at home. Pete had to keep reminding himself of that as he began to get cold. He would have been doing chores, sawing and splitting firewood, spreading ashes on the garden, and whatever else his mother came up with. He didn't mind helping out at the house but there was certainly no adventure in it. *This* was adventure.

Pete picked up his radio. "Stink Bug, this is Wombat."

"Stink Bug?" Charlie replied. *"That's the best you could do?"*

"Sorry, you can try to think of something better. You have any luck?"

"The only thing I can see moving around are birds and they're not any kind I'd eat."

"You want to head back?"

"Might as well. It's cold as shit up here and I don't think the hunting is going to get any better today. We'll try again another day."

Pete got up and walked from where he'd been sitting to Charlie's side of the ridge top. It felt good to move. Sitting still made his muscles stiffen. He'd gotten a little chilled too with his sweat-dampened clothing and the constant wind. Before he left, he wanted to see what the other side of the mountain looked like from this particular point. He hadn't seen it before. He knew that side of the ridge stretched deep into National Forest and backcountry. It was even less populated than Jim's side.

"You got a better view," Pete said. The mountains on Charlie's side rolled off into the distance for miles. From there, he spotted the power line clearing rolling over smaller ridges for quite a distance.

"A better optic would be helpful," Charlie replied. "With a good scope you could see pretty far."

"With a nice long-range rifle, you could hit for a good distance too."

Charlie stood and shook his head. "Stink Bug. That's the last time I let you pick the call signs."

"What's that?" Pete was pointing at a distant ridge.

In the utility clearing, where it crossed a ridge several miles away, there were bright orange pieces of fabric that stood out from the snow.

"I don't remember seeing that," Charlie replied. "If it had been there the whole time, surely I would've spotted it."

Pete raised his rifle and examined the orange shape through his rifle scope. Even at low magnification it was an improvement. "Those are tents. There are people moving around. It looks like they're setting up a camp."

"They're camping in this snow?" Charlie asked.

"Yep. We need to keep an eye on them," Pete said. "They could be headed this way."

10

Jim's wife, Ellen, was at the kitchen table planting seeds in black plastic trays. She knew she'd have to get her seeds germinating early since she just couldn't go to the local Lowe's and buy starter plants this year. She planned on starting them in a nice warm spot by the wood stove. From there, they'd transition them to cold frames in the garden made from old windows. They also had a number of old wooden window sashes with the glass intact that would allow them to make more cold frames if they needed them. She was covering a tray with clear plastic wrap when she heard the radio crackle, then Jim's voice come across the airwaves. They must be on their way back, near the river crossing. Any further than that point and getting a clear signal was difficult.

She placed the seed tray on a shelf near the wood stove and picked up the radio. "I'm here Jim."

"We're on our way back."

It was all he had to say. They'd known each other for so long were so accustomed to reading between the lines and reading each other's minds. They could finish each other's sentences and she could finish this one. She could feel the pain of loss in his voice even from a distance. They were coming home but they were not all coming home. Something bad had happened and someone had died.

"What is it, Jim? What happened?"

There was a pause. She understood Jim was trying to decide if this was something he should say on an open channel or not. Perhaps she shouldn't ask the question on the radio like that but she couldn't wait. She had to know. With the exception of Deputy Ford, whom she barely knew, the others were people she was close to. The loss of any of them...

"Buddy is dead." Jim's voice was hollow, as if putting the reality of it into words pulled something out of him.

It was out there now. No warning or preamble. No effort to soften the blow because how could he? There was no way to make that news less painful. She felt it as a gut punch and her legs weakened. She sagged to a kitchen chair.

It was hard to believe their family had lived within a mile or two of this man for over a decade and had barely known he existed until the world fell apart. In that short time he had become integral to their community. He had become family. She assumed too that to some extent they became family to him. Though the loss of his daughter was too big a void for them to hope to fill, perhaps they had eased his pain a little. Perhaps they had given him something to care about during his darkest days.

Ellen keyed her mic, her voice breaking. "Buddy?" She needed the confirmation, the verification that she hadn't simply misheard him.

Jim pressed his own mic and she could hear him breathing at the other end as he tried to find the words. *"He wanted to spend time alone at the cemetery with his daughter. He said they had a lot to talk about."*

Jim paused, his voice breaking, and he let his mic click off. When he keyed it again, he'd regained his composure. *"I'll have to tell you the rest in person. We're at the creek crossing. We'll be home soon."*

"Please be careful."

"I will," came the flat reply.

Despite the intimacy of the conversation, that transmission was heard throughout the valley where Jim and Buddy lived. At Buddy's house, Lloyd heard the transmission. He shattered the closest thing at hand, a glass jar, against the wall. When it did nothing to ease the pain, he sagged to the floor in a sobbing heap. Buddy had become like a father to him. Lloyd had been able to make the stoic old man crack a smile, which was quite the accomplishment. As the old man opened up about everything he had been through in his life—about his daughter, about how he'd gone into the house of the man who'd let her die and burned him alive—Lloyd began to understand Buddy. He felt that in some small way he helped comfort the man. Buddy had opened his house to Lloyd and given him a place to live. Buddy had helped make him part of this community.

At the Wimmer house, old Mrs. Wimmer cried quietly at her kitchen table. Her family and Buddy were not close, but they were neighbors. In the country, being neighbors almost made them a degree of family. He was also closer to her generation than most of the others that remained there and his death made her even more aware that hers would be coming soon too.

At Gary's home, at the Weatherman home, at Mac Bird's house, people heard the transmission and were sharing the news. There was silence and prayer. There were gestures of respect. Among all the folks there was an overwhelming sense of awe that anything could bring down this old man that the world itself seemed unable to tear apart despite everything it threw at him.

Ellen remembered that Pete was still on the mountain and it was getting late. She hit the transmit button on her radio. "Pete?"

"*Call signs, Mom,*" he scolded. "*I'm Wombat.*"

She had no playfulness in her at this point, nor any way to soften the blow across the distance. "You need to come on home. Something bad has happened."

The alarm in Pete's voice was instant. "*Is Dad okay?*"

"Dad's fine but Buddy was...killed." She dropped her head at the words, still unable to believe it herself.

"*We're already on our way down,*" Pete said. "*It will probably take us about two hours.*"

"That's fine. Just be careful."

Ellen laid her head on the table for a moment, contemplating the world in which they found themselves. She was sitting in a nearly powerless house communicating with her family over handheld radios. She was thinking of a dear family friend who'd likely died in some act of violence for which there would never be a conventional trial and punishment. Trials were instant now, punishment usually swift and final.

Pops was taking a nap. Nana and Ariel were playing in her room. Ellen gently placed the radio on the kitchen table in the silent house. She scooted from the table and walked across the tile floor of her kitchen. She needed to add wood to the fire and start dinner, but she had something else she needed to do first. She went down the hall and pushed open a door, finding Ariel and Nana both sitting on the floor playing a board game. They looked up at Ellen. Both saw the seriousness of her expression and knew that something was wrong.

Ellen looked at her daughter, remembering the special bond she had had with Mr. Buddy. Buddy had been seriously injured rescuing Ariel from a coyote attack. His act had profoundly moved the little girl who played a huge role in caring for Buddy afterward. The two had been bonded ever since. Ariel was not used to losing people. This was going to be difficult. Whatever degree of innocence her daughter had been able to maintain throughout this disaster was about to be shattered. The mere thought of it clawed a wound in Ellen's soul.

"Ariel, sweetie," Ellen said. "We need to talk."

HUGH WAS SITTING at a folding table surrounded by radio gear, dialing his way through frequencies and making notes in a log when his alarm sounded. He checked his watch and assumed it was Pete and Charlie returning from their hunting trip but Hugh never trusted his life to assumptions. He removed his headphones and picked up a nearby shotgun. It was a decent weapon for throwing off quick, hastily aimed shots in dense woods or poor light. The alarm that sounded was another of his battery-operated perimeter warnings. All of the notification tones were set differently so he would know which direction the intruder came from. This tone indicated that the approach was from the logging road to the back of his property, further confirming his assumption that it was the boys returning.

Hugh slipped out the front door, keeping the mobile home between him and whoever was approaching. Before he even got the corner he heard his name being called, the boys remembering his instruction to call out before approaching the house. Hugh stepped from around the corner and threw an arm up to the boys, just now exiting the woods. "Any luck?"

Charlie shook his head

"Buddy's dead," Pete blurted out. "I got a call from my mom on the radio."

Hugh had been so focused beneath the headphones that he'd missed that exchange. He didn't know the older man well, having not been in the valley long enough. He knew, though, that the old man was a keystone of this small group. His friend Jim held tremendous respect for the older man. This loss would not sit easy with the folks of this valley.

"What happened?" Hugh asked.

"They were in town. I don't know the details. I guess they ran into trouble." Pete kept shaking his head. Despite being hardened by current circumstances, this death clearly bothered him.

"Well, you boys best get on home then. Your families are going to need you. Times like this, people need to be together."

Hugh caught the quick look in Charlie's eyes and regretted his words, remembering now that Charlie had no family anymore. Hugh dealt with the awkwardness of his comment head on. No brushing it under the table. No pretending he hadn't said it. "You too, Charlie. You're family now. Don't forget that. These are your people."

Charlie nodded. "Oh, I almost forgot. Before we go, you need to know that there are men camping under the power lines."

Hugh raised an eyebrow, his usual gesture indicating that he required more information on the topic at hand.

"They were setting up camp a couple of ridges away. It looked like they just got there. They could be traveling in the clearing under the power lines or they could be hunters just camping there for the night. Just thought you should know."

That was indeed something Hugh wanted to know. If they were a couple of ridges away, they could potentially be standing in his backyard tomorrow or the next day. That was too close for comfort. Hugh's wheels were already turning.

The boys knew he was lost in thought, processing this new information.

"We better get on home," Pete said.

Hugh patted each boy on the shoulder as they passed him, his mind on the strangers. He couldn't wait until they were closer to decide what to do about them. He needed intel. If these were men with bad intentions, best to just slit their throat where they slept tonight. If they came in this direction, they would soon smell the smoke of his fire, see the glow of his lanterns, or spot the reflection from his solar array. They would find him. Hugh preferred that encounter take place by his rules and not those of the strangers.

He climbed back up the front porch steps and kicked off his boots. When they were clear of snow, he went inside and began assembling his gear. He didn't have the money to buy dedicated snow camo but his low-cost option was several unopened packages of oversized Tyvek painter's coveralls from Lowes. The tough but disposable suits were designed to pull over your clothes during a messy job and then dispose of afterward. Conveniently, they were white.

While Hugh had managed to snag several weapons and a decent supply of ammo in the superstore battle, now he grabbed his personal AR. It was his go-to weapon when the world went sideways. It was a generic rifle he'd assembled from components, including a Primary Arms 1x6 power optic. He knew it inside and out. It was nothing fancy but it did the job.

Hugh had a black tactical vest he had also commandeered from the superstore when he went back to get the radio equipment. He recalled seeing some spray paint in one of the outbuildings behind the mobile home so he went out there and retrieved a can of white.

He sprayed some streaks and globs of white on the tac vest to simulate snow camo, then used the same spray paint to add some hasty stripes to a small backpack. The pack already contained food, water, a blowout kit, and a few survival items.

When Hugh had all his gear on, he began layering on the knives. He was from the *silent but deadly* school of weaponry. While he enjoyed shooting he really had a passion for edged weapons. He carried two folders—a Kershaw and a Zero Tolerance. The Zero Tolerance was an expensive knife. It was more expensive than he would pay full price for but he'd won this one in a dare overseas that he didn't like to talk about.

He carried three fixed blade knives. One on the vest, one on his right hip behind his pistol holster, and one fastened crossways on the back of his belt. Finally were his homemade kiridashi, the small razor-sharp daggers that he made himself and carried in a forearm holster. He'd used those before to kill a man on the roof of the superstore and he remembered vividly that they sank into flesh like a knife into soft butter.

He regretted that he had no night vision equipment. There were several units floating around the valley and had he been closer to some of the other residents he would have looked into borrowing one but there was no time. With a decent moon and the highly-reflective snow, he should still be able to see his way around even without supplemental light.

Before leaving, he double checked his gear. Then he triple checked it. When he was certain he had everything he needed and everything was stowed where he could lay a hand on it without a second thought, he let out a deep breath. Any doubts, any concerns, any fear were pushed out and left behind.

He slipped out the door and into the woods.

11

Crossing the river and coming in the valley by the old farm road led Randi, Deputy Ford, and Jim to his house first. They were a somber and devastated group, having buried someone who had become family over the last several months. They'd barely crossed the gate to Jim's property before he noticed his family filing out onto the porch in the distance. They'd been waiting for him.

Apparently the sight of his group without Buddy was jarring, his absence a glaring reminder of what had transpired in town. Ariel pulled loose from her Nana's hand and came flying down the steps to the snow in her house slippers. She tore across the yard toward Jim. Her composure gone, she was now crying full-steam. Jim dismounted his horse and handed the reins to Randi.

He bent and caught his daughter, picking her up as she clung tightly to him. He was as aware as he'd ever been that there would not be too many years left of this. She was getting bigger and he was getting older. The relief she experienced in his embrace was not a permanent thing. There would come a time when it didn't have the same effect. That awareness crushed Jim, his heart already damaged from the events of the day, and soon he was crying along with her. He cried for Buddy, he cried for Ariel, and he cried for himself.

It was as if Ariel had pulled the plug on what little self-control still remained among the group. Nana, Pops, and Ellen sobbed on the porch. Deputy Ford was crying too. Only Randi, steadfast in her tempered determination to shed no more tears, would not her allow herself the relief of crying. In the absence of vengeance, it seemed that crying was the only solace for such pain and Randi would not grant herself that freedom. Each had to find her own way through this world and she had found hers. She understood the only way she could make it, the only way she could do this, was to bottle the rage and pain and use it to her advantage.

Jim saw movement from the corner of his eye. He spotted two man-sized figures walking down the driveway from the front gate. He immediately recognized the snow gear and the gait, knowing it was his son, with Charlie at his side. He gently set his daughter back on the ground, kissed her head, and held her hand.

He looked up at Randi. "Let's all go inside and warm up by the fire. We'll have a cup of coffee and then we can go tell Lloyd."

The group headed into the house and those who had been in the weather peeled off their bulky outer layers and shed their boots. Everyone found a seat wherever they could find one while Ellen made coffee. Jim had been generous with his coffee, continuing to share it, continuing to make it every day like he had before the world fell apart, but the supply was getting low. He had two 5-gallon buckets of green unroasted beans he had purchased and stored. That was what they were down to now, except for a few jars of instant and some stray packets of hotel coffee. Each day they roasted beans on the stove and ground them in an old-fashioned hand-cranked grinder. When the coffee was gone, Jim would still have a decent stash of tea left, having bought pounds of black leaf in bulk. Even though the caffeine would be welcome, it was just not coffee. Life would not be the same.

Buddy's loss hung over the room like an oppressive cloud but no one dared broach the subject until Ariel asked the question everyone who had not been there wanted to know.

"What happened to Mr. Buddy?"

The innocence of her voice, the sincerity, broke Jim's heart. He didn't want to go into too much detail with his daughter but at the same time felt it was important she understood the danger of the world so she would listen to his warnings and not wander off. One of his greatest fears was that someone might abduct her and try to use her to extort supplies from the family. While they had shielded her from the danger as best they could in order to try to preserve some remnant of her childhood, it was a delicate balance. He didn't want her to fear the world but she had to respect its dangers.

"Somebody who didn't know Mr. Buddy, somebody who didn't know how special he was to us, killed him," Jim said with a sigh.

Ariel's brow furrowed, her face still blotchy and tear-streaked. "Where is he now? You didn't leave him there did you? In the snow?" It was the practical question of a child, an indication of her concern for her friend.

Jim shook his head and opened his arms to his daughter. She came and sat in his lap. "No, sweetie. We didn't leave him. We had to bury him and we did it right there beside his daughter, just where he wanted to be. That's what took us so long. Don't you think that's where he'd want to be?"

Ariel nodded.

"So that's already taken care of?" Pops asked. "I wasn't sure."

Jim nodded. "There was no doubt it was where he wanted to be. We were able to find some digging tools there at the cemetery and the ground wasn't really frozen under the snow. It took a while but we managed to get it done."

"But why?" Ellen asked. "Why was he killed?"

Jim cut his eyes to Ariel. "That story is better left for later."

With the plug pulled on that line of inquiry, silence fell over the room.

"Well, did you find anything out about Mrs. Fairlane?" Nana asked.

With everything that had happened, Jim had nearly forgotten that his original intention of going into town was to try to find more out about his friend's widow. It seemed hard to believe that that he'd even spoken to her today. It felt like weeks ago.

"She's actually doing okay. She was warm and well fed. She reminded us that she was a country woman and grew up this way. She has a little trouble getting around but is more than capable."

"She's a firecracker," Randi added.

"She speaks her mind," Nana said. "She can have a vicious tongue."

"She tell you it was about time you came to check on her?" Pops asked with a grin.

Randi nodded and smiled back at Pops.

"Pretty much," Jim acknowledged. "She basically said I was forgiven, because my entire generation is uncouth and uncivilized."

"Nailed you, didn't she?" Ellen said.

Jim ignored the remark.

"She's right there in town," Nana said. "So many people around. Did she have any trouble?"

"Apparently, but I think she dealt with it. Some of the snowdrifts in her yard were not entirely made of snow. They were more like snowmen, if you know what I mean."

When Nana deciphered that her eyes got wide. "Oh my!"

"I offered to try and help her out but she got a bit huffy about it. She said she didn't want to be taken in as someone's charity case. What she would prefer, and what she thought everyone else in her demographic would probably prefer, was someplace they could live together and help each other out. It makes sense that dividing the responsibilities would help them out, same as it has for us. People could act on their strengths and get assistance where they needed support."

"So what they need is a place where they could live communally that would be suited for this type of situation?" Pops said, looking off in thought. He knew the county well and this was his type of problem.

"Exactly," Jim agreed. "But I told her that the power might be coming back on soon anyway. We'll need to wait and see what happens. She may be fine once things are back to normal."

Pops shook his head. "Not sure if they'll ever be normal again."

There was a radio chirp and a distorted voice began coming from several of the family band radios, all of which were monitoring the same frequency.

"What the hell?" Jim said, picking Ellen's radio up from kitchen table and adjusting the volume. When there was no repeat of the message, Jim keyed the mic. "Can you repeat that last transmission?"

"*You guys back?*" It was Lloyd's voice blaring from the tiny speaker.

Jim hesitated, looking for words. "I was going to head up your way in a few minutes. We need to talk."

"*Save the bullshit. I heard what you said earlier. About Buddy.*"

Jim let out a slow breath and looked at the floor. "I was going to come up there and tell you personally."

"*No use,*" Lloyd said. "*Nothing to say. He's fucking dead. One more dead person. Everybody is either killing or getting killed or some shit...*"

Jim started to retreat to the back of the house then realized this wasn't like a telephone. There were at least a half-dozen more radios in the room all turned to the same frequency and listening in on this conversation. Regardless of where he went, it was not going to be any more private.

"I'll be up that way in a few," Jim said.

"*No need,*" Lloyd slurred.

"I'll be up anyway," Jim said.

Lloyd didn't respond.

"I'm going up there," Jim said to the group.

Deputy Ford got to his feet. "I'm heading home. I need to check in on the sheriff and do a few things around the house."

Randi was already pulling on her cold weather gear. "I'm going with you, Jim."

"I don't know what kind of shape Lloyd is in," Jim cautioned. "This could be ugly."

Randi gave him a look that indicated this was not open for discussion.

Jim shrugged. "Fine." He turned to his family. "I'll be back at some point this evening. Don't hold dinner for me. Call on the radio if you need anything."

Ellen nodded. "I hope he's okay."

"He'll be fine," Jim said. "He's...resilient."

"Everybody has their breaking point," Pops said.

"Pete, can you and Charlie deal with the horses?" Jim asked.

"We're on it," Charlie replied.

"Thanks," Jim replied. He pulled on his gear and followed his companions into the deep slush of the yard. It was already getting dark and Jim checked his pocket for his headlamp, finding it just where he expected. This could be a long evening.

THE EVENING at Buddy's house went pretty much as Jim expected. Lloyd was already shit-faced drunk when they got there. He was crying both because of the loss of his friend and the fact that, in the rage of his grief, he'd broken an entire jar of moonshine his own late grandfather had crafted personally. Randi sat Lloyd down in a chair and cleaned up the mess.

"You don't have to do that," Lloyd said.

"Fuck you," Randi said. "I know I don't but if I don't get it out of the way, you'll step in it tonight when you're stumbling outside to puke."

"Puking is a waste of good liquor," Lloyd mumbled.

"Then you better slow down," Randi warned.

"I don't need any woman telling me—"

That was as far as Lloyd got before the broom hit him upside the head. It was not a playful blow.

"Consider yourself warned," Randi said. "Finish that sentence and I'll kick your ass like no one's ever kicked it. Are we clear?"

Lloyd snapped out of his shock and saluted Randi, eyes wide. She belted him with the broom again.

"Yes, ma'am!" Lloyd cried, cringing and covering his head.

"That's better," Randi said.

They talked late into the night, toasting Buddy. Jim and Randi shared the details of his death and Lloyd could only shake his head in disgust at what the world had become. He absently fumbled for his banjo, seeking solace, seeking distance from this place and this time. He played a *crooked tune*, one that Buddy had remarked on often. Crooked tunes were traditional songs that didn't follow conventional musical structure. They often had extra notes or dropped notes that threw off the rhythm. They were difficult to learn, challenging the musician's ability to let go of the way he expected things to be.

That was where Lloyd and perhaps all the folks in the valley were now. Things were not what they were expected to be. They were a conventional people in a crooked world with life throwing odd notes at one moment and stripping notes from them the next.

Jim stood and motioned at Randi. She joined him by the door. He pulled on his boots. "I'm leaving. You need me to walk you back to your house?"

Randi shook her head. "I radioed my kids. They're fine. I think I'm going to stay here and make sure Lloyd is okay."

Jim straightened up from his boots and raised a questioning eyebrow at Randi. She frowned at him and smacked him on the arm. "I'm a grown-ass grandmother. I can do what I want."

Jim raised his palms and backed off. "I wasn't saying a thing. Don't get your broom."

Randi picked Jim's coat up and shoved him out the door. "See you tomorrow. Be careful."

Jim stood on the porch for a moment, letting the cold air sober him before slipping on his gear. He checked that his sidearm was accessible and slung his M-4 around his neck. He fished his head-lamp out of his pocket and fought to get it on his head. He stared at the pale snow-covered fields. He probably wouldn't need the light at all. The moon was high above the ridge and bold enough to create shadows. There was not a single sound in the world. Smoke floated through the valley from the remaining families–the Weathermans, the Birds, the Wimmers, and a few others.

Jim thought again of the man they'd lost today. He had been a moral compass for Jim. He was the one with the perspective and the wisdom that Jim could trust to tell him when he was on course or if he was being too "Jim," which was sometimes synonymous with being too final and too violent in his decision-making. On his way home from Richmond, it had been his grandfather's voice in his ear that helped get him home. He hoped that Buddy could find some similar way to offer guidance to him from beyond the grave. He surely needed it.

Only Ellen and his children remained to ground him. In his desire to protect them, he knew no boundaries. He would spill the blood of any man–of any thousand men–to protect them. If he killed everyone outside of this valley, he could still find a way to close his eyes at night. The state of the world made things so much simpler in some ways. The day job no longer mattered, school no longer mattered, politics no longer mattered. All that mattered was the preservation of his family and their little sphere of friends at any and all costs.

Jim started walking, following the driveway to the road, and then the beaten path down the road to his own house. He thought of Ellen, of her frequent hints that she felt like he'd always wanted this collapse to happen. He adamantly denied it. In fact, he became down-right defensive when she made those accusations, gentle as they were.

That raised the question of what he would become if the power came back on. He'd wondered for years who he would become if society collapsed. When it did, he quickly found out. He had adjusted. He had risen to the occasion.

But what about going backward? Could he even go back to what he had been? Criminals were used to taking what they wanted and Jim was using to shooting back when they did. He wasn't sure he could cram what he was now back into what he had been. The genie couldn't be put back in the bottle. How the hell did the government think they were going to do this?

Here in the night, in the cold and dispassionate winter, maybe he was ready to admit something to himself for the first time. Maybe he had longed for this simplicity. Maybe he had longed for the ability to solve problems in a simpler way. Perhaps he was okay with what happened with the world. Slogging through the snow, he was aware that he had never felt so alive in his entire life.

12

Jim's internal alarm went off early, and he groaned with self-inflicted misery. His head hurt and he felt about two quarts low on essential fluids. He couldn't remember the last time he'd been out late, come home drunk, and awakened to a fierce hangover. His post-apocalyptic world was full of problems, though this wasn't typically one of them.

It was a tribute to a friend, he reminded himself.

As flimsy an excuse as he felt that was, there was a degree of truth in it. A good drunk was what he'd needed to close out the kind of day he'd had yesterday. That little bit of self-assurance, of justification, made him feel better, but only by a small degree.

He could have laid back down and tried to sleep it off but he had a masochistic streak. He'd done this to himself so he could damn well suffer the consequences. Jim staggered to the kitchen and filled a glass with water from the gravity-fed line at the sink. It didn't have the pressure of the old well system, but it flowed without regard for the presence of electricity and it beat the hell out of hauling water in buckets. He drank two cold glasses of spring water and then filled a kettle for coffee. Normally he would be fine with heating the water on the stove but he needed some caffeine in his body ASAP to fight this hangover. He got his tiny canister stove from the cabinet and took it to the back screen porch. He opened the wire valve, struck a lighter to it, and it took off like a jet engine. In a matter of minutes, it had the aluminum pot of water churning at a boil.

Jim poured the boiling water over the grounds in his H2JO contraption and let it steep. While it was doing its magic, he plodded to the living room and stoked up the fire. He'd heated his home with wood for so long that this was a matter of routine and he could do it with his eyes closed. He shook the night's ashes down into the ash pan, opened the draft, and added kindling to the pile of coals that remained from the previous fire. In less than a minute, he had a roaring blaze and returned to his coffee-making.

He twirled the Nalgene bottle and watched the mixture darken. When it was just the right color, he opened the bottle, removed the filter insert, and poured the dark coffee into a mug. He was inches away from settling into an overstuffed leather chair by the fire when there was a knock at the door.

He paused at first, uncertain if it might have been one of the several other occupants of the house moving around or closing a bathroom door. Either way, Jim grabbed the nearest weapon, which happened to be a Ruger Mini-14 with a red dot sight. The knock came again and there was no doubt it came from the front door. Jim did not want to use the peephole on the door, aware that someone might be ready to shoot through it the minute he stuck his eye to it. He moved to the front window and peered around the edge of the closed curtains. He found Hugh fully kitted out and sipping coffee from a plastic convenience store mug.

Jim frowned and went to the door. He opened the various latches and swung it open. Hugh smiled and raised a finger in greeting.

"Top of the morning to you," Hugh said. "Mind if I come in?"

Jim stepped out of the way. "Come on in."

Hugh took a whiff as he passed. "You smell like you've been brewing liquor."

Jim shook his head. "No. The liquor brewed me this time."

Hugh removed his boots and began shedding gear by the door.

"That's a lot of gear," Jim remarked. "You going on some kind of operation?"

Hugh shook his head. "No, but I can't just run back to the house if I need something. It's like I live in some remote mountaintop village."

Jim went to his fireside chair and Hugh joined him, slouching on the couch.

"Those boys tell you about going hunting yesterday?" Hugh asked.

Jim shook his head. "Never came up. They got home about the time everybody was getting upset about Buddy."

"That's understandable. So I guess they didn't say anything about their trip?"

Jim shook his head again. The motion made him slightly nauseous and he held his head.

"They spotted a camp a few ridges away. Matching orange tents and a campfire. I went up there last night to do a little snooping but they were so far away I decided it wasn't worth the trip at this point. If they get closer, you can be sure I'll pay them a visit. I'll probably go up there tonight to see what they're up to."

Jim glared at Hugh with heavy eyelids and a sour expression. "You came all this way to tell me that?"

"You're not concerned about strangers approaching from the most inaccessible route into the valley?"

"I am," Jim shrugged. "I guess I'm not at optimal processing power at the moment. Is that the whole story?"

"No, but it's relevant. Otherwise you'd probably wonder why the hell I was up on top of the mountain at night."

"I have long since given up questioning what you do, Hugh."

"That's good to know. We may return to that point again in the future. But to the topic at hand, do you have a map?"

"Of where?"

"Here."

"Here as in this valley or this region?"

"Region," Hugh replied. "Southwest Virginia."

Jim got up and went to the bookcase. He removed a folded map stuck into a row of books dedicated to outdoor activities in Virginia–kayaking, fishing, backpacking, and biking. He took a seat on the couch by Hugh and unfolded the map on an ottoman.

"Show me where we are," Hugh said.

Jim pointed to a road, then to his own driveway. "We're here."

"So I'm here," Hugh said, tracing a finger up the slope of the mountain, along a farm road. "And here's where the high voltage line crosses the mountain near my trailer."

Jim nodded. "That's it."

"So I was standing there last night like some kind of fucking hippie, having a moment of reverie and just taking in how cool the world looked up there. Turns out I saw something way cooler than expected."

"A UFO?" Jim asked.

Hugh shook his head.

"What?"

"When I faced north, I saw a glowing area of light at my ten o'clock. It was far off, but it was clearly an enormous area of illumination. Not quite as big as a town, but pretty good-sized."

Jim oriented the map until north was at the top and ran a finger to the ten o'clock position. "That could be the Carbo power plant."

"There was a cloud rising straight above it. I saw light reflecting off the cloud. Place was lit up like a fucking sports stadium."

"I'm not sure how it could have gotten this far along without us hearing something," Jim said. "There would be miners and truck drivers involved, wouldn't there?"

"How many people have you talked to outside this valley over the past couple of months?" Hugh asked.

Jim considered. "Just Mrs. Fairlane, I guess."

"She a miner?"

"Not that I recollect," Jim replied.

"So this *could* have been going on under our noses, really, and us still not see a thing," Hugh concluded.

"I guess so," Jim shrugged. "We might need to lay eyes on it."

"What possible benefit could there be to us verifying this plant is either operating or ramping up to operate? I'm not sure any action on our part will affect the speed at which power is restored to this valley."

"Maybe not but, for one, I'd like to make sure that some of that power produced there goes to our local communities and isn't all funneled northeast to aid in the recovery of Washington, D.C. and its suburbs."

"I guess that's a possibility," Hugh admitted.

"So do you feel like a little recon mission?" Jim asked. "Nothing crazy. Just verifying what you saw last night."

Hugh regarded Jim. "I understand you may not want anything crazy to happen but you do understand that you have no control over that, right? Crazy shit happens despite everyone's best intentions. It happens despite how much care you take. It happens despite your level of preparation."

"Trust me, I completely understand that," Jim said. There was an honest gravity to his expression that made it clear to Hugh that Jim had seen a lot, had gone through a lot, since shit got real.

Hugh shrugged. "I guess we could just walk up to the gate and ask them when they intended to steer some of that power toward town, couldn't we?"

"I guess we could."

"Just who do you want on this mission?" Hugh asked.

"How about just you and me. Let me radio Randi and make sure she doesn't have any problem with us taking a couple of her horses. After the way our last trip went, she's probably okay with staying home."

"Have at it," Hugh said.

Jim picked up his radio and keyed the mic. "Randi, this is Jim. Jim calling Randi."

Jim checked his watch and saw that it was around 8 AM. Randi was probably up by now, probably having a cigarette from some secret stash of hers.

"This is Randi. Go ahead, Jim."

"Hey, sorry to bother you but Hugh and I need to take a little trip this morning. We need to check out something. Do you mind if we borrow two of your horses?"

"I don't mind. But I don't want to go. That last trip to town did me for a long time. I'll just stay here."

"Thanks, Randi."

"You got it. Be careful."

"Hey, Randi!" Jim said quickly. "One more thing."

"What is it?"

"Is that a banjo I hear in the background? Are you at Lloyd's again?"

"Fuck you and the horse I lent you to ride in on," Randi said.

Jim put his radio down and was preparing to get up when it chirped again. *"Jim, this is Ford."*

Jim picked it up and replied. "Go ahead, Ford."

"When you guys leave the valley, swing by my place a second."

"Roger that. It may be about thirty minutes before we get squared away here."

"No problem. See you then."

Jim left Hugh by the fire and went to his bedroom to retrieve some gear for the trip. His intention was to be back in one long day but things didn't always work out as planned so he would gear up for two. Jim woke his wife and explained to her what was going on. This wasn't the kind of world anymore where you took leaving home lightly. Every little trip could be the last trip. Every good-bye could be the last time you spoke to that person. With that fresh in his head, he kissed each of his children goodbye.

When Jim returned to the living room, he was dragging an armload of loose gear. He put on his base layers, his snow pants, his vest, and his fleece. He stepped into his boots, then put on his coat and web gear. He threw on his Go Bag and retrieved a spare pack to strap onto the horses. In the basement, he cracked open a case of MREs and shoved half of them in the pack, along with a half dozen freeze-dried Mountain House meals. Back upstairs, the two men gathered their gear and moved to the porch.

They went around back to the outbuilding where Jim stored his camping gear. The kids called it The Daddy Shack. He grabbed two heavy winter sleeping bags and a 10 x 20 tarp. The tarp could be used to rig an assortment of shelters if it came to that. Jim crammed each sleeping bag into a kayaking dry bag, sealed the top, and then grabbed a rope for attaching them to the horses.

"I'm assuming you need one of these?" Jim asked, holding up the sleeping bag.

Hugh nodded. "Pretty much brought everything else. Hadn't planned on an overnight trip though."

They hauled all of their gear to the barn, saddled Randi's horses, and packed their animals. Despite Jim being a total amateur at both saddling and packing horses, they were out of there in a few minutes. In another ten, they were in front of Ford's mobile home. Ford came to the porch and waved them inside.

"We ain't got time to bullshit around," Jim mumbled to Hugh. "Let's try to make this short."

His mind was already on the journey ahead. He assumed Ford was wanting them to make some side trip for him or perhaps even to tag along. If he was interested in going, he was shit out of luck. Jim and Hugh had not brought another horse with them and they were not interested in waiting while Ford fetched another.

The two men stomped off their boots on the porch and went inside Ford's sparse trailer. Ford greeted the men and without much preamble led them to what must have been the spare bedroom for whoever had once owned this place. There they found a bare mattress covered with the gear that Ford had brought from the weapons locker at the emergency operations center.

"Oh shit!" Hugh's mouth involuntarily curled into a smile.

"I'm not sure where you guys are headed, or what you're headed into, but after what happened on our last trip I wondered if you might want to borrow some of the good stuff. Notice I specifically said *borrow*."

Jim gestured at the bed. "This is what was in all those duffle bags we hauled back?"

"Yep. I assumed all this gear was long gone. Most of the good stuff was at the Sheriff's Department office and this was only a secondary locker. They kept it there in case anything crazy happened. I guess nobody bothered checking it."

As Jim continued to stare wide-eyed, Hugh was efficiently checking each weapon.

"There's body armor too," Ford told them. "Now you can stick a pair of real plates in that plate carrier."

Jim picked up a plate from the small stack on the bed and examined it.

"It's a level IV composite. The pair adds about fifteen pounds to your loadout so it sucks if you're walking long distances. Since you guys are riding, it sucks more for the horse. But that particular plate is rated to stop a 30.06 with armor piercing rounds."

"Maybe that'll save our asses if we come under sniper fire," Hugh said. "I feel pretty exposed sitting on the back of a horse."

"Unless he's a skilled sniper with a good rifle," Ford added. "Then he might take the head shot."

"That's comforting," Jim said.

"What about any of these weapons?" Hugh asked.

"Some of this stuff was confiscations and I haven't had a chance to check it out thoroughly. What are you guys carrying already?"

"M4s and pistols," Jim said.

"Then why don't one of you take the select-fire M4? It's burst, not full auto. The other can take the MP5. It's got a four-position safety so make sure you familiarize yourself with it before you pull the trigger. I've got loaded mags for each of those but you're sticking to the same calibers you're already carrying for consistency."

"Good plan," Hugh agreed. He wasted no time grabbing up those weapons and mags.

"I appreciate this," Jim said. "We owe you big time."

"Don't get all mushy," Ford said. "Just wear the fucking plates and come back alive. I don't want to have to take care of your family because you did dumb shit."

Jim smiled. "I think we're going to get along after all."

Ford helped them carry the stuff out to the living room. He

assisted each man in slipping the composite armor into the carriers each was already wearing. With that done, Hugh and Jim headed back to their horses, stowed the new gear, and mounted up.

It felt like the sun had already pushed the morning above freezing. Hugh pulled a blue bandana from a pocket and tied it around his head, then inserted a dip of tobacco into his lip.

"You ready?" Jim asked.

"Just waiting on you," Hugh replied.

ON THE TRAIL, Jim powered up his Garmin backpacking GPS. He hadn't used the thing in months and was pleased to find that the GPS satellite network was still available. Jim had a paper map, but the various maps and overlays in his GPS contained a lot more information than the paper map did. This could be important since his plan was not to follow the roads but to head cross-country. While this might add to the distance they would travel, hopefully it would reduce the possibility of unplanned encounters with other folks, particularly hostile encounters.

The town sat directly between the two men and the power plant they wanted to see. There was no way for Jim to head toward the power plant without crossing through town unless he was interested in making a broad swing around it, which could add hours to the trip. After their last experience in town, after the loss of Buddy, Jim wanted to minimize those periods of exposure. They would cross directly through town at one of its narrowest points.

Jim had uploaded a variety of local map data into his GPS over the years. The GPS could read various map sets as long as they met certain data parameters. One particular topographical map set not only showed secondary roads but also certain farm and logging roads. It even contained abandoned roads for which the public right of way was still in place. It was one of those old abandoned roads Jim hoped to take out of town.

They approached the small town by means of a farm road and

crossed Main Street without incident. They immediately steered their horses through the old town park and the untouched snow indicated that no one had been there since the storm. They plodded past rusting swing sets, jungle gyms, and picnic shelters.

Jim eyeballed the WWII 155mm Howitzer that had been on display at the park since his childhood. He remembered the barrel being packed tightly with the shattered glass of beer bottles. "If I could improvise some shells for that thing, it might be a nice addition to the valley."

Hugh regarded the cannon skeptically. "You could probably build something equally effective for less trouble."

At the far end of the park was a yellow pipe gate that was padlocked shut. The gate blocked access to an old right of way that had been used since the town was established. As happens with modernization, some of those old pioneer-era paths become official roads and some never do. With the advent of car traffic, people continued to use the rough, unmaintained road as a shortcut from the northern corner of the county. When county officials failed to develop and maintain the road the landowners realized they would never profit from the inconvenience of having people cross their property. They lobbied the county and succeeded in having the road closed down, much to the consternation of those that relied on the road as their shortest route to the feed store.

Jim pulled a pair of folding bolt cutters from his pack and cut the lock open. Once they were through, he closed the gate behind him and arranged the chain to hide his handiwork. Beyond the gate, they had a peaceful hour on a quiet farm road. They saw a lot of birds, including a hawk. They saw a red fox scurrying in the distance and rabbits padding across the melting snow. Although there was plenty of life along the road, there was no sign of people, and that was okay with both of them.

The farm road eventually brought them to a paved secondary road. There were several sets of tracks on this road including ATV, people, and horses. Some folks back in there were still getting around and getting by. This was the area of the county that Hugh had grown up in and he knew it well. Since this part of the county was only sparsely populated, Hugh encouraged Jim to stay on the paved road, which would save them a lot of time and take them more directly to their next route, a dirt road leading to an even more remote section of the county.

Jim was pleased to see signs of life along this road. There were farm dogs still guarding their homes, which made him hope there was life inside them. Some homes had smoke coming from chimneys while others appeared to be burning old seasoned wood that produced very little smoke. Jim couldn't see smoke coming out of those houses but he could smell it. Country people were resilient. They were used to making their own way in the world.

In the remote community of Pickshin, they passed beneath a railroad trestle. The track was supported by foot-square beams and x-bracing fastened with long bolts. Creosote was slathered on the structure to act as a preservative. A change in the wind brought the scent of death to their nostrils. Neither man commented on it, both recognizing the scent, and hoping it was an animal. Still, they gripped their weapons a little tighter and scanned their surroundings warily, pleased that the snow provided something of a muffling effect to the hooves of their mounts.

On the backside of the trestle, Hugh was the first to see the extended arm. His heart immediately surged, assuming it was a threat, but before he could warn Jim he determined there was no threat there. The arm was not held in a menacing gesture but with fingers curled in the supplication of death. Once they'd fully crossed beneath the trestle, they turned their horses. There were ropes wrapped around wooden cross-members, holding aloft the devastated body of a young man who'd wronged the residents of this community.

The words *thief* and *looter* were spray-painted on the beam over his head. The body was bloated and blackened. Crows had removed the eyes with the jagged chiseling of their beaks. One hand had been cut off, as well as both feet. The man was stripped of his clothing and the discoloration of his body made it clear that he had taken a severe beating for his poor judgment.

Neither Hugh nor Jim sympathized with the man. He got what he deserved. If there was anything to be regretted it was that the man had been so dumb as to steal from honest people who worked hard for what they had. Yet perhaps he served more of a purpose in his death than he had in his life, acting as both a warning and a cautionary tale to anyone else entering into Pickshin with bad intentions.

It was two more hours before they reached the town of Cleveland, sitting on the muddy banks of the Clinch River. What Jim had hoped would be a four hour trip had taken nearly six, slowed by slick conditions and their own caution. The town sprouted from the sandy soils at a time when being located on the railroad meant something. When the emergence of the automobile meant that men were no longer bound to those two steel tracks, the town withered like the banded testicles of a goat. Yet the railroad did not die completely. Coal still traveled on those tracks and it was partly for that reason that the power plant was built there.

Jim had driven by the old Carbo power plant several times. He'd even passed it in a canoe twice, so he knew how to access it. Despite traveling through a small town, despite being on a main road, Jim was excited they were so close to their objective. His exuberance overpowered his caution until they hit the railyard at Carbo. One moment they were riding along in the snow, uncertain as to whether there was any human occupation around them at all. Then they turned the corner and found evidence of the massive snow clearing operation. Jim was so taken aback that he just sat there on his horse staring at it. It took him a moment to realize Hugh was urgently calling his name as he steered his own horse off the road and up into a stand in the trees. Suddenly it occurred to Jim that they were standing there in plain sight in what was obviously an occupied, populated, active zone of operation.

Once Jim reached the trees, he found Hugh on foot, scanning the area with a pair of binoculars.

"Looks like they've been using those 900 Cats for snow cleanup," Jim said, climbing off his own horse and tying it off to a cedar tree.

"It's not the yellow machines the concern me as much as those other ones."

Jim followed where Hugh was pointing out a row of neatly parked front end loaders in desert tan and woodland camo. Some were equipped with scraper blades for clearing snow while others had standard loader buckets. "It looks like somebody's opened this place up."

"That may be one of the reasons they chose this power plant over some others. It has tracks going right to it. That's probably an easier way to get fuel than trucking in the coal or trying to make sure the natural gas pipeline is intact. I'm just guessing."

They scanned the railyard, examining graffiti-covered cars. There was a lot of evidence of activity but neither spotted any people moving around.

Hugh gestured to the road with a nod. "My guess is that if we proceed along this road we're probably going to hit some kind of manned guard post.

"The question then is whether or not we want to encounter the guard post."

"That's up to you, my friend," Hugh said. "This is your operation."

Jim twisted up his mouth in thought. "I don't want to take a chance on getting my horse and weapons confiscated."

"Then how about we find some place safe to tie these horses up? You can stay on the road and I'll shadow you in the woods. We find this guard post, you can ask them whatever the hell you want to ask them. If they don't kill you, we'll load up and head back home."

Jim shot Hugh an *eat shit* look. "I would like to talk to somebody. Even a little information about the power situation would be nice."

"If you want information, you may have to offer something in trade. These are hard times and information may be all these poor bastards have. They're not going to give it away out of the goodness of their heart."

"What would you suggest?" Jim asked.

Hugh dug around in the chest pocket of his jacket came out with half a crumpled pack of Newports. "Cigarettes usually work. They're a universal currency."

Jim took the smokes and stared at them for a moment. He took a deep breath and let it out. "Well, let's do this."

Jim ditched his web gear, his body armor, and everything else that was the least bit tactical looking. He felt naked without all his gear but he didn't know what he would run into. He had to remind himself that his plan involved talking and not killing.

After they stowed the horses in the dense woods, Jim stepped back onto the road and walked past the entrance to the railyard. When he escaped the slushy melting mess and his feet landed on scraped clean pavement, he suddenly felt like a new man. Walking took significantly less effort. He felt like he could walk twenty miles again instead of just three or four.

He tried to give up any appearance of caution and apprehension. He wanted to look like any other hillbilly dumbass out walking in the snow. He'd have to come up with some kind of story. Jim couldn't remember the exact distance between the railyard the power plant but he had not gone far when he spotted what was clearly a road-block. A 6x6 military truck in desert tan was parked diagonally, blocking both lanes of the road. Two large antennas sprouted from the vehicle and a water tank filled the bed.

Jim could make out two men sitting inside the cab of the vehicle. The truck was running, the loud diesel carrying across the distance. When he approached they turned it off. They had spotted him. Jim kept walking.

There was a squawk from a rooftop speaker. "This road is closed. Turn around now."

Jim raised his hands to show he was not armed and kept pushing forward.

When Jim insisted on approaching despite the warning, the passenger exited the vehicle. He came around the front of the vehicle with his rifle raised and centered on Jim. Apparently they were nervous enough that he wanted to be ready for a quick shot.

The driver spoke over the PA system again. "Stop where you are or we will shoot. Put your hands above your head and drop to your knees."

Jim did as he was instructed, glad he'd left his weapons and gear with Hugh. They also had the understanding that Hugh would not intervene unless they tried to arrest Jim or harm him. In that case, Hugh would apply the judicious use of force. Jim was certain Hugh had the approaching soldier dead center of his crosshairs at this very moment.

Jim winced as his knees hit the pavement. He raised his hands above his head. The driver climbed out of the vehicle and provided cover with his own rifle while the passenger approached Jim. The passenger drew his sidearm and let his rifle hang from the sling. The men were in full combat loadout with body armor, bump helmets, and were prepared for trouble.

"On your face!" the passenger demanded.

Jim complied and received a hasty frisking, which wasn't so easy in the bulky winter clothing.

"State your business!"

Jim adopted a submissive demeanor and tried to appear terrified. "I live back in here. Back toward Pickshin. I saw some lights last night and decided I'd walk down here and see what was going on."

"What's going on is none of your damn business, hillbilly. Showing up here could get your dumb ass killed."

"This is a public road," Jim said, sounding humble but offended. "I've walked it all my life."

"It's closed now."

"Ya'll fixing to get the lights on?" Jim asked. "That's all I wanted to know."

There was no response. He looked from man to man and it was clear they were not interested in disclosing anything. Perhaps they were uncertain as to how much they should talk about or maybe they even had orders to say nothing. They seemed not to know how to deal with him, as if no one had just walked up to the roadblock before and asked them what the hell was going on. He decided to take another tack.

"Ya'll smoke?" Jim asked.

The men looked at each other. The one closest to Jim, the passenger, looked to be in his mid-20s. He had dark, beady eyes and bad skin. "We like to when we can, but smokes have been scarce here recently."

"You regular Army or a reservist?"

"Regular Army. From the Eastern Shore of Virginia before I got stationed in this shithole."

"How long have you been stationed here?"

"I think he's told you enough." It was other man. The driver. He looked to be in his early 40s and a little shrewder.

"Mind if I reach into my shirt pocket and pull out a pack of cigarettes?" Jim asked.

"That better be all you pull out," said the older man.

"I ain't up to anything," Jim said. He pulled the pack of Newports from his pocket and extended them toward the younger man. "You can have the whole pack. I quit."

The man took the smokes and shoved them in his pocket.

"Can I stand?" Jim asked.

"Go ahead, but keep your hands where we can see them," said the driver.

The younger man stuck a cigarette in his mouth then realized he did not have a lighter. He pointed at Jim with one eyebrow raised in a question.

"Yeah, I got one. Can I reach for it?"

"Go for it," the younger man said.

Jim reached into his pocket and came out with a lighter. He moved toward the younger man, raised his hand to light it, but the younger man retreated and held his hand out.

"Just fucking toss it. Keep your distance."

Jim did as instructed, tossing the lighter to the younger man. He lit his cigarette then tossed the pack and the lighter to the older man who lit one but made a face at the flavor.

"Fucking menthol," he muttered.

Jim shrugged. "You can give them back if you don't want them."

The men made no indication that they were interested in doing that.

"So you guys don't have any idea about the power?" Jim asked.

Both men shrugged and shifted around. The smoked and looked at each other.

"They don't tell us much," the older man finally said. "We're about as bottom tier as you can get in this operation."

"Is the plant operational?"

"You said yourself that you saw the lights," the younger man said.

"I did," Jim said. "But does that mean that the plant is ready to send out power?"

"They been running tests but I don't understand what they're talking about. Doesn't mean shit to me," the older man said. "Our information comes one day at a time."

"How long have you guys been here? I haven't heard anything about this. Not even rumors."

"Months?" The younger guy said, looking at the older guy for confirmation.

The older guy nodded. "Months."

"I have buddies that work for the power company," Jim said. "I'm surprised I didn't hear rumors about this from their families."

"I doubt your buddies are working here," the younger guy said. "Everybody here is from outside the area. In fact, most of them are from outside the country."

That bit of information shocked Jim. "What do you mean *out of the country*?"

"News of the world doesn't seem to make it back here into the sticks, does it?" the older man asked.

Jim shook his head. "There hasn't been much news about anything, but I'm also not a ham operator. If there is news, I'm not hearing it."

"Power restoration is part of the international recovery effort.

There are NATO troops all over the fucking country. French, Italian, Turkish, you name it."

"I had no idea," Jim said.

"It's a different world now, buddy. A different country. You might as well spread the word this area is off-limits. When the snow melts, there will be patrols on the road. Trespassers will be killed."

"There's a new boss in town," Jim mumbled.

"You got it."

"Is there somebody else I can talk to? Maybe an engineer or somebody who has a better idea what the plan is for rolling out the power to local communities?"

The older guy took a drag on his cigarette and blew smoke out his nose. He looked at the cigarette like it was a vile thing whose very existence pissed him off, yet he did not flick it into the snow. "Look, man, there's nobody here you want to talk to. They don't give a damn about you or your power."

Jim was confused. "If they don't give a damn about us and our power, why are they here? Why are they firing up the plant?"

"Just because the plant is here doesn't mean you have a right to the power," the younger guy said. "By the time we're done here, this plant will be sending most of its power to new locations."

"What do you mean most? Does that mean we could potentially keep some of the power?"

The older guy did flip his cigarette off into the snow this time, though he'd smoked it down to the filter. "You've said enough, Hancock." He looked at Jim. "You need to take a fucking hike. We appreciate the smokes but you need to get your ass out here before somebody with more juice comes along."

"So there's nobody else I can talk to?" Jim persisted.

"We're trying to be nice here," the younger man said. "But if you were to get past us then the next guard post is manned by foreign troops. They don't speak your language and they damn sure don't give a shit what you are saying. They'll kill you and throw your ass in the river."

Although Jim was dejected there was nothing else to say. He

decided to give it one last shot before he left. "If I was to give you guys a radio frequency, could I get you to send me an update if you learned anything new?"

The older man raised his rifle and levelled it at Jim. "This is where you turn around and start walking. I don't want to hear another word."

Jim imagined Hugh at this point, somewhere in the woods with his rifle laid across his pack. He probably had his safety off and was taking up the pressure on his trigger. Jim understood if he didn't turn around now and start walking, Hugh would err on the side of caution and drop the soldier. Jim could see how he would take the shot; he knew the crosshairs were resting on the base of the man's neck. Jim reluctantly turned and started walking away.

"Do yourself a favor and don't ever come back here," the younger man warned. "You got lucky this time."

Jim didn't reply. His head was down and his mind was racing. He had tried to live with the awareness that the power might never come back on, or would at least not come back on until vast numbers of people had already died. Still, the little information he'd picked up before the power went out was that, though this attack it been widespread and devastating, it did not knock out everything. There was still oil and there was still fuel, as well as small refineries.

Certainly for a while, demand would outstrip supply, but slowly things would be repaired. The question all along had been whether those repairs would happen soon enough to avoid a large chunk of the population dying off. Now it didn't look like that was going to happen. That realization brought its own set of questions, its own concerns.

And there was no one to ask.

13

This was the most downcast Jim had been since the collapse took place. He'd never faced a situation for which he felt so unprepared. Certainly there were times he'd been scared or worried but he always felt like he had a chance. What chance was there when you were facing an army? The answer seemed clear. There would be no power for the folks in this area. As wrong as it was, the power would be stolen and routed elsewhere to aid another region's recovery.

"What now?" Hugh asked.

"There's a park near here, runs along the Clinch River. They call it Sugar Hill because there was a French settlement there that made maple syrup prior to the Revolutionary War."

"How far?"

"Couple of miles," Jim said. "Maybe thirty minutes' ride in this mess to find a good spot."

It was nearly dark when they crept into the park on the fringes of St. Paul, Virginia. The sun had already dropped beneath the highest ridge and they had only the remaining ambient light to see by. It would not last long and they preferred to find a place to huddle up before dark so they didn't have a ride around with headlamps advertising their position. They hit the river and steered their horses to a narrow riverside trail used by joggers, fishermen, and hikers.

There were tracks here and there, both man and beast. Jim might have suspected that some of the tracks belonged to people hoping to catch their next meal from the river but each bank was lined with a jagged crust of ice that extended nearly a dozen feet from the edge. Only the center of the river ran free, the water a deep green and surging with its own brand of violence.

They rode along the trail, heading deeper into the park where the mountains became steeper and were more likely to offer shelter. Jim stopped abruptly. "Jesus Christ."

Hugh dropped a hand to the grip of his rifle. "What is it?"

Jim pointed to the riverbank, to the frozen crust of ice along the shore. On the side of the river closest to them, a man's body lay on the bank, his head disappearing into the ice. Were his body not limp and clearly lifeless, he would look like a man sticking his head through a hole in the ice to watch for fish.

"Shit," Hugh said. "Haven't seen that in a long time."

"You've seen that before?"

"Unfortunately, yes. It happened on our farm when I was growing up. A cow was drinking from the pond and slipped on a rock. He hit his head and died. By the time we found him, the temperature had dropped and the pond froze with his head trapped in the ice. We hooked the tractor to his legs and pulled him out so he wouldn't contaminate the pond, but when we tugged on him, his head came off and stayed there in the ice for several weeks before it thawed out. Being kids, we went back to see it pretty often."

"I reckon we won't try to pull this guy out then. I got enough bad shit floating around in my head without having that picture in there too."

"Looks like he was trapping beavers or muskrats."

"Let's get out of here," Jim said. "We'll leave him to scare the next son-of-a-bitch."

The men rode on for another fifteen minutes before reaching a fairly remote section of the park where they were not visible from any road or trail. A cliff rose alongside their route, its base strewn with rocks the size of washing machines.

"Reckon we should probably stay here," Jim said. "It's dark and slick and I don't want to end up like old Ice Head."

Hugh nodded, the faintest curl of a grin visible on his shadowed face. "Old Ice Head."

It wasn't quite a cave, but a place where the base of the cliff was back-cut into the mountain, providing a slight overhang that would deflect some of the weather. Appalachian folks called them *rock houses* because they'd sheltered hunters and travelers for eons. Many of the rock faces were scorched by fires that well could have warmed mammoth hunters.

Depending on how the rock house was formed, a halfway decent shelter could be constructed with the addition of a tarp and a warm fire. By building the fire against the back wall, heat would reflect off and provide significant warmth. Hugh and Jim worked together, using the tarp, branches, and a hank of paracord to construct a shelter. They piled a few rocks on the base of the tarp to seal it down to the ground.

Hugh gathered wood for the night while Jim filled a pot with river water. They got a cooking fire going using old birds' nests that they pulled from crevices in the cliff. Within a half hour, each man had a cup of hot black tea in his hand and a pouch of chicken tetrazzini rehydrating at his side. Sleeping conditions would be less than ideal, which was usually the case in primitive winter camping. Even with a foam pad, the cold of the ground would seep into their bodies and make it hard to find comfort. Both men were exhausted, and that would help them find sleep. A day on horseback, fighting the cold and maintaining constant vigilance, was taxing.

As his full belly and the warmth of his sleeping bag caught up with him, Jim mumbled at his friend, "Do you want first or second watch?"

"You go ahead," Hugh said. "I'll wake you up in four hours."

Jim was asleep before he could even agree.

14

The men packed hastily the next morning and were back on the trail at first light. There weren't a lot of options for crossing the river this time of year. With the ice-covered rocks and the vivid image of Old Ice Head, they opted to cross using a bridge. In this rural area, bridges could be twenty or more miles apart. Jim knew from living in the area that the public road crossed the river only a few miles from where they'd camped for the night. They both agreed it was better to hit the bridge early and get across rather than waste time looking for a more private crossing, which may never present itself.

With the cold and early hour, the ride back to the park entrance and the mile to the river bridge was uneventful. The town that lay below the road was an old coal town struggling to find its place in the modern world. Prior to the collapse, there were emerging tourism projects such as ATV trails systems and breweries. Now Jim had no idea what remained of the townspeople. Smoke rose from some houses, a beacon of hope that folks remained alive somewhere down there.

Nearing the river, the pair saw several houses below the bridge and along the river with smoke coming from chimneys. River folks in

Appalachia were no different than river folk anywhere else in the country. They were the swamp people of the hills, resilient and roach-like in the way they bounced back after every disaster. Let their homes wash away, let them lose all they owned, and they would be back when the waters receded. They would erect a new house or pull in a new mobile home. They would throw out a trotline to catch catfish while they slept. They would shoot snapping turtles the size of manhole covers and chop them into stew. They would fry the prehistoric-looking alligator gar and show it who was boss. No societal collapse would cull those folks.

Jim and Hugh remained on the public road for the next couple of miles to see how it went. They made better time on the smooth surface. The snow was already melting as the temperature began to rise. Pavement was already showing through the heavily-traveled sections of the road. Given the early hour and the winter conditions, they hoped people would remain huddled around their fires and allow them to travel in peace.

It was a mile beyond the bridge that they topped a rise and passed a local funeral home. A forty-yard construction dumpster, a steel vessel the size of a shipping container, sat in the parking lot. The green paint was scorched and peeling, fresh rust coating the bare metal. Pallets and fence posts were piled nearby.

"They're burning the bodies," Hugh remarked.

Jim nodded but offered no comment. What could be said?

Minutes beyond the funeral home was the vast acreage of the county fairground. There were stages, parking lots, and agricultural buildings scattered throughout the property. Jim had spent many hours there over the years, buying cotton candy, watching his kids on rides, and checking out the demolition derby.

He was in that reverie, remembering his children when they were smaller, and didn't notice Hugh rein his horse to a stop.

"Jim," Hugh said.

Jim snapped out of it and stopped. "What?"

"Let's go left, through the gate, and to the rise in that field."

"See something?"

"Maybe," Hugh replied. "We'll know in a second."

Hugh took the lead and veered off the road, cutting through the heavily trampled snow of the median. He angled up a road on the opposite shoulder and leaned over to unhook the chain on a red tube gate. He swung it open, then shut it after Jim rode through.

"What is it?" Jim asked.

"I saw cleared snow up ahead, just like at the railyards yesterday. It was piled on the shoulders of the road near the fairground entrance."

"Shit, I wasn't paying attention. I was thinking about taking my kids to the fair."

"Can't let your mind wander out here," Hugh said. "A bullet will seriously fuck up your day."

Jim knew that. He'd preached that. Yet here he was, doing what he'd warned so many people against. He needed to stay switched on. He needed to stay alert.

In fifty yards or so they rode up a rounded knoll that rose from the pasture. A rotting round bale of hay sat beside a round feeder. There were no cattle tracks anywhere. If the owner of the field was cautious, his cattle were safely stashed elsewhere. If he hadn't been so cautious, they'd been feeding the locals since the food supply got tight.

Hugh was the first up the rise and he had binoculars out, glassing in the direction of the fairgrounds. Jim fished around in his pack to find his own pair. Even without them, he could tell the fairground had been the scene of a lot of activity. There were cleared roads, massive tents, and temporary troop quarters.

"There's no railyard," Hugh said. "I wonder how they got all of that here. They didn't use the road or we would have seen the tracks."

"There's no railyard but the tracks go through a field near here. I guarantee some engineers were able to cobble together an improvised railyard in a couple of hours. A dozer, a loader, and a couple of side-dumping rail cars of crushed stone would be all you needed."

"What's the point of this?" Hugh said. "Is this some base providing forward security for the power plants?"

Jim shook his head. "Beats the shit out of me."

"They've clearly been at this a while. There's a lot going on over there. They have facilities for thousands of people."

"And animals, apparently," Jim added.

"You mean the old agricultural buildings?"

"No, those cattle chutes near the entrance are new. They weren't there the last time I brought the kids to the fair."

Hugh studied the area Jim pointed out then lowered his binos. "Those aren't cattle chutes, Jim. Those are for people."

"Bullshit."

"Seriously, we used them when I worked in South America. They expedite the processing of large numbers of refugees. Cuts down on riots."

"Why the fuck would they think they're going to be processing that many people? People in this area aren't going to go for something like that."

"Read the signs, Jim. There are signs at the head of the chutes."

"Either my eyes or my optics are fucked. I can't read that."

The men exchanged binoculars. Jim read the signs and let out a long sigh. There were indeed signs at the mouth of the chutes, directing men toward one area and women toward another, along with instructions to surrender weapons.

"Those draped areas are for searches," Hugh said. "They're not letting people in without searching them."

"This is messed up but how do you fight an army? We don't have enough people for this. We don't have the weaponry for this. I'd like nothing more than to run those fuckers out of town and take our power back for our people."

"That's why they're here—for the energy resources. If we didn't have anything to offer, they'd leave us alone," Hugh said. "Just our luck."

Jim lowered his binoculars and stashed them behind the saddle. "You consider that a camp or a prison?"

Hugh shrugged. "Not sure there's a difference, my friend."

THE PAIR REMAINED off-road until they were well past the fairground area. When they reached a point where the main road was no longer cleared of snow and few footprints had marred it, they rejoined the road. An hour's riding brought them to a paved secondary road heading east.

"Let's go this way," Jim said. "I need to see a man."

The temperature may have been up to the low forties. The snow was melting. It was down to around ten inches deep depending on where you were, however, it remained a slimy, nasty mess that made walking difficult for man or horse. Jim and Hugh rode for four more hours, stopping a couple of times to water the horses and let them rest.

They ate MREs in the saddle. The men were not accustomed to such long days in the saddle and both were aching intensely from a second day of it. They bemoaned the world and bemoaned their circumstances. They bemoaned a government that had reduced them to having to ride horseback. In their moaning and bemoaning they hardened their resolve to not let the government deprive them of power generated locally using local coal.

It was nearly dark when Jim and Hugh passed the youth sports complex for their county, not far outside the town limits. There were two baseball diamonds and several tennis courts, as well as a soccer field. The baseball and soccer fields were packed with an assortment of mismatched cattle. The playing fields were turning into a muddy mess from the wandering beasts. A crude log structure sat in the tennis court providing shelter for perhaps fifteen or sixteen hogs that ambled about in the snow, pawing at the clay court and digging futilely for roots and acorns.

"What the hell?" Jim uttered.

"Looks like somebody in the neighborhood started a mini farm."

"You'd think there'd be a guard since they're this close to town."

"Maybe there," Hugh said, pointing at the elevated announcer's booth with its glass windows looking out over each field.

Jim squinted at the booth. "You can see a sentry in there? I can't see shit."

Hugh shook his head. "Don't see one but that's where I'd put one."

"You're probably right. We should just keep moving along and not show any special interest."

"That's probably best."

A little more than a mile down the road, Jim swung his horse to the right and angled up a steep road. The driveway was steep and the snow contained the tracks of a man and several different animals. Runoff from the melting snow had created a wet track down each lane of the road.

"Is this Kyle's driveway?"

Jim gave a slight nod and Hugh turned his horse, following along. After topping a rise, a log cabin became visible. It was set back deep on the property, resting on the shore of a scenic fishing pond. Smoke curled from the chimney, barely visible in the sea of varying grays.

Jim nudged his horse in the direction of the cabin.

"How do you know this guy?" Hugh asked.

"We went to high school together. He works for the power company. I want to ask him a few questions."

"You feel comfortable riding up on him like this? I mean, he's not going to drop a deer round between my eyes is he?"

"I guess he could, but Kyle's not as paranoid as me. He's regular people. A farmer. You ride up to his door and knock on it, I guarantee he'll come open it to you. He may have a gun in his hand but he will answer the door."

When three Australian cattle dogs came out of nowhere, tearing across the snow at them, both men were startled enough to reflexively bring up a weapon, but Jim caught himself.

"Those are Kyle's dogs. They won't bite us. Just hold onto your horse."

The dogs circled the horses, barking like mad as the pair neared the cabin.

"At least we don't need to announce ourselves," Hugh said. "I'm sure they're on full alert now."

"Kyle! It's Jim Powell! Don't shoot!" he called out when they reached the yard.

Jim slid off his horse and walked through the mass of sniffing dogs. He went through a wooden gate in a picket fence and climbed the steps to the cabin, the dogs still letting out low woofing sounds. He barely had one foot on the steps when a stocky man of around six feet opened the door, filling the frame.

He looked at Jim seriously. "You're brave, man. Your chances of getting shot went way up when you announced your name."

Jim smiled and extended a hand.

Kyle took it and shook. "What the hell brings you out in this mess?"

"I know this will sound crazy but I just wanted to ask you some questions about the power grid," Jim said. "I want to talk somebody in the business who might be able to explain some things to me. This isn't a bad time, is it?"

Kyle shook his head. "No time is any worse than the other right now."

Jim hooked a thumb to the horses. "That's my friend Hugh back there. I met him when I worked at the radio station in town. He's a neighbor now, part of a little community of folks that we've got going in the valley."

Kyle waved to Hugh. "Tie those horses up and you folks come in for a while. It's warm inside and we got plenty of food."

"Don't go to any trouble," Jim said. "We don't need to eat any of your food."

"You going to tell Kim you don't want her food? Try it and see what happens."

Kyle's wife could be a little fiery.

"I'll play that by ear. Why aren't you living in the new house? You did build a new one didn't you?"

"Oh, I was," Kyle said. "Built me a fancy new place a little further back on the mountain. This cabin is where we lived when I first bought this farm. The new house doesn't have any other way to heat other than the heat pump, and I don't have a way to cook inside the house. When it got cold, we decided we'd move back in here. This place has thick log walls and it's easy to heat, and it's got gravity water so the toilets flush."

Hugh reached the porch and Kyle led the two guests into the living room. Jim knew Kyle's wife, Kim. The two had gone to school together. Jim introduced Hugh to Kim, and then to Kyle's two sons who were eight and eleven. Kyle directed Jim and Hugh towards a couch covered with a blanket. The cabin was filled with the aroma of beef stew and the two guests soon had bowls in front of them. They tried to protest but Kim would hear nothing of it. She gave them a look that made it clear there was no arguing.

"We've been blessed," Kim said. "We had a good garden, we have plenty of livestock, and we've always had plenty to eat."

"Do you hear much about what's going on in the world, Kyle?" Jim asked.

Kyle shook his head. "I've got over eighty cows to keep up with, thirty-some chickens, nineteen goats, those dogs, three asshole donkeys, and some other oddball critters I've picked up. I don't have time to talk to anybody now that I'm doing it all by hand. God, how I miss tractors."

"I have an emu," one of Kyle's sons said.

"Do you have any animals?" Hugh asked the other.

He looked at his mother.

Kim smiled at Hugh. "He has a gemsbok but he has trouble pronouncing it."

"A gemsbok?" Jim asked.

Kyle shook his head as if he couldn't believe what he'd been talked in to buying. "It's some African critter with long, straight horns. A couple came up at an auction in Tennessee and the next thing you know I'm hauling them home in the cattle trailer."

Jim laughed. "Back to why we're here, did you know both power plants are up and running?"

Kyle looked at Jim skeptically. "If the damn plants are up and running, where's the power? Why haven't I been called back to work?"

"That's why I'm here," Jim said. "We wondered if anyone made contact with you about the power."

"Like I said, haven't heard a damn thing. All I see all day are critters and these knuckleheads here."

"You're the knucklehead," one his sons said.

"No, you're the knucklehead," Kyle shot back.

Jim finished the last of his stew and sat back on the couch. "That was good, Kim. I haven't had anything but freeze dried beef stew for a long time. It's not quite the same."

"You're welcome, Jim."

"So how do you know both plants are up?" Kyle asked.

"The other night Hugh was up on Clinch Mountain where it runs by our valley. He was keeping an eye on some folks camping in the clearing beneath the power lines. When he started back down the mountain, he could see the glow of lights. When we checked it out on the map it was pretty obvious it was the Carbo plant."

Kyle scoffed. "Glowing lights don't mean the power is back on. It could be a repair crew using diesel-powered tower lights. They could just be working on the plant, trying to get it back up and running."

"That's why we went there in person. We just got back. I don't know to what extent they're generating power because no one would really talk to us, but they've been bringing people in on trains and choppers."

Kyle furrowed his brow. "Hell, maybe they fired me and I just haven't got the email. I guess it could be our people, but you think somebody would have reached out to us local folks. I don't know shit about plant operation but I have a lot of experience getting it from the plant to the people."

"I'm pretty sure it's not your people," Jim said. "These were military folks. NATO troops too."

That struck a nerve with Kyle. "NATO troops? Things in this country so bad that our own army can't take care of it? Our cops and military can't?"

Hugh pointed a finger at Kyle. "That's the problem right there, my friend. My experience tells me that these are problems our people can deal with. So why are foreign troops here? Good question."

"Smells rotten to me," Kyle said.

"Let me ask you a question," Jim said. "Let's say the power was on over at the plant. You think a crew of linemen could get power to the town here?"

Kyle waved a hand dismissively. "I've been through ice storms, hurricanes, and tornadoes all over this country. A good crew of linemen can do about anything. It ain't so easy as just flipping a switch though. Are they transmitting power out?"

Jim shook his head. "Not sure. The guard that ran me off said they intended to send most of the power to Northern Virginia and basically no one cared if we got power or not."

Kyle's face hardened. "That burns my ass."

"Mine too," Hugh agreed.

"If they have power running through their transmission substation to the high voltage lines, it makes our job a little easier. That's power we can steal."

"So we can just tap into those lines?" Jim asked.

"It's not that easy," Kyle said. "That's high voltage. You can't just send that to houses. We need to run it through a distribution substation and step the voltage down. So if we were, theoretically, planning on tapping a high voltage line, we would need to do it close enough to a substation that we wouldn't have to run a lot of line. I've never run it by hand but I'm sure it's going to suck bad and take a lot of manpower."

"Will people at the plant be able to tell we're stealing power?" Jim asked.

Kyle shrugged. "Depends. If they don't have a lot of manpower, they might just assume that power loss between here and Northern Virginia is due to some line damage. The biggest risk of getting caught comes from people running lights at night and being seen. We would need to make sure everyone was careful and used the power as sparingly as possible."

"Then you up for it?" Jim asked. "Or at least to look at what may be involved?"

"We all want power back on. I'd be willing to do my part if it's logistically possible. Without trucks and equipment, I'm not completely sure how much we could do. It would be hard, back-breaking work."

"Like I said, I can get you some labor. It won't be all resting on your shoulders. The main thing I need from you is expertise."

"Let me think about it," Kyle said. "I got some maps here that may tell me where a good jumping off point would be. I need a place where whatever high voltage lines they're using come close to a distribution substation that I can tie us to."

Jim stood. "That's all I ask. Give it some thought. And we appreciate the hospitality. The food was delicious."

"You could just spend the night," Kim said. "It's dark already. It's not safe out there anyway and after dark is worse."

Hugh stood and shook Kyle's hand. "We appreciate the offer, Kyle, but we don't want to impose any more than we already have."

"It wasn't any imposition," Kyle assured them.

"I was away from my family last night. You know how that is. Even with friends around it's hard not to be worried," Jim said.

"I assume you fellas are armed?" Kyle asked.

Hugh grinned. Jim nodded.

"Give me a couple days to think on it and see what I come up with. When I get something figured out I'll come by your place."

"And you all be careful," Kim added. "If you run into anything crazy just turn around and come back here. You can try again in the daylight."

"I think the scariest thing out there in the dark is the fellow right here beside me," Jim said with a grin, nodding in Hugh's direction. "It's everybody else that needs to be worried."

Kim nodded grimly. "I hope you're right about that."

15

Despite his eagerness to get home, Jim knew it was dangerous to cut through town. That was unfortunate, because from Kyle's house that was the most expeditious route home. Going the safe way nearly doubled the length of the trip, but in the valley they'd come up with their own version of that old saying *haste makes waste*. Their version said *haste makes bloody paste*, meaning if you get in a hurry, you die.

Jim and Hugh went in the opposite direction of the road into town, riding for nearly two hours before they reached the old farm road they had initially taken from town. This still required that they cross Main Street when they reached town but it lessened their exposure compared to an alternative route. While the night was cold and damp, the condition of the snow let them know the temperature was hovering right around freezing and not below. The snow stayed damp and slushy beneath the horses' hooves, not freezing into a dangerous layer of ice that would have made progress even more treacherous.

It was after midnight when they finally crossed Main Street. Jim paused his horse over the double yellow line he knew lay beneath the snow in the center of Main Street. Hugh paused beside him. Jim didn't look over at his friend but in the darkness he could sense his questioning. In his head, Jim had instantly been transported to a moment maybe thirty years prior when he and a childhood friend sat on a snow-covered Main Street in the middle of the night and reveled at the silence and solitude. Jim didn't know if everyone had those experiences but sometimes the world blindsided him like that, hitting him with memories and recollections that stopped him in his tracks. It was amazing how much life he'd experienced since that moment all those years ago. Amazing how much the world had changed. He reminded himself that the big difference was they had power then. They had warm homes to return to. Most significantly perhaps, the town in his childhood was not full of the dead, the dying, and those still to die.

Jim nudged his horse on, forcing himself from that time and place. When they were clear of town, he would tell Hugh the story. Hugh might understand, or he might ask Jim what he'd been smoking.

They crossed at a point where the town was less densely populated. They saw no lights and heard no sounds. The fact that not even a dog was barking told its own story. It was the story of the starving people that would eat a dog when they could find nothing else. It was the story of a town that would never be the same even if the lights came back on. How many generations would have to pass before people forgot about the time in which they were eaters of dogs and neighbor killed neighbor?

When they were beyond town, Hugh cleared his throat. "Do you need to radio your family?"

Jim shook his head. "I don't think I'm going to. I'm sure they're all asleep now. Since we have a general overwatch on the entire valley now, we haven't been keeping our watch at the house. I'll probably radio the watch when we get back there so they don't shoot us, then I'll just sleep in the barn or the shop. It's too dangerous now to go sneaking into any house, even your own, in the middle of the night."

They rode in silence for a while, following a paved road, then took a shortcut across a vacant farm that took them behind the superstore. There was the smell of distant fires. The road eventually brought them to their river crossing. Jim paused before heading down the steep bank.

"I'd like to use my light but I don't want to blow my night vision."

"Your headlamp do red?" Hugh asked.

"It does but I'm not sure it's going to help here."

"Then trust the horse."

Jim nudged his horse on, halfway expecting it to wipe out at some point and dump him in the frigid water. It didn't. It traversed the river without pause or stumble, climbing the steep bank on the other side.

Jim sat there waiting on Hugh, allowing his horse to rest.

"You need a place to crash for the night?" Jim asked. "You're welcome to a spot in the woodshop. It's warm when the stove is going."

"I might take you up on that," Hugh said, nudging his horse into motion. As quickly as he started, he reined it to a stop. "You hear that?"

Jim cocked an ear to the night. "I don't hear a damn thing."

"Listen!" Hugh hissed.

Jim did as instructed and then he heard it—the low rumble of a distant engine, barely audible.

"Generator?" Jim asked.

"No. Chopper."

"Helicopter?"

"Definitely. I'd guess a Blackhawk."

"You think it's going to the power plant?" Jim asked. "I've never noticed a flyover here."

"Apparently there's been choppers going to the power plant for some time and we've never been beneath her flightpath before. It makes me think this might be something else."

The sound grew louder, filling the valley, bouncing off the ripples and convolutions that made up the ancient landscape. That echo made it nearly impossible to tell what was going on from the sound alone. Then the chopper sounded as if it was slowing.

Jim checked his watch; it was after 1 AM. He could imagine

people throughout the valley waking and wondering what the hell was going on. "We need a better vantage point."

"Lead the way," Hugh said. "This is your territory."

Jim turned his horse up a steep tree-less hill. The horse struggled in the deep snow with the weight of the rider and his gear. He was headed for the outpost that Pete maintained on the highest point of their property. It was the closest point with a good general view of the valley.

"What I wouldn't give for my old PVS-7," Hugh called out as they reached the vacant outpost.

Jim sprang from the saddle and dug urgently through the pockets of the backpack strapped to his horse. "It's not very good but I've got some Gen I consumer-grade bullshit in here. Maybe with the light off the snow it will tell us something."

Jim found what he was looking for and yanked it from the pack, hitting the power button and shoving the lens caps in his pocket. While he waited for it to power up, he scanned the valley with his naked eye. He had no idea where the chopper might be, though the buffeting of the rotor blades reverberated through his entire body. The acoustics of the valley wreaked havoc with trying to locate the origin of sound whether it was a gunshot, a scream, or apparently a chopper.

Jim scanned the valley with his cheap NVDs. "I got something."

"What is it?"

Jim handed the device over to Hugh. "Check the valley floor at my 1 o'clock."

Hugh oriented himself and scanned in the dim glow the device. "I hope you didn't pay good money for this piece of shit."

"It's better than nothing," Jim said. "You can see can't you?"

"Barely."

"What do you think is happening?"

"That chopper is landing. They've got IR lights designating the edges of the LZ and some kind of IR laser guidance system that probably steered the chopper in. I've seen those used before when the ability to provide precise coordinates was in question. Means you've probably got a pilot flying by night vision."

"So who the fuck are they and why are they landing in my valley?" Jim asked.

Hugh passed the night vision back to Jim, who raised the device to his eyes just in time to see the chopper touch down. The door immediately slid open and a red light emanated from inside. Red headlamp lamps popped on outside of the LZ, telling Jim the ground crew, whoever they were, was not running with night vision. Jim hooked his NVD on the saddle horn and dug out his regular binoculars from the pack. The shitty NVD only had 2x magnification and was practically useless. With the increased optical quality of the binoculars, Jim was able to see what was going on even with just the red light.

"Looks like a supply drop," Jim said. "They're offloading gear. All of it in duffels and packs."

"Maybe it's those folks that were camping beneath the power lines on the ridge."

"If that's the case, they're not a couple of ridges away now. They're right here in our backyard."

"How many do you see there on the ground?"

"Four," Jim answered. "How many did you see on the mountain?"

"They were too far away for me to get a good count," Hugh said. "But I'd bet there were three times that based on the number of tents and level of activity."

"If it was me down there, I'd have three teams working," Jim said. "I'd have one guarding the base, one doing the offload, and one watching over the whole operation."

"I think that's a safe assumption. Are you up to intercepting these guys and asking them a few questions?"

"Let's radio our overwatch first," Jim said. "I don't want to be wandering around out there with no one knowing we're here. If Mack Bird is on watch with his thermal scope, he wouldn't know who he'd shot until he was checking the body."

Hugh pulled his radio from a pouch on his plate carrier. "Valley

Watch, this is Wayward Son returning to base. We're mobile in your area of operations and didn't want to be mistaken for hostiles."

"Roger that, Wayward Son. What's your location?" It was Gary. He must be on watch tonight. That probably meant that Will was there with him. They usually pulled watch together.

"Outpost Pete," Jim said.

Hugh repeated it into the radio.

"Roger that, Wayward. We have you at Outpost Pete."

"Do you have eyes on the chopper, Valley Watch?" Hugh asked.

Gary laughed. *"Dozens of them, Wayward. I think everyone in the valley is up and mobile."*

"Good to know," Hugh replied. "If things go south, we'll all need to be careful with our fire."

Jim held out his hand for Hugh's radio and he passed it over. "This is Wayward Son. Can I get a head count of how many knuckleheads we have wandering around out there tonight? I don't want any confusion."

When Jim released his mic people began sounding off. Lloyd, Randi, Mack Bird, Weatherman, Pete, and Charlie were all awake and geared up.

Jim shook his head. "If that chopper has thermal, we're screwed. I'm assuming they have comms, they'll radio the ground crew that they're surrounded."

"Then we don't surround them," Hugh said. "That chopper will be anxious to tuck tail and boogie home. He ain't sticking around for high fives. We wait until he's clear before we do anything."

When the last voice sounded off, Jim keyed his mic again. "I need you all to listen closely. Here's what we're going to do."

16

—————

When the last gear was tossed out, the chopper door slid closed. The Blackhawk rose and banked away. The men on the ground crouched, shielding their eyes from the stinging snow stirred by the rotors. When the flurry subsided, each man shouldered one of the heavy green duffels while carrying another by the handle. They waded toward the gate they'd used to access the field. The going was slow due to the snow and their general lack of familiarity with the terrain. They all turned their red headlamps off. It would be a long slog back to camp.

From a distant barn, Jim watched through his night vision. Gary monitored the same scene through the night vision scope on his rifle, lying prone in the hayloft of the barn.

"Their second team is pulling out of position and converging near the gate," Jim said.

When the men with the duffels reached that gate, each man handed over a duffel to the men who had been covering their backs. Those men used the backpack straps to carry the duffels while keeping their weapons at the ready. Everyone left the field and started down the valley road. Cattle fencing lined each side of the road, forming a gauntlet. It was exactly what Jim and his team had counted on. There was no escape to either side.

Jim raised the hand holding his radio and keyed the mic. "The cattle are in the chute. On my signal, hit them with lights and strobes. Stay low and don't fire unless you have to. Dead men tell no tales. We want these people alive."

He watched their progress down the road. He didn't want to spring the trap too early or the men would have a better chance of dropping their gear and retreating. Spring it too late and his men, stationed on both sides of the road, would be firing toward each other if things went to shit. Jim placed the night vision in a pouch on his plate carrier and raised the binoculars to his eyes.

"Get ready," he instructed. "Hit 'em on my signal. Count it down. Three. Two. *One!*"

Through the binoculars, he saw the road light up like a nightclub. Weatherman, Bird, Pete, Charlie, Randi, and Hugh hit the approaching men with tactical lights, strobes, and lasers. Some immediately threw up hands to protect their eyes from the blinding lights. Other squinted, shielding their eyes, but maintaining a grip on their weapons.

"Drop your weapons and you will not be harmed!" Hugh bellowed at the stunned men. "You are surrounded. Drop'em now!"

Gary remained in the hayloft, following the action through his night vision scope. Jim ran from the barn with Will trailing him. Jim had trained to run and gun but never in the snow, never with a loaded plate carrier. Lesson learned—train how you fight.

He slipped once and went down but was back on his feet in a second. He and Will put the cork in the bottle, closing off any retreat.

"Drop your weapons now!" Hugh repeated. "Drop them!"

Jim relaxed a fraction as rifles began hitting the ground.

"Now drop those duffels," Hugh ordered.

"You can have the gear but we need our rifles," said one of the men.

"Time to use your ears and not your mouth," Hugh said. "Just shut the fuck up and do what you're told. Drop to your knees and raise your hands over your head."

The men reluctantly complied. Some prayed. Some begged. These men were clearly not a military unit. They were not combat-hardened troops.

Bird and Weatherman looped around behind the men and approached cautiously, rifles raised, moving from one man to the next. With Weatherman providing cover, Bird dropped a feed sack over each man's head and zip-tied their hands. They performed a hasty search, removing any handguns and knives they found, tossing them into a pile. With the bulky clothes and the assortment of pockets, it was understood that they were probably missing things but the hope was that this would be over shortly. If the men had a solid story, Jim would cut them loose. If they had bad intentions, Jim would send Pete and Charlie back home, then he'd deal with these men.

It had become that kind of world. There were no second chances. There was no hoping people might have a change of heart and see the error of their ways. Sometimes it was just a matter of drawing a line through the world. Which side you found yourself on at any given moment could determine your fate. Sometimes it was bad choices. Other times it was just shitty luck.

Jim's group frog-marched their prisoners back to the barn where Gary was hiding. They lined the men up and forced them to their knees on the packed dirt. The building smelled of moldy hay and old manure. Pete and Charlie maintained watch outside. The remainder of Jim's team circled the bound men.

"Which of you is in charge?" Jim asked. He spoke loudly enough to be sure the men heard but he did not yell. If they were scared it would be because of what Jim said, not how he said it.

No reply.

"What's in those duffels?" Jim asked.

Again, no answer. They must have planned for this.

"Dump that shit out," Jim said.

Hugh unsnapped the strap from the ring at the end of the bag, unfolded the grommets, and looked inside. He upended the duffel and the contents dumped onto the barn floor. Jim sorted through it with the toe of his boot. It was mostly dehydrated meals, some clothing, batteries, and socks. Glaringly absent was any tactical gear, ammunition, or weapons.

"You guys just out for a little winter camping?" Jim asked.

No response.

"Okay, who's in charge?" he repeated.

No answer.

"This is getting old. Please don't make me assume you're here with bad intentions. Randi, what happened last time I took men with questionable intentions into a barn and shut the door?"

Randi's face hardened at the memory. "You killed them," she said flatly. She was pissed he brought that up as she felt a degree of responsibility for those deaths.

Jim sighed. "I'm not a patient man. In fact, I'm an asshole. This will be the last time I ask and that's not an idle threat. If I don't get an answer, this will move beyond that point where we can back up and fix things. If I kill one of you, I have to kill all of you. Then we have to track down your friends back at camp and kill them. Do you understand?"

Jim let that hang out there. Let it settle in. The barn was silent. The valley was silent. There was no wind that night, no dogs barking. Only the sound of breathing. Then Jim clicked the selector switch on his weapon. The sound was massive in the small space, like the cracking of a board or the shattering of glass. It was the sound of a hard decision being made.

"I'm in charge," one of the masked men blurted out.

Jim nodded at Hugh and he stripped the bag from the man's head in a single pull. The man blinked at the yellow glare of the lantern light. He looked around the room, taking in the hard faces made harder by the cold night, the late hour, and the grim resolve that they would see men die before the night was done. It was a scene no man kneeling and bound would relish. It was the kind of scene that was often the last men saw before they died. Cold men. Dispassionate expressions. Hard eyes. Men who knew violence.

Men who could stomach death and live with the decisions they made.

"Now we're getting somewhere," Jim said. "Don't make this harder than it needs to be."

"I'll try not to," the man replied.

"What's your name?" Jim asked.

"Scott."

"Scott, my name is Jim and this valley is my home. Last summer I fought my way back here and damned if we haven't had to fight to keep this place ever since. So when people show up unannounced, I get concerned. When people I don't know get supply drops from a chopper, I get concerned. Most people can't scrape together enough fucking gas to start a lawnmower and you have a Blackhawk delivering you long underwear. Explain this to me."

The man on his knees looked at Jim. He made a decision, one that he hoped would keep him alive. He was going to tell the truth. "Have you heard the official radio transmissions talking about power restoration?"

"Yes."

"What do you think about them?"

Jim gave an indecisive shrug. "If you'd asked me a week ago, I would've told you I was pretty damn excited to hear what they had to say. I don't think there's anybody out there who doesn't miss the convenience of electric lights, refrigeration, and television."

"Not to mention all the people who've died and will still die due to lack of power," Scott said.

"There is that," Jim agreed. "But after what I've seen today I'm a little skeptical."

The man honed in on Jim with razor-sharp focus. "What exactly did you see today?"

Jim met the man's gaze. "I saw a power plant up and running. I saw NATO troops providing security and operational assistance. I even talked to a couple of U.S. soldiers, guards who basically told me to get the hell out of there before things got ugly. Then they told me I probably wasn't getting any power."

The man on his knees looked to both sides, as he was looking for a reaction to what he'd been told. All of his team still had bags on their heads so he had no idea how they were reacting to this information. He looked back to the residents of the valley assembled around the room.

"That news doesn't seem to surprise you," Hugh commented. There was no reply from Scott so Hugh continued. "Your jackets and patches say East Coast Power Recovery Commission. Is that legit? I kind of wonder because it makes my bullshit meter peg out."

"Why would you say that?" Scott asked.

"You may have a chopper dropping off supplies but I'm not seeing a lot of standardization in your weaponry, and no government-issue gear. Truthfully, your weapons look like individual shit you brought from home. It makes me think that all is not what it seems." Hugh raised a questioning eyebrow at the man and let the statement linger.

Scott shifted uncomfortably on his knees. "A lot of things are not what they seem."

"You explain that to me," Jim said, "we work this shit out, you're free to go. But you start maxing out my bullshit meter too and things will get ugly."

Scott shifted again. "Can I at least sit back? I'm too old to sit on my knees like this."

"Go ahead," Jim told him.

Scott cautiously eased back until he was sitting on his feet. He took a deep breath. "There's an official notification coming in the next couple of days. Hell, it might've even been tonight for all I know. They didn't give an exact date, but the government is supposed to lay out their plan for energy recovery, which they then link to a national recovery."

"We know that much," Jim said. "We've heard those broadcasts. Hugh is a radio operator."

Scott cut a quick glance at Hugh. That seemed to pique his interest. "They are going to start rolling the power back out but it's not going to be what folks expect. The first places to receive power will be these glorified FEMA camps. Depending on where you are in the country they'll either be called 'comfort camps' or 'recovery camps.' Those camps will have power and folks will be allowed to go there for in-processing, but it comes with a catch."

"What's the catch?" Jim asked.

"When you are processed into the camp you have to bring identification. You also have to bring your all guns with you. These camps have the ability to crossmatch registration records, purchase records, credit card statements — all kinds of stuff — to see what guns people have purchased. Of course, there are always private sales that aren't tracked so the records are not one hundred percent accurate, but basically you have to turn in every gun that can be tracked to you if you want to enter one of the camps. Once you're there, you're there to stay. You can't come and go. You have assigned tasks and you're there for the duration of the recovery. If you leave, you won't be allowed back in and you don't get your guns back."

Hugh and Jim exchanged a look. Scott caught it.

"What? What was that look for?"

"I think we've seen one of these," Jim said. "There were chutes for sorting people. There were lots of signs telling people where to go. It was on the county fairgrounds."

Jim raised his gun to his eye and leveled it at the man. "So if you're part of this fiasco, part of this energy recovery effort, why should I let you live? Sounds like you're taking advantage of the American people, making them give up their rights in exchange for electrical service."

"No!" Scott bellowed. "We're not part of that. Our mission is to get the word out. We're to let people know what's going on and encourage them to stay strong and not go to the camps."

Hugh regarded the man. "You're referring to this as a mission and you obviously have the backing of folks who can set you up with a chopper resupply. You have that expensive infrared guidance system for coordinating your chopper landings. Just who the hell are you people?"

Scott looked at his team, still hooded and bound. "Can you at least take the hoods off my people?"

Jim met the man's eye then saw no subterfuge there. It seemed to be concern. He nodded.

"Take the hoods off."

Hugh, Randi, and Mack Bird stepped forward and carefully removed the hoods from the remainder of the kneeling men.

"I did as you asked," Jim said. "Now tell me who sent you on this mission."

Scott made eye contact with each of his team members. More than anything, it seemed an attempt to verify that each man was okay. When he was reassured they were, he returned his gaze to Jim.

"Regardless of your political affiliation, most things that happen in the world, perhaps even for centuries, are really just attributable to two opposing ideals. You have the people who are loyal to their country and you have the people who feel that the entire world is their nation and they want to run it. The power may stop, the fuel may stop, and everything else might grind to a halt, but that underlying conflict was not slowed in the least by *anything* that's happened in this country since those terror attacks. Forces on both sides have positioned themselves to maximize what they can get from this. That's what it all comes down to. Everyone's plan is now in place and unfolding before our eyes. This is when we find out who's going to win."

"So some shadowy element of the government is in control?" Jim asked.

"Sounds like this goes way beyond the government," Hugh said. "Something of this scale would involve the people who really pull the strings. The people who *own* governments."

"Whether it's conspiracy or not is up for you to decide," Scott said. "What I can tell you is that the restoration of power is going to be directly tied to disarming the citizens of the United States. They'll start with these comfort camps, and when they feel like they have local communities stabilized enough that they can start turning the power back on for them, they'll apply the same metric to citizens in their private homes. You can have your guns or your electricity, but you can't have both."

"Then they can just keep their fucking power," Hugh said.

Scott looked at the faces around him. "That's easy for you to say in a place like this where your neighbors are like-minded folks. It will be much harder for some folks. They have a more devious tactic lined up. They're going to go to neighborhoods, subdivisions, and communities, and they're going to tell those folks that *nobody* gets any power until all the guns in the neighborhood are turned in. Now, not only will this decision impact your own family, but some folks will have an entire community bearing down on them. It's conceivable that, even if you were holding strong to your values, your neighbors might storm your home and take your guns just to get power back on to the neighborhood. I can see this tearing apart families. I can see men refusing to give up their guns and wives pointing at their cold, hungry children and asking if they choose their guns over their family. It will be a tough call. It will break men."

Jim shook his head in disgust. "I'm not sure that choosing the convenience of electricity over self-defense is the path the greater personal safety."

"I'd agree with you there, but think of the massive pressure that can be exerted on individuals around this country. I can imagine that, not since the Civil War, will families be torn apart in the same way. It's a profound moral dilemma for some folks."

"The more you talk, the more this whole thing reeks of a false flag operation," Gary said.

"I'm not sure there's any point to going down that rabbit hole," Scott said. "It's bottomless. It would be impossible to prove, and even if you knew the truth, how would it change anything?"

"He's got a point," Jim said. "Regardless of who initiated this, I'm not certain we can trust the government anymore. Not after seeing NATO troops patrolling our power plant and telling us we weren't getting any of the power they produced."

"There are still parts of the government that can be trusted," Scott assured them. "There are still patriots in our nation's capital. That's why my team is here."

Hugh gave a sarcastic jerk of his head. "And just what are you all going to do? Are you guerrillas? Are you revolutionary fighters?"

Scott fixed his eyes on Hugh. "We're forward reconnaissance. There's a reason that there are NATO troops here. The forces directing this plan are not certain that they have the full support of the military. They've worked for the last twenty years to get officers in place who supported their agenda and those officers are in command of the troops you saw. Commanders they couldn't trust were forced into retirement or put out to pasture. Anyone remaining that they can't trust has been sent home."

"So those commanders are out of the fight?" Hugh asked.

That comment actually brought a smile to Scott's face. "Who do you think is supporting us? There are teams like ours all up and down the East Coast. We're in Ohio and the Tennessee Valley. We're in Alabama. These teams come from different backgrounds but every team is assembled from patriots who don't agree with the agenda that's being put in place as we speak."

Jim looked at Hugh and the men had a wordless exchange, coming to a consensus. Hugh slipped his hand around his back and came back around with a dagger. Some of the men kneeling in front of them were visibly afraid, certain this meant the end. Hugh moved behind the men and efficiently sliced away the zip ties binding their wrists. Some of the men were so relieved they nearly collapsed to the ground.

"Thank you," Scott said, rubbing his wrists.

"I hope you understand my caution," Jim said. "Everything important to me is in this valley. As much as I'm tired of this fight, I will die to keep my family safe."

"You might as well get used to it. I don't think this fight is over," Scott said. "In fact, I think it's just beginning."

The truthfulness of that statement hit Jim with a nearly unbearable weight. It took his breath. While the vigilance and the constant stress were wearing on him, it would not be going away anytime soon. This would not be like the lights coming back on after a hurricane.

This would not be like anything the country had known before. Jim looked back up and met Scott's eyes.

"I'm assuming you have communication with the other men at your camp?"

Scott nodded.

"If you want, you are welcome to this barn for the night. It's not heated but it might beat sleeping in the snow. You can at least dry your stuff out."

"Thank you. We'll take you up on that."

"We'll talk in the morning."

Scott nodded and Jim's people filed out into the night.

17

K yle couldn't sleep that night. The things Jim said were running through his mind. It irked him that power would be available but none was designated for local distribution. It just didn't seem right to him, and above all things Kyle believed in fairness. Local people risked their lives to mine the coal that fired that plant. Local people trucked it to the prep plant where local people loaded it onto coal cars for transportation to the plant. Local people were entitled to a portion of that power. Kyle felt that in the deepest part of himself.

He was up before the sun and had a cold slice of beef for breakfast. He packed a backpack with food for a day, water, and a bottle of tequila. He slid a revolver in his coat pocket and armed himself with his 7mm Magnum deer rifle and a box of shells. He kissed his sleeping wife and children, leaving a note explaining he'd be back that night but not to wait up for him. He'd learned a long time ago that tequila and a strict timeframe were not compatible. Best to not make promises he might not be able to keep.

He strapped on a headlamp and went to the barn. His horse greeted him from its stall, vast clouds of steam puffing from its nostrils.

"Morning, Ranger. Hope you're up for a workout today."

Kyle scooped some hay into a feeder and the horse ambled over to it. While the animal was occupied, he saddled the horse, then worked a bridle onto his head. He threw open the gate and led the horse from the barn. Kyle strapped his pack behind the saddle, threw the rifle sling over his shoulder, and headed toward his driveway.

Of all the people he worked with at the power company, the man with the most experience was Orfield. Kyle was certain if he explained the situation to Orfield they could pore over the maps together and come up with a plan for creating a micro-grid around the town. If the two of them could come up with a plan for how to pull it off, Kyle thought there could be at least thirteen men in the area of town who could help make this happen. Some, like Kyle and Orfield, were employees of the power company. A few others worked for enormous electrical subcontractors that did work all around the country.

It took Kyle nearly two hours to get to Orfield's house, then another hour to convince the man, who was nearing retirement, that it was their duty as Americans to do what they could to restore the power to the local folks. Orfield was apprehensive and it took a fair amount of convincing to bring him on board. When Kyle finally succeeded, Orfield pointed to a quadrant of the map and tapped his finger on it.

"That right there. That's where you want to do it. It'll be a short pull for the wire and easy to isolate."

Kyle nodded, impressed. "That's exactly what I was hoping you could tell me. I knew you'd know just the right place."

"There's still the matter of getting all the wire you need over to the job site, but I think I might have an idea for that too."

"Those spools are pretty damn heavy. I thought about a horse and buggy, though I'm not sure how many horses it would take. And I sure hope you don't have any plans for me and the guys to roll a spool from the shop to the jobsite."

"Nah. You know that frozen food company down there in the industrial park?" Orfield asked.

Kyle nodded but frowned. "Frozen food? What in hell does that have to do with running the power?"

"People looted that damn place early on but got nothing. The place only distributed frozen food so every bit of it melted and went bad before people got there. They still got a fleet of trucks there."

"Hell, our shop's got an entire fleet of trucks but it don't do you a damn bit of good with no fuel."

"Their trucks run on propane."

Kyle slowly shook his head as if it was the most obvious thing in the whole damn world and he was an idiot. "Propane?"

Orfield nodded. "Gas is gone. Diesel is pretty much gone too. Propane is all over the place. We'll probably end up hanging wire off trees instead of drilling for poles but at least you won't have to be carrying the wire in. We can use a spool trailer and unroll it with the truck."

"We'll still need a crew," Kyle said.

"We can find a crew. There's plenty of good guys around. Especially if we've got a truck to haul them in and they don't have to walk."

"Okay, then here's the big question—when do you think we can get on this?"

There was no hesitation on Orfield's part. "I think the sooner the better. We need to check those high-voltage lines. If they're not sending power through them yet this would be the time to get our own lines in place. We could go ahead and run everything then just fuse it off. When they energize their lines we'll close the fuses and we got power."

Kyle chuckled. "I hope it's that damn easy."

"Well, I need things to go back to normal so I can retire," Orfield said. "If there's no power then there's no banks running. If there's no banks, then how does my pension get deposited into my account? Without that pension, I can't go fishing every day and laugh at you poor fuckers who are still working. So I'm not doing this for you, I'm doing it for me."

"I don't question a man's reasons," Kyle said. "Do you want to be foreman on this one?"

Orfield nodded. "Why not? Sure. I'll run it."

With that resolved, Kyle opened his pack and pulled out the bottle of tequila. He cracked the bottle open and passed it to Orfield.

"Let's make a toast to getting switched on," Kyle said.

Orfield read the label and screwed up his face when he saw it was tequila, however, that didn't stop him from taking a drink. He went through a series of facial contortions, tremors, and animated gestures before he was done with the ritual of his first sip. He passed the bottle back to Kyle.

"How about I come and get you tomorrow with two horses?" Kyle said. "We'll take a look at those trucks you were talking about. If we get a couple of them running you can bring one back to your house and I'll take my horses back home. Then the day after tomorrow, we'll pick up a crew and get to work."

Orfield sighed. "As much as I want to retire, *let's go to work* are some the sweetest words I've heard in a long time."

Kyle took a hit off the bottle. As much work as lay ahead of them, this was one of the first positive things he'd heard in a while. Every bit of news they'd heard since last summer was worse than news before it. Violence, death, disease, starvation. Finally there was a flicker of hope. He hoped it was the beginning of the end, and that this would all become a story he would tell his grandchildren one day, the way old-timers talked about the Great Depression or the Normandy invasion. People would recall where they were when the lights came back on the same way they talked about where they were when they heard Kennedy had been assassinated or that terrorists had hit the World Trade Center.

At least that was what he was hoping.

18

Sometime after 2 AM Jim slipped into his woodshop and built a small fire. Hugh decided to push on home. In these days of wood heat, a man couldn't leave his home unattended for too long or things froze up. Jim slept well on the comfortable old couch and rejoined his family in the morning. They were sitting around the fire and were pleased to see him home. It was an ever-present concern that each trip could be your last. There were too many variables to be certain of anything anymore.

It took a long time to explain everything that happened over the course of the two days Jim had been gone. He found it easiest to start at the beginning and go through everything in order. He told them about the power plants and what the guards had told him, about visiting Kyle, and then intercepting the helicopter crew that night. He explained that the story the Energy Recovery folks told seemed to verify what the guards at the power plant had said. Finally, he told them about the comfort camps and the pending announcement.

No one interrupted Jim with any questions as he spoke but the expressions on the faces surrounding him certainly communicated that they had some. He understood. Sometimes a new piece of information only served to raise more questions than it answered. For months the question on everyone's mind was wondering when the power might come back on. Now they had some sort of answer and it only served to complicate things.

"I don't think this leaves a person many options," Nana said. She looked around the room for support.

"I agree," Jim said. "There's no way I could accept conditions like those."

His mother furrowed her brow and looked at him intently. They were clearly on different wavelengths. "Wait a minute. You mean to tell me you would *not* go to the shelter?"

Incredulous, Jim sat straight up on the couch. "Absolutely not! I saw the FEMA shelter system fall apart right after this whole mess took place. People were lucky to get out alive. Going to a shelter is just making the choice to die in a mass grave. There's no way that turns out well."

Jim's mother was not pleased with him. "Well, I just don't see how someone could choose to risk their family's life when the government is making power available to you," she fired back. "It makes complete sense to me that they want people to turn in their guns. Look at what's happening with the world! It's gone crazy. Look at how many people this family alone has killed. I think the only way they're going to get people to start behaving like civilized adults again is to take away their weapons."

Jim took a deep breath, then several more. He forced himself to remember this was his mother he was speaking to. The way she was talking, what she was considering doing, provoked a strong reaction from him and he was trying to curb that reaction. He not want to say the same things to her that he would say to other people in this exact same debate. He didn't care if those other people ever spoke to him again or not, but he planned on continuing to have a relationship with his mother. He reined himself back in.

"I understand if that's what you want to do. I want *you* to understand that I'm very concerned about what could happen to you."

She was not impressed by his restraint. "What might happen to us there is certainly no worse than what happens to us out here. We would be under the protection of armed troops. It should be safer."

"Just remember you might find yourself under the authority of foreign troops who don't speak your language and have no concern for you whatsoever. You would not be under the protection of people who know and love you like you are now."

Nana turned and looked angrily at Pops. "You haven't said anything. What do you think?"

Pops sighed and smiled at his wife. "I will go with you wherever you want to go. My days of fighting are over anyway. My personal preference would be to stay here with my family, especially since they won't even be able to visit the camp. You understand that, right? Jim and Ellen won't be bringing the kids to visit. There's no interaction with people outside of the camp. Once we go when it's just us."

Nana started crying. His mother didn't use tears to manipulate so this was clearly an indication of just how upset she was.

"You don't have to decide right now," Jim assured her. "You have plenty of time." He didn't have the energy for this.

"Are you going to tell the old lady?" Ellen asked.

Jim looked at his wife quizzically. "The old lady? What lady?"

"The lady that you and Randi visited. Near your parents' house."

It suddenly hit Jim that she was talking about Mrs. Fairlane. "Oh yeah. My God, it seems so long ago I'd nearly forgotten about her."

Ellen grinned playfully. "Apparently that would come as no surprise to her. She seems to have pretty low expectations where you're concerned."

Jim frowned. "I've about had it with people and their expectations. I'm starting to understand why people leave their hometowns after high school and never come back."

Ellen looked stung by the remark. "I'm only joking. I was just teasing you."

"Sorry. Guess I'm not in the mood for it."

"Obviously. I still think you should go tell the old lady this news when you have a chance. She might be someone who would choose a shelter."

"She probably would. And it would likely be the best thing for her."

Jim's wife stared at him. She could tell where he was in his head at the moment, what he was thinking, what he was wanting to do. "Listen, I know you want to get away from it all right now, but take someone with you. It's too dangerous to go into town alone. Too many stupid things can happen."

"I will," Jim reluctantly agreed. "Maybe I'll take Ford again. I think there might be some folks he wants to check in on."

"You asking Randi?"

Jim shook his head. "She's done with town for now. Said it's where people go to die and she doesn't want to die."

Ellen understood. Losing Buddy had hit Randi hard. "You thinking about going to speak with her today?"

"I don't think so." Jim laughed. "Riding that horse for two days about wrecked me. Every muscle between my ankles and my shoulders is about to kill me. I need a day just to walk around and loosen back up. I'll plan on doing it tomorrow. Maybe I'll run by Kyle's house to see if he's figured anything out."

"You could take Hugh. He seems pretty handy."

"Hugh is cool under pressure but I could tell he missed his radios while we were gone. He probably spent all night catching up on what he missed. That may be the best place for him, gathering intelligence. He's the only one who can do what he's doing."

"That reminds me," Ellen said, "the sheriff's mother died while you were gone. Lloyd, Randi, Will, and some of the Wimmers went up there and tried to help the sheriff dig the grave but he didn't want any help. He said it was a family thing and he'd take care of it."

"I can almost understand that," Jim said. "It's probably more about closure than anything else. He needs a little physical suffering to go along with the mental suffering he's been experiencing."

Nana's crying had subsided but Jim didn't try to resume the conversation. They both needed some time to cool off and think. Nana and Pops retreated back to the bedroom where they had been staying, presumably to discuss what had taken place.

Jim looked at Ellen and lowered his voice. "You do understand why I oppose this, don't you? I can't handle the idea of you all being at the mercy of the people running those shelters. The people that choose to stay there will just be sheep who are surrendering all ability to make decisions for themselves. Some people want that but I couldn't handle it. I don't want anyone in my family to die. I don't want anything bad to happen to any of us, and I honestly believe trusting your survival to one of these so-called comfort camps is the wrong thing to do."

Ellen stared at her husband for a long time. "I think you're right. I don't think it's going to be an easy way to go though. Things may get worse for us before they get better."

"When has any of it been easy?"

Ellen shook her head. "It hasn't."

JIM STUCK AROUND LONG ENOUGH to have breakfast with his kids, then threw on his gear and went to check on the energy recovery folks. The barn Jim offered them for the night was on a vacant farm with no home on it. It belonged to some folks who lived several towns away and Jim hadn't seen them since he returned from Richmond. After a short walk, he found the folks awake and stirring, cooking breakfast and instant coffee in the dark interior of the barn.

Jim banged on the open door before going inside. "Morning."

He received some noncommittal nods from members of the group. They were either uncertain as to whether it was actually a good morning or not, or perhaps they still harbored some resentment from the previous night when Jim had been a little rough with them. He couldn't blame them for not gushing at his appearance, yet at the same time they had to understand his precautions.

Scott, their apparent leader, seemed to hold no grudge. He approached Jim and held out a hand. It was not the exuberant handshake of old friends but the tentative handshake of new potential allies.

"How did everyone sleep?" Jim asked.

"It's not exactly the Ritz-Carlton but it beats sleeping in the slush."

"Sorry, but this is the best I had to offer."

"And you don't really know us yet," Scott added.

Jim smiled. Scott knew the score. "Yeah, but maybe we can find something better if you're sticking around for a while."

"Not happening."

"If it's not confidential, what's next for you guys?"

"We were supposed to go to the state line, make a U-turn, and head back northwest. The plan was to continue doing the same thing we did here, letting folks know what was about to happen and allowing them to make an informed decision as to whether they wanted to go to these camps or not."

"Supposed to?"

"After what you told us about the presence at the power plants, our plans have changed. Speaking of which, you mentioned you had a radio operator?"

"We do."

"It would be helpful if we could get him to relay a message for us."

"I can't speak *for* him but you're welcome to ask him."

"Our intelligence on a national level is a little scattered right now. We know what the overall agenda is but we really don't know how far the government has progressed toward putting their plans into place. Your information about plants being up and running is new. I'm not sure the folks back at the office are aware they're that close to flipping the switch."

"Aren't you concerned about transmitting that information over open channels? It's possible that the folks at the power plant will intercept your transmissions and know they're being watched."

Scott gestured toward his gear on the ground. "If your radio operator is willing to assist me, I have top end encryption. This device will record my transmission and send it in a burst that will be indecipherable except to parties who have the same device in place."

"I can radio Hugh on my walkie-talkie and let him know what you need," Jim said. "If he's game, I can walk you up there. It's about a thirty minute walk."

Scott smiled. "Is that all? I've been walking for months now. Thirty minutes is nothing. Hell, thirty *miles* is nothing anymore."

Jim got Hugh on the walkie-talkie and explained the situation. Hugh offered to walk halfway down the hill to meet Scott.

While Jim was on the radio, Scott went through his gear. He pulled several items from his pack and shoved them into his pocket, then slung his rifle over his shoulder. He explained to his group where he was going and that they should be prepared to leave when he got back.

Jim and Scott walked the farm road a short distance and then rejoined the main county road through the valley.

"Part of this transmission is a resupply request," Scott said.

"I thought you just got resupplied last night? That's how we found you."

"That was basic gear. We only thought we were in for another month of snooping and pooping down here in the boonies. What you told us last night changes things. I'd like to get some better surveillance gear. I could use a micro-drone, some long-range optics, and thermal blocking gear. Maybe even a parabolic mic for picking up their conversations."

"With that shopping list, it sounds like you have some good resources available to you."

Scott shrugged. "We do, but there's a lot of treachery right now. It's typical beltway stuff, only the consequences are higher. It's not just the fate of a nation, but life and death for everyone involved. Whichever group prevails will probably execute the other for treason. It's that serious."

As bad as it sounded, Jim was glad there were good guys out there who had access to top-level gear. That indicated there were some powerful backers to this rogue group. They weren't just rebels, but the tip of a true patriot resistance.

"Sorry, I got sidetracked. The point of all that was to see if there might be anything you guys needed," Scott offered.

Jim nearly rebuffed the offer purely out of habit because he didn't like to feel indebted to people. Then it occurred to him that, hell yeah there was stuff they needed. "That would be great. There are several things we could use."

Without missing a beat, Scott fished around in his jacket pocket and whipped out a small field notebook and a pen. "Shoot. What do you need?"

"Coffee if you got it. We could also use cases of MREs. Our long-range food is good but we're running out of MREs for people who are out doing guard duty or recon."

"MREs we got. I can hook you up. What else?"

"We could use ammo in all the basic flavors. If you can feed my ARs, AKs, and handguns, we would all feel little more comfortable."

"Got it. 5.56, 7.62, 9mm, and .45 cal."

"How much do you think you can bring?"

"It's not a matter of what we have available," Scott said. "It's more a matter of how much weight we can put on the chopper and not put a pinch on the flight range. I could probably get 10,000 rounds of each without even raising an eyebrow. It was understood from the beginning of this mission that we might have to do some local trading to secure cooperation. We'll just chalk this off as greasing the wheels of local government."

"Whatever makes it happen," Jim said. "Can we get medical supplies?"

"What kind?"

"Medications. Antibiotics, pain, whatever you can get us."

Scott scratched that down on his list.

Jim spotted Hugh in the distance ahead of them and threw up a hand. Hugh waved back.

"There's our radio guy," Jim said. "I'll pass you on to him. I've got a few things to take care of."

Scott extended a hand. "I think we'll be meeting again, but if we don't, keep your head low."

Jim shook the man's hand. "You do the same."

19

I t was early when Kyle showed up at Orfield's house with a spare horse. By midday they were in the industrial park riding down a desolate road between expansive metal buildings. The industrial park looked relatively untouched, likely having none of the things people were most intently searching for.

For Kyle, a frugal and resourceful farmer, he couldn't help but make a mental note of the resources that were potentially available here. There was a hardwood flooring manufacturer. It was likely they had a decent supply of finished lumber which could be a rare commodity in the coming years, depending on how quickly things got back to normal. There was a gas pipeline company and Kyle noticed they had racks of metal stock outside of their facility. There were also semi-trailers stacked high with six-inch well casing. It was a material that in hard times could be used to make a chimney for a wood stove. He figured it was a safe bet they also had oxygen and acetylene equipment inside. Without electricity for arc welding and fuel to run portable welders, gas welding may be the best option for the short-term future. Of course, Kyle sucked at it, but with a little practice he might be able to stick two pieces of metal together.

The warehouse they were looking for was a retail distributor of frozen meals. Their drivers went door-to-door leaving catalogs and selling meals much like the vacuum cleaner salesman of days gone by. It was immediately obvious that someone, or several someones, had ransacked the facility. The freezer compartments on the trucks had been pried open and there were fragments of old packaging evident even beneath the snow.

Because the grid collapsed in summer it was unlikely any meals had survived for long. Anyone who looted these trucks looking for food was certainly disappointed. Other than open doors on the freezer compartments the trucks appeared to be undamaged. The doors were not locked so no one broke out any windows and the tires were still inflated.

Understanding that they would have to get inside the warehouse to find the keys, the men went to the office door and found that it had already been pried open. In typical shortsightedness, the people who had raided the place had only been looking for food and cash. Drawers in offices had been ransacked and the contents dumped in the floor. A heavy safe anchored to the concrete had been pried upon until the door gave way and yielded the contents. Whatever the robbers had found there was likely as useless now as it was then. Money meant nothing at all. Food, gas, and ammunition were the commodities of the day.

"There," Orfield said, nodding at a metal key cabinet mounted on the wall.

Kyle went to the cabinet and swung open the unlocked door. Inside were hangers of neatly labeled keys that rattled against the box as the door opened. "Looks like nobody gave a shit about keys."

"Can't eat keys and the people that came here weren't looking for trucks. They might've been looking for fuel, but when they saw these vehicles ran off propane, they probably just got pissed off and left. Most people were looking for fuel for their own vehicles, not new ones."

Orfield instructed Kyle to take all the keys to all the vehicles, concerned that if they were seen driving around in one of these vehicles folks might come and get the rest of them before Kyle and Orfield could get them. They didn't want the vehicles they were stealing to be stolen out from under them.

"We better just take all of the vehicles today. You can't count on tomorrow," Kyle said. "Maybe once I get my horses home, you can drive me back over here and we'll shuttle all these vehicles to my house."

The men went outside with the keys, and in less time than Kyle expected, they had four of the seven trucks running.

"Good job for an old man," Kyle said, patting his friend on the back.

"I had a little experience with propane vehicles before," Orfield said. "The power company went through this phase fifteen or twenty years ago where they thought about implementing this with their entire fleet. They changed their minds. They rolled us out on a disaster recovery with some of those propane trucks and we couldn't get them refueled. It was a little embarrassing to them."

"I wish there was some way to haul those horses back to my house with the truck. It would save us a lot of time. I'm afraid to just tie them up around here. If people don't steal them to ride they'll steal them to eat."

Orfield frowned at that idea. "Why don't you lock them inside the warehouse? There's plenty of room."

"I ain't so sure my horses would like that."

"What if we gave them a big pile of grass to eat?" Orfield asked. "It will at least distract them."

"I guess we can try it. If they're still jittery when we come back for the second truck I'll come up with another plan."

The two men pulled out their pocket knives and spent the next fifteen minutes gathering clumps of the tall grass that jutted above the snow, sawing the clumps loose at the base, then piled them into boxes they found inside the warehouse. When they were done they had two big boxes of dried grass. It may not have been ideal but hopefully it would keep the horses from getting too spooked.

Kyle unfastened his backpack from the horse and hoisted it over his shoulders. He led the two horses through the door into the warehouse, then went back to the key box and found keys that would allow him to get back into the building when he returned. With the building secured, he met Orfield back at the vehicles.

Orfield kicked at the melting snow. "This stuff is slicker than cat shit on a hot plate. I wish we had some chains."

"We have chains at our shop," Kyle said, referring to the power company shop he and Orfield worked from.

"Maybe we should swing by there and put a couple of sets on. It will take a little time but it sure beats the hell out of getting stuck. Especially when there's no one to call for help."

The snow was melting a little bit each day but it wasn't gone yet. Depending on where you stood there were still six or eight inches of the wet, nasty mess everywhere. The falling snow had been pretty for all of about one day before people realized how much harder it was going to make their lives. Now everyone was praying for it to disappear as soon as possible and for spring to come.

They started the pair of vehicles and pulled out of the lot. After months of foot and horse travel, driving a vehicle again seemed alien. Kyle could imagine this was probably what people felt like back in the early twentieth century when they gave up their horses and rode in a car for the first time. Sure trains had been fast, but it wasn't like you had control over them. They went where the tracks were. To be in a vehicle where you could push the accelerator and turn in any direction you wanted, that was freedom.

It took several stressful hours for Kyle and Orfield to complete their task. When they were done, they had four propane trucks parked at Kyle's farm, though Orfield would be driving one home. Although the trucks were heavy-duty, they were not four-wheel-drive like the power company trucks. Kyle could only hope the tire chains they'd installed would help with traction.

While they were picking up the chains at their shop, Kyle hooked up to a trailer that held an enormous spool of wire just the size they needed. He raided the shop and found most of the tools and safety gear he thought the men would need. Even if he missed something, it would be a lot easier to get it now that they had some working vehicles. Any trip, even just across town, took a long time on a horse.

20

J im and Deputy Ford armed themselves to the teeth and headed into town. Jim still had the MP5 that Ford lent him. In addition, he carried his own M4 and his Beretta 92. Ford was armed with his Glock and one of the Colt select-fire carbines that were designated for Law Enforcement Only. Both men were wearing Level IV body armor and carrying Go Bags with the essentials.

Randi was glad to lend them her horses as long as she didn't have to go with them. She continued to swear off town after her experience with Buddy getting killed. Jim and Ford decided to travel together despite having different goals for the day. Their plan was to make each stop as a team. Jim would check on Mrs. Fairlane. Ford would check on the woman and daughter, Paige and Nicole, he found at the emergency operations center. After those stops, the plan was to hit Kyle's house and see if he made a decision about assisting with getting the power restored to the area.

It was a beautiful day, sunny, with temperatures in the mid-40s. It felt warm and spring-like after the period of cold and snow. Every-where there was the sound of trickling water, a welcome indication the snow was finally melting. The pair wanted to make good time but experience told them to keep a low profile and place caution over speed. The town was so small it couldn't be fully traversed using back streets. There were some sections of town where Main Street was the only route through town, but when back streets were available they utilized them.

With the warmer day, there were more people out moving around than usual. An atmosphere of caution prevailed and both sides were hyper-vigilant. The residents skulked toward cover as they appeared, never certain about the intentions of strangers. At other times, they heard the sound of scavengers breaking glass and prying loose lumber, presumably for firewood. They heard voices from vacant houses and smelled the lingering odor of wood smoke.

There were dead bodies. The deceased were dragged from their homes to yards or porches. Perhaps with thawing ground they would soon receive proper burials, if for no other reason than to reduce the risk of spreading disease. At a neat white house that sat close to the road, what Jim took to be a man sleeping in a lawn chair underneath a blanket actually turned out to be a corpse on second glance. The blanket had slipped from his head and was tucked beneath his chin, making it appear as if he were simply taking a nap. The open and discolored eyes, the rictus of the mouth, bespoke death and decay.

Once at the Fairlane house, they paused at the foot of the driveway and Jim pointed out the men that Mrs. Fairlane had shot. The melting snow of the last few days exposed more of the bodies and the dead looked like hunched zombies rising from a white swamp.

"I always wondered who lived here," Ford said.

"Everybody in this county used to know the Fairlanes. Old Mrs. Fairlane may have already been a shut-in by the time you graduated high school. It never occurred to me how many elderly there were out there like this until she pointed it out to me. There's an entire population whose only contact is with family, their church, home health, or their physician. Those with good health see even fewer people."

"That makes me think of all the elderly we used to do welfare checks on," Ford said. "I wonder how those folks are holding up."

"Probably dead."

"If this lady isn't dead, maybe they're not dead either."

"Maybe."

The pair plodded up the driveway. The horses spooked at the dead bodies now more visible than on their previous visit. Ford stared at each one of them.

"Pretty sure I recognize each one of these assholes. Dope heads and petty thieves. Just the kind of people you would expect to break-in on the elderly."

"No shortage of assholes," Jim agreed.

Jim was relieved there appeared to be no new tracks in the driveway or yard. Hopefully that meant no new dead bodies in the yard. They tied their horses to the porch railing and climbed the front steps, each man making an effort to stomp the wet snow off his boots. After the reception he received last time Jim had no intention of taking his shoes off, but he would at least make an effort not to track snow into the lady's house.

He raised a fist and tapped on the door. He listened for a moment and there was no response. Jim frowned and tried again. "Last time she came to us. We didn't even have to bang on the door. She was out here with a shotgun before we were even at the house."

Ford shook his head in frustration. "Get out of the way. You'd make a lousy fucking cop. Let me show you know to knock on a door."

Ford stepped forward and banged a half-dozen hammer fists against the door. "Police!"

"Dammit, Ford, you probably scared the shit out of her."

"You are the one who told me how tough she is. If she's that tough, banging on the door ain't going to scare her."

When there was no response to Ford's insistent knocking Jim became more worried. "Let's check the back door."

Ford shrugged. "Whatever. It's your show."

Jim led the way around back, to the French doors off the kitchen. There were no tracks, nor signs of forced entry anywhere. He crossed the patio, approached the door, and drew his hand back to knock.

What he saw through the glass doors stopped him in his tracks. Mrs. Fairlane was sprawled on the floor by the pantry, her arm extended toward him in pleading anguish. Her eyes were puffy and swollen, electric from pain and desperation.

"Oh my God."

Ford reached the door after Jim and took in the scene in front of him. He drew his Glock and shattered a single panel in the antique French door. He racked the remaining shards of glass out of the way and stuck a hand through the opening to unlock the lock.

With the pane of glass missing, Mrs. Fairlane's cries were more audible. She was breathing rapidly, nearly to the point of hyperventilating. "Oh God. Oh God," she kept repeating, over and over.

Ford yanked open the door and lunged through the opening. He dropped to his knees beside the elderly woman and put a hand on her face. Jim had never seen the man so compassionate.

"What happened?" Ford asked, holding her hand. "Jim, bring a cup of water."

"I was getting a can from the pantry," she sobbed. "I dropped it, and when I backed up to look for it, I stepped on it and fell. I can't get up. I think my hip is broken." The words poured from her in an emotional surge.

Jim heard those words from the sink where he was filling a glass of water. They shot a bolt of terror and panic through him. A broken hip? What the hell were they going to do with a broken hip?

Jim was back at Ford's side in a moment, dropping to the floor to assist Ms. Fairlane with getting a drink. He carefully raised her head and helped her hold the glass.

"When did this happen?" Ford asked.

"Three days ago."

Jim tried to put the numbers together in his head. Had she fallen not long after he and Randi left? Had she laid here all this time? It was heartbreaking.

"I'll get you a pillow," Jim said, starting to get up.

"Negative on that," Ford said. "Let's try to get her up on the couch or something. She's wet herself and the fire has gone out. It must be forty degrees in here. I'm surprised she's not hypothermic."

"She might've been if she didn't keep most of the house shut off and the temperature around ninety-five degrees."

"It probably saved her life," Ford said.

"How do you want to do this?" Jim asked. "I've never tried to move anyone in this condition."

"You get on the other side of her body. When I give you the go ahead, put one hand beneath her back and the other on her bicep. The first step is to see if we can get her to sit up."

"No! No!" Mrs. Fairlane wailed.

"Now!" Ford commanded.

Both men tried as gently as possible to raise the elderly woman to a sitting position. They had barely raised her shoulders a few inches off the floor when she bellowed out in the most tortured, pain-stricken cry that Jim had ever heard. She latched onto the two men with her claws, screaming for them to stop. Jim looked down and saw Mrs. Fairlane's left hip had rolled away from the body at an unnatural angle. The joint appeared to have broken off entirely with only the muscle keeping the leg hanging in place.

She began to fight violently as they tried to finish raising her upright. Jim tried to reason with her, tried to assure her that it would be okay, but would it? She screamed that they were killing her.

Jim met Ford's eyes and the deputy gave a quick shake of his head. He was throwing in the towel.

"It's not working. Let her down. Let her back," he said urgently.

Jim complied. They'd reached a damned if you do, damned if you don't predicament. There was no making her comfortable. There was no assisting her. And realistically, there was no fixing this. With the state of the world being such as it was, surgical hip repairs could be several years off.

Back flat on the ground, Rosa sobbed hysterically and clutched each man's arm. Ford tried desperately to comfort her. Jim was practically in a state of shock, uncertain as to what course of action to take. Then he realized the only thing he could do.

He asked her, "What do you want me to do? What do you want us to do for you?"

Ford was still in cop mode, used to solving problems and resolving situations. "We can get her some pain meds," he said. "That'll make her feel better."

Jim studied the deputy and saw the panic beginning to tear at the edges of him. The calm, cool, and collected persona of a few moments ago, the man who'd made entry and took control of the situation, was disintegrating. Ford realized there was nothing in his training to help him here. Everything he'd been taught was focused on keeping the victim comfortable while waiting for EMS. This time there would be no EMS.

"What the hell do we do?" Ford hissed.

Jim shook his head. He had no idea either. Meanwhile, beneath them, the moaning and whimpering continued.

"Just shoot me!" Rosa Fairlane begged. "Shoot me."

Ford's eyes filled with horror. He shook his head as if unable to accept a concept so revolting and so contrary to everything he stood for. His reaction only served to increase her level of desperation.

"Just shoot me!"

Ford patted her shoulder gently. "What's your first name?"

When she didn't respond, he looked at Jim. "What's her first name?"

"Rosa."

Ford looked back down at the injured woman. "Rosa, it's going to be okay. We can find a way to get you out of here and we'll take you somewhere where they can make you feel better."

Rosa sobbed harder.

"Rosa, just calm down now." He was using his cop voice now. It was the voice of a man used to taking control and having people listen to what he said. Rosa wasn't listening. "Honey, if you don't settle down there's nothing we can do for you."

"There's nothing you can do anyway!" she wailed.

Ford plastered a fake smile across his face. "Why, of course there is. There are people that can help you."

His statement was so ludicrous that no one in the room believed it —not Rosa, not Jim, and not even Ford himself. His fake smile simply drilled that point home.

Seeing that she was getting nowhere with Ford, Rosa turned her eyes to Jim. "Can you shoot me?" she asked, choking out the words between bouts of sobbing. "You owe me that much. For history. For Charlie."

Jim's eyes got wide and he shook his head in a rapid, involuntary movement, as if he were trying to shake the idea from his head. He was instantly transported backwards in time to when he was in high school and his grandfather had practically asked the same thing. His grandfather, half-paralyzed by a stroke and facing a future of requiring personal care, would not accept that as his fate.

He had asked Jim to help him take his own life. Jim loved his grandfather and could also empathize with his plight. It was not about the law or about morality. It was about Jim and his grandfather. It was about Jim doing something important for a man who would have done anything for him. Jim retrieved the gun his grandfather asked for and smuggled it into the hospital. At some point later, his grandfather used that gun to take his own life. It was something Jim lived with his entire adult life, something he had learned to deal with on a daily basis. While there had been struggles with coping he never regretted his decision. Jim always hoped that if he found himself in that situation he would have someone close to him he could trust to provide that kind of assistance.

So, as revolting as the idea of shooting Rosa Fairlane was, Jim completely understood her motivation. Not taking his eyes off Ford, he said, "Rosa, tell Deputy Ford what happened to people who broke a hip when you were young."

Rosa struggled to speak, fighting the pain and her own desperate sobbing. "If they were my age, they laid in bed and waited to die. The bones never knitted together. They never walked again. They rotted as invalids, sometimes for decades, until death took them."

Deputy Ford looked at Jim as if Jim were undergoing some physical transformation that he could not make sense of. "Surely you're not considering what she's talking about? We can't do that. I can't do that! Breaking a hip is not a fatal injury."

"Maybe under these circumstances it *is* a fatal injury," Jim said.

Ford was livid. "I cannot sit here and watch you murder this woman."

"If you're thinking of arresting me, don't bother. I wasn't going to do it myself. I couldn't. But I could leave a gun and let her do it. And then I could give her a decent burial."

Ford pushed himself away from Jim and from Rosa. He reeled back, pushing himself with his feet until his back was resting against the wall. He shook his head wildly, muttering. The man was losing it.

"What would you have us do, Ford? You going to leave her here because you can't deal with it? Are you going to throw her over the back your horse and torture her with a ride back to the valley, listening to her scream hysterically the entire way? Are you going to put her on a sled and drag her home? If so, what are you going to do then?"

"Something. Anything."

"You saw what the sheriff just went through with his mother? You think you have some better option of how to treat the elderly and the mortally wounded? You have some solution that the sheriff wasn't aware of?"

Ford buried his face in his hands, rambling through his fingers. He stripped his hat off his head, shaking his head in anguish. He clenched his hands into fists, pulling at his own hair, unable to accept the situation. "What the FUCK!"

Rosa's moaning drew Jim's attention back to her. He touched her forearm and spoke softly to her. "If this deputy will let me, I will leave you a gun, but I cannot shoot you. You have to convince him, because he won't listen to me."

Ford's eyes flew to Jim's. "Listen, dammit, what she's asking for is *wrong*. It's against the law and against everything I've been taught as a law enforcement officer. Surely you can't expect me to be a part of this?"

Jim sighed. "I guess I don't really care if you're a part of it or not, but this is what she wants. I hope you won't try to stop it."

"I can't believe you're okay with this!" Ford erupted. "What kind of person *are* you?"

"I've been here before, Ford. I try to be a decent person. I may not always succeed. I'm pretty sure I fuck it up a lot, but I try to be a good person."

"Are you one of those *death angels*? Like those employees in the nursing homes who euthanize everybody they think no longer has any quality-of-life? Do you get off playing God?"

Jim shook his head and stared angrily at Ford. "It's not about me at all, but I can imagine what it would be like to be her right now. That a place you'd like to be? What if it was you laying there with a busted hip, no family, and praying you don't have to spend your life being a burden to someone else?"

Ford was silent.

"Put yourself in her shoes, Ford. Everyone you've known and loved in the world is dead. You've sustained an injury that will create a permanent, painful disability. Your freedom and your peace are gone forever. What would you want?"

Ford shoved himself to his feet and waved a finger at Jim. "You do what you have to do! You do what you can live with, but I won't be a part of it. I'm going on to the operations center and I'll meet you out in front of this house when I'm done."

Ford backed through the kitchen and left out the French doors. It hit Jim at that moment, the impact of the situation he'd put himself in again. He was awash with emotion at the decision he'd been forced to make as a teenager and the long term impacts that might have had on him as adult. He'd never considered it. He had done what he felt was right then and he still felt it was right now. A hand clasped his, pulling him back to the moment. He looked down to see Rosa's yellow-tinged eyes brimming with tears. He knew she was in tremendous pain, yet he couldn't help but think some of those tears were for him, an acknowledgment of the struggle he was going through.

"Thank you," she croaked.

Jim clasped his other hand over top of hers and held them for a moment. "What can I do for you?"

She struggled to swallow. "My daughter's bedroom is at the top of the stairs on the left. You'll know it because the walls are pink and the furniture is white. There's a picture on the nightstand of Charles, my daughter, and I. It was taken one summer when we went out west and it was the best time of my life. Would you bring that to me? I want to hold it."

Jim pushed himself up from the floor, fighting tears of his own, and went through the living room. In the foyer, he turned up the stairs. It was quite cold, and his breath clouded in front of his face as he ascended. He was aware that his squeaking shoes were damp and probably leaving water spots on the beautiful maple steps. Then it occurred to him it likely didn't matter. No one that loved this house and cared about these steps would ever be climbing them again.

At the top of the steps, a carved wooden ball the size of a cantaloupe sat atop the newel post. Its surface was worn smooth by the touch of so many hands that it barely appeared to be wood anymore, assuming instead the polished golden depth of amber or topaz. Unable to stop himself, Jim made the mistake of touching it. It was like being hit by lightning, the sudden awareness of how many lives it took for a piece of wood to become that polished.

He was profoundly moved by that awareness in a way he would never understand. He knew Charles Fairlane had installed those steps himself and he could imagine a younger Charles touching the fruit of his handiwork with deep pride. He imagined that same newel touched by the tentative fingers of a young woman coming up those steps for the first time as a bride and knowing that this was the house where she would raise her family. He sensed within it the trailing fingers of a child who could barely reach it when she moved into the room at the top of the stairs, both excited at having a room of her own yet terrified to be away from her parents. It contained the faith of a man who made this house his own but, ravaged by old age, depended on that newel to stabilize himself before he descended those stairs into the twilight of his very life.

Jim pulled himself away from the emotional wormhole and found the room he was looking for. Opening the door was like entering a fifty-year-old time castle and it was another gut punch to Jim, already reeling from the intensity of the moment. He had been in rooms like this before, left as monuments to the dead with nothing ever moved or changed. It was a tomb in every way except for containing a body. Jim tried to avoid taking in too many details of the room, simply focusing on getting the picture he was looking for and getting back out.

He entered the hall and closed the door behind him. That was when he heard the gunshot.

Jim flew down the steps and tore through the house. In the kitchen he found Rosa bleeding profusely through the gaping wound in the top of her skull. There was a clatter as her arm relaxed and hit the floor, dropping the gun. Jim took in a deep breath as he recognized a dull black Glock falling from her hand. It had to be Ford's gun. Either she'd pulled the gun from his holster or it had fallen out while they were in the floor helping her. In the end, he guessed it didn't really matter.

"Oh, Rosa," he sighed.

Jim found a heavy bedspread and carefully rolled Rosa's body into it, the picture she'd asked for placed on her chest. He did his best to avoid looking at her damaged head and distorted face. He selected a spot in the backyard for her grave. His first choice was by a tree but he knew there would be too many roots to deal with so he selected a spot in Mr. Fairlane's garden. The dirt was softer there and the digging easy. It was a place both she and Charles loved and spent many peaceful hours.

JIM WAS FILLING the muddy grave when Ford came walking around the corner of the house. Jim was muddy to his waist, struggling to toss shovelfuls of dirt back into the hole. He was still two feet shy of ground level and thick mud clung to the point of his shovel, making the work difficult. Jim regarded Ford without comment, then resumed his work. Ford noticed a mattock lying near the grave and used it to rake dirt into the grave.

They worked for several minutes before Jim broke the silence. "For what it's worth, I didn't do it."

Ford raised a hand to silence Jim. "I didn't ask."

"I know you didn't ask but I didn't want you wondering either. I've seen some hard things since this happened. I guess I've seen so much I've become numb to it and I assume everyone else is too."

Ford went back to raking clumps of mud into the hole. "I don't know what the fuck you've seen but I know I never want to see it."

Jim stopped shoveling for a moment, removed a glove, and reached behind his back. He retrieved the Glock that Rosa had shot herself with and extended it to Ford.

Ford immediately pawed at his holster and found the pistol missing. "Where did you find that?"

"I guess she either took it from your holster or it fell out while we were on the floor helping her. I was upstairs looking for a picture she asked for when I heard the shot."

Ford regarded his Glock with a disgusted look. Jim was certain the look reflected Ford's own disgust at losing his weapon. The pair continued to work in silence and shortly the hole was filled. Jim used the bottom of the shovel to pat the surface flat, then spread a little snow across the grave, wanting to camouflage the nature of the hole.

He stretched his back, dropped the shovel, and sat down on a concrete garden bench. "What did you find at the operations center?"

Ford stood nearby, leaning against a tree and staring at the grave. "The woman and her daughter were still there. I told them there was supposed to be an announcement about the power and that they would be able to find food and shelter at the fairgrounds."

"Did you tell them about the rules?"

Ford shook his head. "It doesn't matter. It's a starving mother and her half-starved child. She won't give a shit had about any conditions."

Ford was right. For some people it wouldn't matter.

"What about you, Ford? I've always assumed you'd stay with us but I never asked. You going to stay with us or move to the fairgrounds?"

"I've been a cop for a long time. Before I was a cop I served three years in the military. I can't imagine a world where I didn't have the right to defend myself. So for now, I'll stick with you guys see how this plays out."

"I'm glad to hear that, Ford."

Ford chuckled. "Really?"

Jim nodded seriously. "Yeah, I am. We need people like you."

Ford nodded toward the house. "I wasn't sure after that thing back there. I just haven't had to deal with many situations where my training didn't help out. There was nothing in my experience that told me what to do there. All I could see was my own mom or grandmother laying there and me not being able to do a damn thing about it."

"The training doesn't stop you from being human. Sometimes the irrational, emotional human part forces its way out."

"I noticed."

"I guess I'm getting more able to detach myself when I need to," Jim said.

"You might've made a good cop."

Jim laughed at shook his head. "I don't think so. For the most part I hate people."

"I've heard you say that before, but everything I've seen you do has been *for* people. I think you care about people more than you can admit."

Jim thought about that. "Maybe I like the people I know."

"Maybe. Or maybe you feel obligated to help people and that obligation is what you hate."

"If this is therapy, I'm not interested," Jim said. He looked toward Rosa's house. "Normally I'd want to go through that house from end to end. The only family she has left is a son in California and I don't know if he'll make it back here before vandals pick it clean. She's probably got all kinds of nice items from the old days that would be helpful to people without power."

Ford looked at the house and nodded. "You're too close. Maybe I could come back tomorrow and bring Gary and Randi. Or Will if Randi doesn't want to come. It would be easier for people who didn't know her."

"That's fine with me. I'm starting to feel the same way about town that Randi does. Every trip in brings something worse than the last time. I'm not sure it's worth it."

Before they left, Jim went back in the house with his pack while Ford watched the horses. He stopped on the porch and stared at his muddy boots, then took them off before continuing. He went inside and climbed the steps. At the top, he unscrewed the wooden ball from the newel post and slipped it inside his pack. He wasn't completely sure why he did it and perhaps he'd never mention it to anyone. Yet he knew beyond any doubt that it was the right thing to do. It was an act of preservation. An act of remembrance.

FROM THE FAIRLANE HOUSE, it took them a little less than an hour to get to the intersection where they turned off to Kyle's place. The first thing Jim noticed was that there was much more open pavement there. Several heavy trucks of some kind flattened the snow, making it melt much faster. From there, it took them less than thirty minutes to reach Kyle's driveway. Jim paused there, taking in the information at the scene presented to him. He was confused by the appearance of trucks in their community. He was immediately concerned that the military trucks may have ventured out in this direction.

"The trucks all turned here," Ford said.

"They did," Jim agreed. "Right up Kyle's driveway."

Jim didn't see that sitting there and speculating was helping them figure anything out so he nudged his horse toward Kyle's driveway. At the top of the steep incline he found a large parking area marked by more truck tracks. There also a lot of boot prints and they were different enough that it was clearly not Kyle.

"I don't get it," Jim said. "I guess they could be military trucks. Maybe they came to recruit Kyle to help with the power restoration."

Ford shook his head. "Nope. Not military. Wrong tread pattern."

Jim could see all the way to Kyle's cabin now and there were no trucks in sight anywhere. A tendril of smoke rose from the chimney. The cattle dogs, familiar now with Jim, looked wary but didn't growl.

"Stay here," Jim said. "His wife may be home alone and I don't want to spook her."

"Fair enough."

Jim nudged his horse into motion and it plodded down the muddy farm road toward the cabin. The trucks had not gone this far onto the farm. The snow was marked only by the traffic of human and animals. A muddy stream ran down each track of the farm road, water splashing from the horse's heavy steps.

Jim tied his horse off at the gate and called. Kim came to the door, a dishtowel in one hand, a pistol in the other. She was all smiles, which put Jim at ease. If Kyle had been kidnapped by the military, forced to go work on their project, she would not be this cheery.

"Hey, Jim, what's up?"

Jim smiled. "I was in town and thought I'd ride out here to see if Kyle had an opportunity to think about what we discussed."

"Did he ever. You know how he is. Once he got that on his mind he couldn't do much else. He goes from one obsession to the next. He already got a plan together and put it in action."

Jim was troubled by that news. He wished Kyle had not proceeded without discussing it with him. He especially didn't like the idea of those guys out there running around without a security detail to watch their backs while they worked. This needed to be a coordinated effort.

Jim didn't want to give Kyle's wife the impression that he was not excited about what Kyle was doing. Anyway, he was not so much displeased as concerned. He gestured back toward the driveway. "Does his plan have anything to do with all those tire tracks down there? How did he get access to power company trucks and the fuel to run them?"

She laughed. "Oh, those aren't power company trucks. Those are frozen food trucks from that distributor in the industrial park. They run on propane. Kyle and one of his buddies from the power company were able to get them running. I wish he'd thought of that earlier."

Jim was floored. He had never considered the idea of looking at who may have a propane fleet that might still have running trucks. He wished he'd thought of that earlier too. "It looks like he has several."

"Yeah, he's got a couple of trucks and a whole crew of men. They're working at the substation now. I don't know how late they intend to work he said not to worry about dinner and not to wait up on him."

"I guess he figured out a good place to make a connection to the high voltage transmission system?"

"One of the senior guys, Orfield, knew a good spot. It's up the road toward Belfast."

Jim's stomach sank at the news. Belfast was completely on the other side of the valley from where he was now. It could take him two or three hours to get back to the valley, then another three hours to ride to Belfast. By that time, the crew would probably be gone. There was no way Jim was going to catch up with them today.

"Can I give him a message?" Kim asked.

Jim shook his head. "I guess not. Just tell him to be careful. I may bring some people by there tomorrow to see if he needs any help. If nothing else, we can just keep an eye out while they work."

"Keep an eye out? You don't think they're in danger, do you?"

"No more than anybody else," Jim lied.

Anyone out there operating a vehicle now had a big target on their back. Jim would have felt a lot more comfortable if he had a heavily armed man in the passenger seat of each one of those trucks. If nothing else, the presence of an armed passenger might serve as a deterrent. They could talk about that tomorrow. Jim was concerned that Kyle might become so focused on getting the power back on that he lost track of maintaining security.

Jim said his goodbyes to Kim and the kids. He walked his horse back down the farm road where he relayed the story to Ford. Ford didn't know what to think about the whole mess. Most of his days were about right and wrong, rules and laws. He'd dealt with some crazy situations sometimes but this entire week had been a whole new level of crazy. He didn't know how he was ever going to return to normal life after this. In fact, he didn't know how any of them would.

21

When Boss initially seized the power plant it was a damn good time. He very much enjoyed it. Setting up the entire operation had been exciting and it was the type of fieldwork that he loved. As more people arrived, the honeymoon was soon over. The last couple of weeks his job had taken on the feel of an administrative and management function. It was like he was the regional manager of some bland company, like maybe a fast food franchise.

He knew his ability to function both as a field operative and a manager was why he was in this position to begin with. The folks in charge of the *realignment*, as they called it, needed people like him who could wear both hats. If he had a choice, he much preferred the life of a field operative. Today, he got to return to that role.

Yesterday he had recon teams running vehicle patrols throughout the area. The idea was for the men to familiarize themselves with the area, note any sizable inhabited compounds, and observe anything unusual. The patrols were a mix of foreign troops and Americans. Some of the Americans were military, some contractors, and some came from a federal law enforcement background. Most teams returned with similar reports of looted dwellings, hungry residents, and indications of violence. A mixed team of Americans and Turks had returned with photographs of tracks made by a convoy of heavy, dual-wheeled trucks. That piqued Boss's interest enough that he had to observe the tracks for himself. That meant a field day.

Boss was up before daylight and kitted out for going over the wire. As much he hated it, there were some management duties required before he could get out of office for the day. He hoped his impatience and irritation showed so people would keep their business brief. Even so, it was after 9 AM before he burst through the steel door to the parking lot where his team waited on him.

"Let's hit the road, gentlemen. This is going to be a fucking brilliant day."

Boss's vehicle was a custom job he brought in on the train, based on an Oshkosh L-ATV, or Light Combat Tactical All-Terrain Vehicle. There was a ring mount on the roof with an M240. His team also had a designated marksman carrying a Wilson Combat Super Sniper. The rest of the men, including Boss, carried FN MK16 CQCs.

Boss waved to the team that had found the tracks yesterday. There were two Americans and three Turks in an Otokar Cobra II painted United Nations white. "You take the lead," he told one of the Americans. "Stop at the point you pick up the tracks. I want to get a look at them before we obliterate them."

It took them about forty-five minutes to make their way from the power plant to the spot where the recon team picked up the tracks. Another day in the mid-40s was doing a good job of melting off the road but there was still slush and pockets of snow in the shady hollows of the road. In these steep mountains, there were many of those shady hollows.

When they picked up the truck tracks again, the Cobra II came to a stop. One of the Americans popped out of the side hatch and scanned the perimeter. He was in full load-out, complete with helmet and armor. Boss seemed to remember that the guy was with U.S. Customs. The doors opened on Boss's Oshkosh and his team climbed out, with the exception of the man on the M240.

Boss examined a set of tracks where one truck had turned tight against the shoulder. It was clearer than the other tracks, most of which ran over top of each other.

"Just going off the tires and the turning radius I'd guess that's a commercial vehicle," Boss said.

"And somehow they have enough fuel to run several of them," said his driver, a man named Kerry. He'd left Special Forces to come work for Boss. More action, less bullshit.

"Or it's a single vehicle that's been in and out a lot," Boss countered.

Kerry shrugged, testing the density of the snow with the tip of his boot. "Could be."

Back in the vehicle and following the tracks, Boss pulled a tablet from a pouch on his leg and studied a digital map of the area. "This is farming country, as far as I can see. No factories, no coal mines, no industry of any kind. There's no obvious reason for that much truck traffic, all things considered."

In a matter of moments they were at Kyle's driveway and the team of vehicles stopped again while Boss examined the tracks. "They've definitely been in and out of this driveway a few times but the tracks keep going. Whatever they did here, they didn't stay."

"Which way, Boss?" Kerry asked.

Boss climbed back into the Oshkosh and made a forward gesture with his hand. "Let's keep going. If we don't find anything we can always come back."

They continue to follow the truck tracks for another eighteen miles then turned onto a divided state road they followed for another five miles. With the snow melting, there was a short window of time where the trail would be visible. In another day or two they would be completely gone.

They'd been following the tracks for nearly an hour when they stopped at a four-lane highway. They walked around a major inter-section for several minutes, examining the utter carnage that had taken place there. There were bullet-riddled and burned out cars. What appeared to be human bones were scattered about around.

Boss picked one up and examined it. "Teeth marks. Likely a dog or coyote."

They confirmed the direction the trucks had travelled and got back on the road. Within another three miles, the tracks left the road, turning right onto a county road that led up a steep ridge. Boss constantly referred to his tablet, examining their surroundings and trying to see what lay ahead. This was new country for him. He'd studied the area around the power plants but nothing this far out, except in general terms.

"I'm still not seeing shit," he said.

They drove under a set of high-voltage transmission lines and a man in the back pointed them out. "Is that our power, Boss?"

"There's no power yet, but soon," he replied.

"You think those are our lines though? You think that's how our power is getting back east?"

Boss turned around and looked at the passenger. "I haven't memorized the whole damn grid. Don't be asking me stupid shit."

"Sorry," the man replied, embarrassed.

The road began to get steeper and Boss pulled out his tablet again. "I wonder where the hell they're going." It wasn't intended as a question, just a man with a lot on his mind processing out loud.

Boss scrolled around his tablet trying to figure out what those trucks might be doing in this area. His mapping software showed few houses. In fact, it showed very little at all when he expanded the range of his map. Most of the roads out in this area were dead ends. It was vast cattle country, with big blocks of grazing land that extended for hundreds or thousands of acres.

Then Boss saw a feature on the map he recognized, one he'd seen numerous times in his extensive study of the local power grid mapping. He zoomed in on the feature and squinted his eyes in disbelief. "No, they wouldn't do that."

"What was that, Boss?" Kerry asked.

Boss shook his head. "Nothing. Just thinking out loud."

22

Kyle was pleased with the early progress of his hastily-assembled crew. They'd done much better pulling wire than he had expected. In fact, he'd sent two trucks off the job to retrieve more wire in anticipation of another productive day. If all went well, they would have all the line stretched out on the ground by the end of the day. With things going well, they knocked off for an early lunch. The men had earned it. After lunch, they were sitting around lamenting the lack of tobacco products when they heard the distant rumble of vehicle engines straining as they climbed the steep road.

"Sounds like somebody has got another of the trucks running," one of the crew said.

Kyle and Orfield looked at each other. They didn't think it was one of the propane-fueled freezer trucks. No one else knew about those trucks. In fact, Kyle's first thought had been that Jim came up with a vehicle and fuel in order to come check their progress.

Kim had mentioned that Jim had come by the house. That made Kyle slightly guilty for just diving into the project without even telling Jim he was doing it. After all, it was Jim's project. He'd been the one that had come to Kyle. But to Kyle's way of thinking, why waste time on talking? It was better to just get to work. That was how things got done.

While Kyle's curiosity was piqued by the sound of the truck engines, there was also a nagging concern it could be somebody dangerous. He got up and retrieved his deer rifle from the back of one of the trucks, worked the bolt, and chambered a round. He lifted it to his eye and used the scope to scan the road.

"Oh shit," he mumbled on seeing the first of the military vehicles.

"What is it?" Orfield asked.

"Boys, it looks like the Army has done come to pay us a visit. There's a chance they may not approve of what we're doing."

"What are we gonna do?" asked one of the linemen.

Kyle shrugged and lowered the rifle. "I don't rightly know."

Orfield pointed to the tree line. "We could go take cover over yonder. I doubt those boys are interested in chasing us around these hills on foot."

"We do that, they might take our trucks," Kyle said. "We lose those trucks and tools we might as well throw in the towel."

"So you're fixing to take on the Army with that deer rifle?" Orfield asked. "All by yourself?"

Kyle smiled. "I intend to have this here deer rifle handy while I discuss our situation with the gentlemen from the military. Just for my own piece of mind, you see."

Orfield nodded, considering the situation. Kyle noticed a little distress on the older man's face.

"Orfield, you're practically retired. You're more than welcome to keep an eye on us from cover. We'll call you down when we run them off. Matter of fact, why don't *all* you boys go up there and take cover. It will be okay. I got this."

Orfield gave his old friend a bitter look. "Son, you got the gift of gab. Don't know as I've ever met anyone quite as gifted with gab as you. But I'll be staying here and facing the music with you. Wouldn't feel right to watch from the sidelines."

Kyle tried to convince Orfield to leave but he only succeeded in making matters worse. By the time Kyle gave up, all of his crew had made up their mind stay at his side. Whatever they had to face, they were going to face it together. They would be facing it soon too, since the two military vehicles had already turned onto the gravel road leading up to the substation and were approaching them cautiously.

Orfield pointed to the roof of the Oshkosh. "By God, there's a gun mount up there and a feller pointing a machine gun right at us."

"I see that," Kyle said. "We must look pretty mean from the road."

The Oshkosh approached to within thirty feet and a voice came across a loudspeaker. "Drop your weapons!"

Kyle did not raise his weapon in an aggressive manner but neither did he drop it.

"You drop yours and I'll drop mine!" he hollered back.

Kyle assumed they were behind all that armor and those tiny windows discussing his lack of cooperation but he couldn't tell what was going on. It wasn't long before teams spilled from both vehicles, weapons at high ready and aimed center-mass toward every one of the linemen.

"Don't even breathe," Kyle told his crew.

From what he could tell, the soldiers were not all part of one force. They were several different types of uniforms, no visible insignia, and no flags indicating nationality. The line of approaching men stopped at around fifteen yards, thoroughly covering Kyle's crew of linemen.

No one asked Kyle's crew to drop their weapons again. In fact, no one said a word at all, which made the entire event that much more terrifying. When the standoff had stretched way beyond the uncomfortable point, the passenger door on the Oshkosh opened and a man stepped out. He looked like he was military from the waist up but wore jeans and a pair of snow boots that did not look military issue. He carried a stubby rifle that Kyle didn't recognize but it looked like something from the movies. The man did not immediately acknowledge Kyle and his crew. He checked out their vehicles, their tools, and examined the task they were working on.

When the man had finished his thorough assessment of the

scene, he returned stood in front of the assembled lineman. "Who's in charge of this little group?"

He waited for a response. When none came, Boss tipped his FN toward the youngest of the linemen and dumped nearly a dozen rounds in the boy's chest, neck, and face. He was dead before he hit the ground. The other linemen were too shocked to react. It was also clear at this point that any reaction would likely get the rest of them killed.

"When I have to repeat myself, there's always a price to pay."

The group, particularly Kyle, stared in horror as their friend and coworker bled out in the slush. His name was Nick and he'd planned to get married last fall. They'd put the wedding on hold until the power came back on.

"Now, assuming you all remember the question, are you going to answer before I have to kill another of you fuckers?"

Kyle raised a hand, still unable to pull his eyes away from the dead man. He heard footprints moving toward him, sloshing through the snow. They stopped in front of him but still he didn't look.

"I don't talk to the side of a man's face. You can turn around or I'll turn you around," Boss warned.

Kyle had no intention of ignoring the man but apparently he didn't respond fast enough. Before he knew what was happening, there was a man on each side of him and he took a blow to the arm that numbed it entirely. His gun dropped involuntarily from his hand. One of the men behind him kicked the back of his knees and he dropped to the damp ground. The same put a gloved hand on each side of his face, roughly tilted it up, and made him face the murderer.

"My name's Boss," the murderer said. "No need trying to commit that to memory because you're not going to live long enough for that to matter."

Kyle gave the man his full attention but had no response for what he had been told.

"Now what the hell do you boys think you're doing up here? You aren't trying to steal some of my power, are you?"

Kyle wanted to kill this man with his bare hands. "I reckon we have more right to it than you do," he responded.

Boss smiled. "You'd be wrong about that, shitbird."

"I've worked in this industry all my life. Our people work at that power plant. Our people dig the coal that feeds that plant."

Boss shook his head as if humoring a child. "Being a worker bee doesn't mean you own the honey. I'm the farmer here to take the honey and if you challenge me, you'll get crushed."

Kyle could not believe this was happening. An hour ago they'd nearly been enjoying themselves. It had almost started to feel like any old day on the job before the world fell apart. For a little while they'd been able to forget the trouble, the sadness, and the hunger.

"So what was your little plan here?" Boss asked, looking around the substation.

"We were going to steal a little juice from the high voltage lines," Kyle said. "It wouldn't have been enough to cause you any problems. You'd probably never have even noticed."

Any trace of humor left Boss's face. "There's where you're wrong. Now everyone you wrangled into this little plan of yours is a liability. You're like a bunch of cattle with mad cow disease and I've got to deal with it."

Kyle's shock was beginning to wear off and the seriousness of this whole episode was settling over him. They were going to be killed. "If you have to teach somebody a lesson, teach it to me," Kyle said. "Let these boys go. It was all my idea."

Boss shook his head. "I appreciate you trying to be chivalrous but it doesn't mean shit to me. I got bigger things to deal with and this is just a waste of my fucking time."

"Please," Kyle begged.

Boss turned his back on Kyle and spoke to his men. "We need to make an impression here, boys. I want people to be scared to ever try this again. Let's make it memorable."

23

J im and his team headed out early for what he thought would be a three-hour ride to the substation where they suspected Kyle might be working. Since it was a good distance from home by walking or horseback, Jim wanted to take folks who were capable of a fight if it came to that. He had no idea what was taking place in that part of the county. It might as well have been a different state.

He recruited his friend Gary, who'd walked all the way home with him from Richmond. Gary had been keeping a low profile lately. His large extended family was living in a home that had once belonged to Henry, one of Jim's friends and neighbors. The small ranch house was busting at the seams and Gary was working to ready another nearby home for his daughter and her husband Will. The two would still be close by but the split would make conditions a little more tolerable in Gary's house.

Since they were not returning to town, the scene of Buddy's death, Randi was up for the trip. Jim raised Hugh on the walkie-talkie and he agreed to go also. Gary had a set of body armor he could wear on the trip. Ford had outfitted Hugh and Jim each with a set from gear he found at the emergency operations center. Before they left the valley that morning, the entire entourage stopped by Ford's house and he outfitted Randi with a set as well. Jim felt a little better with everybody armored up but in truth there was a whole lot of body sticking out on all sides of that armor plate. Catching a bullet in an arm or leg was no picnic in the best of times. It could be a death sentence under these conditions.

Jim had a rough idea of where the substation was. It sat on the shoulder of the same mountain range he lived on, a few miles further north. The good news was that reaching the substation from his valley required no travel at all on paved roads. They could take short-cuts through vast cattle pastures. When they reached the higher elevations, they could follow dirt and gravel roads that cut through sparsely populated communities.

The bad news was it was entirely possible the residents of those communities may treat visitors the same way Jim and his neighbors did. It would not surprise him at all to find roads blocked and cut off to outside traffic. Hell, Jim had gone as far as to blow a road up to prevent folks from traveling it. If he encountered a situation like that, he would have to backtrack and hope they could find a way around.

When they reached the higher mountain communities, Jim was pleasantly surprised to see people generally ignored them, making him wonder if the residents were accustomed to folks on horseback moving around. It was a good sign. Maybe these people were weathering the hard times with the same resiliency Jim and his neighbors had demonstrated.

Seeing people made Jim feel very exposed on the open road. He would not have been surprised at any moment to hear the crack of a rifle firing a warning shot, or worse, in their direction. The roads changed from asphalt to gravel as they went higher on the shoulder of the mountain and soon they reached their destination. It sat off the road in dense woods but the oaks, maples, and poplars were bare this time of year. Had it been summer and the trees fully leafed out, they may have ridden right by it.

A flat gravel pad had been bulldozed into the side of the mountain and hundreds of tons of gravel scattered to create the site. A wide gravel road wound its way up to the site. The road was still snow-covered at this elevation and overlapping tire tracks laced their way up the road. This had to be the place.

Jim spotted vehicles but heard nothing. He didn't know the work style of these linemen. Maybe they all had their heads down working hard and didn't have time for chatter. While he was trying to spot the crew, Hugh paused his horse and whipped up his rifle. The sudden motion caused Jim to grab his own.

"What is it? You see something?" Jim asked.

Everyone else immediately went on guard, shifting their horses to make sure all directions were covered. When Hugh whipped his rifle in a different direction, still without saying a word, Jim finally raised his own and began scanning the substation with his optic. Even with the low power optic he was able to spot what had caught Hugh's attention.

"Oh shit," Jim groaned. "Oh shit."

Jim slid off his horse and started tying it off to a bush.

"I'll take him," Randi said, extending a hand for Jim's reins.

Gary and Hugh were right behind him, handing over the reins to Randi and hurrying to catch Jim. He was on high alert but moving quickly toward the trucks. They had to run to catch up.

"What did you see?" Gary puffed. He was running a red dot with no magnification on his rifle and hadn't been able to pick up what all the fuss was about.

"Bodies," Hugh muttered.

They moved steadily to the rear-most freezer truck, the first cover available to them. Several of the freezer compartment doors were open and various electrical tools hung out of them. Hugh signaled he would take the right side of the vehicle while Jim and Gary should move up the left side.

Once past the front of the vehicle, they used the same approach to move around the next. Beyond that truck it became a struggle to remain vigilant while also taking in the macabre scene they found before them. The bizarre sight that originally got Hugh's attention from the road and was unavoidable, as well as incomprehensible, at this distance. The bodies of the crew hung from the wooden utility poles erected around the jobsite. Somehow, whoever had done this vile act strapped each man to the pole by wrapping his own lineman's belt around his neck.

Jim looked from man to man but did not see anyone that he recognized, particularly Kyle. He had to have been here when this happened. Perhaps he lay dead somewhere else on the site. Worse yet, perhaps they took him with them.

"Jesus, they're all missing their hands," Gary said.

While nobody had noticed that detail until Gary pointed it out, it was true. Each man's hands had been cut off at the wrist.

"Why the fuck would somebody do that?" Jim asked.

"It's an ancient message," Hugh said. "In its simplest form it means *hands off*. It means someone tried to steal or take something that wasn't theirs."

"None of these men are Kyle," Jim said. "We need to find him."

"The hands," Gary said, pointing ahead of them. On the ground was a canvas lineman's bucket with a rope handle, the type the men used for raising tools up and down on a rope. It was heaped high with the severed hands of the dead linemen.

Jim shook his head. "Those fuckers."

Hugh brushed close to the fender of one of the trucks and snagged the sleeve of his coat on a jagged curl of metal. That was when he noticed the bullet holes riddling the engine compartment of the vehicle. "They shot up the trucks."

The group hurriedly examined each of the freezer trucks and found that a burst of full auto fire from a large caliber weapon had destroyed each engine. Even if they were repairable, it wasn't likely they would be able to find the parts to do it. Jim shook his head in disgust.

When they rounded the front of the last truck, Hugh found a man zip-tied in a seated position with his back against the front bumper. His clothes were blood-soaked and his face battered. "I've got another body."

Jim rushed over. "It's Kyle!" He propped his gun up against the truck and checked his friend's neck for a pulse.

"He's alive," Jim said.

Kyle's wrists were zip-tied to the bumper as if he had been crucified. Another, tightly strapped around his neck, forced him to keep his head back.

"They made him watch," Hugh said. "I've seen that before. They strapped him there and made him watch."

Kyle had been severely beaten and the zip tie around his neck had restricted his breathing. Had he completely lost consciousness, he'd likely be dead. While Hugh held Kyle's head, Jim sliced away the thick zip tie that held his neck to the grille of the truck. He then sliced the ties holding each wrist and Kyle collapsed against Hugh.

Jim knelt beside his old friend and rolled him over onto his back. Kyle was semi-conscious and mumbling incoherently. Jim ripped open the Velcro strap on his belt, pulling a water bottle from a pouch. He put a hand under Kyle's head and elevated it slightly, pouring some of the water between his lips.

The water immediately came back up in a spray of bloody vomit.

"Get Randi up here!" Jim said.

Hugh called to her.

"What happened?" Jim asked

Kyle's eyes fluttered open and words came out they made no sense.

"He's probably in shock," Gary said. "Who wouldn't be if they had to watch something like this?"

Randi reached them, handing the horses over to Gary.

"Let's get him out of the snow," she said. "He's probably close to hypothermic."

Jim grabbed one arm, Hugh the other, and they lifted Kyle. As they did, his flannel shirt fell open, exposing a belly covered in streaks of blood and deep scratches.

"What the fuck?" Hugh spat.

"Did they torture him?" Randi asked.

No one answered. No one knew.

Hugh, in a better vantage point to see the wounds, spoke up. "No, it's writing."

A plastic tarp was laid out to the side of one of the trucks, providing a dry spot for the linemen to sit and eat their lunch. They stretched Kyle out on the tarp and Jim immediately threw his shirt back to read the writing.

In scabbed, scratchy letters, the statement was carved into Kyle's flesh: *Don't make us come back.*

"Those bastards," Jim mumbled. He got up and went to his horse. He had a bivy sack there. They needed to warm Kyle up.

Everyone had blowout or trauma kit somewhere in their gear but no one carried a comprehensive first-aid kit in their Go Bags. The pooled their resources while Randi tried to get another drink of water down him. This one came up as bloody vomit, same as the other.

Randi gave up on the water, instead checking Kyle's wounds. Despite the volume of blood, none of it appeared to be from life-threatening injuries. It was mostly from cuts, torn skin, and his broken nose. There were nasty bruises, some of the worst she'd ever seen outside of a car accident.

When Jim got back with the bivy sack, they stretched it over Kyle.

"Can you understand me?" Randi asked the injured man.

Kyle gave an erratic nod.

"I want you to take another drink but I don't want you to swallow it. Just rinse your mouth out and let's try to get some of that blood washed out of there."

She and Jim helped Kyle lean his head up and she tipped a water bottle to his mouth. He followed her directions, rinsing his mouth out and then spitting. As he did it, she saw that two teeth had been broken off at gum-level. Both his tongue and the inside of his lip were also split.

"Those sons-of-bitches," Kyle mumbled hoarsely. With his nose broken and swollen shut, his throat was probably dry from having to breathe through his mouth.

"Let's just focus on you right now. Where are you hurting?" Randi said.

"Arm. Ribs."

"Is that all?" Kyle's eyes fluttered and he winced. "Nuts," he groaned.

Randi furrowed her brow. "Do you have a groin injury?"

Kyle nodded.

"Hit? Kick? What?"

"One solid kick in the balls," Kyle said sheepishly. "I think it was just one."

Randi turned to the men standing behind her. "Hugh, I need you to find some type of bag you can pack with snow to make a cold compress. We don't have a catheter and we need to make sure the swelling doesn't cut off the flow of urine."

"Roger," Hugh said.

Randi turned back to her patient. "I know it's chilly but can I get your shirt off of you for a second? I want to check your wounds."

"Okay," Kyle muttered.

"Jim, let's sit him fully up. We'll probably need to help him slide his shirt off."

They both placed arms beneath Kyle and eased him into a seated position. Seeing Kyle's expression, the wincing at the movement, made Jim think that he probably did have some broken ribs. They slid his shirt off and Randi examined his arm, prodding it gently with her fingers. The bruising she found made her think a fracture was likely but it didn't feel displaced.

She examined the bruising on his torso and traced his ribs, determining that two may be cracked. With Jim's help, she laid him back and probed his abdomen but found nothing to indicate internal injuries. Without access to advanced diagnostic tools or a skilled trauma physician, there were still a lot of things she could be missing.

Hugh found a wide roll of electrical tape on one of the trucks and they used it to wrap Kyle's ribs. They helped him dress, putting his gore encrusted shirt back because they had nothing else, and then putting his coat on over that. Hugh and Gary helped him to his feet, then held his arm long enough to make certain he was not going to pass out when they had him standing.

Maybe the pain of standing acted as a stimulant, but he seemed more alert now. He regarded the bodies of his friends and crewmembers. "They made me watch. They said they were leaving me alive to tell the story."

"Who?" Jim asked. "Who did this?"

"They looked military, but maybe not our military. Some of them were speaking a foreign language."

Jim shook his head with disgust and looked at Hugh. "It has to be those bastards from the power plant. It has to be."

Kyle nodded. "They said something like that. They said the power was theirs, that we had no right to be messing with it."

Jim paced angrily. He needed something to do, somebody to kill. Somebody needed to pay for this. He waved desperately at the bodies and looked at the people around them. "Is there any way we can at least get them down? Can we even get them down to bury them?"

Kyle's eyes filled with tears. "They destroyed our gear. I don't know how you get up there without it. The damn pole is covered in splinters and would eat you alive if you tried to climb it."

Jim studied the pole and saw that Kyle was right. With a belt and spurs he may have been able to do it but without the proper gear it was a recipe for disaster.

Over his outburst, Jim faced his people. He'd choked down the emotion now and made it work for him. He was in his cold, calculating place. The place he went when determining how to make men die.

"We have to make them pay," Jim said. "There's no other way. This is not something we live with."

"We don't fully know their capabilities," Hugh said. "We've seen a lot of vehicles and a few mixed troops, but they could have access to gunships. They could have all kinds of missile and drone capabilities that could reduce this valley to a scorched hole."

Jim stared back at Hugh, his face a mask of determination and cold hatred. "All that tells me is that we can't get in a protracted war with these people. If we strike first and we strike hard enough we could put a serious dent in their effectiveness."

"Won't they just send more people if we attack?" Gary asked. "I'm also wondering about the consequences if they track this back to us. If they do, we're all dead."

"They're only here for one reason and that's because we can generate power. If we take away their ability to produce power I would venture that this whole thing goes away. They're not going to take the time to rebuild that plant right now. They'll just move somewhere else."

"Let me get this straight. You're talking about taking out the power plant?" Kyle asked. "Aren't we just cutting off our nose to spite our face? If we lose that power plant it could be decades before we get power back here again. I want to make them pay too, but I don't know about taking out the plant."

Jim shrugged. "It might be worth the trade, because I'm not living with an occupying army that does shit like this." He stabbed a finger at the bodies for emphasis.

Kyle sighed. "Then I'm with you. I kind of feel like some of this is my fault. We just jumped on this without even talking to you. If you hadn't come looking for me, I would have died right there on the bumper of that truck. I don't know what would happen to my family then. I feel an obligation to avenge these guys because I asked each and every one of them to be here."

"Every man makes his own choices in life," Jim said wisely. "It could just as easily be my fault for coming to your house and bringing this whole thing up in the first place. Maybe I should have just kept my mouth shut."

"Then let's make it right," Kyle said.

"If we do this, it *better* be right," Gary insisted. "There may only be one shot. If it fails, everyone in the valley may pay the price."

24

A fter leaving the substation, Jim's entire group headed back to the valley. It was a long ride back to Kyle's house and the valley was the halfway point. Randi and Gary had to double up on a horse to make room for Kyle. The injured man held up well despite his injuries, but occasional grunts of pain escaped him when the horse took a misstep on the slick ground. The three hour ride took nearly four and a half hours, putting them back in the valley just as the sun was setting over the patchy white earth.

They turned their horses over to Pete and Charlie. Gary headed home to check on his own family, while Randi took Kyle into Jim's house to better tend his wounds. Hugh stuck around because he didn't want to miss anything. When the group entered the house, Nana took Ariel to a back room so she wouldn't have to see Kyle's injuries and overhear any discussion. Pops stuck around to hear the story of what had taken place.

They assisted Kyle with removing his shirt and Randi cleaned his injuries with rubbing alcohol and applied a topical antibiotic to the cuts and scratches. She didn't re-tape his ribs because the electrical tape seemed to be adhering well.

"Where's the bag of snow I gave you for your groin?" Randi asked.

"It melted," Kyle said.

"Hugh, go get him another one, please."

Hugh did as he was asked.

"I'm serious about this," Randi said. "Keep that in place as long as you can. You do not want the swelling to shut off the flow. That's a painful death."

"It's going to be just as bad if the pipes freeze," Kyle said. "That snow is cold. I'm completely numb."

"You'll be fine," Randi said. "You're not going to freeze with those clothes on. It should be just the right amount of cold."

Kyle looked doubtful.

Pete stuck his head through the front door. "Dad, that guy from the barn is here."

Jim frowned. He'd forgotten about those guys.

"I think their supply drop is supposed to be tonight," Hugh said. "They're supposed to be bringing the supplies we asked for."

Jim nodded. "I'll go see what he wants."

Pete held the door open for his dad while Jim slipped on his snow boots. He strode out to the porch where he found Scott waiting for him on the steps. Scott had found the one step that was free of snow and dried from the day's sunlight. Jim's ass had not adjusted to all the horseback riding. He was too sore to sit. He walked stiffly down the steps and faced the seated man.

Pete continued to hang out on the porch.

"Are you done with the horses?" Jim asked his son.

Pete scowled and shook his head. "No." He clearly wanted to eavesdrop.

"Then get to it."

When Pete was gone, Jim returned his gaze Scott. "Sorry about that. What can I do for you?"

"It's okay, I've got kids. I know how they are. Anyway, we noticed you guys traveling by the barn earlier. I know it's none of my business but it looked like you might have an injured man. I was curious what kind of trouble you ran into. If our gear gets here tonight, we're going to head out of here in the morning. I'd like to know what I might be dealing with."

Jim's stomach knotted at the memory of what Scott and his people might be dealing with. "The injured guy is my friend Kyle. I've known him a long time. He works–*worked*—for the power company and we had been talking about a plan of how we might redirect some of that grid power to our own community when it was restored. Kyle went ahead and implemented the plan without letting me know, so he didn't have any security in place. Somehow the guys from the power plant tracked him down and decided to send us a message."

"What kind of message?"

"They tied Kyle to a bumper and made him watch while they killed his entire crew. They cut off their hands and left them in a bucket for us. Then they hung those men from the utility poles. They're still there. We didn't have any way to get them down."

Scott shook his head bitterly. "Jesus."

"Yeah, no kidding. It was messed up even by current standards."

"I think your guy ran across someone known as Boss," Scott said.

"The boss?"

Scott shook his head. "Not *the* boss, just Boss. It's his name, call sign, or codename. Nobody seems to know for sure, but that's how everybody knows him."

"What the fuck is he?" Jim asked. "CIA? Military?"

Scott shook his head. "You remember Ollie North?"

"Of course," Jim said. "That whole Iran-Contra thing."

Scott nodded. "This guy operates at that same level. He's a one of those shadow government guys who makes things happen. I don't know who he works for but he's good at what he does. He's not the only guy like that running around loose either. There are people taking advantage of this disaster to realign the country and they've pulled out all the stops, bringing out every nasty bastard they can find. They've built a whole army of crooked operators, greedy mercenaries, fixers, and private security. They've turned over every rock and hired everything that crawled out from under it."

"So where does this guy's allegiance lie? He can't be a patriot and do what he's doing."

Scott shrugged. "I'm not sure he has any allegiance, other than to whomever is putting the gold in his pocket on any given day."

Jim nodded slowly, processing all of that information. "Well I don't give a fuck who he is. Boss needs to die."

Scott couldn't stop an outburst of laughter. "You know how many people probably said that same damn thing? There are dozens of people on every continent who have tried to make that happen yet he's still out there walking around. If it was that easy he'd be dead already."

"Yeah, I get that but it doesn't change the fact that he needs to be taken out."

Scott shook his head, incredulous. "Are you dumb or just have a death wish?"

"Neither. I'm a dad. I'm a husband. Sometimes I'm an asshole."

"You know you're significantly outmanned and outgunned, right? These are soldiers. They may not be American soldiers but they're still trained soldiers with weapons *and* the backing of the U.S. government."

"They have the backing of this globalist faction that's trying to pretend they're the U.S. government," Jim said. "That doesn't mean they're my government. There are times the government doesn't represent the people or their best interests. This is one of them."

"Look, I'm not saying I disagree with you," Scott said. "I'm just saying you can't butt heads with this guy and come out of it. This dude could come through here and kill every man, woman, and child, and no one could lay a finger on him."

Jim shook his head bitterly. This pissed him off on all levels. He hated bullies. "What about these people that are backing you? Where are they in all of this? Why can't they just launch a drone strike on the power plants and take that asshole out?"

"I don't think that will happen. As ridiculous as this may sound, they're trying to do this without it turning into full-out civil war. It's on the cusp of happening, but it won't be good for anyone. Right now this is just a political battle and they'd prefer to keep it that way."

"It's not just political here," Jim spat. "They hung these men and cut off their hands."

"Yeah, but it's political in the beltway. Even if those guys are operating under generator power in lockdown conditions, it's still D.C. I'm not sure they get all the details of what's happening in the field. Then there's the concern over the infrastructure."

"What?"

"The infrastructure. The plants. I think they want to protect the plants."

Jim was floored. "So they won't take him out if they think there's a risk of damaging the plants?"

Scott nodded.

"I don't give a fuck about power plants," Jim said. "I would take them out tomorrow if I could send that asshole up with them."

"Think about what you're saying," Scott warned. "How long do you think it will be before any more power plants are built? If you destroy a plant, it could be a decade before power is restored here."

Jim mulled that over. "So if I opt for the convenience of power, then I have to give up everything else? Self-respect, security, and freedom?"

"That's basically it," Scott said.

"That's no fucking choice," Jim said.

Scott stood. "It's a bitter pill. Just don't do anything rash. The effects can be far-reaching and they don't only impact you."

Jim didn't respond. He was looking off toward the orange sky of late evening, thinking.

"The announcement is supposed to start running tonight," Scott said. "That's what they told us when we radioed for the supply drop. Six PM, just like the evening news. You should try to listen."

"We'll see," Jim said, starting back up the steps.

"I'll talk to you later," Scott said, heading across the yard.

"Scott!" Jim called from the porch. "You've never said where your allegiances lie. What do you choose? Is it freedom or security? I mean, you're here representing someone who has different interests than whoever is taking over the plants you're trying to talk me out of destroying."

Scott stopped and turned back to Jim. "I never said I was against destroying the plant. I just want to make sure you fully understand the ramifications. Besides, it's not like you have artillery at your disposal, and that's about what it would take."

Jim considered what he said, then went back inside. He returned to the living room where he found Kyle bandaged up and dressed. He was warming himself by the fire and discussing the logistics of restarting a coal-fired power plant with Pops.

"There's so many moving parts to a coal plant," Kyle said. "You have to have coal trucks, drivers, fuel for the coal trucks, and a system for getting the coal from the trucks into the plants. That usually involves more men and more machines."

"They should have gone hydroelectric like everybody else was doing," Pops said. "But all the talk around here was about coal jobs and what those jobs would do for the region. They were right. Those coal jobs did prop up the economy for several years. It wasn't all to support our power plants, of course, but those plants helped."

"Did they ever seriously consider hydroelectric power?" Jim asked.

"Sure," Pops said. "At one time they talked about putting in a pump station where water would be pumped up to Hidden Valley Lake at night when demand was low and then run down through a hydroelectric plant during the day when the demand was higher. Local residents threw a fit about that and it died on the vine."

"What about a dam and a lake?" Jim asked. "It would've been nice to have grown up with a lake around."

"Oh, they talked about that, back in the 1950s and 1960s. They even did a big study about how they could dam the Clinch River. They looked at who would be flooded and how big the lake would be and all that. Those plans got scuttled because it would take away coal jobs."

"Where were they going to build the dam?" Kyle asked.

Pops pointed like that would instantly explain where they were talking about. "There's a gorge down in Wise County where the river goes through a narrow channel. The plan was to put a dam in there. The whole area where the power plant is now as well as the surrounding towns would be on the bottom of a lake."

With those words, an idea struck Jim with such ferocity it was like an explosion took place in his head. It was a staggering aneurism of awareness. He suddenly knew how to make a lot of things happen, but he would need some help.

JIM SENT Pete and Charlie around to let the families of the valley know about the announcement on the radio. They carried hand-written invitations put together by Ellen and Ariel. It was probably the biggest social gathering in the valley since the terror attacks took place. Certainly since winter arrived, people were getting out less. They were all invited to come to Jim's barn and listen together with the others if they were interested. Jim had a fire pit at the barn and an old pot-bellied stove inside that would provide a little heat for people standing close to them.

Jim wasn't sure what other families knew and he wanted to gauge their reactions to the idea of comfort camps. He wanted them to know what happened to Kyle and his crew though. He wanted their support in coming up with a plan to deal with these invaders. He hoped to find a way to help them decide that occupying this region of the Appalachian Mountains was not worth it.

Kyle was bandaged up and dressed but accepted Jim's offer to stay long enough to listen to the broadcast with them.

"After that, I've got to get on home," he said.

"That's no problem," Jim said. "I'll either send someone with you or I'll go myself."

"That ain't necessary," Kyle protested. "I can bring the horse back tomorrow."

"It's not about the horse. It's about getting you home in one piece."

"I appreciate that, my friend."

Jim shrugged. "Not a problem. You sit down and take it easy until then. Stay close to the fire and rest."

"That ain't easy for me to do. I'm a doer not a rester."

With Kyle situated, Randi returned home to check on her family while Hugh and Jim made preparations for the event at the barn. Jim found a couple of radios that had emergency bands on them. Hugh verified they all had signal from the barn.

They started a fire. Having a nice bed of coal by the time guests started showing up would help keep everyone warm. Jim kept a pile of bonfire wood beside the log yard where he split firewood. The bonfire wood was those pieces that were difficult to split by hand. When he had a gas-powered hydraulic log splitter he could split about anything. That was not the case now. Pieces of wood with twisty grains were a waste of energy when they failed to split after several blows of the maul. He tossed those aside for outdoor fires.

Hugh, never one to miss an opportunity to hone his bushcraft skills, whipped out his fire-making kit and went to work. In a short time, he had a strong fire going from a ferro rod and Vaseline-soaked cotton balls. He added kindling that Jim stored in an old camper top sitting on four cinder blocks, then bigger wood stored beneath ratty, frayed tarps.

It wasn't long before Lloyd showed up. Randi, who had left to visit her family, somehow mysteriously arrived at the same time. Lloyd was dressed in a vintage German officer's coat that came down to his ankles and carried his banjo slung around his back on a length of brown twine. He had on a furry trapper's hat and looked like someone that might stagger into a remote Alaskan village demanding a shot of vodka. Lloyd took a seat on a maple stump by the fire and removed two jars from beneath his coat. Despite the clarity, Jim suspected it was not water.

Lloyd made small talk for a few minutes then was drawn into the strings of his banjo. His playing had comprised the background of so many social gatherings since his arrival in the valley. It harkened back to a time before radio, before television, and before constant noise.

After Lloyd, more showed up. All of the Wimmers, except for the children and one adult left to watch them, came in a line that stretched off into the darkness of the night. Gary and his family came. The Weathermans, the Birds, Randi's daughters, and all the generations of Jim's people.

They talked and stood close to a bonfire that burned twice the height of a man. Inside the barn, the pot-bellied stove glowed cherry-red and the older folks sat around it in the odd assortment of chairs that found their way to the barn. Hugh lingered on the fringes of the crowd, listening to the radio and waiting for the announcement they'd been told to expect.

Then it came.

"Hey! Pipe down!" Hugh bellowed.

He cranked the radio volume up, then ran into the barn and did the same, letting them know the announcement they'd been waiting for was starting.

All sound fell away except for the crackling of the fire. The voice that came over the radio was a generic announcer's voice, not immediately recognizable as anyone in particular. Not a celebrity, not a government official. The voice conveyed reassurance and unquestionable honesty. It was a voice you could not help but believe.

Unless you knew the truth behind those words.

Jim wondered how many people would listen with unconditional trust and comply with every element of the government's demands. The answer to that question could well determine the fate of the Republic.

"...comfort, safety, and security of our citizens is the primary concern of the United States government. Over the last several months, diligent efforts have been underway to restore power. Multidisciplinary teams have been working to troubleshoot the electrical infrastructure, get power plants up and running, and determine the most efficient manner in which to distribute electrical power to the citizens of the United States of America.

"Unfortunately, restoration of power is not so simple as just flipping a switch and sending power back to all the areas that previously had power. It has been determined recovery shall take place in the following manner.

Power will initially be restored to specific facilities and institutions which are determined to be critical to the recovery effort. Reestablishment teams have also been hard at work building comfort camps in regions throughout the country. Beginning tomorrow, maps, flyers, and leaflets will be distributed in the county seat of all counties affected by this disaster. Those leaflets will explain the details of what a comfort camp is, will include directions to your regional comfort camp, and will include instructions for admission.

"Please be aware that the primary criteria for admission into any comfort camp is the surrendering of any and all firearms possessed by the person seeking entry into the camp. Federal and retail databases will be checked by Recovery Team personnel to ensure the honest compliance of each citizen seeking entry. For the safety of individuals residing in comfort camps, these facilities will be isolated from any outside interaction. Once you have entered the camp, you will not be allowed to leave unless you choose to do so permanently. There will also be no visitation between the residents of comfort camps and those residing outside in the community at large."

The announcer's voice took on a placating tone. *"You can be assured that there is no state of martial law, nor is this an effort to take away your Second Amendment rights. The voluntary surrendering of personal firearms is simply an attempt to quell the widespread violence that has been taking place since the initial terror attacks occurred. The only way the United States can move safely forward is to get a handle on violence and make this country safe again.*

"American citizens should know that distribution of the written materials about comfort camps is such a vast effort that it could not be conducted alone by U.S. forces. A NATO relief effort is currently being undertaken in the United States to assist us with national recovery. Foreign troops should be afforded the same respect and authority as American troops. Should persons fail to comply with this directive, please understand that NATO troops have the authority to arrest or kill to carry out their mission."

25

Before the gathering at the barn even wore down, Jim built a fire in the stove of his woodshop and threw together an impromptu table out of sawhorses and plywood. As people began to wander off, Jim spoke to a few to gauge their reaction to the announcement. He'd been with these folks long enough to think he knew how they would respond but you could never be certain. Like with his own mother, there were people who would choose the comfort and ease of a life with electricity to the alternative. Jim had no name for that alternative originally but had decided that very night to refer to it as *dark freedom*. It was the choice to keep your rights in exchange for not receiving electrical power. He was comfortable with the choice.

Jim invited Scott, Hugh, Ford, Randi, and Gary to stay for a discussion in the woodshop. Kyle stayed for the announcement but was clearly exhausted. Jim tried to send him home several times but he didn't want to go until he heard the discussion that was going to take place. He wanted to be a part of it. He wanted revenge.

Weatherman and Bird were also recruited, simply for the purpose of discussing the plan. If they heard it and wanted out, they were free to go with no judgment and no hard feelings. The shop was toasty warm by the time everyone gathered there, taking whatever seats they could find. Despite the long day, Jim was too amped-up to sit.

He spread out a regional map on the plywood table and set a heavy structural steel bolt down on each corner to hold it flat. "First, I just want to know how many of you think that government announcement was bullshit?" he asked. "I can understand the need to prioritize power restoration as part of a national recovery effort but what I cannot abide is tying power restoration to disarming the population. This goes way beyond turning the lights back on."

It was clear there was a consensus in the room, giving Jim the impetus to proceed.

"Then I want you all to hear an idea. I know it's probably bat-shit crazy, but I need you to listen. There's a whole multitude of reasons why we need those people occupying the power plant out of here. It's not just what they did to Kyle's crew. If they're that kind of people, we don't need them here. We either need to make them leave and not want to come back, or we need to kill as much of the crew as we can so they can't come back."

Jim let that last part sink in. This would be an ugly job, however it went down. There would be killing, and likely death, on both sides of the fence.

"I've been trying to think of a way we could run them out of here without putting ourselves at risk. The last thing I want is to bring any more pain and destruction into this valley. These guys are seriously armed so we can't go toe-to-toe with them in battle. We're not trained or armed for that and they are. We *can* outsmart them, and I think I may have come up with the way to do it."

Jim looked around for comments or questions, finding none. They were intently listening, wanting to know what he had up his sleeve. He nodded in Kyle's direction.

"For those of you who don't know, that's my friend Kyle. He and I went to high school together and he worked for the power company. Once we learned that this team of people at the plants was going to turn the power back on and send it upstream to Washington, D.C., he and I discussed trying to get the grid back up for our own community.

We had an idea that we might be able to tap into the grid and intercept power in a way that they wouldn't be able to detect. Somehow these people intercepted Kyle and his crew today. They killed his entire crew, then hung and mutilated their bodies. They left Kyle alive to tell what happened."

Jim could tell that Weatherman and Bird had not heard this story from the looks on their faces. They were clearly shocked and appalled.

"After you left my house earlier, Scott, I walked in on a conversation between Kyle and my dad. They were talking about different types of power plants and why we had coal over hydroelectric here in our region. My dad mentioned that there had once been a plan to create a dam in Wise County and flood sections of our region to form a lake. He mentioned that if this had taken place, the entire area where the power plant is now would be underwater.

"That gave me an idea. What I'd like to do is see if I can put that dam in place right now and flood the power plant. The Clinch is a big, fast-moving river in a narrow gorge. If I can block the gorge that water will shoot up overnight and they won't have a chance. We have to make sure they don't have any roads available to them for evacuating. We have to block those or take them out. We'll also have to take out their choppers with sniper fire so the head guy, a man named Boss, can't escape. He's the head of the snake."

"Building a dam is a big project," Weatherman said. "How do you possibly think you can complete that before they notice the water rising and just come shoot your ass off whatever piece of equipment you're operating?"

Jim shook his head. "Not building it like that. My plan is to blast the gorge shut. If I can shoot off one big explosion in one of those narrow gorges, I think we can make a lake and drown an invading army."

"What kind of explosives are we talking?" Hugh asked. "Blasting isn't as easy as it looks in the movies."

"I was considering a truck bomb," Jim said. "We go back for another one or two of those freezer trucks that run on propane, then pack them with barrels of diesel and fertilizer. We've got both of those here in the valley. I could use the old diesel that has some water contamination. It should be fine for these purposes."

Jim noticed Hugh shaking his head. He'd known Jim a long time and had no problem being blunt with him. Jim also understood that Hugh had a lot more experience with explosives than he did, even though he'd never admit where that experience came from.

"Something wrong with that plan?" Jim asked.

"Everything," Hugh said. "First off, there aren't a lot of paved roads in that area. It's mostly farm roads—two tracks of mud and cowshit. The volume of explosive material you'll require will make that truck so heavy I don't think you'd be able to get it where you need it. I think you need a much better plan of how to direct your charge to put the debris where you want to put it. Think of the difference between putting a firecracker on an apple versus sticking a firecracker inside an apple. You just park a truck bomb at the base of a cliff and you might not accomplish anything but knocking over a few trees. You're needing to move thousands of tons of rocks and dirt."

"Sounds like you might have a little experience in that arena," Bird remarked.

Hugh winked. "I can neither confirm nor deny."

"I think your choice of explosive is fine," Bird said. "I used to work in the mines and I saw a lot of blasting done with ANFO, which is the commercially-packaged version of a fertilizer bomb. But like Hugh said, it needs to be placed for effectiveness. You'll also need a primer charge. Blasting caps alone aren't usually enough for an ANFO mixture."

"Where would I find a primer charge?" Jim asked.

"A mine," Byrd said. "Or a quarry. You'd need a little Tovex or pentolite."

"There's a quarry down that way," Jim said. "It's right by the road. They run gravel trucks out of there all day long."

"They'd probably have everything you need if it hasn't been looted already," Hugh said. "Of course, you have to find the blasting shack and get inside it. That might take a cutting torch. You may even find some commercial ANFO in bags you can add to the mix."

"Excellent," Jim said. "I'll be heading out tomorrow morning to see if I can get those trucks running. We'll get them back here and get them outfitted."

"I want in on that," Kyle said. "I know what my buddy Orfield did to get them started. I might be able to help."

"You need to be taking it easy," Jim said.

"You need to kiss my ass," Kyle replied.

"If you're strong enough to talk shit, then I guess you're strong enough to help out," Jim said. "I'd be glad to have you."

"There's still more to this operation, Jim. You can't just lay explosives on the surface of the ground and cross your fingers. You only have one shot at this. You need to go about it a little more scientifically," Hugh said.

"I don't have any way to drill for charges if that's what you're suggesting."

"Then you need to take advantage of some natural passage or a cave."

Jim paced the room, rubbing his chin and racking his brain. He'd used the map to locate the narrowest point along the river but that would not be the ideal spot if he couldn't get his explosives there or if he couldn't get them into a position where the blast would be most effective. He paused and smiled.

"I took Pete on a canoeing and fishing trip down that way once. He was probably seven or eight years old. We took a bathroom break in that area. Pete pointed out this cave halfway up the cliff face on the opposite side of the river. It was a big round hole in the rock face, like an Anasazi cliff dwelling or something. There were some ledges beneath it and someone had made homemade ladders out of branches for getting up in the cave."

"Did you guys go in?" Gary asked.

"No. We paddled across the river and looked at the ladders but they were rotted. They must have been forty years old. It looked cool.

Pete was convinced there had to be treasure in it, or at least a skeleton."

"You can't carry the volume of explosive you need up a ladder," Hugh said. "I don't think all of us in this room could even if we combined our efforts."

"We wouldn't have to," Jim said. "I ran into a rock climber once when I was hiking near there. I asked him if he'd ever seen the cave and he said it was a common rappelling site. He said there was a road near the top and people parked there, then rappelled off."

Hugh stood. "Let's see it on the map."

It took them a few minutes to find the spot. Since Jim had only seen it from the river, there weren't a lot of identifiable landmarks he could recall. They eventually narrowed it down to what he was certain must have been the spot.

"The rock climber was right," Hugh said. "There's a road near the top."

Jim looked around the room. "Before we go any further, I need to find out who wants to be a part of this. If you don't, this is your opportunity to leave with no hard feelings. If you stay, you'll be given an assignment."

No one left.

"Any concerns?"

Gary raised his hand.

"What?" Jim asked.

"I agree with everything you've said but I don't like the idea of drowning innocent people who are struggling to survive just like we are. I'd like to warn the people who are in the path of the flooding."

Jim considered this. "I don't have a problem with that but we can't do it too early or someone might take it upon themselves to warn the people at the plants."

"That's true," Gary agreed.

"Pete, Charlie, and I could get a couple of those canned air horns and ride around spreading the word," Randi suggested. "If we used the horns, people might come outside to us and we wouldn't have to risk knocking on any doors."

"What would you tell them happened?" Bird asked.

Jim shrugged. "A landslide. Act of God. Blocked part of the river and causing flooding."

"I'm good with that," Gary said. "I'm in."

"Kyle?" Jim asked.

Kyle nodded somberly. "After what I saw today? You better believe it."

"How about we get you home now?" Kyle shook his head. "There's no point. My family knew I might have to spend the night on the jobsite. There's no point going home this late at night and disturbing everyone."

"You're sure?"

Kyle nodded.

"Scott, what about you?" said Jim. "You want to get out of here before we go into detail?"

"If I was to call in, my people would tell us to stand down and get out of here. They may even give Boss a warning just to avoid this escalating. We'll support you in any way we can but I think I'm going to have to sit this one out. If it helps, we can assist with security here in your community until you get back."

"We'll accept that offer," Jim said. "Coordinate with Gary's son-in-law, Will."

"Got it," Scott said. He stood and gathered his gear. "I'll see you guys when you get back. Good luck."

Ford, unusually quiet up to that point, spoke up. "Have you told the sheriff about your plan?"

Jim shook his head. "I haven't seen or talked to him in some time. I think he's lost in his own head right now. He's cracking up. So no, I haven't told him."

Ford nodded. "Then I won't either."

For the next two hours, the group hashed out the details of their plan. Assignments were laid out until everyone knew exactly what they needed to do and when it needed to be done. Work would start at first light and the operation would be launched the following day. No need to waste time.

26

At first light the next day, Jim and Kyle rode out of the valley for the frozen food distributorship. Doing exactly what Orfield had done days earlier, Kyle got both trucks running. In a move that had not occurred to Kyle and Orfield, Jim drove one of the trucks three miles to a local farm supply store and borrowed a cattle trailer, which he hooked to the hitch on the freezer truck. While he was at the farm store, Jim could not help but notice several pallets of fertilizer shrink-wrapped on pallets beneath an open shed. He would be returning for those.

He drove back to the industrial park and they loaded their horses onto the trailer. Since the industrial park was home to several other businesses, the two men went to a gas pipeline company and a tool and die shop to look for cutting torches, gases, and rigging equipment. After using the bumper of one of the trucks to push open several garage doors, they came away with two sets of torches and hoses, two masks, two acetylene tanks, and three oxygen tanks.

The tool and die shop had a small overhead crane system for lifting heavy items. They had several crates of gear for rigging items to be lifted. Jim and Kyle took it all, coming away with several slings made of yellow webbing, a bucket of hooks and shackles, and a few odd lengths of chain.

When they left the industrial park, Kyle went home to spend some time with his family. He was going to explain to them that things at the substation had not gone as expected but he would not go into detail. He preferred not to worry his family. Once this was all over, they could sort it out. Over a jar of liquor, he would share the details he didn't want to get into today. Once he'd had a nap and said his good-byes, Kyle was going to return to the valley so that his truck could be outfitted for the next day.

Jim drove the freezer truck with the livestock trailer back to the farm supply store. He felt very exposed being in a vehicle. Once he parked, he did not set down his rifle even when loading fertilizer. He did not want to take any chances at this late stage in the game. The mission ahead was too important. If he ran into any trouble, his first response would be to shoot.

In full gear, including body armor and carrying a rifle, Jim loaded two pallets of fertilizer. Most went in the forward compartment of the livestock trailer, which was the lowest and therefore easiest place to put it. Some went into the freezer compartments of the truck, which were high and strained his muscles after thirty or so bags. He knew he'd be sore tomorrow. He only hoped he was so busy he didn't have much time to think about it.

WHEN HE MADE it back to the valley, Jim was tired, sore, and sweating through his clothes. He drove the freezer truck to Mack Bird's house, which was not as easy as it sounded. With all of the bridges into the valley destroyed as a safety precaution, they had to take the trucks overland on a slippery farm road. It required putting the tire chains on and took a lot longer than driving through the river near the superstore.

Mack had a shop behind his house and was responsible for the next stage of readying the truck. Jim unloaded the horses and headed back to his house while Bird and Weatherman worked together on the truck.

Using the cutting torches, they modified the bumper to accept a heavy-duty winch that Bird pulled from a rock crawler he'd built several years ago. Extensive redneck engineering went into making sure the winch was tied into the frame sufficiently that it could lower heavy loads without breaking loose.

When that task was completed and tested, Bird set about using old pipe and round tubing from his scrap pile to build a protective bumper for the front of the truck. He would have liked to build armor for the truck too, but knew from his own shooting experience that bullets would penetrate any of the plate steel he had laying around his shop.

While Bird was welding like a fiend, Weatherman was dealing with the freezer compartments. The truck bed wasn't a single box but chopped up into over a dozen smaller compartments that made it easier to organize the contents, though all those compartments made the truck less efficient for nearly everything else. A reciprocating saw with a long blade would have been the ideal tool for dealing with the sheet aluminum and foam insulation but there was no power to run one and every generator in the valley was empty.

Weatherman climbed onto the top of the freezer box and attacked it with an ax. The sandwich of aluminum and foam was around five inches thick but yielded easily to a powerful chop.

"Don't hack your fucking foot off," Bird warned.

Weatherman wiped the sweat from his face with the back of a sleeve and gave Bird the finger. He was breathing too hard from playing Viking to verbalize a response. When he had a line hacked around the entire roof, he waved the ax over his head and roared in victory.

Bird turned off his torch and helped him pry the top off. It took Weatherman another two hours to hack out the interior dividers and to hammer over the edges. They were so sharp that just leaning over one had the potential to open a catastrophic gaping wound. With that done, he stretched a blue plastic tarp over the roof and stretched it tight with bungee cords. The plan was that folks would be riding in the back of this vehicle and that top would give them a little protection from the wind and any precipitation.

Bird and Weatherman were worn out when they were done. Bird's face was smudged from cutting with the torch and doing his best to gas weld, something he'd never been good at. Weatherman was soaked in sweat and covered in dozens of cuts and scratches from the sheet metal. They were relaxing and drinking cups of water in an old van seat that served as a couch when they heard the rumble of an approaching engine. Moving to the garage door, they saw an identical truck come to a stop behind the first.

Kyle eased stiffly out the door and smiled, looking over the truck they'd just completed. "You guys ready to do mine?"

Weatherman and Bird looked at each and sighed.

GARY WAS PACKING GEAR. He carried gear around the valley every day, both as he moved around and as he performed sentry duty, but this was different. He was actually going on an operation tomorrow and he was a little antsy over it. He packed a larger Go Bag, one that would sustain him for a few days if he got separated from the group and had to walk back to the valley.

He cleaned his pistol and, with Will's help, loaded every magazine he had. He had to take the heavy .338 Lapua because Jim was counting on him to use it to disable the chopper. There was only a single Blackhawk according to Jim and Hugh. Hugh had already coached Gary on the specific location he should place rounds to disable the chopper. The plan was that he would not fire unless they tried to use the chopper. Otherwise, he would just maintain surveillance on it.

Not wanting to be limited to the .338 bolt-action and a handgun, Gary had an AR pistol he'd built himself. As part of preparing his gear, he switched the pistol brace over for an actual stock and converted the rifle to what was legally considered a Short Barreled

Rifle. It was a minor change that carried serious legal implication in normal times since an SBR required extensive paperwork and approval. What it meant for Gary was that he now had an AR with a 10.5 inch barrel that would be a little easier to carry but effective to shoulder and shoot.

"I want to go with you," Will said.

Gary shook his head.

"Why not?"

Gary waited a long time before answering. He popped a take-down pin on his rifle and examined the mechanism, closed it back up, and slid the pin back in place. He confirmed the optic was functional then laid the weapon back on the table and began pushing rounds into a magazine.

"I've come too far with these folks to not participate," Gary said. "I could never look Jim in the eye again if I didn't go with him. Even if I didn't believe in the mission, I'd go because he'd do that for me. But the only way I can go away and do that is if I'm comfortable that my family is in good hands. I need to know there's someone here who can protect them and hold them together if I don't come back."

Will nodded. "I understand that, but I'd like to be a part of this."

"Not happening. We need you on sentry watching the valley tonight with the Wimmers and Lloyd. End of discussion."

Gary was never that firm. He was an easygoing guy and never shut down conversations like that. That he did was an indication of just how concerned he was about this operation.

"I need to check the .338," Gary said.

He picked up a walkie-talkie from the table and keyed the mic. "This is Gary. I'm going to check zero on my .338. I may have to fire a couple of shots if I need to adjust the scope. Just wanted to warn everyone not to be concerned by the shooting."

There was a chorus of acknowledgements. Satisfied, Gary picked up the rifle and went outside. A distance from the house, the valley road crossed over a bridge. A sign there read Narrow Bridge. Gary's rangefinder gave him a distance of 653 yards from the back porch of the house.

He laid prone on the carport, dropped the Atlas bipod, and flipped up his lens caps. He adjusted the turrets for the distance and returned to the scope. He placed the crosshairs on the letter "O" in the word "Narrow." He chambered a round, flipped off the safety, and returned to position. He exhaled, and between breaths he squeezed the trigger.

The .338 boomed and a cloud of dust erupted from the porch floor. There was a sound that resembled a tiny click and a hole appeared dead center of the letter. Gary could not help but smile.

ELLEN WAS UPSET with Jim on all fronts. She was upset he'd come up with this plan of attacking a military force and somehow felt like it was a good idea, and upset that he'd set this entire thing in motion without even having the courtesy to tell her he was doing so. She was extremely upset that he had included Pete and Charlie in his plan, assuring that she was not only going to lose her husband but she was going to lose her son too.

To make matters worse, Nana had teamed up with her. In addition to Ellen's lecture, Nana was explaining to Jim that he really should be considering turning his guns in and taking his family to the safety of the comfort camp. Instead, he was basically committing an act of terror against agents of the government and making his son an accomplice in his whole sordid plan.

When he'd heard enough, Jim raised his hands to silence the room. "I'm leaving at first light. If this is my last day on Earth, is this how you want to spend it?"

Jim thought that might make everyone chill out and relax. Instead, they apparently became hung up on the idea that he was going to die. In less than a minute, everyone in the entire house, except for Jim, was sobbing.

Jim, who struggled with compassion on the best of days, had no idea where to go from here. He stood up.

"I'm going to split some wood."

27

Everyone creaked to life around daybreak the next morning. Any lingering hard feelings with family were put to rest since everyone understood the gravity of good-byes anymore. They hugged, kissed, and cried, then each warrior hardened his resolve and geared up. Be they farmers, IT professionals, office workers, nurses—none of that mattered now. Each was a soldier in a war to preserve the country they knew and loved. Their country was dark now and its people beaten down, but as the folks of this valley rose to their feet, hopefully more would too. If they didn't, and if all from the valley perished in their fight, it would be for nothing.

Laden with gear, they assembled at Jim's barn. The night had remained above freezing, though just barely. A cold fog lay over them but should be gone by mid-morning. There was now more ground showing than snow and, though it was a muddy mess, it was a welcome sight.

Folks pitched their gear into the back of the first truck. Ford, who'd driven trucks in the Army, was driving with Gary riding shotgun. Jim would be driving the truck hauling the explosives with Hugh as his wingman. Ford's truck was going to tow the horse trailer with mounts for Pete, Charlie, and Randi. The three had hit several stores yesterday and scrounged up a couple of dozen air horns. Apparently in the looting that had ensued since last summer, no one had seen a dire need for air horns.

A critical step performed just before dark last night was the loading of the explosive components. The bags of fertilizer Jim had obtained from the farm supply were packed into the truck, along with every barrel that could be found in the entire valley. Pete, Charlie, Gary, and Will had scrounged the valley for the barrels, and also five gallon buckets with lids that could be used to transport the diesel fuel. All of the ingredients were packed onto Jim's truck and Hugh would supervise mixing the ingredients when—and *if*—they reached the cave.

Despite his intention of not going on the operation, Scott showed up with three of his crew, all carrying boxes of MREs for Jim's team. They divvied them up and gave each person several meals for his pack.

"We're burning daylight," Jim announced when it seemed that everyone had accomplished the preliminaries. "Let's head to the quarry next. Maintain radio silence unless you see something hinky."

"*Hinky*?" Pete asked.

"Fishy," Jim clarified. "Something you think the others might need to be aware of."

"Got it."

The teams wished each other luck and loaded up. Pete gave everyone a long hug and there were more tears. Jim hugged and kissed his family, promising they'd be back by morning.

THE SILVERSTONE QUARRY was a twenty-five minute drive from Jim's house in the best of times. After around nine months or so the roads were looking like crap. There were abandoned cars, trash, and tree limbs around every corner. On several occasions they had to get out and drag large limbs out of the way.

The quarry itself lay along a barren section of road. The quarry was old, having been worked sporadically since pioneer days. The road leading to the office area was open but the yellow pipe gates leading back to the working area of the quarry were locked. Ford backed his truck up to the gate and Bird used the oxy-acetylene torch to burn the lock off.

Parts of the quarry were flooded. Those seemed like old works that hadn't been reopened. Jim wondered if anyone had stocked them. Someone had once told him that quarries made good trout waters.

They reached a second gate and Bird jumped out to cut it. Jim left his truck idling and joined him. "Any idea where the blasting shack might be?"

"They refer to it as an *explosives magazine*," Bird said. "We should be close. I don't think we're to the working face of the quarry yet. It probably looks like a red shipping container."

After a few more minutes of sloshing around the gray mud of the quarry road they found what they were looking for. It was exactly like Bird had described it. He already had Ford spinning his truck to back up to the door. Jim started to pull up beside him but Bird waved him off.

"You should take everyone back to a safe distance until I get this cut open. It should be safe but we don't know what's in here. There could be some volatile stuff that might react poorly if a spark gets inside."

"Then be careful," Jim warned.

Bird grinned. "I got this."

Jim did as he was told, backing his truck and taking everyone with him while Bird cut the lock free, then swung the door open. Jim immediately drove his truck back to the explosives magazine and backed it up to the door.

Bird was coiling the torch hose back up and storing it away. "No matter how fancy these things get, most of them still rely on a padlock. Once you burn the padlock off, you're home free."

Jim stuck his head in the door of the container. "So what are we looking for again?"

"Tovex," Bird called as he finished with the hose. "Could be in cardboard boxes or even in tubes that look like sausage."

Jim shined a flashlight around the inside of the container. There were quite a few things in there and he could figure out what most of it was. Bird and Hugh, however, were sharing glances with an evil gleam in their eye. Jim knew that Hugh had some dangerous tendencies but he'd always known Bird as a laid-back farmer who just liked to shoot a lot. A *whole* lot.

"Can we use any of this?" Jim asked.

"We can use *all* of this," Hugh said, shining his own light around. "As a matter of fact, we should take this even if it means putting some of it in the other truck. Some of this is the prepared ANFO that doesn't require adding diesel. There's both Tovex and dynamite here for detonating the ANFO. There's det cord, cast boosters, detonators—everything."

"That shit means nothing to me," Jim said. "Can you guys sort it out and let us know what to take?"

The two men nodded.

"Give us a line of folks and we'll start passing," Bird said. "Treat everything very carefully."

Jim assembled a line of folks stretching from the explosives magazine to the back of one of the trucks. Bird and Hugh were talking among themselves in the darkened container, pointing at stuff and comparing options. When they had a plan, they started handing stuff to the man nearest to them and it worked its way down the line to the truck. When they were done, there wasn't much left in the red metal container and both trucks were sagging on their suspensions.

"We'll have to be careful if we hit rough road," Jim told Ford. "I don't want to break anything we can't fix."

"No shit. The ass-end of that truck is practically dragging. How much farther do we have to go?" Ford asked.

Jim pulled out his GPS unit from a pocket on his vest. "It's twenty-two miles to where we think the cave is."

"Then we better get back on the road," Ford said. "That could be another hour or two depending on how bad the road is."

"Load up!" Jim called out.

When everyone was back in the trucks, they crept back along the slimy gray roads of the quarry. Everything here, even after months of disuse, was covered in the same rock dust. When they reached the first gate they'd come through, Gary slipped out of Ford's truck to push that gate back open. They'd closed it behind their convoy just in case anyone came along. Gary stood at the gate for a moment, not doing anything.

"What the fuck is he doing?" Jim asked.

Then Gary was running back toward the trucks, running a finger under his throat in a gesture that was clearly instructing them to kill the engines. Ford complied, then Jim did the same. Gary hopped up on Jim's running board.

"There are engines on the main road. They're loud. I could hear them over our trucks," Gary said.

Ford leaned out his window. "What the hell is going on?"

Gary ran forward to let him know. While he was standing on Ford's running board, the vehicles slipped by on the four-lane highway. The freezer trucks were likely lost in the clutter of the quarry. It would have taken someone a moment to locate them even if they were standing at the entrance to the facility and scanning with binoculars. A moving vehicle on the highway had little chance of spotting them.

Still, it was clearly a military patrol of some sort. Two vehicles moving slowly, a gunner on top. The vehicles were painted in a blotchy deep green camo.

"Hugh, go forward and take a look. I don't want to pull out just as more of them are coming along."

Hugh slipped out and took off at a run, heading past the gate and toward a hill near the quarry entrance. He hunched low and moved slower as he reached a more exposed position. He spent nearly a minute scanning before he waved an arm for the vehicles to move forward. When they reached main road, he appeared at the driver's window of Jim's vehicle.

"They're gone but that would seriously fuck up our day if we run into one of their patrols. I'm not certain that gun would detonate these explosives but I'm not certain it *wouldn't*," Hugh said. "Any chance of an alternative route on a back road?"

"Tell Ford to let me pass and I'll lead the way," Jim said. "I think I know a different way but it will take a little longer."

"I'll tell him," Hugh said, dropping from the running board.

Jim studied his GPS and confirmed a few things. He was fairly certain he knew an alternative route but he wasn't sure exactly how it connected to his destination. By the time Hugh was back in the cab of the truck, Jim was squared away.

"You figure something out?" Hugh asked.

Jim nodded. "I'm on it."

28

It took them over two hours to make the trip. The heavy snow had done a number on the wooded back roads, dropping trees and useless power lines across the winding road. Some of the debris may have been there from fall storms. At one point, debris littering the road became so frequent that Pete, Charlie, and Randi walked ahead of the truck, tossing limbs as they went. Gary and Hugh rode on the running boards providing security.

This area was sparsely populated. They ran across few houses and in most cases it was difficult to tell if they were occupied or not. Only one farm was clearly active, with a man and a boy that was likely his son carrying buckets from a barn to a house. When they spotted the trucks, they threw the buckets down and ran. Jim was saddened to see that the buckets were full of milk. Even though it wasn't his milk or his loss, any waste in this time of deprivation seemed especially cruel.

As they closed in on the area where Jim suspected the cave would be found, his eyes moved between the road and his GPS. He was examining topographic data, looking for the spot where the lines indicated a cliff. In better times, this would have been a crime, driving in a distracted manner. Yet it was likely the smallest of the crimes Jim would commit today. That thought almost brought a smile to his face, an inside joke that only he would ever get.

Nearing what he thought was the spot, Jim spotted a wide pull-off on the shoulder of the road. He suspected this was it. As more and more climbers showed up to spend time on the cliff, the state eventually accommodated them and expanded the shoulder. The area was probably wide enough for a dozen cars but just barely provided enough room for the two freezer trucks and the horse trailer. Jim was forced to laugh at himself again as he tried to pull his truck fully out of the road by force of habit. Then he realized it was pointless. There would be no traffic.

Jim killed his engine and hopped out of the truck. Ford did the same.

"Ford and Gary, you guys keep an eye on the road. We might have attracted some attention. Keep an eye out for anyone following on foot. Pete and Charlie, you guys take the road to the front of the vehicle. Stay in sight of the trucks but keep an eye for anyone who might be coming in this direction."

While those guys went about their duties, the rest followed Jim to a point where the hill started sloping steeply down.

"You guys stop right here," Jim said. "This ground is really slick. If you go down and start sliding, you might not stop until you hit the river."

Jim had brought a climbing rope and he tied it off to a nearby tree with a bowline. He pulled a carabiner and a figure 8 belay from his vest, hooking it to the D-ring on his rigger's belt and then clipping into the line. The rigger's belt wouldn't be ideal for an actual rappel but it should be sufficient for a safety device while walking on the steep, slippery terrain.

Jim unsnapped his rifle from the single point sling and handed it over to Hugh. "Hold my beer."

"Famous last words," Hugh replied.

There was a trail worn through the moss and thick branches. Neat cuts where branches had been pruned to open the path helped assure Jim this was the correct route. He just had to be certain it was actually the route to the cave and not just to a popular climbing spot. Then he was at the edge, the trees leaning off at acute angles and fragments of old abandoned ropes hanging in tatters or embedded in trees.

He took up the slack in his safety rope as he neared the edge. He got a gloved hand on it, ready to arrest his fall if went down. He edged closer and closer. There were still pockets of snow between the rocks and his heart beat faster as he stepped on them, certain his feet would fly out from under him at any moment. Jim loved climbing but heights scared the absolute shit out of him. He stared over, unable to stop himself from looking at the ground, and a nauseating wave of vertigo hit him. He choked it back, taking a deep breath, and focusing, trying to occupy his mind with anything but the awareness of the open space in front of him.

Then he saw it. Perhaps twelve to fifteen feet down from where he stood was a ledge at the mouth of the cave. While not spacious by any means, the ledge would be sufficient for one or two folks to stand on and receive the explosives. Although it would be nerve-wracking work, constantly aware of the seventy foot drop at your side, it would be manageable. If he could get down there first and secure ropes and anchors he would feel much safer about someone working with that kind of exposure.

He backtracked, reeling himself in until he reached the rest of his group. "I found it. There's a ledge that will hold two folks. It's going to be a lot of work but I think we have everything we need to pull it off. I just need to get down there and put some safety lines in place."

"We've been talking about this," Hugh said. "Bird and I are going."

Jim frowned. "You guys have no climbing experience."

"You have no explosive experience," Hugh and Bird responded simultaneously.

"Besides," Hugh added, "I do have climbing experience."

"Well how the fuck am I supposed to know that?" Jim grimaced. "You won't ever give a straight answer on anything further back than last month."

"That's need to know shit," Hugh said. "You don't need to know."

Jim took a deep breath and let it out slowly.

"I'm going to set a fixed line from where we're standing to the edge," Hugh said. "Anyone working past this point has to be clipped into that line at all times. I'll drop a rope and anchor it a little closer to the edge. I'm also going to set an anchor for a belay. I'll rappel down and we can belay Bird down."

"If that's how you want to do it," Jim said.

Hugh and Bird nodded.

"Then let's get with it. Hugh, you get your lines in place. There's a red duffel with climbing gear in the back of the truck."

"I brought some too," Hugh said, jogging off to the truck.

"So, how do you want this all dropped down to you?" Jim asked.

"Weatherman and I welded a steel basket together. It has a hinged lid. It almost looks like a rescue basket for helicopter rescues. Once we get this winch line in place and protected so it won't fray on these rocks, we should be able to lower a couple of hundred pounds at a time. We have to be careful though. A winch isn't a hoist. We don't want to push our luck."

"Got it," Jim said.

"What can we do?" Weatherman asked.

"I guess the rest of us can start carrying all of the stuff in the truck to this point where we're standing," Jim replied. "Like the man said, past this point you'll have to be clipped to the rope for safety."

Jim helped Bird rig a steel cable between two stout trees on the edge of the cliff. They brought a snatch block, a pulley with a hook on it, and hung it over the line. The pulley would give the winch a straighter pull and maybe keep the winch line from fraying so much. Working from the fixed line, Jim pulled the winch cable, fed it through the snatch block, and clipped it to the metal basket.

Hugh already had his ropes and belay anchor in place. "Rappelling!" he called out, then dropped over the edge. The man climbed with a fearless confidence that told Jim Hugh definitely had more climbing experience than he did.

Bird clipped into a harness and Jim tied him off with a figure eight knot. He fed the rope through a locking carabiner on the anchor and then through a belay device that was anchored to a different tree. The devices all multiplied the force that Jim exerted on the rope, allowing him to easily lower Bird to the ledge below. Hugh had already set an anchor inside the cave and had two safety lines for he and Bird to clip into.

"How far back does it go?" Jim called.

"We can walk back about fifty feet," Hugh said. "It looks like you could go a lot farther if you're willing to crawl."

"Fifty should be good, shouldn't it?"

Hugh shrugged. "I hope so."

Jim double-checked the connection of the winch to the basket, the snatch block to the cable, and the cable to the trees. He found that there were dozens of plastic bags of explosive powder and various other items waiting on him. He put three bags of the manufactured ANFO mixture in the basket and signaled Weatherman to hit the winch.

Weatherman was standing by the bumper with a remote. He hit a button and the winch started whining, the cable taking up the weight of the basket and its contents so Jim could swing it out over the edge. The winch slowed a little as it began to labor. The anchor trees Jim had affixed the steel cable to bowed inward slightly. The cable went taut and sang with tension. It slipped along the bark under the power of the winch, startling everyone for a split second, but nothing fell.

Jim let out a breath, not realizing he'd been holding it. He pushed out on the cable with his foot, trying to keep the basket from snagging as it dropped.

"Keep an eye out," he warned. "It may bring rocks down."

Hugh and Bird took the warning to heart, pulling their heads back in the cave until the basket was at eye level. The pair rolled the bags out of the basket and signaled for it to be raised while they carried their load back into the recesses of the cave. It seemed to take forever for the basket to make it back up, but when it did, Jim pulled it back as far as he could and immediately loaded it with four bags this time, over two hundred pounds of ANFO powder.

They repeated the process exactly as before, and everything went smoothly. Seeing that their system was working, Jim moved to some of the heavier items, sending down the diesel fuel, then starting on the bagged fertilizer. He wanted to get the heaviest stuff down first since things were going smoothly. If all else failed, he could rope stuff down with the belay as a last resort. He certainly didn't want to have to lower every single bag of fertilizer and ANFO powder down by that method.

"Hold up," Hugh called as Jim was starting to load the basket again.

Jim peered over the edge. "What's up?"

"We've been checking out the base of this cliff between loads," Hugh said. "It looks like it may be undercut enough that we should put a charge down there."

"I thought there was no point in that."

"There is if the base is undercut enough," Hugh replied. "Especially since we've got all this additional explosive we didn't expect to have."

Jim wasn't able to see the base of the cliff from his position. "What do you want to do?"

"I've got enough line to rappel down," Hugh said. "I want to go down and check it out. If it looks promising, Bird will start rigging this charge and you can start sending loads down to me."

Jim examined his setup. "We may have to reset up here so we miss the ledge."

"Then you look for a spot where you can see the base while I'm headed down," Hugh said. "Just don't dislodge anything on my head."

"I'd feel better if you were wearing a helmet," Jim said.

"Well all I've got is a hard head with a soft mind," Hugh said. "I'll have to work with it."

Jim left the partially filled basket sitting, retied his safety line, and checked the top of the cliff for a better spot to set up the winch. He found one about forty feet away. It was not a straight shot with the winch and would require running the cable through a maze of trees and brush. There were no anchor trees for using a snatch block, so

Jim would have to use a log to protect the winch cable from abrading against rock.

He double-checked that his safety line was secure and looked over the edge, again fighting the vertigo that threatened to drop him to his knees. Hugh was moving around among large boulders.

"How's it look?" he called down.

Hugh gave him a thumbs-up. "Perfect. Start'em coming."

Jim let out a sigh. Easier said than done. He returned to the ledge and sent Bird the last of the materials he would need to rig his charge.

"Give a yell when you're ready to come back up."

Jim got Weatherman to help him move the winch cable and re-rig the basket. He had some doubts about the path of the cable through the woods. There were several dead trees the cable would be riding against. He hoped they could stand up to the pressure.

With everything set, Jim started the next basket on its way. He went light since this was a new route. Even so, it dislodged a rock from the top of the cliff on its way down.

"Hugh!" he shouted. "Heads up!"

Hugh was able to dodge out of the way. Fortunately, the winch cable was long enough for the job. They lowered over six hundred pounds of material before the winch started smoking.

"Fuck!" Weatherman said.

"What is it?" Jim asked.

"Damn winch burned up," he said. "I guess we exceeded the duty cycle."

Jim groaned and went to the back of the truck. They had off-loaded all of the manufactured ANFO explosive but still had some fertilizer, diesel, dynamite, and a few other items they'd picked up at the quarry.

"Let me talk to Hugh and see what he thinks," Jim said.

He went to the edge and conferred with his friend. Hugh felt that they had enough material to go ahead and rig the charge. They were directly on the riverbank, so the hope was that everything they dropped would roll right into the river. Jim sent down a sack with the remainder of the items Hugh needed for setting his charge.

While Hugh was busy, Jim and Weatherman raised Bird to the surface as he unspooled wire behind him. When they got a safe distance from the edge, Bird began putting together his detonator assembly. Jim and Weatherman took down the lines and rigging from their operation.

"I'll walk the base of the cliff and meet you on the road about a half mile back," Hugh told them.

Jim called everyone together back at the trucks.

"This is the calm before the storm," he said. "Everything gets crazy from here on out. Just remember that your safety is paramount. None of you are replaceable."

"This where shit gets mushy?" Weatherman cracked.

Jim looked at him. "Okay, maybe one of you is replaceable."

That got a small laugh from the nervous group.

"From here, we go back to the main road and we'll unload the trailer. Randi, Pete, and Charlie, head out on horseback to warn the folks in the communities along the road. Tell them to spread the word themselves. Do not approach the houses. Set off the horn and give them the message if they come out. Don't tell them to leave because they might think it's a trap. Just tell them to be alert for rising water."

"Got it," Randi said.

"Gary, we get you in place on the hill across from the plant. Your primary job is to keep the chopper from taking off."

Gary nodded.

"Bird, we drop you and Hugh off with Gary. The three of you work your way in together. When Gary finds his hide, you two head for the bridge into the plant. The plant is built on the isolated side of the river. There are no roads in and out except for that old steel bridge. Take the legs out from under it and we trap them there."

"Got it," Bird said.

Jim looked around at the blue-gray sky then checked his watch.

"It's 5:35 PM now. We blow everything at 9. Both the bridge and this whole fucking mountain. Got it?"

There were nods around the darkening circle.

"I don't think they'll suspect we've dammed the river until the water starts coming up," Jim said. "They'll hear the explosions, but if we keep them busy enough they won't be able to do anything about it."

Jim looked around at the faces of his friends and family. His team. "Then I want everyone to eat and drink. I'm not sure when you'll have another chance and I don't want you distracted by hunger."

"What about the rest of us?" Scott asked.

The group wandered off to choke down MREs and rehydrate.

"Pete and Charlie!" Jim called. "You guys stick around a second."

The boys were nervous and made more so by being singled out. After everyone left them alone, Jim put an arm on each boy's shoulder.

"I'm proud of you guys. I want you to listen to Randi. Do everything she says, regardless of what you think about it. She's good at this and she'll keep you alive. Don't try to do anything brave and don't do anything stupid. I've got ARs and pistols for both of you. More than anything, I want you to both come home at the end of the trip. You got it?"

They looked sheepish, as boys that age are prone to when things get intense.

"I'm serious," Jim said. "I love you guys and I can't go home without you. You understand?"

They nodded this time and Jim hugged both of them. While he wasn't a hugger, it was what needed to happen at that moment. He didn't want to miss an opportunity in case the worst befell them.

29

At approximately 8:30 PM, two hastily painted kayaks slipped under the bridge at the power plant. The kayaks were a "donation" from an abandoned house along the river. Despite having power and outside lighting, there was no one watching the water and no one watching the bridge. The kayakers used the ambient light from the plant to drag their boats out of the water as quietly as possible. With their cargo of explosives sealed in the dry hatches of the boats, Bird and Hugh efficiently assembled charges. They had discussed this, piecing together their two sets of knowledge to come up with a plan of how best to demolish the bridge. Many lives depended on their success.

While they were assembling their charges, two small stones flew from the night and plunked into the dark waters. It was a signal they were expecting. A signal not to shoot the men about to cross the bridge. Hugh and Bird continued about their business, listening as four sets of feet crossed above them. If nothing had changed, those feet would belong to Jim, Kyle, Weatherman, and Ford. They were to cross the bridge, take cover, and remain in hiding until after the fireworks.

The men under the bridge made quick work of their assignments, not wanting to prolong their exposure any longer than required. They installed wireless detonators, tested and double-checked everything, then relaunched their kayaks into the powerful current. Each floated without paddling, only steering, carefully watching for rocks and sentries with equal vigilance before beaching their boats. The water was cold and despite both of them wearing water-resistant hiking boots, neither was wearing appropriate footwear for wet-entries in a river frigid with snow runoff.

The riverbank near the plant was covered in rip-rap, an erosion inhibiting stone, to prevent the edges of the road from washing out. Each man struggled his way up the bank, trying to find a spot where he could see the bridge but low enough that he maintained some cover in case sentries were monitoring the road.

With one minute remaining, each man turned on his detonator switch and watched as the wireless components shook hands with each other, connecting the remotes in their hands to the receivers under the bridge. When the units paired, Bird and Hugh flipped the safety covers out of place and waited for 9 PM, counting down the seconds. At the same exact moment, each man triggered his explosive.

Despite the seriousness of the moment, each found it impossible not to be awestruck at the power of the charges. Neither had enough experience to know what to expect. If Hugh did, he wasn't admitting it. The old steel bridge blew loose from its mooring at the roadside, twisted, then leaned into the water with a shuddering groan. When it encountered the strong current, the waters tugged on the bridge, pulling it further askew.

The camp erupted into life with several men streaming from connex sleeping quarters. Generator-powered light towers burst to life and the shouts of men could be heard as they tried to figure out what had taken place. In the midst of all this chaos, the very earth shook under their feet from a massive two-pronged explosion further downstream. It was followed by a low rumbling that continued to shake the ground as chunks of ancient limestone the size of cars tumbled into the narrow valley and closed it off to a height of nearly forty feet.

Hugh and Bird now knew that their charges back at the cliff had detonated but had no idea if they'd achieved the desired effect of blocking the course of the river. They should know soon. Southwest Virginia was not like Mississippi where floodwaters could spread for tens of thousands of acres. The Clinch River valley was nothing more than a narrow rut between ridges. Once blocked off, the water would rise quickly. If their explosives had dammed the river, they might see water rising very soon.

"Showtime," Jim said into his radio, breaking silence for the first time that night.

Bird and Hugh moved to the top of the riverbank, looking over at the road. They'd stashed their detonators in pockets, exchanging them for rifles. In seconds, they heard the roar of an approaching engine. Blinding headlights came around the corner and the men closed their eyes to preserve their night vision. The vehicle locked up its brakes when it found the bridge it was aiming for was no longer there.

It was the white Otokar Cobra II with the UN markings. The drivers were silhouetted in the headlights as they stared over the river at the camp.

"Left," Hugh said.

"Roger that," Bird replied.

The men shot within a fraction of a second of each other and their targets fell into the river. Whether they were peacekeepers or an invading force depended on your perspective. To the armed men crouched on the roadside, they were the first drops of a torrent intent on extinguishing the fires of liberty.

BEYOND THE BLOWN BRIDGE, Jim and his team crouched in a sea of spare transformers, easily camouflaged in the shadows and irregular shapes. A steel door flew open and a half-dozen men streamed out, rifles in hand and pulling on gear as they ran. They were headed for the chopper.

Jim pulled out his radio. "Heads up, Gary. It's your show."

The group had no intelligence on how many men were at the camp. Jim had assumed they were spread thin since units were assigned to so many different plants around the country. He'd been hoping that was what he would find. So far his best estimate was that there were less than two dozen men here with half or more being foreign troops. They were running all over the place, jabbering at each other in their native languages.

The chopper doors were opened and the men scrambled inside. Jim wasn't certain if they were intent on getting an overhead view of what was taking place or if the intent was to flee. Neither was happening.

"What the fuck is taking him so long?" Ford asked.

"Quit checking your data," Weatherman mumbled. "Just shoot the damn thing."

A whine erupted from the chopper as they engines started. Seconds later, the first loud boom from the .338 Lapua rang out, echoing through the valley like thunder. The folks in the chopper didn't move, uncertain as to what was happening. The engines were still going.

Boom!

The second shot hit something vital and the sound of the engine changed. It began to wind down erratically. The chopper doors opened back up and men spilled out. The .338 barked again and the pilot's head vaporized into jelly.

"Oh, now he's just showing off," Weatherman said.

"No, he's dialed in," Jim said.

The men who were hurriedly disembarking discovered a new urgency with the sniper focusing from mechanical to human targets. They scrambled in all directions, seeking cover where they could find it.

"That's him!" Kyle said, pointing at a man in jeans. He wore tactical gear over a dark hoodie and carried a stubby rifle. "That's the bastard that killed my men."

Jim craned to get a look at the man, thus not seeing Kyle was unable to restrain himself. Kyle threw up the rifle Jim had given him and began dumping rounds as fast as he could pull the trigger. This created some confusion among Boss and his men, who had no idea they had combatants inside the wire. It didn't take them long to adjust.

Burst of rifle fire erupted from the group and impacts sang out all around Jim's people.

"Hit the fucking deck!" Weatherman yelled, grabbing Kyle and shoving him down.

Boss's men opened up with full auto, burst-fire, and whatever they had. Holes opened up in transformers all around Jim's group, spewing oil both onto the ground and onto the men.

"We've got to get out of here," Jim said, firing back. "We need better cover."

A smoke grenade popped between the groups and fire subsided, but there were enough rounds still flying around that everyone stayed low.

"What's going on?" Ford asked.

"There!" Kyle yelled, spotting a runner to his ten o'clock.

Ford tore off a shot and hit the man in the hip, dropping him into a screaming mass. A second round from Weatherman shut him up.

"They're going for that vehicle," Ford said.

Jim saw they were right. The man was running for some type of armored military vehicle.

Ford tried to stand up and heavy gunfire erupted again, pinning the group down.

"They're going to go for it," Weatherman said. "If they take that vehicle, we're sitting ducks. We have to beat them there."

Jim started to say something but didn't get a word out before Weatherman was off, sprinting like only a semi-retired farmer can. Boss's group targeted Weatherman, chasing him with rounds and tearing up the ground at his heels. Jim's group opened up with all they had, drawing their fire. Weatherman reached the green vehicle, threw open a door, and climbed in.

The fire dwindled again. Jim took the opportunity to load a fresh mag. He looked at the vehicle and saw movement above it. "What the hell?"

"Is he trying to climb out?" Ford asked.

"They had a gun up there," Kyle said.

Then Jim saw that was exactly what Weatherman was doing. He'd found the gun inside and was trying to affix it to the ring mount. "You think he knows what he's doing?"

"He's a Marine," Ford said.

"A former Marine?" Kyle asked.

"You're never a former Marine," Ford replied. "You're always a Marine."

The smoke was clearing and Boss's people must have noticed the movement. They began peppering rounds at Weatherman. They were unable to get a clear shot and it didn't deter the man from his task. All fell silent as the rhythm of the battle hit a lull. Then Jim heard a sound that even he, as a guy who was never a Marine, recognized—the metallic snap of the feed tray cover shutting on a belt-fed machine gun. It brought a smile to Jim's face and he wondered if the other side heard it. Then from the fog and smoke a voice rang out.

"You know why they call me the Weatherman?" it yelled. "Because I make it fucking rain!"

With that battle cry, Weatherman pulled the trigger on the M240 and opened the fires of hell on Boss and his people. Men were scurrying in all directions, diving for fresh cover as the M240 chewed up the crates they hid behind.

One of the crawling men was cut in half. Another caught rounds across the back that bypassed his armor. Jim felt a weird sensation, a sudden coldness, and wondered for a split second if he'd been hit. The ground looked strange and he reached down to find water.

Ice cold river water.

He looked around and saw the leaden reflection of the water

coming up all around them. Items were starting to lift from the ground and float away.

Then Weatherman's belt ran out and his curses filled the air. Jim threw his rifle up to bridge the gap but he was too late. Two men sprinted from the shattered crates.

"That's him!" Kyle yelled, bolting after the retreating men before Jim could pull him back.

"Fuck!" Ford yelled, starting after him.

"Watch out, Weatherman!" Jim yelled into his radio. "We have friendlies on the move."

"Clear'em out!" Weatherman yelled. *"I'm reloaded. We can end this."*

Jim's radio chirped. *"You've got UN guys closing on your six."* It was Gary.

Jim spun in time to see four men closing at a run, their feet splashing in the rising water. The .338 boomed, catching one of the men in the back and knocking him off his feet. Weatherman heard the transmission too, spinning on the attackers and dropping the hammer. Fire erupted from the barrel and empties clinked off the body of the armored vehicle. The entire line of attackers crumpled into the icy water.

"I'm going after them!" Jim yelled into his radio. "Cover us."

Weatherman went idle with no active targets. Jim could hear him on the radio talking to Gary.

"Give me a heads-up if you see anything, buddy."

"I'm on it," Gary replied. *"Bird is with me and he's got eyes on."*

"Bird is the word," Bird added.

"Whatever the fuck that means," Weatherman grunted.

That water was just above Jim's ankles now, just enough to slow him down. He'd lost sight of Boss and the other man, but saw Kyle in the distance with Ford just behind him. Gunfire erupted from ahead of him. Kyle leaped for cover behind a front-end loader and Ford was trying to reach him.

There was a burst of full-auto fire and Ford staggered, his gait going wonky, and then he dropped into the water. Jim took cover, his eyes moving between Ford on the ground and Kyle behind the loader.

Kyle threw his AR up over the loader arms and began pounding rounds at Boss. Jim took the opportunity to scurry to Ford and grab him by his drag handle.

When he got to the closest cover, Jim hit the man with the red lens of his headlamp and saw that his eyes were open and fixed, his mouth a puddle brimming with blood.

"Shit," he muttered.

He heard a yell and looked up. He had no idea what had transpired but one of the men Kyle had been chasing now had him in a chokehold while the other was punching him in the face. Jim couldn't hit the choker at this range but he could damn sure hit the puncher. He raised his rifle and dropped a red dot on the puncher's neck. He pulled the trigger.

The puncher flinched and dropped away, running for cover. The round must have hit armor. They took Kyle with them and Jim couldn't see any of them now.

"We've got more hostiles," Gary said into the radio. *"I count five total."* The .338 Lapua boomed. *"Make that four. Four hostiles."*

30

The man choking Kyle was not fucking around. He was seriously trying to put Kyle's lights out. Then he started backing up, dragging Kyle from his feet. Kyle tried to backpedal and keep up with him, but the man tripped over something beneath the water and they both went down. Kyle tried to take advantage of the opportunity and roll away but the man holding him was too fast. A series of stunning elbows pounded his head and left him reeling.

Then he was being pulled backward through the water, one man on each arm, and they were taking him somewhere. With his arms being tugged over his head, the pain in his ribs was excruciating. He could barely breathe and cried out from the pain, which only earned him a boot to the head.

They reached a set of metal stairs and began ascending one of the tall structures alongside the smokestacks. He felt himself being pulled from the water, then his feet bumping against steel treads as they dragged him upward. When they reached the first tier, they dropped him onto the catwalk and Boss was on his chest, the tip of a large combat knife resting dead center of Kyle's forehead.

"You're the guy from the substation," Boss spat. "The witness we left."

Kyle's voice was nearly gone from the choking but he croaked a sound to the affirmative.

"Didn't the shit you saw make it clear how serious we are?" Boss asked. "You think we're fucking playing?"

Kyle shook his head, eyes wide. He completely understood they weren't playing.

"Who's with you?"

"Friends," Kyle croaked.

Boss shook his head in disbelief, unable to stop a smile from curling his lips. "Friends?"

Kyle nodded.

"What the hell kind of friends do you have?"

Kyle shrugged, knowing his death was imminent. "Good ones."

"Four assholes gnawed up," Weatherman said into his radio. "Any more coming?"

"I see no movement," Bird replied.

"I only got two ammo cans left," Weatherman said. "This better be most of the party."

"Ford's dead and they took Kyle," Jim said over the radio.

There was no response but Jim could imagine each man cursing and shaking his head.

"Where's Hugh?" Bird asked.

"I assumed he was with you," Jim replied.

"Haven't seen him," Bird replied.

"He'll turn up."

"That water is getting higher," Gary chimed in. *"Debris is starting to move around. It could get sketchy over there."*

"I'm not leaving Kyle," Jim said. *"I know his wife. I know his kids. I couldn't face them."*

"You need my help?" Weatherman asked.

"Not yet. You stay on that gun just in case we get more company."

Jim paused and pocketed his radio. He listened intently. The sound of the water was getting louder. It was nearly to his knees now. It was his handiwork but it only increased the pressure of getting the job done. Then he heard a clank, metal on metal. He looked around, trying to pinpoint where it had come from. He heard it again and focused on the network of catwalks and metal stairs near the smokestacks. He heard a grunt of pain and he knew where he had to go.

The deeper water made progress slow. He couldn't run in it. He tried a slow jog, moving stiff-legged, and found he was getting closer. Then two things happened in quick succession that changed the game. One, there was a loud pop and the power faded away, leaving the smell of ozone in the air. That brought a smile to his face for just a moment, then the second thing happened. He stepped in a hole that was invisible beneath the surface of the water. That in itself was manageable. He wasn't injured but dropped to his waist in the frigid water. When he tried to get out, he found his ankle stuck in a steel grating.

He yanked on it but found no give at all. He bent at the waist and grabbed his foot with both hands, trying to pull it free, only succeeding in soaking himself fully.

"Shit!" he hissed.

He tried pushing down with his other foot but felt no movement at all. He bent and felt it again. There was a piece of rebar on either side of his foot pinching his ankle between them. The pressure made it impossible to pull his foot out or to even remove his foot from his boot.

He was stuck and he was starting to get cold. A chill passed through him and he knew that shivering was not far off. He sucked down his pride and pulled out his radio to call Weatherman in for help. When he pushed the transmit button, he heard nothing. He checked the display and found that his cheap-ass family band radio was full of water. It was dead and completely useless. He drew back his arm and threw it as far into the blackness as he could.

The grate he stepped in was at least a foot or two below grade.

The water was nearly to the bottom of his ribs. He thought of turning his light on and trying to signal for help but he was afraid the only thing he'd catch would be a bullet. Despite his friends and what they'd accomplished today, he suddenly felt very alone. With all the things he'd faced since last summer, with all the expectation he'd die a violent death, he was now facing the possibility that drowning and hypothermia were in a race to see who could kill him first.

With his hands going numb, Jim groped around the ground, feeling beneath the water for anything that he might be able to use. His hands landed on useless items—rocks, a hardhat being swept away in the floodwaters, and plastic bottles. He felt a nudge at his side. He felt around and discovered a tree branch about four inches in diameter. He started to shove it away, then his impaired mental functioning gave way to a spark of clarity.

Pry with it.

There was not enough strength in his hands to make the muscles obey. He pinched the log between two clubbed hands and pulled it to him and shoved the branch into the hole, poking blindly at the grating. He was frustrated and shivering. In a burst of determination, he ducked underwater and guided the end of the branch into the grate beside his foot.

He burst up from the water, which was now up to his chest. When he shoved against the log with all his might it slid free of the grating without accomplishing anything. Frustrated, he pushed it into the grating again, bearing down with all of his weight to wedge it in. He shoved against it again, levering it like a crowbar, growling with the effort.

While he didn't feel like he was making any gains, his foot suddenly came free and he fell to his side in the icy water. He had no time to waste. He was dying, if not dead already. He staggered numbly to his feet, looking for somewhere he might go to get out of the water. He could barely think and his ability to move his body was fading quickly.

Above him, rising into the dark night sky, were the smokestacks.

With the power out, they still poured steam and smoke into the night sky.

Smoke. Fire.

He staggered in that direction, certain that somewhere near those smokestacks would be a power generation boiler, which was basically a furnace. There would be heat and lifesaving warmth.

The building connected to the smokestack was forty long feet away but Jim moved in that direction with dogged determination. A set of concrete steps rose from the water. His stiff legs didn't want to climb but he pulled on the yellow handrail and managed to get himself up, finally free of the water. It ran from his clothes. His Go Bag was sagging with its weight.

Jim said a silent prayer, turned on his headlamp, and reached for the doorknob. Fortunately it was a lever handle, more easily manipulated. He had a new appreciation for that.

And it was unlocked.

He tried to yank the door open but his muscles did not cooperate. He had to use both hands to open the handle, tug, and then shove his body into the opening. A wave of heat hit him in the face as he collapsed through the door and onto the concrete floor. Tears came with the relief that he might actually survive this night after all. He couldn't give up yet.

He got to his knees and dumped his pack, struggling with numb fingers to remove his armor, his sodden coat, and shirt. When all of the upper layers were gone, he started on the bottom—boots, socks, pants, base layer, until he was standing naked in the stark industrial building. While it was damn warm, he had to admit it felt a little strange.

Grabbing his rifle, he carefully trod barefoot, going further into the building wearing only his headlamp. He was still shivering, but despite the dark and the silence, his body was guiding him toward the warmth. He came to another door, the same industrial steel door as the entrance, painted in the same battleship gray. He opened this door and could hear the sound of the boilers. He didn't know enough about the facility to know if power was being generated or not but the facility was dark and the lights were not working.

This room was the warmest yet and he was finally beginning to feel his feet again. It was a painful pins-and-needles sensation that made them difficult to walk on. The room was larger than he could illuminate with his headlamp. He hit the touch pad for his weapon light, hoping the extra money he'd paid for a quality waterproof light had been worth it. He was pleased to see it burst to life. Until it illuminated two foreign soldiers, both staring at this naked intruder in shock.

Jim flicked the selector and sent a round into each man, then backed up and did it again. It was purely a reaction at this point. Had they been Americans, he hoped he might have paused a bit longer, however, the battle lines were becoming blurred. He checked each man and confirmed they were dead. Touching their dry clothes, he had a brief thought that he might take them but decided he'd rather be naked. His folks would shoot a foreign soldier on sight. A naked man might make them pause, if for no other reason than to scratch their head in wonder.

THE TIP of Boss's blade rested on Kyle's forehead. It had pierced the skin and muscle and was resting directly on bone. Kyle was grimacing and blood ran from the wound, tracking down his temple and into one eye.

"All I have to do is smack the butt of this knife with my fist and you've got a lobotomy," Boss said. "These friends of yours have no idea what they've done. They've fucked with the federal government and will suffer the full wrath of that government. After I've killed you, I'm bringing in air support and I'll vaporize a circle around this place until I'm fully satisfied."

"This place will be underwater by tomorrow," Kyle said. "It will take months to clean the mud out of everything."

Boss gave a sharp twist of the blade, a drilling motion that tore flesh and scraped bone. Kyle screamed in pain. A heavy splashing sound in the darkness drew everyone's attention. Boss flicked his headlamp on and Kerry did the same.

Boss motioned into the darkness with a gesture of his head. "See what that was."

Kerry nodded, flicked off the safety on his rifle, and fired up his weapon light. He raised it to a high ready position and started down the steps.

In the darkness below the catwalk, Hugh stood in waist-deep water waiting on the man. He'd thrown a fire extinguisher into the water, trying to imitate the sound of a man moving around. When he saw the approaching light, he eased back into the shadows. The man coming down the steps played his light around in the rising water, looking for anything out of the ordinary. In truth, everything was chaotic. The water bobbed and reflected the light, debris was floating everywhere and bouncing off the structure. A flotilla of steel drums came along and banged off everything in their path. Weird, indecipherable sounds came from everyone.

As the man neared the bottom, Hugh lashed out with his heavy kukri, striking between the stair treads and slashing the man's Achilles tendon. The razor sharp knife cut through boot and flesh with no hesitation. The leg bearing most of his weight crumpled beneath him and he hit the water before he could get a cry out.

The water was three feet deep now, and the man flogged the water with both arms, trying to get to his one good foot, but Hugh was on him in a second. He pressed his pistol against the back of the man's head and pulled the trigger, shooting him beneath nearly a foot of water. There was a small eruption from the water but the sound of the shot was distorted and unclear. The man quit struggling and Hugh shoved him away.

Hugh slowly mounted the steps, the freezing water running off his body and through the mesh treads. He climbed quietly but efficiently, taking the steps two at a time. On the catwalk, he cleared his head, pushing away all thoughts. He saw one man atop another, a cone of light shining into the face of a man he recognized.

Kyle.

Blood poured from his face. A heavy knife was cutting into Kyle's forehead. His attacker had a hand drawn back over his head and Hugh could only see one reason for that—to drop his palm onto the butt of the knife and drive the blade through Kyle's skull.

Hugh lashed out with the kukri again and caught Boss in the wrist. The heavy blade, able to slash tree limbs like a machete, did the same to the thinner bones of the human wrist. The hand fell free and dropped onto Kyle's chest. Kyle recoiled in fear. While Hugh could not see Boss's face, he imagined what it must be like to see your hand dropping into your lap before the pain even hit you.

Boss spun, not even attempting to stem the flow of blood from his wrist. He had dropped his knife and was unable to reach any of his weapons, both of them set up to be retrieved by the hand that was now missing. He stared at Hugh, engulfed in rage. Hugh's arm was just starting the backswing, his intention to catch Boss in the neck on the return.

Boss read the move and pushed back with his feet, rolling across Kyle's body. Kyle found the dropped knife and lunged for Boss, stabbing repeatedly but only hitting the metal grating as the man scuttled backward. Hugh leapt over Kyle, the kukri drawn back for another slash, and Boss rolled himself through the catwalk railing.

Hugh and Kyle stared in shock as the man dropped into the shallow water, then floated to the top, his headlamp blinking out as he disappeared into the night.

"Fuck!" Kyle bellowed.

"It's okay," Hugh said. "With that freezing water and the blood loss, there's no way he'll survive."

Kyle was tempted to dive into the water himself and pursue the man. He wanted to see him die. Wanted to see it up close and personal. He shifted his body and stepped on something. He looked down to find the severed hand. He started to kick it off into the water but didn't. As vile and disgusting as it was, he would take it back with him. When he spoke to the families of the men in his crew, he would show them the hand and tell them of his revenge.

"Let's get out of here," Hugh said. "This water is getting higher. We need to get across it and into some dry clothes."

Hugh turned the volume back up on his radio. "This is Hugh. I have Kyle. We're going to head back your way. Try not to shoot us."

"Roger that," Weatherman said. *"You seen Jim? He's disappeared on us and I'm starting to get worried."*

"We'll check it out," Hugh said.

31

Int was a little after 1 AM when everyone loaded back into the truck. Hugh and Kyle found Jim wading back toward Weatherman. With the cold water rising higher and higher, there was no way they could swim across the deeper river channel. Bird tossed a rope that they caught after several attempts. They used the rope to run the two kayaks back and forth until everyone was safely onshore. While this was taking place, Gary went after the truck and got the heater running. By the time everyone got there, the cab was superheated. Everyone changed into their spare clothes and loaded into the cab. The sight of Ford's bag of spare clothes reminded everyone of the sacrifice he'd made.

In thirty minutes, they were pulling alongside the other truck and the horse trailer at the appointed rendezvous. Jim sprang from the cab of the truck, having become more and more anxious as they neared the spot. He was overjoyed to find everyone was okay. When he asked them how it went, they all looked at each other and said there would be stories to tell. Tomorrow.

Jim hugged his son, then hugged Charlie. He even hugged Randi for helping to make sure everyone made it back.

It took longer to make it out of the Clinch River valley and back toward Kyle's house. Due to the late hour, they drove him as far down the muddy farm road as they could and kept the lights on him until his wife opened the door to him. He threw a hand up in good-bye and went inside to the people that loved him.

Jim thought about the hand that Kyle had shown him. It was justice in the truest sense; an eye for an eye, a hand for a hand.

The sun was nearly up when Jim and his group finally returned to the valley. With all the bridges gone, they had to use a muddy path through one of the farms. When the truck got stuck, they left it where it sat instead of putting the chains back on it. They unloaded the horses and led them along, hanging as much of the gear from them as they could.

They came to Gary's house as the sun broke over the mountain. His wife and Will came out to meet him while the wide living room window filled with sleepy faces. A little farther past Gary's, they lost Weatherman, and then Hugh. Randi and Charlie peeled away from the group next.

When they came to Jim's house, he and Pete opened their gate and took the horses in. Jim was too exhausted for words, beginning to stumble and slur from the exertion.

They headed straight for the barn, pulling the saddles from the horses and settling them in for some rest. They barely had the barn door slid open before Ellen came running across the yard in her snow boots and bath robe. She was crying hysterically. At the sight of her desperately running to reunite with the son she probably feared dead, Jim found himself crying too.

They worked together to stable the horses, then walked back to the house. Jim and Pete stood by the woodstove and Jim felt warm, truly warm, for the first time that night. He could not be certain if it was the stove warming from without, or the presence of his family warming from within. Suddenly, he could stay upright no longer and he staggered off to his bed. He peeled off his clothes and climbed beneath the heavy blankets, falling asleep before he could even straighten his pillow.

32

S cott and his people departed the valley the following day. They sent an additional secure transmission from Hugh's radio and informed their base that there had been a firefight at the Carbo plant between Boss's team and unknown assailants. It was suspected that Boss and all his team had been killed, as well as any foreign troops providing support. At last report, the facility was flooding and had sustained significant damage.

"So you're not ratting me out?" Jim asked when Scott came to tell him he was leaving.

"No. I'm not sure what the reaction would be," Scott said. "It's entirely possible that if this incident triggers a conflict between the two groups, my leadership would offer you up as a scapegoat to keep the peace."

"I appreciate you not putting me out there as the sacrificial lamb."

"I think you and your group are much more useful as allies."

"We're glad to provide you support in whatever role we can, as long as it doesn't place our families in danger."

Scott nodded at that.

"You really think these two groups can work this out?" Jim asked. "Their core philosophies are so different that I can't imagine that happening. One wants to sacrifice the nation to control the world. One just wants to be left alone and let the nation and the world sort themselves out. Where is there any middle ground in there?"

"We're not going to solve it," Scott said. "But we may well find ourselves fighting the war that solves it."

"I feel like I already fought in that war."

"That may have just been the first battle of many."

"If I have to fight it so that my children don't, then I will," Jim vowed.

Scott stuck out his hand and Jim shook it. "If I can get more supplies to you guys, I'll do it. We'll drop them in the same field. If we do, I'll leave a message with it."

"We'd appreciate it. You guys stay safe. Watch out for the crazies."

Scott laughed. "I'm never sure which ones are the crazies."

"It's a safe bet that you should avoid anyone who acts like the people in this valley."

"I'll remember that."

TWO DAYS LATER, temperatures reached into the sixties and crocuses pushed up through Jim's yard. The snow was gone now and the grass was just a shade greener. Jim and Pete armed up for a road trip. They walked Ellen, Ariel, Nana, and Pops to the freezer trucks they'd abandoned in the field.

Jim had to put the tire chains on them to get them turned around and out of the field, but they eventually got back onto the road. Staying as much to the back streets as they could, he drove his family toward his parents' house. When they passed the Fairlane house, Jim looked to see if there were any changes and found his parents looking too. They didn't know what had happened on that last day Jim visited the house except that he and Ford had found Mrs. Fairlane dead. Jim didn't know if they entirely believed that or not. They seemed to think that there was more to the story. Ford, the only witness, was dead now, and Jim wouldn't ever speak of it to anyone.

At Nana's house, Jim and Pete checked for any signs of forced entry and found none. Nana wanted to spend some time at her house, and she thought of getting more of her spring bulbs. Since they had the large truck, Jim told her she could get anything she wanted.

Leaving them there, Jim and Ellen walked the short distance to the emergency operations center. Jim had an errand he felt he had to run on behalf of Deputy Ford. He went to the broken window, the one where Ford had nearly been shot, and called inside. He kept to the side, out of range, and explained who he was and that he was there with his wife to relay a message.

After several minutes with no response, he called out, "Since I'm not sure you're in there, we're going to leave now."

The door to the room opened then and the woman came into view.

"Nicole?" he asked.

She nodded.

"Deputy Ford told you a little while back about some relief camps that were opening up at the fairgrounds. Do you remember that?"

"Yes. We heard it on the radio. We were going to be headed that way in a few days."

Jim took a deep breath. "Those camps aren't going to be opening after all."

Nicole looked confused. "They're still playing the message on the radio."

"I know," Jim said. "They are still opening in some areas but they're not going to be opening here anytime soon. There was a problem at the power plant and the power isn't coming back on."

Nicole sagged to a dusty conference chair and started crying. "I told my little girl this was nearly over. I told her we'd have food soon and a warm place to sleep, and she wouldn't have to be scared any longer," she sobbed.

Jim nodded at his wife. They'd discussed this. The offer would seem less threatening coming from her.

"Deputy Ford was killed," Ellen said.

Nicole covered her mouth. "I didn't know him well, but he seemed like a nice man. He was good to us."

"He was a good man," Jim agreed.

"He was living in our community," Ellen said. "He had a nice mobile home with a wood stove and running water that came off the mountain. It's a decent place and you're welcome to come live there if you want. You and your daughter would be safe. There are other children she could be friends with."

Nicole still looked crestfallen, staring at the wall, as if she were ready to burst back into tears.

"We can give you some time to think about it, if you want," Jim said.

Nicole spun in the chair. "No!" Her voice was urgent, filled with fear.

"It's okay," Ellen said, trying to calm her.

"You never know if people are coming back," Nicole said. "You never know from one day to the next if promises will still exist or if the people who made them are still going to be alive."

"If you want to come, get your things together," Ellen said gently. "We'll be waiting outside. Our daughter is up the street with my parents. What's your daughter's name?"

"Paige."

"You can tell Paige that another little girl, Ariel, is waiting to play with her," Ellen said.

Nicole stood up. "We'll be right out. Please don't leave."

"We're not going anywhere," Jim promised.

Ellen and Jim helped them carry their meager belongings back to Nana's house. The truck already had a pile of items that Nana and Pops had decided to take back with them. Ellen made introductions while Jim loaded Nicole and Paige's things into the truck. Ariel and Paige played together while Nana and Pops finished gathering the last of the things they wanted to take.

When they were done, Jim stood in the yard with his parents, staring at the house where he'd grown up. It was where he'd become who he was. For his parents, it was entirely something different and he could only imagine the thoughts going through their heads.

"This was ours. It was a nice place," Nana said. "It was the old life."

Those words resonated with Jim. Everything he knew was the old life. They were all on the cusp of a new life and had no clue what to expect. He herded his family into the truck and backed away from the old house.

From the old life.

ABOUT THE AUTHOR

Franklin Horton lives and writes in the mountains of Southwestern Virginia. He is the author of the bestselling post-apocalyptic series *The Borrowed World* and *Locker Nine*. You can follow him on his website at franklinhorton.com and sign up for his newsletter with updates, book recommendations, and discounts.

ALSO BY FRANKLIN HORTON

The Borrowed World

Ashes of the Unspeakable

Legion of Despair

No Time For Mourning

Valley of Vengeance

Locker Nine

Grace Under Fire

Random Acts

Please Enjoy This Sample From

RANDOM ACTS
By
Franklin Horton

RANDOM ACTS

The thick hood over his head prevented Mohammed Karwan from seeing anything, but the dank smell reaching his nose convinced him he was standing on the earthen floor of one of Frankfurt's ancient buildings. He suspected his two other roommates were there with him but when he tried to ask in the back of the van he had been struck in the head with a fist. Although not an injurious blow, it was substantial enough to clarify that conversation would not be tolerated. He would have to wait as patiently as a hooded man could wait to see what fate lay ahead of them.

Mohammed and his roommates each received a text message several hours ago asking them to be at their flat by eight P.M. Fifteen minutes after the appointed time, a man they did not know arrived at the flat and instructed them to be at the mosque in thirty minutes. There was no confusion as to which mosque. There was only one mosque to which they were ever summoned.

"Do you think something is wrong?" Machmud asked. He was the most high-strung and nervous of the roommates, always concerned that he was in peril. Perhaps he was not cut out for this business of theirs, but that was irrelevant. This was their life. This was where they found themselves.

Mohammed, the senior of the men, shook his head at Machmud's question. "I don't know, my brother. I assume we will find out in due time." He was the stoic one, his fatalistic attitude the result of a life filled with brutality and violence.

Machmud did not speak again. The men filed onto the street and loaded into the used Renault Megane they shared when a vehicle was required. When they reach the mosque, they parked in an alley and entered through a side door. They were met by four men who gestured for them to turn around and face away from them. These were strong, menacing men dressed as laborers. They were not men to be argued with.

The laborers placed a hood roughly over each man's head. Mohammed was startled.

Machmud tried to twist away and face the laborers. "But why?"

The man attempting to place the hood on Machmud's head twisted his mouth in anger. He let loose with a powerful jab that sent Machmud staggering into the wall. The man twisted Machmud's stunned body and shoved him face-first into the wall.

"That was not a request," he growled.

The man made another attempt with the hood and this time Machmud did not protest. Mohammed was grabbed roughly from behind, his wrists clamped together by a strong hand before being bound with flex-cuffs. From the ratcheting sounds surrounding him, he could tell the other roommates were being cuffed also. Mohammed knew he'd done nothing wrong, but he still found the circumstances to be terrifying. He was also painfully aware that innocence was no guarantee he would return home this night. People in his line of work disappeared all the time and no one ever asked questions.

They were marched out the back door and shoved into the rear compartment of a windowless work van. Mohammed heard Machmud protest again. It was followed by the dull thud of a physical reprimand and the accompanying cry of pain.

Mohammed apparently failed to learn from Machmud's treatment. "Is everyone okay?" he asked. "Are you all here?"

He was rewarded with a blow to the head that rattled his brain and made his eyes water.

Mohammed chose to remain silent from that point and focus on the right and left turns. He was familiar enough with this area that, for a while, he was able to keep track of their direction of travel. It became clear the driver was attempting to confuse them, and he eventually succeeded.

The drove aimlessly for hours before Mohammed found himself standing on the packed dirt floor somewhere in the city. He assumed the location to be an abandoned factory or warehouse. The city was full of them. All he could tell with his senses muted by the hood and the noise of the van was they'd entered through a pair of rolling doors and parked inside the structure. When the engine was turned off, the van doors were opened and they were shoved out into a heap.

When the hoods were yanked from their heads, the roommates found themselves staring at six robed men seated in folding chairs. Propane lanterns were scattered around the room, providing a bright yellowish light that created long shadows and did nothing to reduce the grave appearance of the seated men. Mohammed recognized two of them. One was their handler, the man who came to the roommates for progress reports and updates. He was the man who brought them their instructions, the man he assumed carried news of their progress–or lack of it–to the leaders of their organization. If he were a betting man, Mohammed would assume these unfamiliar men in front of him were part of that senior leadership, fellow Syrians from back home.

The other man he recognized was the Imam, the prayer leader from the local mosque. Dressed in traditional robes and with a long gray beard, the Imam kept his hands folded in his lap, his eyes moving between the faces of the roommates. To the side of the seated men was a crude wooden table. A cast iron kettle sat atop a small stove, flames spilling out around it as the kettle heated. Mohammed did not expect they were going to offer him a cup of tea.

A man Mohammed had not met before addressed him. "Do you know who I am?"

Mohammed nodded, a slight bow of deferral. "We have not met, but I think I recognize you." He thought the man was a leader within his organization. Perhaps a man named Miran.

"Do you know why I am here?" Miran asked.

Mohammed shook his head.

Miran stood. He appeared to be in his forties, beginning to gray but still dangerously strong. He moved like a soldier, efficient and powerful. He walked to the wooden table and lifted the wire bail from the lid of the kettle, peering inside. He appeared to be satisfied with what he found as it brought a slight smile to his face. He looked from the kettle to Mohammed.

"Did you know an apartment with four of our brothers was raided yesterday?"

Mohammed nodded. "I saw the story on the news."

Miran left the table and stood directly in front of him. Mohammed didn't feel as if he'd done anything wrong but this man made him question that. This was a man who would not hesitate to kill someone who had failed him.

"Their arrest makes you our most senior group in the field. That's unfortunate for us because you've not produced any fruitful results. It's unfortunate for you since the pressure of a successful mission now lays upon *your* shoulders."

Mohammed did not know how to respond.

"We do not have the deep pockets some organizations have," Miran said. "We cannot support people living in expensive city apartments and not producing results. Many men work hard to allow you to live this life in the city, to allow you to work with computers instead of stone and concrete."

"We are working hard too," Mohammed said. "Work is all we do. Exactly as we were instructed. As we were trained."

Miran tilted his shoulders in a gesture that indicated he thought the sincerity of the statement was questionable. He gave Mohammed a disbelieving look. "Well, I think not *all* of you work as you should."

"We do," Mohammed assured him.

"Are you willing to stake our life on that?" Miran asked.

Mohammed looked down. "I assume it to be so. I do not look over every shoulder."

"Wise decision, not staking your life on it," Miran said. "Your fellow man will disappoint you as often as he will impress you."

A pop from the kettle drew everyone's attention. Miran smiled at Mohammed and rubbed his hands together. "Ah, it's ready. Finally."

Miran went back to the table, peering into the top of the kettle again. He reached into a pocket of his robe and drew out a potato. From a sheath on his belt he drew a traditional dagger, its point curved and wicked. He placed the potato on the table and cut it into slices. All eyes were on him, some curious, some terrified.

Miran stabbed the tip of the dagger into one round slice of the potato and dropped it into the kettle. There was a hiss and pop.

"Oil," he explained. "If you thought I invited you over for tea, you are to be sadly disappointed."

Miran walked back around the table and faced the three roommates. "Which of you is Machmud?"

"Why do you ask! I've done nothing!" Machmud burst out.

Mohammed turned and regarded his roommate. Why was the man so agitated?

Miran approached Machmud and smiled broadly. "Why are you so upset, my brother?"

"I feel like I'm being accused," Machmud sputtered. "I've done nothing."

"Perhaps that feeling is the jagged edge of your guilt sawing against your guts?" Miran said, leaning close to Machmud. "Perhaps your body betrays what the mind tries to cover up?"

Miran walked back to the table and used the blade of his dagger to fish the potato slice from the oil. It was browned to a crisp. Miran looked past the roommates to the silent row of laborers who'd delivered them here.

"Bring him to me."

There was no hesitation on their part. Instantly, a man was at each side and they dragged Machmud forward. He protested and kicked at the men. This was not well-received. One laborer stomped his heavy steel-toed boot sadistically across Machmud's calf, forcing a scream from the man.

"I've done nothing!" Machmud sobbed.

Miran ignored the protests. He walked around the table. "Stand him up!" he ordered.

The men pulled Machmud to his feet but his injured leg would not support his weight. He was weaving and leaning onto his captors.

"Where were you when you received our text message tonight?" Miran asked. "Where were you when we asked you to return to the apartment?"

"I was with a contact," Machmud said urgently. He was sweating profusely and tears cut paths through the dust caked on his face. "I was cultivating a relationship."

"What type of relationship?" Miran persisted.

"A contact. That's all."

Miran grabbed Machmud by the hair and raised the dagger to his throat. "Do you think we are so stupid as to turn you loose with no way to monitor you? Did you not realize you were always on a virtual leash? That we tracked all your movements both in the city and on the internet? That we know every website you go to and every message you send?"

Machmud's panic rose another notch and he tried to protest. "I've...done...nothing...wrong."

"Your job was to make inroads we could exploit. Your goal was to cultivate relationships and nurture those relationships into assets we could manipulate. Instead, all you've done is pursue your own *deviant* pleasure." Miran drew the word deviant out, relishing the way it sounded on his tongue.

"I did nothing."

"Do I need to read the transcripts out loud?" Miran yelled, getting in Machmud's face. "Do you I need to read the messages aloud? Do I need to show the pictures you exchanged?"

Machmud sobbed and went limp. The men supporting him allowed him to drop to the ground. His hands still flex-cuffed, he curled up and sobbed. "I am sorry. She tempted me and I could not resist."

"Did she tell you things you liked to hear?" Miran mocked. "Was she a temptress?"

Machmud moaned. "Yes. Yes!"

"Then we will make certain you do not hear things that tempt you again," Miran spat. "Hold him down!"

The men at Machmud's side slid on thick leather welding gloves which they used hold Machmud down. One of them, a thick man with arms like tree trunks, placed one on Machmud's neck and another on his forehead, crushing his cheek into the dirt floor. Miran went to the kettle of boiling oil and returned with it. He crouched over Machmud's ear.

Machmud whimpered and cried, still not completely certain what was about to take place. He could not see what Mohammed saw. He struggled but he could not gain ground against the strong arms holding him. Miran tipped the kettle to Machmud's ear.

Machmud screamed. He kicked and fought like an animal, but Miran continued pouring until the ear was full.

"Flip him over," Miran ordered.

The gloved men did as they were told. As they rolled him over, Mohammed could see Machmud's eyes wide with pain, shock, and terror. He tried to scream again but no scream could release the explosion of pain inside his head.

Once rolled to his other side Miran leaned over Machmud and whispered into his ear. "Remember my voice. It is the last you'll ever hear."

Then he poured the other ear full of the burning oil, deep frying everything within the canal. Miran returned to the table and placed the kettle beside the burner. "Take him away!"

The gloved men grabbed Machmud by his arms and dragged him away into the darkness. Mohammed wondered what would become of him. Would they kill him? Would they return him home? When Mohammed returned his eyes from Machmud to Miran he found the man staring at him.

"Have I made myself clear?" Miran asked. "Are you aware now of how serious and how urgent our mission is?"

"We understand," Mohammed replied.

"I will return in two weeks. You have that long to develop an actionable plan. Should you have nothing for me, what you saw tonight will look like the easy way out."

"We will not disappoint you," Mohammed said.

Miran's look indicated he was not convinced. "Get them out of here," he hissed.

The hood was thrown back over Mohammed's head and he was shoved from the room. He felt a sickness deep inside that made him want to throw up, though to do so with the hood on his head would only increase his suffering. He had not known Machmud well and had not known of his activities on the computer.

He also had not known they were being monitored so closely. That concerned him. There were times he watched a stupid video to blow off steam and relax. One thing was certain; he would type each word now with the understanding that he might one day have to stand before Miran and explain it. He would type each word with the understanding his life may one day depend on it.

22128397R10165

Made in the USA
Columbia, SC
24 July 2018